"THE RELUCTANT TORTURER"
by Andy Sparrow

2nd Edition published by 116comics Copyright © 2023

This is a true story.
Only the Who,
the What,
the Where,
the When
&
the Why
have been changed.

Friday - 31st October 2003 - Halloween.

The beaten-up Nissan Estate wound its way through the icy backstreets of London's Kensington, as its driver scanned the grand, double-fronted houses for signs of life. Not signs of the opposite like usual, but life; and not just lights on and shadows moving against blinds, but real lively life: A party. He rounded a corner and there were many costumed people standing in the street, waving, and climbing into cars, not out, so the party was finishing and no good to him, and anyway it had been a kid's party: An excited Disney Princess and a Sugar-rushed Fairy skipped down the path with their ugly sisters in tow, and piled into a big sedan; a Sleeping Beauty draped over her Frankenstein father's shoulder as he waved goodbye to his hosts. A little Monster ran out in front of the Nissan and he braked, swearing under his breath. Kids could be so annoying; they were the worst thing about Halloween, and should've been confined to quarters, not allowed to roam the streets like packs of rabid dogs. Still, he was glad of them in a way - Halloween wouldn't be half as fun if the children hadn't continued to dress up as they grew into adults.

The car's heater was bust, but he was still sweating; a fear-based sweat. Was he stupid to be gambling his life on such a far-fetched plan? He could be burgling right now and be raising the money he needed for tomorrow, but then he'd have to find a fence tonight and... no, he liked this idea. It *was* a gamble, but he loved a gamble. That's what had got him into this nightmare in the first place, but as they say 'you win some, you lose some', or in his case 'you lose some, you lose some'. Tonight though, he had a good chance of winning; of killing two birds with one stone

At the T-junction with the Old Brompton Road, he stopped to check his Nokia. Two texts from his crew needing supplies. He didn't reply. He was saving all he had for his gamble.

Across the road he spied two cute girls walking west, dressed as cartoon characters, or superheroes? One had a skullcap with pointy ears, a black bodystocking and a wired tail which wagged in the wind; the other had a tiara and a cape which flew around her. He liked them and found himself licking his lips - something he was trying to avoid doing. Where were they going? Not home surely? They looked excited, like they were just starting their evening, not finishing it, and were going to a grown-up fancy-dress party; somewhere, where he could quickly make

some serious cash. He decided to follow them so
overtook them, parked his car and killed the engine.
He took a deep breath while he watched them approach
in the mirror.

He was already wearing most of his outfit, so he
pulled on his mask and grabbed his hat, before
remembering he'd forgotten his 'First Aid Kit'. He
leant forward and felt around the steering column and
up inside the dashboard until he found the pouch
jammed amongst the wiring. Opening it, he scanned the
contents for something that might make him more
charming, or less un-charming? He retrieved a blue
pill from its brothers in a bulging baggie and
swallowed it, then stuck a licked finger in another
baggie full of white powder, which he then sucked on.
Yeah, that might do it, along with a couple of shots
of something warming in a pub nearby?

He pocketed the pouch, then, holding his hat for
fear of losing it, he got out of the car into the
biting wind, pulling his own cape tightly around him.
He trotted to catch up the girls, who continued until
they were stopped by a red light on the junction with
the Earl's Court Road, so he hung back and looked in
Martian Parson's window. There was a property for sale
for a quarter million billed as a 'Potentially Stylish
Studio' but to him it looked just like the garage he
was living in, but his was free, albeit in Burnt Oak.
The lights changed and the girls continued straight on
for thirty paces, but then turned right into the gates
of a red-brick Mansion Block. He wasn't quite ready to
follow them in so carried on walking, making sure he
saw which bell they pressed, then crossed the road,
heading for a functional looking pub. He was about to
enter when the door opened and two moustachioed blokes
exited, also dressed in costumes, but theirs were
leather and bondage gear, which led him to believe
they probably dressed like that every day. As the bar-
door was swinging shut he noted that most of the
occupants were in similar uniform, so thought better
of entering. He leant against the wall and tried not
to look at the sight before him: Their exposed
buttocks, one pair tanned and taut, the other pair wan
and woolly, shivered in the wind. He shuddered and
averted his eyes to the mansion block.

He guessed the party was on the third floor.
There, on the balcony, was a Batman laughing with a
Banana Split, and a Snowflake snogging a Snoopy. He
set off across the road and arrived at the door as a
Supergirl and a Jack Sparrow were just entering. They
smiled, holding the door for him and as the lift
wasn't available, they started walking up together.

Supergirl's bag was open and her wallet was on display, and as she bounced up the stairs various items fell out. In an uncharacteristic mood he called after her and handed them back.

"Hello Zorro, and thanks," said Supergirl, "are you a friend of Hannah's or Dasha's?"

His answer was already prepared, as was the middle-class accent to match her own.

"Neither. I'm meeting my girlfriend here," he said, in a voice an octave higher than usual, "what about you Supergirl?"

"Mainly Dash," she said, "we both sing and dance in 'A Forest'."

"What's that?" he said.

"The West End's longest running animal-based musical." she said, before the Pirate added,

"Except for Cats & the Lion King."

The young couple skipped on up the stairs and he fell behind, unable to keep up their pace. He could hear the laughter and music floating down from above, but he was in no hurry so took his time. He checked himself in a mirror on the next floor, straightening his mask, making sure the glue on his facial hair was holding, and setting his hat at a jaunty angle; then climbed the last set of stairs. There was a chance they could all turn out to be Mormons, but the music told a different tale. Would Mormons be listening to House music?

The door was open, and he walked into exactly what he was looking for: Everyone was in costume and looked well-healed; plenty of money to be made here, and maybe he'd leave with a new friend? How could he fail? Tonight, he was Zorro! He felt the drugs kicking in. He smiled and twirled his waxed moustache around his finger while scanning the long, high-ceilinged room with the tall sash windows on the left and the open-plan kitchen on the right.

Before him, two sofas were packed with various characters from history and culture: An Einstein flirted with a Marilyn; A Nixon passed a bong to a Churchill, both ignoring the idiot who'd come as Hitler. Fuck! Even he wasn't that stupid! Behind them was a table of canapés which were being devoured by a Dinosaur. Other characters stood around in groups drinking and passing joints. There seemed to be many men wearing shades, dressed in black suits, ties and undersized fedoras, but he wasn't sure what they were supposed to be. Beyond them more seating, then at the far end a space had been cleared for dancing, and that was where most of the girls were, whooping and reaching for the ceiling in a synchronized routine.

Among them, he caught a glimpse of the Pointy Ears and the Tiara which had brought him here in the first place.

HANNAH looked about her packed apartment and smiled as she danced. Her party was already a great success and it wasn't even closing time. Almost everyone had made a great effort with their costumes, except for some of the guys who'd done the minimum and come as Blues Brothers. That included quite a few of her clients, but, as their Footsie 100 companies would be putting in enormous orders on Monday, they could be forgiven.

Among other colourfully costumed characters, she was dancing with her business partner, Ben, dressed as Liberace and her close friend (and new lodger) Dasha, a beautiful Russian clad as a blue mutant from the X-Men movies, appropriate for her athletic body. Hannah herself though, being less than five feet tall, was dressed as Minnie Mouse in signature red smock with white polka-dots. The costume though, had come from the child's department and was meant for someone even smaller than her, so she was falling out the top, while it barely covered her bottom.

A new track mixed in and everyone cheered as they recognized an old classic: "There's Nothing I Won't do," by JX.

Yeah, she thought, there's nothing I won't do. There was a joy in abandoning all boundaries, being open to anything. Alcohol was the great 'opener', brushing aside reason, and even fear. But that wasn't always appropriate: A mix of other ingredients, sometimes was needed. A little grass could mellow her out and made her think 'creatively'; an 'E' could made her way more loving, or just plain horny; and a few lines of coke could make her more sociable, if that was possible. A party obviously required all of these, and other ingredients: An experimental punch which was always needing tweaking to boost one feeling or counteract another; a balancing act which was working superbly in that very moment.

She had a flashback to last year when she dressed as Raquel Welch's character in '2000 years BC' wearing a suede bikini; they'd been dancing in the back bedroom and the whole room had been blacked out - no lights except a tiny spot on the DJ's decks, thus anyone could do anything, and she had, sometimes without knowing who she was doing it with.

There's nothing I won't do.

Like another 'E' perhaps? But wait, didn't she
just judge the cocktail as working superbly? She did,
but it could always work
extra superbly. But maybe she'd done a bit too
much coke for the 'E' to work at all? She could do an
'E' and then take coke later and it almost
complimented it, but not the other way around; there
was just no point. That had never stopped her in the
past though. She'd been looking out for Jerome, her
dealer, who was coming as Toulouse Lautrec, but no
sign thus far. Fuck it! She'd have another line while
she waited. She grabbed Dash's hand and dragged her to
her bedroom.

ART sat at his drawing board, staring out the
window of his eerie, while waiting for inspiration.
Below, to his left was the junction with the
Portobello Road and his old haunt the Black Cross pub,
where it looked like they were having a hot and sweaty
lock-in.
    Art wasn't hot or sweaty, even though he was
still wearing his winter motor-cycling gear, as he'd
got in and found the flat's heating was not working.
He had removed his helmet though, as keeping it on
would've been silly (and would've made eating soup
impossible). Instead, he wore a lumberjack hat, to
guard against the icy wind swerving through the old
sash windows, rattling in their frames. A fleck of
snow flew past the window and Art stared enviously at
the block opposite with its new double glazing.
    On the ground floor, Joyce opened her window and
called to her many, many cats; above her, Fran and
Zoe's windows were steaming up from their vigorous
exchange of bodily fluids, whilst mostly naked; as was
their neighbour Melvin, who was such a messy eater
that it saved on laundry. Above them, Janine was
packing her belongings into removal boxes, which was a
shame; he'd enjoyed watching the unfolding tableau of
her family's life through these windows and in the
community: The horrible kids; the un-house-trainable
dog; the carousel of lovers/clients? But she and Art
had never spoken in the street; never even
acknowledged one another. In fact, she didn't even
know Art existed as she rarely took her eyes off the
TV long enough to look out of the window, let alone
into the flats opposite; and her name probably wasn't
Janine (unless for an uncanny coincidence). Art spent
so many hours at his board, mulling over ideas; and
was so easily distracted that he'd turn his
imagination's eye on to every passer-by and occupant,
giving them names, jobs, quirky characteristics and

even occasional deformities beneath their clothing. He scanned the rest of the windows, but nothing was stirring.

Down to the right of the block was a small playground where he'd used to take his daughter Aji when she'd been small. Since then it had been overtaken at night by a group of belligerent alcoholics called God, Piss, Alf and Amy (probably not their real names). At that moment they were picking Joyce's many, many cats' shits out of the sandpit, readying for bed.

The phone rang, then stopped and rang again, meaning it was Zal, his agent in Los Angeles. Zal didn't really need to do the code anymore, as he was almost the only person to call Art on his landline, but it was reassuring. Art turned down the volume of his new favourite song, playing on repeat ('Twist' by Goldfrapp), then picked up.

"Artie-fartie-so-fartie! Fee-fi-fo-fartie! Bananna-fanna-fo-fartie! Artie!"

Zal was drunk.

"Artemis Grime! How's the work coming?"

Art looked down at his drawing board and reviewed the rough pages he'd drawn for Zal, or more accurately, for his long-running serial: 'Invasion of the Bobby Snatchers' in Sex-Doll-Horror Monthly. His latest frame featured a semi-naked Japanese schoolgirl running from invading alien Octopoids.

"Five pages down, three to go."

That was a lie. Why did he lie?

"So the roughs will all be done tonight?" asked Zal.

"Fingers crossed—"

"Tomorrow latest?"

"Fingers crossed—"

"Well, they're very happy with you! They love your scripts and the evolution of your style over the past six months, and it's popular with the readers. What's your secret?"

"Going to less meetings? I find my mind works differently, less constrained maybe? More extreme?"

"But you've always extolled the virtues of Recovery to me—"

"Absolutely. Without it I'd be dead, and for the first few years I needed to be less extreme and more constrained."

"Hmmm," hmmed Zal, for once sounding like the grown-up; a weird role-reversal that made Art feel like explaining himself,

"When I was using, we'd say 'this is an all-or-nothing situation' and of course it was always 'all'.

Then I was in Recovery and it was always 'nothing': No drugs; no dishonesty; no extremes, but I think I also muffled the extremities of my imagination—"

"The pervy extremity?" Zal suggested, "and the outlandish, the eccentric, the preposterous and the leftfield?"

"Or maybe I've just unleashed the obsessive-compulsive gland that drives those parts—"

"But you're still clean right?" said Zal, "as your agent I want your work to be as popular as possible, but not at the expense of your sobriety. If you relapse, I won't be making any money out of you—"

Art laughed.

"Plus, of course, I care for you as a friend, obviously..."

"Obviously..."

"So when you say less meetings, how many is that exactly? Thirty being one a day in the last month; zero being none ever."

"Er... Four."

"I know I don't have a leg to stand on, but aren't you skating on thin ice?"

"That's the fun of it," Art said, allowing that high-pitched hysterical laugh to escape from his throat for a moment.

"Shit," said the hypocrite, taking another swig of booze.

"Oh! I have news!" said Zal, "your 'Head' book, sorry, I mean I'm Keeping my Head has gotten interest from a few movie studios! Someone - I shall remain nameless - started a rumour about Spike Jonze coming to London to track down the illusive Artemis Grime, when all he had to do was call me! The Zal Kleminson! And now they're bidding on the option! We're up to $10,000! Isn't that exciting? We could make some serious money here!"

"For a year's option?" asked Art, "that is exciting!"

He heard Zal glug something, then burp.

"And it's I'm Keeping the Head," corrected Art, "the Head."

"Whatever," said Zal, "I imagine they'll probably want to change that anyway, not snappy enough. So, what do you think? It'll make me stop hassling you about promoting it if you accept?"

"That would be nice," chuckled Art.

He had hated doing readings at Book Festivals in the summer. Was it his pride? Did he think he was above such shameless promotion? Or was he too humble, and didn't like reading his own words out loud or talking about himself so much? Probably both, or neither: Come to think of it maybe it was because he'd never before done any public speaking sober?

"Also," Zal continued, "whoever buys it will fly you over here, all expenses—"

"Unfortunately, I'm banned remember? Over ten years ago?"

"Ah, yes, on your Anthology's book tour, for faking your own death in front of a live audience—"

"I didn't fake it, I accidentally overdosed—" [1]

"Don't worry about that. We can do a conference call, or with video on this new thing? Skype is it? So what do you think?"

"I don't know. I'm not sure it's a great idea though. Films never do books justice do they?"

"Who gives a fuck? We could be talking six figures if it goes into production!"

Zal made a robust case. Art needed the money, but:

"Look at Trainspotting - it was a film about junkies, but they weren't even pinned—"

"Pinned?"

"Heroin makes your pupils contract to the size of a pin—"

"Are you comparing your little book with Trainspotting?"

"No, but actors mimic accents, wear costumes and put on make-up to appear realistic, why wouldn't they wear contact lenses or whatever to make themselves look pinned? It ruined the whole movie for me."

"Do you want me to write that into the contract? That the actor who plays Tony must actually be on smack?"

"No..."

"Okay Artie, sleep on it okay? Seriously, this could be a chance for you to buy somewhere, to secure your future, and Aji's."

"You make a good point Zal. I will sleep on it." They said goodbye.

Art walked three paces into the kitchen, turned the kettle on and put some bread in the toaster. While waiting he went back to staring out of the window, while envisioning his next page. He checked his script for speech bubbles and had an idea for a pleasing composition for the page: Big frame bottom right surrounded by smaller frames to the left and along the top.

After two cups of hot tea, four rounds of toast, and half-an-hour of browsing eBay for stuff he didn't know he needed until he bought it, he started to sketch the bottom right frame, where the girl had been caught, and was being given a stiff talking to by the Octopoid.

The female form was his favourite thing to draw, followed by motorbikes, cars, guns and architecture. Men? They came near the bottom alongside trees and ponds and bicycles - didn't mean he couldn't draw them, just that he didn't enjoy it as much - not that he was often required to draw a man throwing a bicycle into a pond surrounded by trees. No, he was more often required to draw porn, or hentai, as his Japanese clients called it; though he didn't know why they insisted he draw every erect penis, when they always pixilated them in the magazine?

Sex-Doll-Horror arrived on his doorstep monthly, but he didn't archive the magazines like he had with the mags at the height of his cult-status. He wasn't proud of them - not very 'recovery' oriented - so he donated them to God, Piss, Alf and Amy, who couldn't read Japanese but enjoyed the pictures (except Amy).

Was 'not being proud' the same as 'being ashamed'? No. Surely if he *was* ashamed, he wouldn't even give them to the homeless. But of course, they didn't know he was drawing the stories.

Yes, it was shame; because he had also added a felt cover to his drawing board, which he could pull over when his daughter came home.

He seemed to spend an inordinately large amount of his time sitting at his drawing board, even when he wasn't drawing. Was this his life? Watching people passing by, watching his neighbours, watching Aji get older, watching from the side-lines.

When he'd come into Recovery a dear old friend had bet him fifty quid that he'd be a football fan within six months. He'd replied (rather pretentiously, in hindsight) "I'm a doer, not a watcher," but then he had been. In his previous life as a Gonzo journalist he'd partaken in every experience, alongside anyone - drug smugglers, war lords, slavers, arms dealers, dungeon masters, and worst of all...

politicians.

He'd travelled the world looking for trouble and invariably caused it (2) then got paid handsomely to write about it in a best-selling men's magazine. But since he'd got clean most of those experiences were to be avoided if he didn't want to return to the gutter from which he came. But was there regret? Life did seem a little monotonous without his career as an adventure journalist.

The 'Head' book (as people annoyingly called it) had been based on a series of events that had happened to him a few years earlier in 1999. It had been published in the spring, but its sales were disappointing and had alienated him from his old friends Mickey and Hannah, who had been featured heavily much to their embarrassment. Maybe he should have done more than just change their names?

It was Halloween, and as usual Hannah was having what surely would be yet another legendary party, with Dash and all their glamorous friends (and this year also Aji); but he had not been invited. Hardly surprising, but annoying as he quite liked the idea at that moment.

At nine years clean and sober he didn't feel so at risk in social situations. He didn't mind being around wasters and found them quite amusing in their sloppiness, though since getting clean, he'd never tested his resolve by being around piles of heroin or bags of weed. It was weird that he was even thinking about it.

He wondered what Dasha was doing. Probably dancing; having fun; laughing; drinking... and he was drawing porn and staring out the window and waiting for her yet again.

They'd been getting closer and closer over the past few months and finally she'd left William, but the next step had still not happened; they hadn't run into each other's arms among the fruit stalls of the Portobello Road, and kissed passionately as the camera craned up to the blue skies...

Maybe they were already to entrenched in the Friend Zone? Shit.

HANNAH and Dasha sat at the dresser in the plush bedroom. Red velvet was Hannah's latest theme. She watched their reflections as she expertly racked the lines of coke on the glass surface. Dash's demonic contact lenses were freaking her out. She looked away and focussed on the coke.

"Coke always makes me horny." she said, thinking aloud.

"Everything makes you horny." said Dash laughing, which set off Hannah too.

"It's true, though in fact I don't really need anything to make me horny. It's just my default setting now-days," she shrugged, "and you've brought a lot of beautiful boys with you this year, from 'A Forest', I assume? They're not all gay, are they?"

"No, quite a few have hit on me since they heard I'd split up with William—"

"So, have you taken advantage?" Hannah asked, "or are you as horny as me?"

"It's only been a few weeks," said Dash, "but it was great to know I could walk out on him and move straight in here. Thanks Sweetheart."

Hannah smiled and looked around for something to snort through,

"Have you got a note on you?" she asked.

Dash unzipped her costume revealing her cleavage, which cradled a blue silk drawstring bag. She retrieved it and decanted the contents onto the dresser. Inside was her little Sanyo SCP-5300 flip-phone, her door keys and some notes.

"Now I understand why you wanted such a petite phone!" said Hannah, taking a twenty-pound-note.

Dash laughed and nodded,

"It is perfect!" she said, "it does everything I need, and is a quarter of the size of my last one."

"Yup," said Hannah, "small is good!" She rolled the twenty into a tube and snorted a line. The coke was zingy, and she felt her brain do a little dance which she nodded along to. She gave the note to Dash who half-heartedly snorted a third of a line then made a face. Hannah tried not to show her disapproval but failed:

"Come on, you can do better than that," she implored.

"You just said 'small is good'!" protested Dash, "I can feel it already thanks, that's all I need."

Hannah never understood people like Dash, the lightweights of the world. What was the point in having half a line? She took back the twenty and snorted the rest of Dash's line, then one of the others.

"Hmm, I think it's a toss-up between the Red Indian Chief and the Pirate?"

"As to who you want to have your way with?" said Dash, "well the Pirate came with Valerie? Supergirl? So I think she may have drawings on him."

"Drawings?" enquired Hannah, quite used to Dash's malapropisms, "you mean designs? Valerie has designs on him."

Dash nodded,

"Designs; attraction; concupiscence; fancy; hunger; lust—"

"Very impressive, the Guardian Crossword is doing wonders for your vocabulary. Lust: That's the one for me. Valerie's probably more in the fancy ball-park."

"Yes, she's a lot more self-contained than you."

"So she fancies the Pirate. Shame, but I guess that makes my decision easier. The Red Indian Chief it is."

"I'm not sure we say 'Red Indian' anymore—"

14

"Oh-for-fuck's-sake! This is P.C. gone mad!"
hissed Hannah, "what do we say these days then?"
     Dash thought for a moment then said,
     "Why not call him the Big Chief?"
     "Yup, that fits. Want to share this last line?
No? Well then we don't want it to go to waste do we?"
she said, snorting the rest. Her nose went fizzy for a
moment and she closed her eyes and shook her head,
     "Come on, let's go!" she said, jumping up and
taking Dash's hand.
     Dash had looked like she was about to load
everything back into its bag but, pulled along by
Hannah, abandoned it all on the dresser.

     ART thought about getting into bed, but the idea
of taking off even his fleece-lined leathers was
unthinkable. But a better idea occurred to him: As Aji
was staying over at her friend Margot's house after
Hannah's party, it meant he could borrow her electric
blanket. He went to retrieve it. Aji had totally
consumed his life for the past decade. She had been
everything to him, his very reason to live. She still
was, but at thirteen she didn't seem to need him in
the same way. She really just needed his money.
     He thought back to his daily wait in the Primary
School playground for the three-thirty bell to ring
and the kids all flooding out in a wave of joy. It had
been his favourite moment of the day and in retrospect
he felt lucky he'd become unemployable, giving him the
opportunity to experience Aji growing up. "Every Clown
has a Silver Lining," as the lovely Dasha would say.
His 'Clown' had been his addictive tendencies from
which he'd managed to make a good living by
documenting his terrible behaviour. But as his
addiction had taken grip, he'd found it harder to do
the documenting, and was just left with his terrible
behaviour. He would sit in front of his laptop staring
at the blank Word doc with a fag hanging out his mouth
(trying to recall the night before, or decipher his
mumblings into his micro-cassette recorder), until his
eyes slowly closed and, like Aji's Drinking Bird toy,
he would dip forward and another letter on the keypad
had a hole burned into it.

     DASHA was dancing again but suddenly felt
exhausted and had to sit down. She'd done rehearsals
and the show, then come straight to the party and had
hardly stopped dancing until then, when she had to
stop moving. That line had given her a momentary lift
but since then it felt as if it had sucked away all
her natural energy. She guessed that was why Hannah

just continued to shovel the stuff up her nose, but really, wasn't it better to just not start in the first place? She grabbed a bottle of water and flopped onto a free chair next to a man dressed as Zorro. He turned to her:

"You look all pooped out," he said.

She drank as she tried to decipher the meaning of his words all pooped out. She didn't want to ask - it sounded awful - she'd have to look that up in her little book of 'Idiotic English Idioms'.

"So is that a costume?" asked Zorro, "or did you just spray yourself Mutant Blue?"

Dash smiled and said,

"I painted my hands and face and put in contact lenses - the rest is just a very skin-tight suit."

Beneath his magnificent moustache, Zorro's lecherous smile revealed an incomplete set of grey teeth. He scanned the dancefloor,

"There's a lot of great dancers here," he said, "are they from your show?"

Dash nodded,

"Yes, there's quite a few here. See there's a few giant inflatable heads on the dancefloor? They came straight from work."

"A Forest? Named after the Cure song?"

"No, sadly. It would probably be a lot more interesting if it had been. It's actually based on a Japanese video game called Animal Forest—"

They were interrupted by Morty, one of Hannah's clients (dressed as a Blues Brother), who approached saying,

"Are you the man with the E? Snoopy says they're great! Can I have two?"

Zorro nodded and got out a pouch containing zip-lock bags of various pills, powders, and vials.

"You've got quite the selection!" said Morty, as they did the exchange.

"Something for all tastes - uppers, downers, inside-outers," Zorro said, turning to Dash, "you want anything Mystique?"

She waved away the suggestion, saying,

"Not for me, I'm—"

"Dash!" cried Hannah as she jumped on to her lap, "have you seen a black Toulouse Lautrec around?"

"Jerome? No, he's not here yet, but Zorro here can help you—"

"Really?" said Hannah, turning the full power of her charm onto Zorro,

"Got any 'E', dear Zorro? That I can borrow? Until tomorrow?"

Dash had to cling on to Hannah to stop her from climbing all over the guy, who was opening his pouch.

"No problem, Minnie. It's free to you cuz I know you and Mystique are the hostesses."

Hannah was almost salivating at the selection:

"Ooh! What's the purple stuff in the glass vial?"

"That's to help you come down when you've done too much coke."

"Ha! Excellent! Well maybe later - for now, just an 'E' please."

Zorro placed a small pink pill in her hand which she immediately popped in her mouth, glugged some of Dash's water then said,

"Maybe just one more?"

Zorro held another in front of her mouth between thumb and forefinger. Was he hoping she'd put her lips around them and pull the pill in with his tongue? It wouldn't be out of character for her to, but Hannah stuck out her tongue, onto which he dropped the little pill. She smiled, took another swig of Dash's water and went back to the dance floor.

Dash looked around the room and found Morty, downing his 'E' with a large Scotch. She pointed at him then said,

"He just said, 'Quite the selection', instead of 'Quite a selection'."

"Yeah, it might be a recent development, I think—"

"And what's the difference?"

"Whether the speaker is a fucking gay, or not?"

Dash winced and tried to look beyond his mask to see if he was joking, but all she could see were black irises staring at the dance-floor, and even with the disco ball there was no lights reflected back; like black holes, no light escaped, and there was no smile curling his moustache this time. She was about to leave him when Zorro got up and said,

"Okay, I'm gonna do a little chemistry in the toilet but I'll be here if you need me."

Dash watched him as he bobbed through the crowd, occasionally stopping to dispense some fabulous pharmaceuticals.

Ben sat down beside her.

"How's it going?" he asked.

"Good, though I don't like him," she said, pointing at Zorro's back."

"Well Zorro and all your friends from 'A Forest' are very popular with our clients!"

He scanned the room,

"And how's Hannah? She seems really on one tonight - bouncing like Tigger!"

Dash didn't know who Tigger was but looked over at her pogoing on the dance floor.

"She's been like this every night since I moved in!"

"Like Tigger? Oh shit!" he said, shaking his head, "you think she's close?"

"I don't know, she seems so happy, then I hear her crying in the night..."

Ben looked philosophical:

"I think she's close. She's not functioning properly anymore. She can't do her job, except this part, the part that'll kill her. She needs treatment..."

They nodded and watched as Hannah climbed the Big Chief.

ZORRO sprinkled some of the purple crystals among the tobacco then picked up the joint and licked its gummed edge. Expertly, he folded it over, rolled the paper and glued. He put the joints in his fag packet, unlocked the toilet door and peeked out. The plush red bedroom (which was supposedly out-of-bounds, according to the sign) was still empty, but would it have mattered if it hadn't? Everyone here loved him! He was having a great time. He walked through and scanned the living room. There were so many good-looking girls at the party. Mainly gazelle-like, professional dancers apparently. He really was spoilt for choice. He'd liked the Middle Eastern Minnie Mouse a lot. She wasn't the best looking, but she was the sexiest with her overt flirtiness and those awesome boobs sprouting from that tiny brown frame, he could've picked her up and popped her on right there. He'd also liked the Snowflake; the Marilyn and the Teddy Bear, and of course the blue mutant, who had just avoided him. Maybe it was his crack about the gays? But who gave a fuck? If he wanted her, he'd take her; she looked like she'd probably put up a good fight, which was always a bonus. But none of them perfectly fitted his requirements. His eye was always drawn back to the Pointy Ears and the Tiara, neither of which he'd had a chance to speak to yet.

The girl in the Catsuit was the first of the pair to break away from the herd, and he followed her first to the noisy kitchen, where she grabbed a bottle of water, then to the queue for the main toilet, behind a couple of horny looking penguins.

He wandered past her along the hall and opened the end door. It was a deep wardrobe packed with rails. He turned back and opened the door opposite the red bedroom. It was occupied with a number of his

Ecstasy customers, who were disrobing each other, but when they saw him they paused to cheer. He bowed and backed out into the hall. A swift check revealed the red bedroom was not occupied and neither was its toilet. He went back to his quarry and stood behind her and she looked him over while opening her water.

"Zorro. Very nice."

He smiled. She was perfect.

"Thank you - er - Kitty? Pussy-Willow? er..." he smirked.

She laughed and corrected him,

"Catwoman. Not as professional as yours but it was very last minute."

She didn't look like a woman to him. She looked... He felt his tongue emerging between his lips and quickly retracted it.

"Have you got a cigarette?" she asked.

He pulled out a packet, thumbed it open and, like a card sharp, forced her choice.

"Ooh, I'll have one of your joints please," she said, reaching out, but he pulled away, saying,

"I'm sorry, those aren't for everyone; they're 'special' ones; have a straight instead."

"No, I like the sound of the 'special' ones, if you don't mind."

He shrugged and let her 'choose' for herself. It really was his lucky night.

While she lit up, he crossed the hallway,

"You know, there's a free toilet in this bedroom here," he said, opening the door while standing in front of the 'No Entry!' sign.

"Thank God! I'm bursting!" she cried, running over, joint in one hand, water in the other, as she tried to undo the poppers between her legs, turn on the light in the loo and lock the door. He followed her then sat on the red velvet, king-size bed and listened as she finally let out a very long sigh, then laughed,

"What is in this joint? I thought it was going to be grass... It's got me all..."

He said nothing, just listened as she continued to talk, her speech getting more and more slurred.

ART had finished putting Aji's electric blanket on his bed and was plucking up the courage to disrobe when his phone pinged. It was Aji texting:

> *"Cum get me dad NOW please X"*

He texted

"coming x"

then put on his helmet and gloves while leaping
down the stairs four at a time. His yellow squint-eyed
BMW burst into life and he was away, through the back
streets of Notting Hill and down towards South
Kensington. The traffic was light and the whole
journey to Hannah's only took a few minutes, aided by
the frantic tugging of his heart strings.

Outside Hannah's he parked on the pavement and
ran inside. The lift was busy, descending from a few
floors above but he couldn't wait so he ran up the
stairs, scanning the costumed guests lounging on the
carpeted steps. Inside, he scoured the packed room for
Aji, examining every female as, shamefully, he
couldn't remember what she had planned on wearing. He
tried calling her as he stomped through the apartment
in his massive Wesco boots, but there was no reply.
Maybe she was passed out somewhere, he thought,
searching under the tables and behind the DJ's station
at the far end. Where were Hannah and Dash? He pushed
his way into the kitchen, past a Harry Potter sharing
slammers with a Victoria's Secret Angel, who looked up
at him and said,

"What've you come as? Judge Dredd?"

He looked back at her blankly before realizing he
was still in his full biker gear, including helmet.
More panicked, he continued the search; down the hall
to the loo where a couple of Penguins were making out
(with much difficulty). Then to the spare room, in
which there seemed to be an orgy, but by shifting a
few lithesome limbs (to much outraged objection) and
shoving a hairy butt aside he was able to ascertain
that Aji wasn't partaking. For a moment he was
confused: Was he relieved his jailbait daughter *wasn't*
having sex and thus still missing? Or if he'd found
her under that hairy butt would he have been angry or
just happy she was alive? He apologized and backed out
the room. Next, he checked the end room - the one
Hannah had turned over to her clothes. He pushed aside
the coats as he advanced until he came to the
clearing. Hanging rails, drawers, shelves, and boxes
surrounded him. He heard a muffled cry from a corner
and investigated. A couple were screwing on a pile of
coats, but it wasn't Aji. He left and closed the door
behind him.

That only left Hannah's door, decorated with a No
Entry sign. He noticed his heart racing. He hadn't
seen Hannah in ages. He took a breath, trying to

prepare himself for whatever debauchery he was bound
to see inside, then knocked and entered.

Hannah, with a big red polka dotted bow in her
hair and matching smock, sat at her dressing table
with a Native American Chief, racking up a few lines
of coke.

"Hi Hannah. Where's Aji?"

Hannah turned and saw him and raised her
eyebrows,

"Well, well, long time no see," but then she
seemed to clock the stress in his voice,

"Dunno, sorry. We were all dancing together only
an hour ago? Maybe less?"

Art looked wistfully at Hannah and the drugs then
shook the notion from his head, striding across the
room to the en-suite and pushing on the door. A squeak
came from inside, and there, sat on the loo was a
naked Dash, with blue face and her one-piece costume
around her knees. Art froze for a second (maybe more),
before shaking his head and saying,

"Sorry Dash - I just got an S.O.S. text from
Aji!"

Dash didn't cover herself, just said,

"Did you call her, Arthur?"

"Yes, but no joy."

"Shall I try Margot?" suggested Dash.

"You have her number?"

"Of course! If I can find my phone..."

Dash had babysat Aji since she was in primary
school so knew all her friends better than 'Arthur' as
she called him mistakenly. (3)

"Okay, and I'll try Margot's mum," he said.

Art was closing the loo door when he noticed the
lock was broken. There were splinters of wood on the
floor. It looked like it had been forced.

ZORRO was ecstatic. Was that the ecstasy or his
situation? He had almost sold out, but also the girl
in the cat-suit was very pliable. Hadn't the previous
two put up much more of a fight than this? He'd told
her he was going to a much better party and she was
seemed happy to go along. Maybe he could put her in
the car then come back for the other one? As he led
her down the hall, he saw the Supergirl.

"Oh you found her then?"

"Yes, but she's a little worse for wear, so..."
he said, wrapping his cloak around her as she giggled
and waved.

When he led her into the lift, all she'd asked
was 'Will there be cake?'

As they left the building, they passed a big yellow motorbike parked on the pavement, the engine clicking as it cooled down in the icy wind. It was the one like who's-it had ridden around the world on? The dude from Trainspotting? He'd always wanted one of those. Maybe soon. She seemed to notice it too and opened her mouth as if to speak, but nothing came out. She shivered so he wrapped his cape tighter around her as they walked to his car, him almost carrying her by the end. At the car, he checked the surroundings for onlookers then opened the back door, saying,

"Now you can lie down in the back and sleep."

He lifted her in and she lay down on a thick fleece blanket without realizing she was lying on the back of the folded down seats. She snuggled in.

"Thank you," she said, then, "what's your name?"

He thought for a moment. It didn't matter anymore so said,

"It's Grody. Now go to sleep."

He got in the front and for a moment felt like sleeping too; or at least just shutting his eyes and listening to the dance music on Radio One. The 'E' was very good. Finally, he took the Motorola from the glove compartment while he waited for her breathing to settle.

He clicked on 'Messages', then on the only text saying,

'wrong number'

He started to type a reply:

"30 mins..." when he heard the girl in the back start to snore. He smiled then leant through and tipped up the seats, neatly rolling her into the boot. It was TOO easy. Fuck yeah! He would go back for the other one. Without sending the text, he dropped the phone on the passenger seat and started the engine.

HANNAH's buzz was ruined. She just felt drunk, and however much she resented him, drunk was no good to Art, who had frozen in panic and was staring at the broken lock on the loo door. Hannah snorted a line, then the other meant for her Big Chief, who looked miffed. She glanced at him wistfully and handed him the packet, before she felt the coke kick in and give her a moment of anger about her splintered door, then, an idea,

"Art, did you see Margot outside?"

Art shook his head.

"So don't you think she left with her?" Hannah asked, "they've probably gone to Margot's and then had a stupid argument and Aji just texted you in a huff."

"Maybe," said Art, "I hadn't considered that, though I thought she'd grown out of that sort of behaviour years ago—"

"Where's my phone?" Dash said, emerging from the loo in full costume, "Oh, Hi Nigel!" she said to the Chief. She spotted her phone on the dresser, grabbed it and called.

"Margot's is going straight to voicemail. Did you call her mother?"

"Shit!" Art said, while finding the number and pressing 'Call'.

He stood in silence waiting, but the landline just rang out.

"You get down there Art, and set your mind at rest," said Hannah, trying to sound confident, "you'll probably find them all tucked up in bed; but we'll keep trying the phones, and call you if need be."

Art thanked them and ran out. Dash looked at Hannah and the Big Chief, who'd just snorted a line, making his headdress shake like a peacock's tail and said,

"When you said 'we', you meant 'me' right?"

Hannah kissed her, pushed her out, then locked the door and leant against it. She looked the Big Chief up and down, and he in return, eyed her in her tiny Minnie Mouse costume. From the look in his eyes, the Big Chief wanted to do to Minnie, what Hollywood had been doing to Native Americans for a century. She smiled.

DASHA followed Art as he picked his way through the apartment.

"Don't forget to plug your headphones in Arthur."

He paused on the landing to take off his helmet and find the wire. She could see the fear in his face, and it made it more real to her. Until that moment she'd believed Aji was with Margot in Battersea, but maybe something had happened to her. She felt a pain behind her eyes as tears began to well up and she feared it would be even worse for Art if he saw. But he didn't notice and was gone. It was relatively quiet on the landing so she tried Margot again, but it went straight to voicemail. She decided to go to her room and call again.

HANNAH wedged a chair under the door handle, just to be sure of no interruptions. The Big Chief sat on the side of the bed and loosened the drawstring on his nubuck pants. She stood before him, only a little taller than he was sitting.

23

"As we have a houseful of guests, and we're both characters from the Silent Era of cinema," she said, "we have to express ourselves without words." He smiled and nodded, his headdress doing all the talking. She pushed him back and bent forward, exposing even more cleavage. Putting her hands on his thighs, she leant her weight on him and squeezed her boobs together. He jiggled his thighs, causing her breasts to do the same, until her nipples peeked into view. He smiled and brought his mouth up to meet them; his lips were soft; his tongue was swivelly. She hugged the back of his head and shut her eyes, as she felt his hands move inside her knickers and slowly push between her buttocks.

ART jumped on his bike and started it up. He was about to drop off the pavement between two parked cars when another car pulled into the space, blocking his exit. A swashbuckling dude jumped out and said, "Cool bike man!" then disappeared into Hannah's mansion block. Art swore under his breath then found another exit. He took the Earl's Court Road and sped towards Margot's, south of the river. He made an illegal right on to Albert Bridge and was at Margot's in moments. The house was dark, but when he thumped on the door a light went on in a bedroom. When Margot's mother opened the door and saw Art she burst into tears. Then he did too.

DASHA had found her room to be full of naked sweaty bodies, and though they offered to make room for her on the bed she declined and left.

Hannah's door was closed. She knew what was going on but she couldn't hear any of the usual screaming, just the sound of the headboard damaging the expensive wallpaper.

Then she kept getting accosted by friends saying goodbye, bar-staff needing advice, and neighbours complaining who she reassured it'd all be over in an hour as she led them back to the landing. As promised, the party was beginning to wind down, with dishevelled characters making their way out. Dash tried Margot once more and this time it rang.

"Hullo?" said Margot.

"Margot, it's Dash, where are you? We've been worried."

"At the party - sorry, our phones died and there was a queue for the charger."

"Where at the party. I don't see you."

"Not at your party. We left an hour ago and went to another on High Street Ken—"

"And is Aji okay?"

"Yeah, but she's making out with some boy in a room and he's locked the door—"

"What's the address Margot?" Dash asked as she raced down the stairs.

"I can't Dash, Aji made—"

"Aji sent an S.O.S. text to her dad! Tell me now!"

"We're at Wendy's."

By then, Dash was hailing a cab in the Old Brompton Road.

HANNAH's Minnie Mouse ears were becoming askew as she bounced up and down. The Big Chief lay on his back, miming the action of a mechanical bull; Hannah mimed a cowgirl, one arm clinging to his shirt, the other waving in the air above her. Her thighs gripping just enough not to be flung across the room, but not enough to stop the delicious slidey action going on inside her. My, he was a 'Big Chief'. Her polka dot costume was gathering around her waist as she was bucked up and down. 'Buck me Big Chief, buck me!" she mouthed, in a Silent Era style. He seemed mesmerized by her boobs as they bounced so perkily, never losing their 'C' cup perfection (maybe he'd never seen the artistry of Doctor Nina Van Horn of the Maddox clinic before. They had a lifetime guarantee).

Oh! There! That was it! That! Oh! There! Her mouth formed a big 'Oh' as her thighs gripped him to keep him in that spot while she came; a big shuddering glowing orgasm that went on and on... and on.

DASHA called Art from the back of the cab. He was consoling Margot's mother.

"I found them. I'm on my way to get them—"

"Where. We want to—"

"No! You're both too emotional - I'll deal with this. Got to go, I'm here."

Dash told the taxi to wait, ran up the steps to the front door just as it was being opened by a boy with his cheeks puffed out. She neatly pirouetted around him as he puked on the porch's mosaic, adding an interesting second mosaic on top. She felt like kicking some butt, mainly her own, for letting Aji out of her sight.

The flat was packed with a bunch of drunken teenagers, including many she recognized as she weaved between them. Wendy, in what was left of her 'Alice in Wonderland' outfit, sat in a corner sobbing. Margot was on the phone to her mum and pointed Dash towards a closed door at the end of a hall. Dash ran and karate-kicked the door by the handle. It gave way and inside she found Aji on the bed, fending off an aggressive, drunken boy. Dash grabbed him by his hair and pulled him onto the floor, pinning him down with a knee on his chest.

"Mystique," the boy whimpered.

"Marcus Taylor, from two years above," sneered Dash.

"I didn't do it."

She looked him over and noted his pants were pulled down and his shrivelling willy flopped against his leg. She grabbed it by its wrinkly foreskin and stretched it out, examining it for signs of usage, but it was clean and dry.

"But you tried, you little cun—"

"Dash?" Aji said, as she re-laced her bodice, "can we go please?"

Dash pulled on the foreskin until it wouldn't stretch any further, making him scream.

"Maybe I should tie a knot in it, like you do when you've blown up a balloon," she said, exaggerating her Russian accent for effect, "or castrate you so you never try tha—"

"Dash!" Aji shouted.

Dash turned her mutant lenses on Aji and said, "I'll deal with you later! Go!"

Aji fled, grabbing Margot, who had entered and was documenting the event with her camera.

Dash gave the foreskin one final tug and the boy screamed again, then she let go and it snapped back, spattering tiny droplets of blood on his Dracula T-shirt.

ART was in bed, luxuriating in the warmth from the electric blanket, when he heard the door, and chatting and the voices of Aji and Dash. Aji poked her head around his door and said,

"Sorry Dad."

He steeled himself to stay calm then peeked at her over the duvet.

"You're okay?"

She nodded.

"Yeah, bit drunk, another lesson learnt, sorry to scare you all," she said, hugging herself, "God, it's freezing in here. Has the heating shut down again?"

"Yes, and I've taken your electric blanket as penance for your deceit—"

"What!"

"Mmm, I'm toasty and all snuggl—"

"It's probably the water pressure again," she said as walked away, "it shuts off automatically if the gauge gets too low."

Art heard the broom cupboard open, the turning of the two squeaky taps, then a gurgling from the radiator and moments later the whoof of the boiler as it fired up. However angry he was in that moment, he was also very proud of her. Dash entered with a cup of tea and sat in the armchair next to his bed. Art noticed she'd taken out the fiery contact lenses.

"Did you kick butt?" Art asked.

"Butt, of course!" she answered, offering him a sip.

He nodded and as she came closer, he whispered, "So what happened?"

Hearing Aji in the hall, she looked at the door, then moved closer and whispered,

"A boy might have got her drunk. Or she did it herself, then she was out of her depth—"

"Who?"

"No, I'm not telling you. I've dealt with it."

"Is she hurt?"

"Not physically."

Their faces were so close he could feel her breath on his cheek.

"I like you in blue," he said, "it makes your eyes even more intense."

"Thank you."

"And I noticed earlier, when I burst into Hannah's loo, that you didn't cover yourself up?"

"I'm not shy," she said, "around you."

"Then kiss me."

She looked at the door, then at him,

"Here?"

"No, here," he said, pointing at his mouth, "you're single now. Nothing left to stop you."

"I guess that is true," she said, moving towards him, looking at his mouth. Their faces were so close he could feel her breath. He pushed his lips towards hers and they touched. So soft. He could smell her. She smelt of home. Aji shouted,

"Goodnight!" from the hall and Dash was on her feet immediately and opening the door. She looked at Aji, then at Art, then at Aji, then she was gone.

Art heard the front door slam, and Aji stood there smiling at him.

"Awwww," is all she said before swaying away to wash her teeth.

HANNAH sat on the loo, looking at the broken door. The one bit of damage from one hundred people partying in her apartment. Not bad really, she reckoned. One good thing about having friends in their thirties. The caterers and bar staff had done a great job cleaning up after everyone, and the DJ had just finished taking his equipment downstairs and said goodbye, so she was alone; which she didn't much like. Where was Dash? And what happened to her Big Chief? She spied a half-smoked joint on the floor and picked it up. It looked clean, but who was she kidding? She would've smoked it even if it had been lying in a puddle of wee. She lit it up and dragged on it, expansively.

DASHA had fallen asleep in the back of the cab. She awoke when the cabbie stopped outside her mansion block and announced his fare over the speaker. She unzipped her costume but only found her phon.

"My money's upstairs. Be five minutes okay?"

The door downstairs was ajar, so she took the lift then realized she'd also forgotten her keys. She rang the bell but there was no answer. Maybe Hannah and her new boy were still at it? She opened the window on the landing and got out on to the ledge while hanging on to the security grill, then shimmied around it and jumped on to their balcony. She tried the sash windows in turn, but they were all locked. If she couldn't get in, she thought, she could get the cab back up to Art's and snuggle in with Aji; or maybe this might be the perfect moment to—

The door at the far end was ajar, dammit! Inside, everything was back in place and there was no evidence of a wild party, though she did wonder if anyone had thought to change her sheets. Hannah's door was open and she peeked in. The lights were on and she could see the bed was empty, so she took her money and keys and put them back in their bag.

"Hannah!" she called, "where are you?" She pushed on the broken loo door. That's when she saw Hannah lying still on the floor, a purple-tinged joint between her blue lips.

(1) (2) (3)
See Appendix

Saturday - 1st November

ART sat at his drawing board and stared out the window. Below, Saturday's Portobello Road was packed with street performers and gawking tourists from the four corners of the globe despite the weather. Very annoying. Also annoying - he'd forgotten to buy coffee, which meant venturing out among the stinking masses. He could fight his way through the crowds to Best-Save for a box of Lavazza, or ride to Lisboa (the best coffee in Portobello), but of course Dash, having left William, no longer lived in the area, thus he wouldn't 'bump into' her there. He'd been up most days assuming she'd still want to continue the tradition but he hadn't seen her. So it had to be Mike's Café; close by, passable coffee and delicious food.

He thought about waking Aji but decided against it. He wrote her a note then went downstairs. He stood on his stoop, while he zipped up his coat and surveyed the scene. It was much noisier at ground level, and the FecoBurgers smelt even more rancid than usual so he decided to turn right, away from the Portobello road and take the back way. He did so, then immediately crossed over and turned left along the 'relatively' deserted street by the little playground.

There, he noticed 'Janine' and son carrying boxes to a hire-van. So they *were* moving out. 'God', 'Piss' and 'Amy' sat on the wall watching over proceedings, while 'Alf' searched the pavements for butt-ends.

At the end of the block he turned left, passed Rough Trade (his favourite) record shop, then was back at the Portobello Road, but it was bearable as he just had to contend with a moment of crossing the main flow then he was almost at Mike's. The usual mob of tourists were taking pictures of friends posing outside the Travel Bookshop; some with the pervy Hugh Grant lookalike. His sandwich board proclaimed:

> *Picture with Hugh   = £5.00*
> *Picture with Hugh + 1st Base = £10.00*
> *Picture with Hugh + 2nd Base = £20.00*

Inside Mike's, the place was bustling but he found a free booth at the back and slid into the rear bench so he had a view of the entire room. There were many locals and a quantity of tourists sharing the big tables, and Art hoped that no one would want to share his booth.

Mike brought him a large coffee as he took out his new phone and admired its chunky silver frame with a big screen and no keypad. It was o2's 'X.D.A.' which was the latest pinnacle of technology, running Windows

Mobile, with 64 megabytes of WAM, or was it RAM? It had a big screen on which one could write or draw with its own stylus. He'd bought it using the excuse that he was attempting to drag himself into the 21st century but really it was just another example of his shop-o-holism. He opened a document and started to write about the previous day - Zal and the film rights; Aji's deceit and almost kissing Dash. He'd perfected using the stylus to write in one spot and loved the way he didn't have to look; and when he did, it had magically turned his scrawl into the popular typeface *Comic Sans*.

JOSEPH stood behind his dais in the foyer of Ebury House and watched the people emerging from Sloane Square tube station, pulling their hats on as they hit the icy wind. The tube wasn't busy, compared to a weekday morning, but there were still a lot of traffic. He saw a young couple, fashionably but inappropriately dressed for the weather, heading towards him. He walked over, opened the door and ushered them inside.

"Come in, come in!" he cried.

They did so and smiled as he shut the door, cutting out the wind.

"Are you the porter? Mr Joseph?"

"I am indeed Sir."

"Eva told us you could let us in to Karen Ford's apartment?" he said, handing an envelope to Joseph, who pocketed it, replying,

"Absolutely, everything is at your disposal." he said, handing them the fat catalogue as he led the way into the lift, "I'll show you up and then you have two hours, in which time you can make yourself at home," he said, closing the grille and punching a button, "eat from Karen's fridge; drink her favourite teas; listen to her favourite music, and marvel at the work of art which is her apartment, just as she left it all those years ago."

"Do you believe she was taken and killed," asked the boy, "or that she ran and survived?"

"I choose to believe she's alive sir, as I couldn't bear the idea that she's dead."

"So were you the porter then? It sounds like you knew her?" asked the girl.

"I was, and I did Miss. She was more beautiful than her photos, but such a down-to-earth character. Such a shame."

"I'm a model too," she said, "Karen inspired me to be one; I used to look at my Mum's Vogues and Elles and she had such presence you know? Like some of the others look absent, vacant even, whereas Karen's life-force shone out of every picture. And in her movies? Terrible she only got to make three." she said, looking awed and sad at the same time.

Joseph nodded and smiled. The girl was probably about the same age as his grand-daughter and beautiful, but not a patch on Karen. But who was? She'd embodied the phrase 'The face that launched a thousand ships'.

As the lift slowed, through the grille, Joseph saw Mr Gustav buttoning his expensive overcoat and placing his trilby over his balding pate.

"Ah, Sir, may I introduce a young couple who are viewing your neighbour's apartment."

Mr Gustav, twirling his handlebar moustache, looked them up and down as they swapped places, then said,

"Viewing eh? Is it for sale?"

Joseph's heart raced as his mouth acted before his brain,

"Yes, Sir."

"They don't look like they could afford it."

The couple both opened their mouths to speak, but Joseph jumped in first,

"Appearances can be deceptive Sir."

He closed the grille for Mr Gustav who pressed the button and descended.

"Sorry," said Joseph, wiping beads of metaphorical sweat from his brow, "he doesn't know we're charging for the pleasure of being in Karen's home. He'd stop us if he knew."

They walked from the lift and Joseph unlocked the door and stood back as it swung open, revealing the cavernous hallway. The couple hesitated, seemingly awed by what was before them; but finally, they tentatively stepped over the threshold. Below a giant Samurai chandelier, was a life-size photo of the iconic Eighties model.

"Oh my God!" said the boy, "this is the photo taken by Weber from this exact spot we're standing in! It's almost as if she is greeting us."

"In the red, black and gold hall," the girl cried, "inspired by
Tawagoto shō, the obscure Japanese Jet Metal Band!"

The boy raised his camera,

"Stand next to Karen," he said, snapping away.

"Remember, photos are for your own memories. You've agreed not to publish them anywhere."

They both nodded.

"Call me when you're finished," Joseph said as he shut and locked the door. At the lift he was reminded of Mr Gustav. That was the first time he'd bumped into him while with visitors, and he'd forgotten his prepared speech. Maybe he should tell Eva?

In the lift he checked the contents of the envelope. All there, including a print-out of the emailed reference from her employer. It was amazing to him that people were still so obsessed with someone who had disappeared over a decade ago. Karen Ford had, of course, been one of the most famous women on the planet at the time (along with Princess Diana and Madonna) and apparently the World Wide Web was awash with pages devoted to her memory, to sightings of her, and conspiracy theories about what had happened to her. He wondered if any of them came close to the truth.

GRODY, sat in his usual spot in the Greasy Spoon on Watling Avenue, Burnt Oak, his face clean-shaven. The sky was darkening outside as black clouds rolled in from the north. He thumbed the newspaper while racking his brains, trying to think of another way to acquire cute girls. The Halloween idea had been a stroke of genius, but how was he going to maintain that level of quality?

He wished it could be Halloween every day, so he could truly dress to express his feelings: One day Zorro, the next Freddie Kruger. And if he had a house and it was Halloween every day, he could have a good excuse for giving cute girls candy, laced with a little of the Purple. But it wasn't, so he'd have to think of another way.

He'd tried simply approaching them but that never went well - he was ugly and charmless, and he knew it. His only options were drugs or a Flintstones-like club.

Parties were a great place to find them, but how else could he be invited into parties and be invisible? He had a moment of inspiration and turned to the Classified Ads, found the Catering section, and started searching for any with potential.

He heard his Nokia bleep, so retrieved it from his pocket and saw a new text:

> *"You know what today is. Bring it all, 2pm.*
> *Also I'm moving today and need your*
> *help/car.*
> *I'll make it worth your while. Revox"*

Revox, his wholesaler, always moving, like Saddam staying one step ahead of the Cruise Missiles.

Grody thought about his options: Last night had gone well but even selling all his stash (without using his crew) hadn't covered his entire gambling debt to Revox. Could he ignore the text and the deadline? No, that would just add another 25% per week interest and get Maurice *No Mercy* Morrison on his tail. He could try double or nothing again? But that was what had landed him in this nightmare in the first place.

But he had another iron in the fire. He checked his other phone, the Motorola. Nothing. Why hadn't he heard from them yet? Had something gone wrong? Or maybe they didn't have another car available? Last time he'd had to wait three days!

He'd have to ignore Revox's text and hope for the best. He went back to scanning the classified ads. He found one Event Management agency that sounded ideal. It required Catering/Bar Staff URGENTLY for the party season. He circled the advert and ordered another cup of tea.

ART, on his second coffee, was enjoying his new gadget, while he thought about Dash, and their 'almost' kiss the night before. But he was still slightly tormented by guilt. Was it ever okay to go after your school-friend's ex? Especially so soon after they'd split? Maybe they could start a secret affair, like so many of his previous relationship had been. Why was that? Not all were nefarious, but it definitely added another spice to the already exciting early days of dating. Hannah, from a couple of years ago was a prime example and also Frieda more recently, who he hadn't wanted Dash or Aji to discover. Why? Was he aware, even then, of his simmering feelings for the beautiful Russian.

But maybe that was what made this different? Maybe he should talk to William (who had already admitted he and Dash had nothing in common), tell him that him and Dash were so better suited, loved so many of the same things; that whenever they were together they were chatting endlessly, sharing opinions on politics, books, movies and songs.

It was so unfair. If he'd arrived first at One-Nine-Two that night everything would've been different. But, late as usual, he'd been beaten to it by William, who'd met Dash first and invoked that stupid schoolboy code. Jeezus, *he* sounded like a schoolboy with the *It was so unfair!* What was he doing? Trying to justify his recent behaviour in encouraging Dash to leave William?

Out of the corner of his eye he noticed a silhouette approaching, so employed his usual defence of picking his nose and coughing gutturally.

But, seemingly undeterred, a voice said,

"Is this seat taken?"

He still had his finger embedded in his nostril when she slid onto the opposite bench.

"Find anything up there?" she said, smiling. Art also smiled, but sheepishly, and removed his finger. Her accent wasn't English, maybe a bit Latin American? But she didn't look it - more Irish, with green eyes and shiny copper hair pulled back in a ponytail. Her face was pleasant in a child-like way, with many freckles clustered on her tanned skin.

Was she a tourist, or here on business?

"Mmm, the food all looks great," she said, scanning the room.

Or was she searching for her Irish father who'd abandoned her on a mountain in Ecuador as a child; or was she a Bolivian beekeeper, in London for a conference on 'hive mentality'?

"What do you recommend?" she asked.

Or a cat-burglar, doing her annual round of the ten richest cities on Earth?

She perused the menu and when Mike came over she ordered double mushrooms (well done) on toast. Mike turned his gaze onto Art, but he didn't want to say his order as it was identical.

"Your usual?" asked Mike, raising an eyebrow.

Art was relieved by the man's ingenuity and nodded. But then he realized it didn't solve anything as their food would still be identical. Would that seem charming? or creepy? He should've ordered Egg and Chips.

"Are you alright?" she said. Art attempted to speak but his mouth was dry and he just croaked, so glugged his coffee. She waited, then, looking at him out of the corner of her eyes, she said,

"Are you a bit 'special'?"

Art laughed, spraying coffee onto the table.

She laughed too, while miming wiping coffee off her face.

"No, I'm fine, I just haven't quite woken up yet," he said, taking another slug of coffee, "not enough sleep last night."

"Out artying?"

"Say again?"

"Out partying?"

"No, but my daughter was, and she gave me a scare, so I was out looking for her 'til the early hours."

"How old is she?"

"Thirteen."

"Tricky age."

"Indeed"

Their food arrived. She looked at their identical plates then up at him and said 'snap', then muttered something that Art couldn't quite hear? Was it 'No change there then'?

They ate in silence. He tried to avoid wolfing his food as was his habit, but she seemed intent on stuffing her face and finished way before him.

She was watching him eat and he felt self-conscious so put his cutlery down, but the moment he did, she opened a Time Out and perused the cinema listings. So he continued, until she dropped the magazine and said,

"I've gotten so out of touch, surfing in Tahiti for the last couple of years. What would you recommend? Have you seen Maid in Manhattan?"

"With Jennifer Lopez? I have seen it, with my daughter, but I wouldn't recommend it. It's a bit girly."

"But I am a girl," she said, smiling and turning her head to the right.

"Oh really?" Art smirked, "then you may well find it more palatable than I did."

"So what would you recommend?"

"Out of the other films I've seen with my daughter? I can't remember their names but... There was the moving tale of orphans, taken in (in both senses) by an old pervert in a wheelchair, who dressed them in skin-tight latex and forced them to perform circus tricks."

"That's an X-Men movie? No thanks."

"Okay... er, there was one about a sexy vampire dressed in skin-tight leather fighting werewolves with moving tails? It's more moving than I-"

"Underworld? Non merci."

"How about the moving tale of girls who play football-"

"Bend it like something?" she suggested.

"Beckham."

"What's a Beckham?"

"Never mind," said Art, shaking his head, "next?"

She smiled and nodded. He said,

"There was that Pixar animated fishy adventure - the second best film I saw this year?"

"Finding Nemo? So what was the best?" she asked.

35

"Bellville Rendezvous?"

"Oh yeah, I've read great things."

"Yeah, so good I need to see it again."

"Well, maybe we..."

Art waited for her to finish her sentence but she tailed off, and he didn't want to finish it for her and guess wrong so he remained silent.

JOSEPH was back at his desk. He had never really paid any attention to the decoration of the apartment. He'd realized it was extraordinary, but he'd barely listened when Karen had explained the latest piece she'd commissioned for her life's work. He'd just marvelled at the astronomical sums involved, and watched in awe as enormous pieces had been craned in through various windows.

He fished out another catalogue and read the blurb on the back. Each room was inspired by an album from one of her favourite bands, mainly by the artwork on the cover, but also by the mood of the music itself.

He turned on the monitor, activating the CCTV, then scrolled through the cameras until he located them, taking photos in the corner room with the high windows overlooking Sloane Square and the crescent. He leafed through the catalogue until he found it. The Purple Room, it was called, which seemed obvious to him as all the upholstery and curtains were that colour but apparently it was inspired by a band called Deep Purple, and in particular their album entitled 'Machine Head'. The album cover was a photo of shiny metal into which the words had been stamped. That accounted for the furniture then; more forged than sculpted, it was all stainless steel with various words embossed, but it was the size that made it all so outlandish. All the furniture was enormous, more suited to a giant, in the cavernous room. This was so, Karen was quoted, when you entered you felt like a child in a grownup's room.

He flicked through the catalogue, past various rooms he knew intimately: The red and black bedroom with demonic furniture inspired by Sabbath Bloody Sabbath, the gold and purple study after Prince's 1999, the blue and gold Screening room (Can's Future Days), and his least favourite, one of the spare bedrooms decorated with a thousand moths, after TalkTalk's Colour of Spring. When he looked at the monitor again the young couple were in the main bedroom which had two large windows overlooking Sloane Square; except that one would never see the view as the black velvet curtains were fixed in the closed

position. Everything was black. All the furniture was
mahogany and on every surface there was an intricate
pattern finely carved. The wavy lines were apparently
a famous design from the cover of Unknown Pleasures by
Joy Division.

The couple had been taking photos (in-between
kissing) last time he looked but now they were in
Karen's bed, making love under the covers in the
missionary style. He was about to turn over when they
swapped position and she was sitting on top of him,
exposing her cute body to the camera. She was wearing
one of Karen's wigs; the short black pageboy bob that
had been her trademark. Her partner looked enraptured.
Joseph took out his thermos and sat back...

GRODY had narrowed it down to two adverts which
fitted his requirements. He was about to call one when
finally a text arrived on his Motorola:

> *"P Reg Ford.*
> 35 Stag Lane
> *Good Work"*

'P' reg? Was that 1996? So that made it even
older than the Nissan for fuck's sake! Still, this
could easily clear his debt and then everything could
change if his new idea could keep things regular. A
smile begrudgingly curled across his mouth. He got up,
paid, left a tip (amazing the waitress and even
himself), then excitedly walked/skipped away, while
fragging the Motorola and chewing on the sim card.

ART found the girl's face familiar (and her
mannerism of turning her head as she ended a sentence)
but couldn't place it.

Then she spoke again,

"So I'm gonna do that awful American thing and
ask you what you do?"

"But we were getting along so well!" objected Art
with a faux frown. She smiled and he said,

"I write and draw, or," he corrected himself,
"draw and write?"

"Write what?"

"Well I used to write for some big magazines,
about the sub-cultures in cities I visited, but really
they were about myself mainly," he said looking at the
table, "I think it is known as 'Gonzo Journalism'."

"Artemis Grime?" she asked, turning her head away
and looking at him out the corner of her eyes.

He nodded. She smiled.

"You know I used to read your stuff all the time in my twenties, and I even bought the anthology when you overdosed and 'died'," she said, air-quoting, "and then it wasn't for a few years until I found out you'd survived."

"Yeah, my publisher thought I'd sell more books if I remained dead. But I'm glad you enjoyed my work."

"Yes! You kinda opened my eyes. I'd spent my life being shipped around the world with my parents and I'd stoically refused to integrate or explore these new places. Your inquisitive nature made me want to revisit them and see what I'd missed."

Art was flattered,

"I like the idea that I inspired you, it's been a while since I'd had any affirmation."

"But you wrote that book?" she said, "The *twisty mystery* set in 1999? 'I keep losing my head'—"

"I'm *Keeping The* Head! Why is that so hard to remember?"

"Because it is?" she said, stealing a mushroom, "but you must've gotten affirmation from that?"

"Of course," he said, "but a thousand strangers saying it's great is easily counteracted by your two best friends disowning you."

"Hardly surprising," she said, leaning forward, "you told some pretty embarrassing stuff about them in that book."

"Indeed - even though I asked their permission before—"

"Not all of them," she said, stealing another mushroom, "but I liked the book and I liked your tenacity. You didn't give up until you'd found your man. That's why I'd like you to take on a mystery for me."

GRODY was exhausted by his speed-walk to Stag Lane. His heart sank when he saw a rusting grey 'P' reg Ford Mondeo Estate parked outside number 35. It really did look like a piece of shite, though he knew from experience that underneath, all the mechanics would be perfect. Getting on his knees, he checked around the nearside wheel arch for a magnetic key-box, and sure enough, there it was. He got in and started the engine, then drove the mile back to his lock-up, in the lane behind the Greasy Spoon.

He thought about going into the garage and making sure everything was okay, but decided against it.

Instead, he looked in the glove box, where he found a fat envelope full of cash. He smiled: There was more than enough to pay off his debt to Revox, and to restock. In fact, much more than he'd been expecting. He wondered how the payment was calculated? It seemed completely random, but he resolved to ask, if he ever got a chance. Also in the glove box was another vial of purple crystals and another old Motorola, with only one text from a number, saying:

"*3?*"

He put it in his pocket and took out his Nokia. He fired off the same text to four numbers:

"*4!2%1! 3£3!1%3*5*4* 1800*"

then sat back, reclined the seat and closed his eyes.

Blackness. A dark forest. Voices. Murmuring and a familiar voice; a pleading voice; pleading for beer. It was dark and uncomfortable. She'd cricked her neck. Just one beer?

"Here, take some money? In fact, If I give you a twenty you can buy me a six-pack and keep the change okay?"

"Don't be ridiculous Miss Samuelson - you almost died last night—"

"But it's just beer!"

DASHA opened her eyes and saw Hannah propped up in the hospital bed, haranguing the nurse, who was pulling the curtain around the bed. Dash cleared her throat and Hannah turned and smiled saying,

"Wow! Still in your Halloween costume - been up all night?"

"well yes, I have been - with you."

Hannah seemed shocked then shook her head slightly and said,

"Can we get out of here please?" asked Hannah, "I really need a drink!"

"You're kidding."

"No!" she said, "Look at my hand. It's shaking. I need a drink now."

"Do you remember what happened last night? Why you're here in the hospital?"

"I didn't lose the rest of my pancreas did I?" she said, feeling her stomach.

"I found you dead on the bathroom floor. You were blue. I BeeGee'd you for ten minutes before the paramedics came! You were in 'Toxicology' 'til an hour ago. Your body was poisoned! You nearly suffered complete organ failure."

Hannah looked down as she scrunched the sheet between her fingers. Finally she said,

"I don't remember but I'm sorry. I must've scared you horribly."

Dash nodded,

"I didn't tell anyone."

"Huh?"

"You came round for a second and the one thing you said was 'Don't tell *anyone*'."

"Thanks, now where are my clothes?"

"If you leave this hospital I will tell everyone, including your parents."

Hannah leant back and looked at the ceiling through hooded eyelids. Dash stood up, then retrieved Hannah's polka-dotted dress and said,

"I'll bring you your phone and some things from home before the matinée okay? I have to return the costumes soon, so I need to go now. Promise me you'll stay in bed 'til I return?"

HANNAH nodded. She really didn't want Dash telling her parents. She watched Dash leave the ward in her blue skin-tight costume. Hannah liked the way Dash's butt had indents on either side, sculpted by endless hours of dance. She wished she had such a perfectly sculpted body, but she really couldn't be bothered to even use the stairs in the mansion block, let alone go to the gym. Luckily for her she was naturally thin and sometimes bought her clothes at kids stores. The only thing perfectly sculpted about her body was her perky C-cups that she'd had done so people would stop mistaking her for a child. Her hands were still clasped tightly around her bedsheet. She unfurled them, revealing a twenty pound note she'd borrowed from Dash's cleavage. She examined the drip feeding into her arm and disconnected it, then looked around the ward for some clothes.

ART stared at the girl as she spoke but he hardly heard her.

"...I was born in the States, but we moved all over the world while I was growing up, and for a few years I went to school here in London, very near here..."

Art was confused: She wanted his help with a mystery? He wasn't a private detective. What was she talking about?

"...my father was a powerful man who was distant and intimidating and my mother was ineffectual and unable to stand up to his bullying..."

Why would she want him to investigate anything? He'd been incompetent.

"...we had a lot of staff who came and went below stairs, and I was actually closer to the Cook than my own family, including my twin-brother..."

40

She obviously hadn't actually read the book! He'd blundered along, most of the time not even knowing what was going on, until, through happenstance...

"...but then, someone started visiting me in the night. He wore a hood so I never saw his face and he was much bigger than me, so I was easily over-powered. He threatened me, saying if I told anyone he'd kill my family..."

Art had tuned back in and had heard most of what she had just said, but it sounded like a dream he'd had once and was finding that distracting.

"I couldn't sleep anymore, waiting for him to come. I started camping out in the many attic rooms and sometimes I'd hear him coming and he wouldn't find me, or I'd manage to slip past him and hide at my friend's house at the bottom of my garden. We'd cuddle in his bed and that was the only time I felt safe and slept well. Sometimes I wished for the man to come just so I could run to the safety of my friend. Sometimes I pretended he had for that very reason—"

"Lori?" said Art, tears collecting among his eyelashes.

Art saw that Lori was tearful too and he leant across the table and held her hand.

"I'm sorry I didn't recognize you, I—"

"No, why would you? We were just kids then," she said, "though I was reasonably sure it was you the moment I saw you coming out of your house—"

"How did you know where I lived?" asked Art, intrigued.

"It's pretty obvious from the book. There's only a few houses diagonally opposite the Black Cross, so I just waited in there, where your old friend Tony sat..." she said, tailing off.

Tony, he hadn't thought of him in ages, then he popped up twice in twelve hours. Art shrugged, then asked,

"And your mystery? Do you want to find your abuser? Is that why you're here?"

"Other than to berate you for telling my story in that book, for no good reason."

"I'm sorry. I felt I needed to get that out."

"Well, at least you gave my dad a different job and didn't call us by our real names, but I've still gotten some questions about London and specifically Holland Park from friends and family who knew I'd spent two years here. But yes."

"But yes, what?" asked Art.

"Yes, I'm here to find him and I need your help."

Art nodded and was about to speak but tailed off as he was distracted by a bright red coat outside. He sat up as he saw Aji walk into the café.

DASHA was sitting silently by the hospital lifts, scanning the newspaper and trying to resist the urge to go pee. She really should have gone before she sat down, but the one-piece Halloween costume discouraged her. How long had it been? Twenty minutes? The paper was full of Guantanamo Bay, America's latest descent from the moral high ground. Extraordinary Rendition was the new buzzword. That Bush moron had flouted the Geneva Convention as though it didn't apply to America, and Britain was complicit, allowing itself to be bullied by the ever-self-righteous Yanks.

A boy, maybe ten, was sitting close-by with his mother. He kept glancing over at her. She'd forgotten she was wearing her Halloween costume. She smiled at him. He said,

"Are you an alien?" She nodded.

"Where do you come from?"

"Far far, away," she said.

"From a black hole?"

"No one comes *from* a black hole. The idea that a black hole is a portal is crazy—"

"Lots of stories have black holes in them, why is that crazy?"

"Well okay, you know that a black hole is made when a star explodes into a supernova then collapses in on itself?"

He nodded.

"It's all the same stuff, but the gasses and liquids are compacted into solids, yes?"

"Yes," said the boy, "its gravity is so strong it pulls everything in so tightly and becomes a solid ball."

"For sure, so my theory is that the gravity is so powerful that even the atoms cannot spin anymore."

"The atoms?"

"You know an atom is mainly nothing yes? They're tiny balls, (the electrons), spinning around other tiny balls? (the protons and neutrons), and my theory is that they are crushed together. Imagine you have a packet of marshmallows and you put one in the centre of your bedroom on your bed, and another by the door and another by your window. Those two are spinning around the centre with all that empty space in between. That is an atom. It might look like a ball but it's mainly empty."

He nodded.

"So get those three marshmallows and squeeze them into a little ball on your bed and something that was once the size of your bedroom is now the size of your sticky palm. I think that is what happens when an atom is crushed inside a black hole. How else could a ball of gas thousands of times bigger than Earth collapse to the size of an asteroid?"

He nodded.

"So nothing moves inside a black hole, and anything that comes into its orbit will be sucked against its surface and flattened to the size of one electron, proton or neutron."

"I've never heard of squeezing an atom before."

"That's because we can't do it, but it doesn't mean it can't be done. They never thought they could split an atom until the 1940s, but they did."

"And they thought the earth was flat before that."

"For sure, so that's my theory - smushed atoms. And have you heard of the Big Bang?"

"Yes, when there was nothing and then an explosion."

"Yes, they say there was no time before the Big Bang, don't they?"

He nodded.

"Well, I think it's because *before* the Big Bang, there wasn't *nothing*, there was just one gigantic black hole. A black hole that had sucked all the other black holes into itself until it just hung there, with nothing moving inside it. If there is no movement, there is no time. You can't measure how long that gigantic black hole hung there, because nothing was moving. The atoms were crushed into their single components, like a gold watch with all its tiny cogs, which had been ticking away, was suddenly melted down into a solid block. That's why, in my opinion, they say there was no time before the Big Bang."

"So you're saying there was a universe before ours and stars died and black holes formed and they sucked in the whole galaxy spinning around them and then there was nothing left but many other black holes that were gradually sucked into each other and they merged into one big black hole?"

She nodded.

"So what made the big black hole blow up again?" asked the boy.

"I don't know, but maybe one electron in the center got restless and started squirming and it set off other around it, until—"

"Boom!" shouted the boy.

"Yes, and that was the start of our universe, one that is still expanding, but that will eventually collapse in on itself again, into one gigantic black hole, and again, time will not exist."

The boy looked satisfied with her explanation and went for a wee.

She looked up every time someone approached to check if it was Hannah absconding. A little old Rastafarian tottered down the corridor, pushing a Zimmer frame, muttering under his breath. His dreads were all collected into a big beany, the weight of which seemed to bend him double as he headed into the lift. It was only then that Dash noticed his hands had very smooth skin for an old man and his trousers were a good six inches too long for his tiny frame. Dash jumped up and leapt for the lift but the doors shut just before she got there. She ran for the stairs, bouncing down the five flights in time to catch sight of the old man, trousers hiked, jogging through the revolving door, without the Zimmer frame. She followed him out on to the Fulham Road just in time to see him go into the little Tesco. She found him in the alcohol section: One empty beer can lay at his feet as he glugged back a second, while trying to retrieve a bottle of top-shelf vodka.

"Can I get that for you?" Dash said, holding the bottle just out of Hannah's reach.

AJI spotted her Dad sitting at the back and wandered over. Her head was thumping which she guessed was a hangover. When she saw he was with someone, seemingly interacting, she was surprised. In the morning, he'd normally ignore anyone he had to share a table with (except Dash), though she could see why he had changed tack - she was cute, for an oldie. When he saw her approaching, he sat up straight and put his hands under the table.

Aji smiled at her Dad, who said,

"Lori, this is my daughter Aji. Aji - Lori."

Lori said 'Hi' and scooted over, inviting Aji to join her,

"Ah yes, I read about you in your dad's book—"

"Nothing libellous I hope." she said squinting at her father who laughed.

"Nothing compared to what he wrote about *me*," said Lori pointedly. Aji raised her eyebrows and said,

"Really, do tell," as she sat down.

"Er, no. It's quite humiliating actually, so I wish I hadn't told you now." Her dad looked shocked and she was about to comment when her phone buzzed. A text from her third best friend Dora:

44

"Amber is missing. Call me!"

Aji waved apologies then walked out onto Blenheim Crescent while waiting to connect. Dora was already mid-sentence:

"...I don't know what happened we were all dancing at Hannah's then you and Margot snuck off and then Amber went and I was dancing on my own and I've still got Amber's bag with her makeup, credit cards and keys and she just vanished and there's no answer from her phone or at her place and she hasn't rung me and I guess I thought she'd gone off with a boy but she wouldn't have left her bag and she would have called me by now and I'm supposed to be covering for her cos she told her mum she was staying at my place but her mum doesn't care cos she's in Bali anyway with her personal trainer and her dad's always in L.A. so I don't know whether to call them but even if I did they'd probably say she'll be back in a week she does this all the time which is true but this time it's different she'd never leave her bag however out of it she was and my mum's gonna kill me cos I lied to her this morning and said she was still sleeping and now we've gone to see my gran so I'm safe for now but what happens later I can't tell her cos she'll kill me—"

"Dora, stop!" said Aji, "I'm going to speak to my Dad and I'll call you back," then she hung up. Her ear ached as well as her head. She often found Dora exhausting. She was like a new puppy that found everything exciting, that always wanted your attention, was constantly yapping, and prone to occasionally weeing on the carpet. Aji walked back into Mike's and sat down.

"Sorry Dad, that was Dora—"

"You're third best friend?"

"I'm not doing that anymore."

"What about her?"

"She and Amber also came to Hannah's last night, but Amber just vanished from the party and Dora still has her bag with her makeup and credit cards, which of course she'd never go anywhere without."

"Have you called Hannah or Dash? Maybe she's stumbled in there recently."

"Good thinking. I'll do that."

She nodded to Lori then walked out, texting Dora her plan. She tried calling Dash as she walked round to the chemist on Elgin Crescent, but it went straight to voicemail. She bought some Solpadine Plus, munched two, then walked home while trying Hannah's phone, which rang out; as did Amber's. What was wrong with these people? Did they not have their phone glued to their hand like she did?

Upstairs, she crawled back into bed to wait for the Solpies to kick in. They were her favourite painkiller she'd discovered when she first got her period. She liked the little buzz the codeine gave her, but she had to hide them from her Dad. Many years earlier, he'd been a heroin addict so avoided any opioids including codeine. Even that little buzz could apparently start a snowball effect which might end with him returning to the gutter, or worse?

HANNAH was back in her hospital bed. The traitor Dash had carried her back kicking and screaming, literally.

"So you didn't trust me and spied on me, it's outrageous!"

"I was just sitting by the lifts; I wasn't spying on you—"

"You lied to me! Now I think of it the costume hire place isn't even open on Saturdays!"

"That you actually disguised yourself and then walked right past me is your own fault and proves that you—"

"I just wanted a drink, that's all. I'm not an alcoholic, I can stop anytime!"

"Then stop now—"

"I could, but I don't want to!"

"You sound like me. When I was thirteen!"

"Oh Fuck off! and Fuck off! You don't care about me!"

Dash raised her eyebrows, then slowly bent closer until their noses were almost touching. She placed her hand on Hannah's then started to prize Hannah's fingers apart, retrieving her £20 note. Dash announced that she would go pay for the beers and walked out, and for a moment Hannah felt a pang of guilt. Her hands were no longer shaking though, and so far she'd only thrown up once. Lately, her routine had been to buy a six-pack of cheap lager and a two-litre bottle of vodka, then drink two of the lagers and wait to throw up, then drink another can and maybe throw up. Once her stomach was settled, she'd start on the vodka and be able to get on with her day, aided by some coke or speed. Admittedly, this was the worse she'd ever been, but it wasn't *that* bad. From her previous time in Alcoholics Anonymous she'd met hundreds of drunks that had lost their families and their jobs and their homes, so really could this little incident be her rock-bottom? It certainly didn't feel like it. Of course she only had Dash's word that she'd given her

mouth-to-mouth and pumped her chest to the beat of 'Ah
- ah - ah - ah - staying alive - staying alive' for
ten minutes while waiting for the ambulance. Hannah
herself had no recollection of that, but other little
details were slowly emerging from the haze...

ART watched Lori eat her pudding in silence. He
felt so many things all at once, he wasn't sure he
could pinpoint just one.
Maybe shame? Shame that he told her story and she
felt humiliated by it.
"I'm so sorry Lori. I didn't think—"
"It's my fault. I'm so sleepy I blurted it out
before I realized what I'd said. Whenever anyone asked
me about your book (normally friends of my mother) I
always denied it was me, so I've never had to deal
with the truth, in the real world, outside of my
groups."
"But if I'd never written the book, you wouldn't
be here now."
"I still would've been abused Artie, and living
without closure," she paused, then said, "and it
didn't seem like Aji had read the book anyway!"
He laughed and shook his head. Aji had never read
anything he'd written. Sitting before him was his
first love, his best friend's twin from when they were
all together at primary school, and neighbours in
Holland Park.
"So, will you help me Artie? Help me find him?"
Art felt sceptical and didn't want to make any
promises he couldn't keep.
"We hardly spoke of it when it was happening."
"No, I couldn't, sorry," she said, looking at the
table, "I didn't know how to express it; and I kinda
thought it was my fault."
"Do you feel okay talking about it now?"
"Sure," she said, looking him straight in the
eye, "I've had a lot of therapy and attend a shitload
of support groups so I'm way past the shame." Then she
leant across the table and said,
"But I'm not past the anger Artie, I need
closure."
"Okay, I guess we can try," he said, "let's start
at the beginning."
Lori nodded.
"When did he first visit you?"
"About three months after we arrived in London."
"Which was a month after me and Richard (and you)
became friends, and started crawling through the hedge
between our gardens?"
Lori looked behind her then said,

"I see you put me in there as an after-thought?"

Art shook his head.

"No... but I guess Richard was my friend first—"

"And I was his annoying twin, who followed you both about—"

"But if it's any consolation to you, I have rarely thought of Richard since, whereas I've thought of you every day."

He waited for her to speak, but she just smiled.

"Did I take your twin away from you?"

"Kinda. You were his first great school-friend and being our neighbour too made it almost constant."

"Was that why you were so surly with me?"

"Was I?" she said, fluttering her eyelashes, "I thought I was always so lovely!"

"So these are love-bites?" he said, showing her his scarred arm.

She looked pained, and said,

"Wow! I never imagined they'd still be there after all this time! I'm so sorry."

"It's okay. I kind of liked them because they reminded me of you."

"Yeah, and I thought of you every time I bit into a bloody steak!"

They both laughed, then Art said,

"That first time you purposefully hurt me was in Holland Park, when we were playing hide and seek and we ended up hiding in the same place, do you remember?"

"Not really."

"You had that look of contempt on your face - the one that made me feel confused - and you dug your nails into my leg 'til I bled and said something like 'That's for not protecting me'."

Art examined her face, but she said nothing, so he continued,

"I didn't really understand what you meant at the time, but I thought you were talking about Richard - the way he'd beat you up constantly for following us around - so I tried to protect you from him."

"Which you did valiantly."

"But it wasn't until later, when you turned up in my room, that I realized it wasn't Richard you were talking about—"

"No, it wasn't him."

Art liked the sensation of Lori running her fingers along the scar on his arm. Finally she said,

"Okay, I guess I was taking it out on you cos maybe I didn't know how to express my fear and pain, and I didn't have anyone else who'd take it the way you did," she said, looking sheepish, "but it was different after I sought refuge with you, wasn't it?"

"I suppose," he said, thinking back, "yes, you definitely bit me less, but you were more diffident, which was sometimes more painful, because every time you fled to my bed, I fell a little bit more in love with you."

Lori said nothing.

"I'm sorry," said Art, "that sounds incredibly selfish but it was what I was feeling at the time and of course I had no idea of the horror of what you were going through so . . ." He tailed off.

"You were in love with me? The girl who followed you everywhere—"

"Making disparaging comments and poo-pooing our every move."

"The girl who held your hand—"

"Then bit it."

"The girl who kissed you—"

"Then kicked me."

"The girl who pulled her knickers down to get your attention—"

"Then slapped me for looking." They both smiled

"Well; maybe not love exactl—"

"Don't minimize. I'm sorry Artie, I had nowhere to run, then one night, while I was hiding in the attic waiting for the inevitable, I thought of you, warm in your bed and wanted to be there with you, safe in your arms. Then he came, but I managed to slip past him and make it to you. The one place where he'd never think of looking for me."

Art was struck by a revelation:

"So you hadn't just been..." he couldn't say it, "cos you were crying so hard—"

"No, I think it just might've been relief."

Art remembered that night well. She'd turned up in his bedroom after midnight, crying, and had ran to him and he'd held her until she'd fallen asleep. They'd spooned all night, with Artie too excited to sleep until dawn. But when the alarm rang, he'd woken up alone, and from then on she'd refused to speak about it.

He finally said,

"So who do you suspect?"

Lori looked at the ceiling then said,

"We had a few people who came with the house including the Butler, who we called Silver Surfer for some reason, and the gardener which were both a bit weird towards me; then there was the neighbour on our left, he was famous; and one of my Dad's security team called Johan."

49

"Well, that's a good start. How old do you think they were?" he asked, "the Butler for instance."

"It's hard isn't it? When you're twelve everyone looks old."

"Say he was forty? So that would make him 60? He could still be butling."

"Is that even a word?" she asked.

"The gardener was a bit younger wasn't he? In his thirties? Maybe."

"I guess we could look for agencies?" she suggested.

"But to start with, maybe we should revisit the scene of the crime?"

"Or call Catherine? The Cook? She was so kind to me. I think I can track her down."

"Let's do both," suggested Art, "we're gonna have to visit there eventually?"

She looked nervous, then slowly nodded.

Mike came to collect their plates.

"So you still love mushrooms on toast I see?" said Lori, smiling.

Art held his hand over his face.

"That really freaked me out." he said, laughing, "and of course I now get your pun—"

"Which pun?"

"When I said I'd been up late, you said 'Out Artying', which I just thought was me mis-hearing you at the time."

They got up and walked outside. Lori said,

"Let's go back to your flat. I want to see if it is anything like the bare description in your book."

"And you can tell me about the places you've revisited?"

"There's not much to tell really. I'm not a *journalist* like you, *and* it's way past my bedtime."

DASHA hailed a cab in the Fulham Road and shut her eyes on the way back to Hannah's. She knew it was the addict in Hannah making her behave this way: The anger, the denial, the minimization of the problem were all classic characteristics that she'd been through with her own partner William. She'd walked out on him a few weeks earlier, and Dash was hoping it might push him into realizing he needed to do something.

At Hannah's, she got out of the Halloween costume and showered, then plugged in her tiny phone to charge and got into bed. Exhausted, she lay back and shut her eyes.

GRODY awoke from his nightmarish sleep and found
himself in a strange car. It took him a moment to
remember where he was before seeing his 'home' outside
the window. His home, the 'potentially stylish studio'
set in the delightful surroundings of a dank back-
alley bedecked with abandoned cars, broken fridges and
the smell of his own shit. He checked the time
(thirteen-hundred-hours), fired up the engine and set
off for Revox's. What should he ask for this job? £50
off his debt, per trip? plus all the drugs he could
consume during the move? The thing that galled him was
that he'd taken £2000 at the party and he'd have to
give the cunt all of that anyway, plus a large chunk
from the glovebox envelope. Still, if everything went
well, he'd be out of that garage soon enough. But did
he really want to move? Could he see himself living in
one of those pristine blocks? Was he too far gone for
civilization now?

DASHA was awoken by a ringing and turned over to
grab her phone, but it wasn't ringing. Maybe it was
Hannah's phone? She walked across the hall and the
ringing did get louder as she entered the room, then
even louder as she went into en-suite bathroom. But
Hannah's phone was sitting on the sink and wasn't
ringing. It was another phone. Dash finally found it
behind the loo, hidden by the brush. She answered and
said,
    "Hello?"
    "Dash?"
    "Yes."
    "It's Aji. Why are you answering Amber's phone?"
    "Am I? Sorry, I just woke up."
    "Where are you Dash?"
    "At Hannah's."
    "And I take it Amber isn't there?"
    "No, she's not."
    "Dora said she disappeared from the party last
night."
    "I just found the phone on the floor behind the
loo."
    "Oh shit, hang on, me and Margot are coming
round."
    Dash hung up. She scrolled through the list of
calls and saw Aji and Dora had called a lot, but no
one else at all. The same with the texts. So, Amber's
phone had been dropped on the floor in the same room
where the door had been forced open. Were these things
connected?

HANNAH hoped Dash would come soon with her phone, then she'd be able to call someone and charm (or bribe) them to bring her a bottle. She was itching for a drink. Her tummy had that empty feeling, like being hungry except much more empty. Empty all the way to her sides. Hollow. Then she remembered telling Dash to fuck off. Surely she didn't take her seriously? Surely she was going to return? No. The fiery Russian wouldn't be back. Hannah disconnected the drip and got out of bed, but this time she didn't even bother to steal some clothes. She just headed straight for the stairs.

ART and Lori walked around the back to avoid the crowds. He'd been trying to get her to talk about herself but she wasn't keen. Also she was a little sleepy so took his arm and leant on him. God, Piss, Alf and Amy were arguing over fag-butts, but stopped to let them pass. Ever since Art had bellowed at them for scaring his daughter, they had been very wary of him. A car was unloading furniture and taking it into the block opposite his home. Maybe Jeannine's replacement? They walked up and Art put on the kettle while Lori looked around, commenting on her vision of the flat and the reality. She then perused his record collection and played a few tracks from various L.P.s while they chatted. She wasn't very forthcoming when he asked about the recent past, happier to steer the conversation back to Artemis Grime.
     His eye was caught by his new neighbour who had installed a shelf unit and was filling it with ornaments.
     "Lori, look. Look in the window opposite." She did so, watching the man pick objects out of a box and place them on the shelves.
     "Yeah, he's moving in," she said, "so what?"
     "He's using a polaroid as reference for where to place the ornaments."
     "Then he's a removals man," she shrugged, "that's what they do when someone pays for the full service." Art shrugged too. He'd never considered such a service existed. So that man with the polaroid wasn't his new neighbour.

DASHA, Aji and Margot looked at the loo door in Hannah's room.
     "Do you think the broken lock has something to do with Amber's disappearance?" asked Aji.
     "Well it would be quite a coincidence if it wasn't—"

"And now we know something bad happened to her,"
said Margot, "she might have forgotten her bag, but
she'd never ever go anywhere without her phone."

"But you don't think it's worth calling Amber's
parents?"

Margot shook her head, as they walked back to the
living room,

"No, they won't care."

"Then *we* should call the police-"

"And say what? A girl, who's notorious for
running away from her uncaring home has gone missing
again?"

"But her bag and phone must count for something?"

"Who's legally responsible for her while the
parents are away?

"Their housekeeper."

"Have you spoken to her?"

"Dora tried but the woman was drunk. She's been
drunk since Amber's mum left on Tuesday."

Margot examined the abandoned Ericsson T610,
scrolling through the Calls and Texts. Then she looked
in the Gallery at the photos. Dash silently cursed
herself for not thinking of that, though cameras were
relatively new on phones.

"Look at these," said Margot, "this first one was
taken in Hannah's bathroom mirror." Amber was standing
a bit crooked, as she photographed herself with one
hand and pulled her leggings up with the other. Her
face was also crooked.

"Is she winking?" asked Aji, "or semi-conscious?
And look, what's that in the corner of her mouth? Is
it a joint"

Dash squinted at the tiny screen. It was the same
purple-tinged joint she'd found in Hannah's mouth. She
was about to nod and tell them about Hannah but
decided not to. She'd respect Hannah's wishes for the
time being.

Dash saw their faces drop.

"So now she's taking drugs too! She's probably
over-dosed and is lying in a ditch somewhere!" Dash
said,

"Let's not jump to conc, conc,"

"Conclusions," said Aji.

"She's probably with some guy and is still
asleep," said Dash, "she'll call any minute."

They nodded and Dash tried to distract them,
saying,

"So this photo being the first in the gallery,
means it was the last one taken?"

The teenagers nodded, as Margot started to scroll. They bent in and examined the low-resolution images on the tiny screen.

The next ones were pictures of the party, featuring all of them:

Amber dressed as Catwoman, Dora as Wonder Woman, Aji as Madame de Tourvel (from Dangerous Liaisons) and Margot as Helen Levitt (her favourite photographer, though Dash had thought she was meant to be Annie Hall) in various poses, plus lots of indistinct figures in the background.

"They're pretty shit," said Margot, "compared to my thirty-five mill."

Dash and Aji looked at one another, then at Margot.

"So how many rolls did you take last night?"

"Half a dozen or so?" she replied, squinting at the screen, "it's a real shame these aren't better quality because we'd probably be able to find some clues, don't you think? Like the ones of them walking to the party? There's someone in fancy dress behind them in these two shots but they're so blurry it could be Batman or Robocop or..." She looked up and found them both staring at her.

"What?"

HANNAH was freezing. She was running barefoot along the side-streets of Fulham in nothing but her paper gown which only intermittently covered her modesty, let alone her butt. She zigzagged her way north and west towards Earl's Court and her home, but when she finally arrived on the Old Brompton Road she veered into her favourite pub where she knew she'd get a warm welcome. The Leather Boys of the Colherne were devoted to Hannah, so it only took a few minutes for them to warm her with cuddles and hot toddies. Then they found her some clothes (leather, of course), and the spare keys to her flat. When she was leaving, she saw Aji and Margot exiting her building, and they ran over to say hello. They hugged her and held her hands. From them, she learnt that Amber was missing and that Dash was still upstairs.

"Don't tell her you saw me okay girls? Please?"

They promised, escorted her back into the pub, then said goodbye.

GRODY arrived at Revox's block in Shoot Up Hill and looked for a spot to park. He recognized Jimmy-Jimmy-ah!, an old rival carrying boxes to his car, which already looked full. Was this a coincidence or had Revox enlisted other dealers for this mission? It made sense. To move all of Revox's stuff would've taken him days. Jimmy-Jimmy gave him the finger as he pulled out and Grody took his space then walked up.

He hated Revox, and found his appearance repulsive, with his pallid skin and white hair; was that cuz he never went outside? But then he had almost no colour in his eyes, like a white rabbit. What did you call someone like that?

He found a gaggle of other dealers in the half-stripped flat, filling boxes and suitcases with Revox's belongings, all pretending to listen 'intently' to their wholesaler's pronouncements, while he scanned world through a crack in the curtains,

"Now Jimmy-Jimmy has gone, Dorfmeister, you take your stuff down, ah, Grody, you got something for me?"

Grody nodded nervously, handed him the envelope of cash, then backed into a corner and stood at ease. Revox passed the envelope to Maurice who counted it quickly:

"It's all here, plus the interest," he said, impressed.

Revox looked disappointed and returned to his crack in the curtains.

"Unless you'd like to go again? Double or quits?"

Grody's heart leapt. His mouth opened automatically to say 'Yes!' but he felt a poke in his back. He turned and spied an old 'friend' Harry, filling a box with ornaments. He was raising his eyebrows and shaking his head almost imperceptibly.

"Er, better not, thanks Revox."

Harry Houdini, who dealt out of a squat in 'Hangover' Road was a weaselly Rocker with skin like ancient parchment and breath like the Dead Sea Scrolls, or was it the other way around? Harry's side-job/claim-to-fame was that he had customized a certain wet/dry carpet cleaner to aid constipated junkies in evacuating their bowels.

"It's like an industrial enema, but it doesn't just flush - it sucks too!" he'd proudly announced, handing Grody his card, which had a photo of Harry performing his service on an anonymous butt in a grimy bath, "call me, and I can be with you in twenty minutes."

Grody had never used his service, but, like an insurance salesman Harry couldn't stop talking about it:

"Nozzle width," he'd whisper, "uniquely tailored for each client, that's the secret." Necessity being the mothefucker of something-or-other.

Revox perused his notepad, "Grody, that gives you the books and the sound equipment, cos you have an estate car, like a real nuclear family man. So, use this polaroid to take a couple of pics to remember where all the cables and plugs go, then dismantle the sound gear and be ready to go in about an hour."

"But what about my order?" he asked, "I've got over two grand—"

"We'll sort that at the other end," said Revox, "oh, and leave the passenger seat free. I'll be coming with you."

Revox swung round to take a peek out the curtains. Maurice said,

"And we're offering you twenty in cash for the move, or thirty off your next purchase?"

Grody sighed. He should've ignored the text. He had more important business than pandering to this paranoid psycho. He signaled the thirty, found a box and went over to the bookshelf. Did these qualify as books?

None of the classics. Just pulp fiction by Jeffrey Archer and Jackie Collins and writers he'd never heard of: Dan Brown? Robert Harris? Irvine Welsh? Artemis Grime? Shit.

AJI and Margot left Dash to prepare for her matinée. As they were hit by the biting wind, they saw Hannah coming out of the pub opposite. She was dressed in leather and looked cute, but was swaying dramatically. They ran over and grabbed her, holding her up, as she was obviously drunk, even though Hannah claimed it was the wind that made it hard to stand up. It was difficult to decipher her speech, but they understood that Hannah didn't want them to tell Dash that they'd seen her. They promised, then carried her back into the pub, saying their goodbyes.

They walked quickly with the icy wind behind them.

"So do we need any supplies? asked Aji.

"No, got everything we need. We'll just do contact sheets to start with, then have a look at what we've got.

Aji's hangover was fading. But she still felt like shit. She was embarrassed that she'd fallen for Marcus's line about loving her. She'd been warned that he was a dick, but she'd thought she knew better.

"Can we do the last one's first? I want to see if you got a good one of Dash yanking Marcus's willy."

Margot laughed.

"I think I must have! I took enough!"

Aji nodded and walked on in silence.

"What's wrong?" Asked Margot, "I mean other than Amber being missing, and that little prick Marcus?"

"It was weird. I went to Mike's Café to meet my dad for breakfast and he was sitting with a woman and I could swear there was something going on between them."

"Ooh! What was she like?"

"Strawberry blonde, freckly, skinny, with a maybe Brazilian accent?"

"Was she beautiful?"

"Not exactly, but pretty... for her age."

"Which was?"

"About the same as him - ancient?"

"And what do you think was going on between them?"

"There was a tension?"

"Sexual tension?"

"Ugh! Maybe..."

"But isn't that a good thing?"

"I guess." said Aji, shaking her head.

"You're always saying how you want more independence. If he had a serious relationship, he wouldn't be thinking about you so much anymore."

Aji liked the idea; and didn't like it,

"Yeah, but I don't want him to think about me any less."

"You want to come home whenever you please."

"Yeah, but I don't want to find a new step-mother there."

"You want to experiment with the opposite sex."

"Yeah but I don't want my dad doing it!"

The only real constant in their home had been Dash, her long-standing baby-sitter. The three of them made up the closest thing to a family unit that she had ever known and they seemed to be getting closer and closer. What would happen to them if he got a girlfriend?

DASHA was preparing to leave for the hospital. She was closing a window when her eye was caught by a bright red coat below in the street. It was Aji, standing with Margot and someone in leathers? She looked closer and realized it was Hannah. She sighed, then went and put Hannah's phone back by her bed.

ART was intrigued by the block opposite. Another couple of cars had been and gone and they'd all done the same thing in unloading then unboxing and using a polaroid to arrange the objects accordingly. Surely a professional outfit would have one big truck? Lori had fallen asleep on the sofa and was gently snoring just like she had when they were kids. That time had stamped the template of how he'd viewed love: She ran

to him in need and he fulfilled that need; then she
ignored him or punished him by withholding, until she
needed him again. All his teenage relationships had
followed the same pattern. Was it his behaviour that
had made the girls react like that, or had he
unconsciously chosen girls who would fill that
criteria?

GRODY wound the speaker wires back and forth
between his hand and his elbow, then fastened them
with a cable tie, while watching Revox weigh his order
on the scales.
    All the other dealers had left except for Milton,
a chatty Irishman, who had foolishly engaged with
Revox in a stupid, coke-fuelled rant about his ex
throwing him out. Why did Milton have to take it? Why
did he? Because Revox had the drugs and he knew it.
Did Grody treat his crew like this? Lording it over
them? Pontificating? Treating them like shit? He
didn't think so, but that meant he wasn't sure. He'd
have to check himself when they came round later to
re-stock.

JOSEPH was happy, even after the incident in the
lift with Mr Gustav. His life had taken a strange turn
since Eva had opened the apartment to visitors. He
found he had a disposable income for the first time
since he retired. He could, if it appealed, take a
cruise in the winter, or spend two weeks in Morocco?
But who'd watch the desk and let in visitors? Baz, the
night porter couldn't be trusted. He'd sat in for
Joseph when he'd been ill, but Karen Ford's apartment
was a different matter. Once Baz knew about it, they'd
have to pay for his silence continually. Maybe Eva
would have to meet the guests somewhere else, then
bring them in with her? He'd mention it to her later.
    Outside, he saw Eva pull up on her scooter,
unfold her long limbs then retrieve her phone and
start tapping away at the keyboard with her thumbs.
Maybe he'd buy a Blackberry like hers? The QWERTY
keyboard would certainly make texting his grand-
daughter easier. And, of course, he could afford it.
Eva's thumbs moved so fast they blurred. What was she
writing? A novel? She was wearing her trademark outfit
of black hoodie and skinny jeans with her black wavy
hair protruding from her open-face helmet. It was
remarkable how physically similar she looked to Karen
Ford (though up-close Eva was pretty, as opposed to
drop-dead gorgeous); but Eva would never countenance a
career in modelling; she was a dancer in 'A Forest',
the West End's longest running animal-based musical*.

58

She'd recently given Joseph tickets and as the curtain rose, he was surprised by the audience's reaction, like the cast were superstars. He couldn't make out the story, but as it was apparently based on a Japanese video game, he didn't suppose there *was* much of a story.

Eva finally walked into the foyer, smiling at Joseph.

"How's it hanging Joseph?"

Joseph did not know how to respond to her American slang.

"I do not know how to respond to that Miss, but I so enjoyed your show the other night. I thought you were all brilliant."

"Aw, thanks Joseph, could you tell it was me?"

"You were the Bunny. I recognized your beautiful voice during your solo. I wanted to ask how you sing inside the giant head?"

"Oh, it's all pre-recorded unfortunately, though as some of the dialogue is in Japanese that can be a blessing."

"And is the head heavy?"

"They were originally made of papier maché and had to be supported by your shoulders, but now they're inflatable. We just pull them on, blow them up a bit more so they grip our head nicely, then we're good to go."

"But if you're head's inside a balloon, wouldn't it slowly deflate?"

"Our head isn't inside the balloon. The balloon has an indentation in it where our head goes."

"Of course. That makes much more sense. And can you see well?"

"Yeah, the balloons are translucent so we can see out, but you can't see in."

"Well it was marvellous Miss," he said, handing over an envelope stuffed with cash, "as are the visits to the Karen Ford Museum. Our new scheme of locking them in has killed any idea of sneaking out with a valuable souvenir, so it's a lot less embarrassing for all."

"That's great Joseph, thanks!" she said, squeezing the envelope, "and they're happy to pay the fee? No grumbling or passive-aggressive asides?"

"None Miss. They seem honoured."

"Shall we raise the fee?"

Joseph shook his head.

"I don't think so. There's no overheads other than groceries, so best not get greedy."

"Speaking of which," she said, holding up a Tesco's bag, "I'm gonna replenish the fridge. See you later!"

She ran and leapt up the stairs two at a time, then stopped and looked back at him through the caged lift-shaft.

"We've gotten another visitor coming on Tuesday afternoon if that's okay with you Joseph?"

Joseph smiled and said,

"The more the merrier, Miss."

*(except for Cats and the Lion King)

EVA unlocked the door and carried the groceries through to the kitchen. She replaced the empty box of Jasmine Tea, which seemed popular with Karen's fans (hardly surprising as there was a photo by the fridge of her drinking a cup in one of her first campaigns).

Eva looked around and was proud of what she saw. Karen had started something fabulous, but a lot of it had been half finished so Eva had completed it. She'd even commissioned pieces that Karen had sketched, like the giant 'Sun' lamps in the Music room, and the Hippo in the Hallway. Was it weird that she was following so closely in Karen's footsteps? Living with Karen's ex-boyfriend? Decorating her apartment?

While replacing the bin liner she saw the rolls of wallpaper she'd gotten for the 'Life on Mars' loo. She thought about having a crack at it, but then remembered she had a matinée to get to.

JOSEPH said goodbye to Eva then went back to examining the catalogue. He'd never paid it much attention in the six months since Eva had got it printed, but he was finding it fascinating. As their porter, he had known Karen Ford and her partner Michelangelo, and had a few stories he had contributed to the catalogue, but most of the stories were directly from Michelangelo himself, including how in 1987, he and Karen had met in Milan when she was still an unknown model, details of their tempestuous affair, and his account of the day she disappeared:

"Unfortunately, Karen's address on Sloane Square was common knowledge and she was often accosted by fans on the doorstep. She also attracted criminals who knew how wealthy she was. Somehow, in 1991, two managed to enter our home and take us hostage. They locked Karen in the Music Room, then tied me up and tortured me for information of where the valuables were. Finally, after I'd lost a litre of blood I cracked and told them. They escaped with ten million in Bearer Bonds, and maybe a million in diamonds. And maybe Karen too. I have no idea what happened to her. I woke up in hospital, my jaw wired shut, my nose flattened, covered in stab wounds, and with many bones broken. Ironically, the police suspected *me* of killing *her*, even though I was the one found unconscious in a pool of my own blood. Once they'd realized their error, and I could leave hospital I returned to my hometown in Italy, where I lead a peaceful and unglamorous life."

    This was the first time Joseph had read that story in the catalogue and he understood why it was only half-true.

    It was true that Michelangelo had been found in the Purple Room almost dead (Joseph still remembered it vividly), and it was true that there was no trace of the world-famous model, but his claim it was a home-invasion by opportunistic thieves was not true. Neither was the claim that Michelangelo had moved back to Italy. In fact, after a trip to Switzerland for rehabilitation and reconstructive surgery, he had returned to London a new man with a new, much better-looking face.

    Joseph, now he came to think of it, was probably the only person who'd known Michelangelo *and* the new improved version, named Mickey.

    MICKEY sat in the one good swivel chair in the Helpline office, slowly swivelling, scanning the maps, notices, and meeting information on every vertical surface (plus one map of London Postcode Areas stapled to the ceiling).

    Only ten minutes into his shift and the phones for Narcotics Anonymous had hardly rung and he was mildly bored. Normally he'd get a few calls on a Saturday afternoon, which would take himself out of himself: Some addict (in Recovery) looking for advice; or a first-time caller who he could try to inspire into getting to their first meeting. Or a heart-rending story from a tearful family member. Yeah, this wasn't ever a busy shift and the main reason he'd agreed to it was because Eva did a matinee on Saturday Afternoons.

    Finally, the phone rang. He picked it up and said,

    "Hello, how can I help?"

    The caller introduced himself as a Policeman in Nottingham, then asked,

    "How do I get attendance records for the meetings in our city?"

    "I'm afraid there's no such thing," Mickey explained, "it really is anonymous - there's no registration or fees and people don't even have to give their real name—"

"Seriously?"

"I'm afraid so—"

"So how do you keep track of members?"

"We don't. They're not classes, so they don't end up graduating with a diploma. They're support groups, which we regularly attend to help us get clean and stay clean."

"So you can't help me find this guy? I've got his name and address. His name is John Burling?"

"Sorry, it's the weird thing about the groups: We sit in these rooms and others pour out their darkest deeds, weirdest thoughts, and deepest fears week on week, but we may know nothing about their most basic details. It's one of the many dichotomies about the fellowship. But it's one reason we're so successful. If it had cost money, been monitored or required registration I wouldn't have come."

The policeman accepted Mickey's explanation and said goodbye. Mickey always tried to enlighten outsiders when he had such an opportunity, hoping they'd be able to pass the message on to someone who needed it.

The Doorbell rang. Mickey looked on the screen and saw Eva, so he buzzed her in. He heard her bounding up the stairs, then she rounded the corner and fell into his lap, making the swivel chair swivel. She kissed him then looked at the walls as they continued to turn.

"So you haven't ripped down the Wall of Paper yet?"

The Wall of Paper: Ninety-plus A4 sheets, pinned onto cork tiles, featuring all the N.A. meeting information for Great Britain. When additions or changes came in on the phones, the volunteers on duty would write it on a pink sliver of paper, then pin it over the old info. This happened a lot, and it was someone's job to transcribe the handwritten slivers into the computer, then print the edited page and pin it on the wall. He was doing a shit job compared to when Art did it, but that was the nature of rotating commitments.

Mickey hugged her,

"Well that was always Art's dream, to build a Meetings Database, but it could be years before they agree to spend that kind of money."

"And how is Art?" she said, pointedly.

"You know I don't know the answer to that—"

"What's that phrase? *Cutting off your nose, to spite your face.*"

"Never heard of it," he said, smirking.

"Look, Art's book threw us both a curve-ball," she said, "for you, excruciating embarrassment and fear of reprisal from Milan; and me to a lesser extent as no one really knew me, but we did both sit for long interviews and give him permission to write it—"

"But changing the name of the only world-famous supermodel who ever mysteriously disappeared was pointless!" hissed Mickey. "For anyone who was a regular at A.A. or N.A. meetings in the King's Road, it was easy to put two and two together—"

"Or either of your 'families' in Milan!" agreed Eva, "but it's all turned out okay now, hasn't it?" Mickey nodded. "So why don't you call him? Invite him to Blacks tonight!

He nodded. She smiled then checked the clock and got off his lap, saying,

"Shit! I'm almost late! I have a matinée to get to. She kissed him, put on her helmet and ran out.

Mickey watched her disappear and smiled. Maybe his old Chelsea friends would have forgotten the gory details by now? Be able to say 'Hi' without adding some stupid joke? Be able to stay in the same room as him without fearing he might turn violent?

Maybe he'd go to a West London meeting that evening and test the water? He looked at the listings for London - Saturday and saw the Emperor's Gate meeting which he used to frequent. Yeah, he'd go there. What's the worst that could happen?

ART stood in his bay window and watched with some amusement as yet another car pulled up and started unloading boxes. This guy, though, also hung some net curtains in the window which slightly disappointed Art. His view was obscured.

Lori had woken from her snooze and they were listening to one of her favourite tracks called 'Session' by Linkin Park. He liked it.

"So are you still clean?" asked Lori, sitting up, looking refreshed after her nap.

"Yup," he smiled, "nine years clean of all mind-altering substances now."

"Still going to the meetings?"

"Not so much."

"Why not?"

"Well, I guess I felt it was impinging on my creativity?"

"How so?"

"Er... A lot of addicts are extremists. We either love something or hate it, especially when we're using. Then we come into recovery and go to lots of meetings and it calms us down and we're less extreme; and that's exactly what I needed to start with..."

"But?"

"But when I started writing the 'Head' book, I just didn't think I was doing the story justice. My style was too bland for the storyline. Then I went to visit my old friend Hew in Palma for a month and neglected to go to meetings, and I felt the old me bubbling up inside. Now that is dangerous for a full-blown, ten-out-of-ten addict, but the work I was producing made me realize I could sit on the fence and have the best of both worlds: Still be clean, but have the twisted imagination, the pervy mind, the dark humour..."

"It sounds like so many creative skills - you have to learn the rules before you can bend them—"

"Exactly!"

"But it sounds like a difficult balancing act. How do you know when you've gone too far? When you're at the tipping point?"

"I can notice the difference in me. I start to become less positive... a bit resentful... more territorial... more selfish—"

Lori gestured for him to hurry it up with the winding finger motion.

"and more impatient," he said raising his eyebrows. She pretended not to notice.

"So for me, I think a meeting every two or three weeks is good. If I get too hateful or snarky, I know it's time to go to an extra one. Or when Aji tells me to. But I like the way I think now - back to being slightly more extreme - and it shows in my work, it's more edgy?"

"What are you working on now?"

"Enough about me," he said, instinctively leaning on the felt that covered his drawing board, "tell me about surfing in Tahiti?"

"Show me," she said, walking over.

He sighed and lifted the cover and she laughed,

"You're drawing porn! And pretty extreme porn! Maybe your theory is correct?"

Art watched her eyes scanning the rough pages and was surprised that she hadn't stormed out, or thrown up on him. She was actually smiling,

"They're pretty good. Do you write it as well?"

Art nodded, less embarrassed.

"And do you do the ink as well?"

"No, I used to ink as well but they keep upping the pages so I don't have the time any more. I send them to Antoine in Amsterdam who inks them and applies the halftones."

"Halftones?"

"They're the tiny dots that create shading in old newspaper photographs, and you can also buy them in sheets that you can cut out or rub, transferring them on to your artwork."

"But you must be able to do that on a computer nowadays?"

"Yeah, but Sex-Doll-Horror monthly is very old-school—"

"Sex-Doll-Horror?"

Art nodded. She was still leaning over him and he could smell her hair which was falling in his face.

"Artie, I don't know... I'm a bit surprised. In the *Head* book, you were uncomfortable about Aji knowing you were drawing porn and said you wouldn't do it anymore."

Art nodded.

"So what's changed?" she asked.

"I guess the pervy part of my head is slowly strangling the moral part?"

"And what about the sex?" she asked, "in the book you'd had trouble keeping it in your pants hadn't you?"

Art laughed and said,

"Yeah, it had become a painful obsession which I needed to knock on the head, so I took up eating instead—"

"No, I meant now."

"Oh right. Well, I go to an S.A. meeting once a month which seems to keep it in my pants."

"So are you celibate?"

"No, I've had affairs, but according to S.A. I have to be monogamous, and respectful of how often she wants to have sex; I can't coerce her into it—"

"Sounds healthy," she said, "except you said 'affairs' which implies you're cheating on your partner which doesn't sound very monogamous?"

"Oh, I don't have a partner," he said, "and no one is being cheated on. I guess I used the word 'affair' because they're secret from Aji."

"Why?"

"Because, like most teenagers, the idea of her dad having sex disgusts her."

"It's not just teenagers Artie."

"Plus I think she still harbours a desire for me and her mother to get back together?"

"Don't all kids? I know I did, even though Dad was an asshole."

GRODY lugged Revox's boxes downstairs and into the Ford. The back seat of the car was almost full so went to the boot and saw the bicycle and suitcases in the boot. He should have left that in the garage before he left. He opened the boot and they lifted with the door, exposing the lie that the boot was full, when only small parts of the bicycle and luggage were glued to a panel. Below was the large empty space where a sleeping girl could be hidden. He took a fleecy blanket and threw it over the top of the panel, then loaded the sound system into the boot. When Revox deigned to come down and squeeze in, all he said was,

"Portobello Road", adjusting the mirrors so he could see behind.

Grody tried to zone out Revox's paranoid ravings ("...it's so obvious they'd installed microphones..."), and his justifying of his exploitation of his minions ("...so the police won't know I'd moved this way..."), and his wife ("...she blames me for our daughter running away even though we haven't lived together in a year..."). Revox spoke as though they were friends but Revox didn't have any friends – only obsequious customers who hated him, and, like Grody, were waiting for their moment.

Grody reached for a cigarette from his pack and Revox motioned for one too. Passing them over, Revox noticed the pre-rolled joints and lit one up. Grody was about to warn him then thought better of it. Maybe that would shut him up. As the car crawled onwards, Grody smiled. Revox's ranting were slowing to a relaxed rambling. Normally, it took only a few drags to put a girl out, but Revox was sucking on it like it was a thick shake from SvenDonald's. Maybe he'd feed the rest of them to him? Maybe he'd finally shut up? Forever...

DASHA arrived at the theatre, entering through the stage door on Greek Street. She'd fallen asleep on the tube and missed her stop, so was late, but only by her own standards; she was still earlier than some. Her friend Valerie greeted her, from below the dressing table, where she was searching for something.

"Great party last night! Your costume was amazing!"

"Thanks Val. So was yours. You looked great as Supergirl. Did you get it from Angel's too?"

Valerie nodded and held up her lost lipstick,

"Yeah, so did you have a good time?" she said, clambering up, "it's hard sometimes when you're the host, isn't it?"

Dash nodded as she sat down next to her friend,

"I've only been there a few weeks, so I didn't really feel any of that, and it was great until I lost someone. You saw Aji and her friends there yes?"

"Sure," Valerie murmured while she looked for her eyeliner, "is Aji okay?"

"She is. But her friend Amber went missing. Just vanished from the party."

"What was she dressed as?"

"Catwoman."

"Catwoman? Oh yeah, I remember her. Cute. Didn't she have an older boyfriend there?"

"Did she? It's possible, she's quite advanced for her age. Did you see the boyfriend?"

Valerie stared at the ceiling while squinting her eyes,

"Yes, I kind of recall speaking to him, though I was already pretty drunk when I arrived," she said, smirking, "yeah, I think we walked up together. I was with Jake? Third Panda?"

"What did he look like?"

"Jake? You know him surely? He's a hunk but I fear he might be as gay as—"

"I mean Amber's boyfriend."

"Oh, I dunno darling."

"What kind of costume?"

"Sorry, a lot of last night is a blank."

"But you say you walked up together? Was he with Amber then?"

"No, I don't think so.

"So how do you know he was her boyfriend?"

Valerie looked blank.

"Sorry darling. I've got nothing. Maybe it'll come back to me, once I've got a few vodkas inside me later? Have you seen my blusher?"

Dash felt disappointed. Even though Valerie was a brilliant dancer who never forgot a move, in every other part of her life she was an air-head; and why did she make herself up for every performance when she was only going to cover her face in an enormous inflatable head. But, Dash loved her, and of course, Valerie had given her a lead.

Once Valerie's head was inflated, she hooked her head up to the pump then set off for Jake's dressing room, stopping by large metal vent that went all the way to the roof. Wally, from the Dimmer Room nodded to Dash as he approached, held his phone against the vent for a moment, heard a ping, then walked away. It was the one spot in the bowels of the theatre where anyone could get reception on their phone. She composed the text,

> *"Valerie (Supergirl) says Amber's*
> *older boyfriend might've*
> *been at the party?"*

then held the phone against the metal and pressed
'send'.

AJI sat in the red-lit darkroom, watching Margot
cutting the negatives into strips and laying them on a
sheet of glass. Aji loved watching Margot performing
all stages of her passion, including the darkroom. She
was in her element, working efficiently in the
blacked-out bathroom in Battersea. Aji didn't have a
passion. She was good at a lot of things, but she felt
passionate about none of them. When the career
counsellor had asked her what her main interest was,
she'd said 'TV and Films'. The counsellor had looked
encouraged and said she might be able to get a job as
a runner in any of the hundreds of Production
Companies in London to learn the trade. No, she'd
replied, you misunderstand me, my main interest is
watching TV and films. She also liked Boys? Could
there be a career in watching TV and films with boys?
Probably not.
    Margot was already fixing the first contact
sheet, then hanging it up to drip-dry.
    "Do you think Marcus is going to keep quiet about
last night?" Aji said, examining the tiny black and
white pictures for a good one of Marcus, dressed
poorly as Dracula, being taught a lesson by Dash in
full-on Mystique Mother-fucker mode.
    "I doubt it somehow," said Margot.
    "Then could I have a few prints of number
thirteen please? I think I might pop one through his
letterbox later, as I'm south of the river."
    A text from Dash popped up. Aji read it aloud,
    "Did Amber have a boyfriend at the party last
night?"
    "Not that I remember," said Margot, "but come
look at this. She's in the background of this shot,
queueing by the loo door. Let's do a big print of this
one, and see more."

DASHA found the new boys' dressing room and
knocked before entering. She got a cheer from the guys
as she picked her way through the chorus.
    "Jake? How are you feeling?"
    Jake saw Dash in his mirror and smiled,
    "I'm good thanks Dash, I only had a couple of
drinks so no hangover."

Dash sat next to him as he turned to her, looking very earnest.

"I hear you've left William?" he said, "I'm sorry, but if you'd like a shoulder to cry on, or someone to go dancing with, or..." he leant in closer and whispered, "anything. Anything, okay?"

She smiled and thanked him, then,

"Do you remember you and Valerie arriving at Hannah's?"

"I'm not with Valerie, we just thought we'd go together—"

"No, I just mean do you remember walking upstairs?"

"Sure."

"Did you walk up with another guest?"

"Yeah, he said he was meeting his girlfriend there."

"And what was he dressed as?"

"Zorro."

AJI and Margot watched the print develop, and as the contrast grew, they could see the partially hidden profile of a costumed character.

"Zorro!" they cried in unison.

DASHA texted Aji once she'd returned to the vent. She sent a one word text, and received the same text from Aji moments later. As she walked into the dressing room, Valerie shouted the same word at her.

"Darling I remembered! I was just telling Eva she missed a classic at Hannah's last night, and it suddenly came to me!"

Eva smiled, as she squeezed into her Bunny costume.

"Yeah, I'm sorry I couldn't make it now. So who's this Zorro?"

"He told me he was meeting his girlfriend as we walked up," said Valerie, as she tried on her giant inflatable head, "then later I saw him with Catwoman, as they left together."

"So he wasn't carrying her out?"

"No, they were walking out together. He said she'd had a bit too much or something. She was giggling."

"That doesn't sound like someone who was taken by force."

"No it doesn't darling," Valerie agreed then changed the subject, "has my neck got thicker? The collar on my head felt really tight last night..."

Dash went back to the vent and texted Aji the news.

AJI read the text aloud:
> *"Valerie now remembers Amber*
> *walked out with Zorro.*
> *Seemed happy about it. x"*

Margot shrugged,
"She's done it before..."

On Ladbroke Grove, GRODY followed Revox's mumbled directions to turn left. The first joint had slowed him down but the second had hardly affected him at all. Maybe the Purple had a short shelf life? Maybe that was why it came in a glass vial? They arrived in a sea of people on what was (according to the sign) 'THE WORLD AMOUS PORTOBELLO MARKET'.

"Fucking tourists... Lucky they only come... on Saturdays otherwise I'd... have the fucking Remington out... pretty fucking quick... Just slowly edge forward," mumbled Revox, waiving him on, "they'll part... like the fucking sheep they are."

Grody did so and then was told to park. He saw Milton the Irishman about to pull out of a space next to another of those yellow BMW dirt bikes he was lusting after. Maybe it was a sign? He parked then got out and looked across at where Revox was pointing: A block of flats.

"It's Flat 3b up there," said Revox, almost falling out of the car "but there's no lift... so mind your back with those boxes of books," he smiled (sarcastically?) at Grody, "you see? I do care," then as an after-thought, "and don't drop the sound gear or I'll skin you alive."

Grody immediately wanted to drop the sound gear. Why didn't he? He could find another wholesaler. He took the last fag from the packet and mused upon the pre-rolled joints inside. Shrugging, he tipped them into the gutter then, prompted by a disgruntled Revox, picked up a large speaker and hurried across the road.

ART sat at his drawing board reviewing and tweaking his work. He liked having Lori there with him. A lot of his life had been spent drawing while chatting with friends who he had his back to. They never seemed to mind.

He finished another page and popped it in the scanner for digitization. Sex-Doll-Horror still paid well, compared to some magazines which were losing readers to the internet, and thus paying less for content. But his earnings were falling year on year, and he worried that if the decline continued, he may have to find another line of work, or accept the offer from Hollywood?

His 'Head' book had sold moderately well (but nothing compared to his Anthology when he was at the height of his fame, and 'dead'), so that wasn't going to pay the rent. Perhaps Zal was right about the option? Let them develop it, hope they made it. Take the money and run. Never see it.

Lori was stretched out on the sofa, half dozing, half watching 'Popular' on the TV, half staring at the ceiling, when she asked,

"Hey, did you ever dig up our time-capsule we buried in Holland Park?"

"No, it's still there as far as I know."

"Shall we go and dig it up?"

"That sounds like fun," he said.

"What was that rhyme we made up to remember where it was? The one with the farting?"

"You mean the one *without* farting," he corrected her pedantically (something he was trying to avoid doing).

Art hadn't thought of that in so long, but as with so many rhymes they were never really forgotten. Somewhere, it was buried deep in his memory. He dragged it to the surface:

> "The Frog-Pond squares is where you'll start,
>> then walk downhill but do not fart,
>> for fifteen steps, then take a left,
>> fifteen more then take a breath,
>> turn right and let gravity play its part,
>> for fifty steps into the heart,
>> then right behind the sycamore tree,
>> is where the time-capsule will be."

"Well done!" she said, "all I remembered was the 'do not fart' line. Are those square ponds still there?"

It had been an age since he'd spent any time in Holland Park, as Aji was no longer interested in outside pursuits, but he did walk through occasionally, to and from the specialist Gin-monger on High Street Ken for his father.

"I think they are. But it has changed quite a bit. Further down the hill they've put in a Japanese Garden which is cute, but it's really cut in to the wilderness that we used to play in."

He scanned the room for a photo of his Mum and him when he was nine. He spotted it and retrieved it from the wall, then sat down on the sofa next to Lori.

"I also drew a map," he said, turning over the frame, "on the back of this picture."

Lori pulled herself up, close to Art, staring intently at the detailed drawing, more an aerial view from a forty-five-degree angle, than a map.

"It's so beautiful!", she said, running her fingers over the Indian ink, "I remember you used to do a lot of these secret drawings on the back of pictures. Can I take a photo?"

Art nodded and smiled. She took out a little Sony and snapped away as he spoke,

"The sycamore was only as tall as us then. It will be enormous by now, if it's still there."

Lori sat up.

"I think I need to go sleep properly. I'm still on Tahiti time, so it's halfway through the night for me."

"Where are you staying?"

"The Portobello Hotel." she said standing and stretching.

"Which room?" he asked, "they're all different but I've stayed in most of them over the years."

"I don't know the number, but it's gotten an enormous four-poster bed?"

"With the French windows overlooking the garden? I love that room. Shall I walk you? "

She nodded and they made their way downstairs.

Outside, yet another guy was moving stuff in to the block opposite. He was lugging an enormous speaker across the road while being shouted at by a white-haired man of indeterminate age.

Art and Lori walked up the hill in silence, until Art had a thought and said,

"So it stopped when you went to Lima?"

"Yes."

"So who didn't come to Lima?"

"Those ones I already mentioned."

"So you predicted correctly?"

"What do you mean?"

"When you came to me that last night, you said you wanted to reset, start again, meaning you knew it was going to stop."

Lori walked silently for a while then said,

"I don't remember saying that."

He said goodbye to her at the doorstep and waved, saying,

"Call me tomorrow."

He wandered home circuitously, avoiding the tourists on the Portobello Road. She didn't remember saying that. There were a few things she hadn't remembered, which were etched into his head; momentous memories which just didn't hold the same weight for her. That was probably common to all relationships?

His phone vibrated in his pocket. It was Aji.

"Hi Dad, bad news. It looks as if Amber did leave the party with a man dressed as Zorro. Which sounds normal except Dash found her phone in Hannah's loo, and the door looks as though it was forced."

"I remember! I was the first to notice it when I came round looking for you."

Art waited for his daughter to speak. Finally she said,

"Sorry again for scaring you Dad—"

"Hang on. Zorro? Didn't I see someone dressed as Zorro as I'd been leaving?" Art looked at the sky, "Yeah, the guy who double-parked and blocked my path? But he'd been arriving and the loo door had already been forced."

"So you're saying it wasn't him who kicked the door down?"

"I guess, which makes sense if you're saying she wasn't taken? That she actually left with him?"

"Good point."

"And isn't she prone to that kind of behaviour?"

"Unfortunately, that's why we're dithering about calling the police."

"Understandable. And are you okay?"

"Been better. Listen, I'm south of the river with Margot, so I thought I'd stay with Mum tonight, okay?"

"Sure Sweetheart, but you know I'm gonna phone her and double-check—"

"Dad!" she shouted, "why do you have to be like that?"

"You realize you lied to me only last night? Claiming you'd be sleeping at Margot's, while she told her mum she'd be sleeping at ours—"

"Oh. Yes. But—"

"Anyway, that's good cos I've got a lot of work this evening. Speak later?"

They said goodbye and Art wandered on. When he got home, an ambulance was parked opposite, loading someone onto a gurney. Was that God, with Piss, Alf and Amy watching on?

MICKEY walked up Gloucester Road and looked at his watch. It was already 7.30 so the meeting would have started, but he was only minutes away from Emperor's Gate so he would be okay. He was never normally late - maybe he didn't really want to go? Maybe he should turn around and go to Dino's instead? He hadn't been to a meeting in Kensington in ages because of the humiliation caused by Art's book. Maybe this was a mistake? He'd never liked any of them anyway.

Then he was outside the building and the smokers greeted him like an old friend and he felt a little better; then he walked down the stairs and heard the murmur of addicts and felt like he was coming home.

He recognized a few faces in the gloom who nodded and smiled. So far, so good. No pointing and laughing. He sat back and listened to the addict at the top table tell his tale. It wasn't so different to his own - a slow descent until all self-esteem had been stripped away. One thing that jumped out for him was when the guy spoke about his 'negative head':

"I've been around a good few years now, but I haven't changed that much. I can't get rid of my addictive personality and the little voice that tells me 'I'm shit', 'everything's shit', so I come here to get a better perspective on my life. That doesn't necessarily mean a rosier view, like arriving at a meeting hating or fearing everyone and leaving loving everyone. It means, for me, that I can get a greater understanding of myself, and maybe how to improve. So maybe, instead of a better perspective, it should be a clearer perspective?"

That was weird. Like so many times before Mickey had arrived at a meeting fearing everyone! And already he was feeling better about things. A 'Clearer Perspective'? Yeah, he needed that. He knew he was so lucky and had so many things to feel grateful for, and his banishment of Art was causing him more pain than relief. They used to come here together every Saturday night then go into the West End and meet Eva and Dash at Blacks. It would be nice to re-establish that tradition. Maybe it was time to call him?

He started stacking chairs as was his habit at the end of a meeting and a few old faces came and said hello, asking him how he was, and how was living in Hampstead. There were no jokes or any strange comments. Maybe everyone had forgotten?

He said Goodbye, went outside and got out his phone.

ART sat at his drawing board staring out of the window.

His phone rang. He saw Mickey's name and smiled; first time in eight months! He pressed the green button and said,

"Hi Mickey, how are you?"

"I'm over it."

"Oh, tha—"

"I mean it's not like you didn't ask my permission is it?" said Mickey.

"Well—"

"I just never thought anyone would read it!" said Mickey.

"That's—"

"Especially anyone in the fellowship who knew me, or anyone in Milan who knew me!"

Art didn't bother to try to speak.

"Forcing Eva and me to move to Hampstead!" he hissed.

Art winced,

"Sorry Mickey - you're obviously not over it—"

"I am, I am! You did me a favour actually, because my parents got in touch in the spring, and we met up in Paris."

"Oh - I'm so happy for you," said Art, acting surprised, even though he knew.

"And they've met Eva, who they love, so..." Mickey tailed off.

"And your other family?" inquired Art.

"All clear. My old bodyguard? You remember me telling you about him? Chico? He runs Milan now, so I'm not in danger anymore."

"That's great Mickey," said Art, "I'm—"

"But how are you? What's new with you?"

"Well, talking of my book—" Art stopped. It wasn't the time to tell him about it being optioned. He heard the sounds of Mickey getting in a cab and speaking to the driver. When would be a good time to tell him? Never! Maybe this was a sign? Which did he need more? Mickey or the money?

"Sorry," said Mickey, "what about your book?"

"Er..."

"Come on."

"Okay, er, remember I wrote about my first love?"

"Lori?"

"Yeah, well she turned up today."

"At your place? Why?"

"Well, ironically, to give me a hard time about writing about her!"

"Ha!"

"Yeah, I thought you might find that funny."

"Does she hate you for it?" said Mickey mischievously, "did you ruin her life too?"

"Er, well her life had already been ruined."

"Sorry. Bad joke. But does she hate you for it?"

"No, in fact she was very sweet and asked me to help her find her abuser."

"You? You're no detective!"

"I know!" agreed Art.

"So is she everything you hoped?" asked Mickey.

"What do you mean?"

"Didn't you write about her in the hope she might come to you?" asked Mickey.

"No!" said Art, but thinking about it, "...maybe..." he whispered, "...subliminally?"

"And is she everything you hoped? Subliminally?"

"She's tall, tanned and skinny. Still blonde and freckly. Still cute—"

"So you're going for it."

"I don't know. There's Dash to consider—"

"Oh for fuck's sake! You're still pining after the unavailable?"

"Well, she's not unavailable anymore."

"Oh yeah, which makes her less attractive to you?"

"God no," said Art, "I just feel a bit torn now."

"You're always torn about something aren't you? Can always see both sides of the argument."

"Another word for that in 'indecisive'."

"Anyway, want to come into Soho and meet me and Eva and Dash after their show? It'll be just like the old days, or do you have Aji?"

"I don't have Aji, so I guess I could, but..." said Art.

"So come! Or are you with Lori now?"

"No, she's jet-lagged at her hotel, and of course it goes without saying that—"

"Of course!" said Mickey, "*I* can keep a secret," then he hung up.

Art looked at his phone. That was stupid. But he didn't lie exactly. More a lie of omission. He went to make a cup of tea.

When he'd written about Lori, had he ever imagined she'd turn up in his life again? Was it a fantasy of writers that their heroines return to visit them? Maybe lots of authors wrote about their exes with that in mind. Had he done that?

EVA and Dash were in the Ladies loos in Blacks, touching up their make-up. Eva saw a text arrive:

> *"I have spoken to Art. All good.*
> *I did invite him to Blacks x"*

Dash yawned.
"Are you sleepy darling?"
"Yeah, I was up late last night—"
"I know - almost kissing Artie!"
Dash nodded but remained silent.
"So are you still on the pill?"
Dash shook her head and said,

"No, I came off it ages ago. There didn't seem to be any point."

"Then you need some condoms!" Eva said, getting out some coins and feeding them into the machine. A box dropped into the tray.

"Here," she said, passing them to Dash, "you never know when you might need one."

Dash smiled and said thanks.

MICKEY paid the driver and got out on to Dean Street. Even in the cold the street was packed with people standing around. Smokers mainly, but Mickey didn't mind the occasional whiff being blown his way. He used to smoke forty a day and couldn't judge anyone their habit. He knocked on the black door of the black house and was welcomed into the warm. There was Eva and Dash sitting at the bar, getting looks from all the guys, while they chatted and sipped their cocktails. His drink was waiting for him (Tonic Water with Angostura's bitters, ice and lemon) so he leant between them and took it. They both welcomed him and they all stood, backs to the bar, surveying the crowd. Some beautiful people, many so young it made him feel slightly out of place. He wouldn't come here on his own. Eva was his passport to anywhere, legitimizing his presence. Two beautiful women on his arms made him feel superhuman.

"So you spoke to Art and made up?" asked Eva.

"Yes, and I invited him here."

"So you've made up?" asked Dash, "that's quite the development."

They both looked at her.

"Just trying something. No?"

They both shook their heads.

"Does he have Aji?"

Mickey shook his head.

"So is he coming?"

Mickey shrugged.

"Aw, that means no, yes?"

Mickey nodded.

"I'm disappointed," said Dash, "this would have been the perfect location for us to make our acquaintances, if you know what I mean."

Mickey and Eva nodded and laughed. They were the only ones who knew about the mutual admiration that had been simmering between them for years.

"So," said Dash, "if I'm not going to get to smooch tonight, I'm going to dance!" and she skipped off into the dark. They consulted one another with their eyebrows, then followed her.

77

Sunday - 2nd November

HANNAH awoke being defibrillated. She liked the buzz. But she didn't like the wetness or the cold, or the tepid green uniforms of the two brutish men leaning over her. She looked around and realized she was lying on wet grass in a cemetery. In fact, in the Brompton Cemetery, just a few hundred metres from her home. What had happened to her? There was a hobo standing nearby (can one still use that word?),

"I called them for you Hannah! That was some night! But I woke up this morning and you were blue! So I had to call them! And I BeeGee'd you till they came."

Hannah nodded and tried to smile as she was lifted onto the stretcher and carried to the ambulance. BeeGee'd? Where'd she heard that recently?

ART sat at his drawing board making changes to his Sex-Doll-Horror pages, listening to 'Session' by Linkin Park on repeat.

He looked at his alarm clock on the windowsill. It said 11am. He should have put it back an hour, like all the other clocks, but this one he kept on British Summer Time. He'd found, over the years, that forcing his body-clock back an hour induced a mild jet-lag, as his body was used to going to bed at midnight, and he was suddenly going to bed at 1am. So when it said midnight he knew it was time for bed (even though it was actually 11pm according to the world outside). This, he surmised, accounted for everyone else's foul mood in November as their body-clock had to adjust to the whims of government.

He jumped when the doorbell rang, then squinted at the wing mirror mounted outside his window to see who was below. He recognized the platinum blond crop, so opened the window and dropped the tennis ball to Dash, then automatically started counting (one elephant; two elephant...) He put on the kettle, then pulled the felt over his drawing board.

Dash was slow today. Her record for the five flights was thirty elephants, but she was obviously not in an exuberant mood. She came in and slumped on the sofa.

Art examined her face for clues, then finally said,

"Are you okay?"

"Yes, but I was in Lisboa—"

"You were in Lisboa?"

"Yes, well I thought maybe—"

"I didn't think—"

"No, of course—"

"But—"

"Hannah's in hospital! They just called me."

Art was speechless.

"So will you give me a lift down there? She'll be out of I.C.U. soon."

"Sure," he said, standing up, "what's wrong with her?"

"She overdosed again—"

"Again?"

"On Friday night, after I left here, I found her on the floor passed out, so called an ambulance. I thought she'd 'just' drunk too much but they said she'd overdosed. I stayed with her overnight with all the wires and tubes sticking out of her, then she woke up and straightaways went to the mini Tesco's for a bottle of Vodka."

"Why didn't you call me? I would've come—"

"She asked me not to tell anyone, but that was then. I told her I wouldn't as long as she stayed there, but first it was Tesco's and then I saw her outside the pub opposite her flat?"

"The Colherne—"

"Yes, but that was yesterday afternoon and she never came home. Her phone was still by her bed this morning. And now this."

Art got his gear and the usual helmet and leather overcoat for Dash.

"Let's go."

REVOX surveyed his new home and cursed his minions for having arranged his belongings so shoddily. Maurice pointed at the clock. It was time for their first customers to arrive. Revox thought he heard their car and peered out through the crack in the curtains. No car below, but directly opposite sat that bloke in the window again. Revox said,

"He's there again, staring at us."

Maurice didn't take his eyes off the scales as he sprinkled the 28th gram into the freezer-bag.

"You're imagining it."

"He's making calls. Ratting us out. Fucking pig."

Maurice shook his head,

"Seems a bit fast since we've only just moved in."

"It's not an outlandish idea," said Revox, "in fact it actually reinforces my theory that I am constantly being watched, and justifies my constant moving between locations."

Maurice sealed the freezer-bag and shook his head,

"Maybe we should move then?"

"I've never seen the surveillance teams before," said Revox, "never imagined just one bloke being so blatant about it. I'd always imagined a team with high tech gear staking me out."

"And that you was always just too smart for them."

"Yeah."

The car pulled up below. Revox went to get his Forty-Five.

DASHA held Art tightly as they rode to the hospital on Fulham Road. She loved riding pillion as it was the only time she could hug him and squeeze her thighs against his.

They parked underground then went to admissions and found which ward Hannah was in.

The Ward Nurse greeted them,

"Oh hello Miss Petrova, I remember you from last time. She's out of danger. Her stomach has been pumped, she's on a drip to hydrate her and she needs a rehab immediately. She's obviously suicidal."

Dash nodded, though she found it hard to take. They walked over and sat by her bed.

"Suicidal?" Dash asked.

"Well I guess so," said Art, "though probably not consciously? I guess that my rock-bottom was similar. I would never've killed myself, but I didn't want to go on living the way I was. It was too painful."

ART looked wistfully at Hannah lying there with tubes coming out of her face. They had become great friends when they'd met in the rooms of A.A. and N.A. but then, after five great years, Hannah had relapsed and her drug-piggery had made it difficult for him to see her anymore. He'd never have gone to her Halloween party unless it was an emergency as he knew what he'd find. Walking into her bedroom and seeing her chopping the coke had simultaneously made his heart leap and his stomach fall out of his bottom.

He looked at Dash then around the ward. Were these all overdoses? In one of the beds he recognized the bearded face of God. Or was it Piss? He could never tell them apart. Those names that he'd bestowed upon his four homeless neighbours had originated decades earlier in the Games Arcades of the West End. The Space Invader machines which he and Hew were addicted to would only allow a three-letter name on the high-score chart so GOD, PIS, ALF and AMY were their chosen names. They had made it their mission to get those names in top place on every machine in London.

When, many years later, he'd clocked the four of them, it had seemed serendipitous that there were three men and one woman, so the christening had taken place. But now it seemed wrong. He wondered what his name really was and went over to ask.

A nurse was tending to him and she looked up and smiled.

"He's my neighbour," Art said, "I see him from my window every day."

"Oh really? So do you know his name? He had no I.D."

"I call him God," said Art, as if that was at all helpful, "or Piss, or Alf. But never Amy." He cringed then said,

"Sorry, I don't know his real name." She smiled so he asked,

"What's he in for?"

"Poisoning. He nearly died. He was on a ventilator all night. Weirdly the last case of this same poison was on Friday night and was your friend Hannah over there. The very same poison."

"Do you think it's worth alerting the police?"

"Hannah told me the last thing she remembered of Halloween was she'd been sitting on the loo, picked a joint off the floor and smoked it, so it would seem accidental?"

"But someone put poison in a joint?"

"But a lot of *street drugs* are poisonous to humans, it just depends on the quantity." Art nodded and thanked her, then went and told Dash.

EVA stood shivering in the high-ceilinged kitchen of the Hampstead House. She was boiling a kettle to fill a hot water bottle and make tea. Mickey didn't seem to feel the cold like she did. She watched him in the high-walled garden below, with two men in thick coats. They looked like identical twins. They were both shivering identically while Mickey stood there in his button-down shirt. Were they his new security team? She opened the window and shouted,

"Hi Darling! Would your friends like a 'cuppa'?" in her best Cockney accent.

They looked up and both nodded their heads; then looked at Mickey; then back up at Eva and shook them.

"They've got to leave now thank Evie. But I'll come up and have one with you?"

Mickey shook hands with them and let them out the security gate.

"Who were they?" asked Eva when he arrived in the kitchen.

"Sponsees."

"A.A. or N.A.?"

"Neither. D.A."

"D.A.?"

"Debtors Anonymous. I'm teaching them how to manage money; and giving them the odd job to help them become solvent."

"Well done," she said as she passed him his Jasmine tea. Jasmine tea. She wondered who had liked it first? Mickey, or Karen Ford? She wanted to ask but wasn't sure it was a good idea. She was never sure how he'd react to questions about Karen. Not that he'd be angry, but sometimes it made him sad? No, wrong word. Introspective.

HANNAH woke to find Art and Dash leaning over her. The last two people she needed, but the first two she'd thought of while lying on the wet grass in Brompton Cemetery. They were talking, but the rushing in her ears made it impossible to understand. Was this it? Was this her rock-bottom? Waking from blackouts? Waking from overdoses? Waking, and being disappointed that she was still alive? But she couldn't just stop. She was going to need help this time. She needed to be locked up. She needed a detox in the sticks, and some structure in her day. It was weird the way Dash's mouth was lip-syncing with her thoughts. She didn't need to tell her parents anything. The rushing in her ears was fading...

"...and we thought maybe Klaus House would be good? It is out of the way in Wiltshire, and they have a place for you today. What do you think?"

Hannah nodded and felt a relief flood over her.

"That's great," said Art, hugging her, "welcome back."

Dash hugged her too,

"I'm gonna ask Eva if we can use their car to go down there later okay?"

Hannah burst into tears.

DASHA and Art pulled up outside his place.

"...so because of rehearsals for these new songs, I'm not going to be around much next week," said Dash. He nodded as he parked and they got off. Art pointed at the three characters sitting on the wall nearby:

"Shall we tell God's compatriots?"

"I'll do it," said Dash, "you put the kettle on."

Art agreed and she went over and introduced herself, then said,

83

"We noticed your friend in hospital. He was on the same ward as my friend, so I wanted to tell you he's out of Intensive Care."

They looked up and stared blankly at her.

"Your friend?" she said, "the other one you always hang out with?"

"That greedy cunt?" said the female (the one Art called Amy), "he's no friend of mine."

"Nor mine." said (Piss).

"Nor mine." said (Alf).

"Okay, sorry, it's just that he was poisoned and so was my friend. My friend picked up a joint and smoked it and she almost died—"

They started laughing and wouldn't stop. She looked up at Art's window, and there he was, smiling and giving her the Thumbs Up.

"Why are you laughing?"

"Because that's what happened to him!" laughed (Amy), "he found a joint in the gutter right outside your house and wouldn't share it!"

"What a cunt!" said (Piss) laughing 'til snot came out of his nose.

"Was it purple?" asked Dash.

"Not to begin with," said (Alf), "but after he lit it up it turned purple."

Dash raised her eyebrows and (Alf) suddenly looked serious.

"But he's out of danger you said?"

Dash nodded.

"That's great. I love that guy," he sobbed.

"So do I!" cried Amy.

"So do I!" said (Piss) crying 'til snot came out of his nose.

"You're upset," said Dash, "by your poor friend, I'm so sorry; I'm going to get you a couple of bottles of that cider you like. The White Diamond, yes?" They all perked up and she jogged off to Best-Save. That was intri— intruig— interesting. Both poisoned by a purple joint, and Zorro had a little glass vial of purple among all the other drugs in his purse. He'd said it was a sedative. That was what he'd put in the joint that sedated Amber and nearly killed Hannah!

She rang the bell to Art's flat, (Piss), (Alf) and (Amy) glugging cider on the wall behind her. Art threw her the tennis ball with the keys inside. Upstairs, she met Art in his hall, putting on his helmet. She said,

"I have news! God is in hospital because of the same poison that put Hannah in there. Isn't that weird?"

"Yeah, the nurse told me that; and it is weird."

"And who's the only person that connects the two?"

"Who?"

"You!"

"So you're suggesting I poisoned them?"

"Yeah, you laced their joints with purple poison!"

"You got me! Bang to rights!"

"Bang to rights?"

"Er - caught red-handed."

"Red-handed?"

"Oh shit - sorry Dash; I have to go."

"Where are you going?"

Dash perceived a short pause before he said,

"Er, I'm actually going to see my father, but stick around if you want. Aji will be back soon."

He leant down and kissed her cheek, like she was his auntie, then he was gone. Strange. What just happened? The other night they had kissed. Or nearly kissed. What had changed? Was it Hannah?

ART fired up his bike and got on. He had only just noticed that he'd lied to Dash (his third lie in as many days. What did they say? A slippery slope). He pulled away and made the short journey to the Portobello Hotel in less than a minute. Lori was waiting for him in Reception, nodding off in the armchair. They hugged then set off on the short but hilly walk to Holland Park.

"I thought you were going to bring a helmet?" said Lori.

"Oh... Yeah... Sorry... I...."

"Doesn't matter. Not exactly in a hurry to revisit the place," she said, clutching his arm as they ambled onwards.

Her old home was a double-fronted mansion on the crescent running alongside the north end of Holland Park. Her family had lived there for the duration of her father's posting to London.

As they rounded the crescent they saw it was unoccupied and covered in scaffolding, which on closer inspection, they found to be alarmed. Neither of them spoke. Art glanced across at her, trying to gauge her mood. Finally he shrugged and said,

"Shall we go round the back?"

Lori did not look happy, but finally nodded and they set off back down the hill. A left-hand turning led them into the Mews behind the mansions where Art's father still lived. They climbed the steps, then as they had done as children, used the wisteria to clamber on to the flat roof. From there, they had a perfect view of the rear of the mansion. Lori found his hand and gripped it hard as she stared at her old bedroom window. Art squeezed back, hopefully in a reassuring manner.

"Let's go see my dad then we can get closer to your house," said Art, turning and pulling her toward the sky-light. But she let go of his hand then said,

"I see our tree is still here," she said, turning her head away and looking at him out the corner of her eyes.

Art turned back and then, just like when they were kids, she jumped off the roof onto the branch. Art was shocked, but impressed as he watched her lower herself to the ground. She smiled up at him then found the hole in the hedge and entered her old garden.

Art followed her route into the tree, then through the hedge. The scaffolding wasn't alarmed on this side so Art shimmied up a pole then let down a ladder for Lori to climb up. Art tried various windows as they continued up to the third floor. Lori peered into her old bedroom.

"It's much smaller than I remember," said Lori. Art nodded then tried lifting the sash window but stopped when he heard shouting from below.

DASHA sat in Art's living room, waiting for Aji. She had made lunch for them while musing over her career and her choices recently. When Gonks had come to a close, both Eva and she had been offered parts in 'A Forest' and had jumped at it. But it had dawned on her that it wasn't very good, and that the audience was mainly made up of Japanese businessmen. Sometimes one would wait at the stage door and bow, saying 'Kigurumi Zentai?' with photos of all the characters from the musical. She'd helpfully point to her own character and they'd smile and bow and hold out a pen for an autograph then scurry away; but she'd never found out what Kigurumi Zentai meant. Maybe it was something to do with the costumes that attracted them? It certainly wasn't the songs, though they were getting some new ones on Monday.

Aji came in and they hugged, then sat down to eat. Dash told her about Hannah, which didn't surprise Aji. She hadn't seen much of her recently but had been updated by an increasingly worried Dash, and then she was hilarious at the Halloween party, but really did look like she was crashing and burning.

After lunch Aji produced a box from her bag, out of which she took a photo.

"Look at this," she said, showing Dash the picture of her dressed as Mystique and Marcus screaming as his foreskin was stretched beyond its capacity.

"Oh shit!" said Dash.

"I got Margot to make up a few for me, in case Marcus tries to say he fucked me. Good one yes?"

Dash understood the situation, but,

"I feel the shot is more likely to incrim, incrini—"

"Incriminate."

"Incriminate me of a sex crime against a minor, than it is to hurt Marcus."

"But he's not going to show it to anyone," said Aji, "he'll be too ashamed. He's probably burnt it already!"

"You have already given it to him?"

"Yes, I stuck it through his door last night, and now I think we should call him. In fact, you should call him."

"Why me?"

"Because you're scary. And your threats will mean a lot more than mine."

"Okay, we will do it after lunch."

ART heard the call and turned towards it, seeing an old gentleman with white hair, moustache and goatee in the next-door garden. They waved then started descending, Art asking,

"Is this one of our suspects? The neighbour?" Lori nodded, not meeting his gaze.

"He looks like Albert Einstein, doesn't he?" Lori nodded again.

They stopped on the first level, so they were still able to look down on him, then said Hi.

"May I ask what you are doing?" the old man said.

"Just looking," said Art, "this is Lori, she used to live here many years ago as a child, and I knew her then as I lived in that mews house with my father who still lives there. We're just reminiscing about the 'old days'."

The old man looked shocked, staring up at Lori as she stood there. Finally, he spoke:

"Ah yes, I remember you," he said to Lori, ignoring Art, "you were always fighting with your twin brother, weren't you?"

Lori nodded.

"And your father was a complete bastard, wasn't he?"

Lori laughed nervously and nodded again,

"You tell it like you see it," she said.

"No time for pussyfooting at my age—"

"You have a very good memory, considering all the families who must've passed through in the intervening years?"

"Well, you were kind of special," he said, making Art's ears prick up, "why don't you join me for a drink?"

Art looked to Lori for a decision and she nodded, so he pulled up the ladder and dropped it over the wall so they could descend.

"I'm Albert by the way." Art nudged Lori and smirked.

They climbed down which was when Art realized Albert was taller than him. He'd always had a problem with the 'taller' since he was at school and had to do what he was told by the 'grown ups', even though he had no respect for them; and to top it off this old man pretended he wasn't even there.

"Come in, and let's have a drink," he said ushering them through the big bay window doors into a humongous living room. Hovering by the bar he said, "What's your poison?"

"Vodka, rocks, double please," said Lori.

Albert poured two generous glasses and looked to Art, who waved away the offer.

"And I believe your father was posted to Lima after London?"

Lori nodded as he passed her the vodka.

"Not exactly a promotion?"

"No," agreed Lori, "it was dreadful. Kinda lucky my dad had a heart attack, and we were brought back to D.C.—"

"Lima," said Albert, "where the Conquistadors chose the location of their capital city on the advice of the indigenous people: In a boggy valley where the mosquitos were the size of locusts."

Lori downed her drink in one, handed it back for a refill. Art decided to change the subject,

"Do you remember the cook or the gardener or the butler who worked next door around then?"

"Ah, let me think," said Albert, pulling on his goatee, "maybe I'm imagining it, but I think the gardener still works there once a week and I see him do your father's little plot at the same time and the butler, Silvert came to work for me for a few years then died sadly, but I have an idea about the cook—"

"You used to stare at me," blurted Lori, "you used to watch me in a creepy way."

"I did? I'm so sorry. I didn't mean to scare you."

"I didn't say you scared me, I said you were creepy."

"Oh god, I'm so sorry," said the old man, "you reminded me so much of my own daughter who was the same age as you. You were very similar with the blonde hair, the green eyes and even the freckles."

"So why not stare at her?" Lori asked.

"Because she had already been taken from me, before you arrived in London."

"Oh, I'm so sorry."

"Taken from you?" said Art.

"She disappeared, while we were taking a holiday on the Continent."

"Abducted?"

"In a service station on a Belgian autobahn. A year went by. The most unbearable year that my marriage didn't survive, and then there you were. For a week or so I was convinced you were her, and I had hope. But once I'd spoken to your brother and the butler..."

Art didn't know what to say. Lori drank more vodka.

"But even though I knew it wasn't her, I still found solace in watching you from my window, fighting with your friends in the garden. Looking at you now gives me a good idea of what she looks like today—"

"You think she's alive?" asked Art, which prompted Lori to elbow him in the ribs.

"I hope so, yes. Somewhere, living a good life. Maybe not even remembering she was ever taken? Hopefully happy? There's a chance of that, isn't there?" They both nodded vigorously.

"I'm so sorry for your loss," said Lori, downing the rest of her vodka.

They sat in silence for a moment before he said,

"So, do you want to get inside your old house, to have a look around?"

They both nodded.

"Then if it's all locked up the only way is via my house - you'll have to go to the attic," he said, leading them to the stairs, "follow them all the way up, then head to your right. There's three rooms that have windows that will look out on your old house. It's a small jump from eave to eave—"

"Jump?"

"Yes, but it's only about four or five feet? If it were a puddle you wouldn't think twice about leaping it. Just don't think about the sixty-foot drop."

They looked at each other then back at him.

"Then, if there's no open window, there's a couple of low-slung chimneys that are so wide even I could climb down them."

They thanked him and started up the swirling staircase.

Art looked at Lori and whispered,

"This guy is so obviously our man. How could he not realize he was handing us evidence of 'opportunity' on a plate?" Lori mused for a moment then agreed,

"I guess so. What do you think of that story then? Was it bullshit?"

"I don't know, he sounded sincere and even got a bit tearful so I believed him at the time."

"Same," she said, "but maybe we might dig into his past a bit? There was scene in your book where Eva, the American girl goes and looks at old newspapers? In a library?"

"Yeah, the London Library in St James. We can do that. I recognize him as a conductor I think, who was famous even back then, so it would've definitely made the papers."

They had reached the top floor, a warren of little rooms designed for servants. At the end of the corridor was a room with a window facing Lori's old home. Directly opposite, across a void of two metres, was an identical window.

"I'm a bit drunk now," said Lori, "so maybe I'll stay here and watch."

Art opened the window and climbed out. The ledge he was standing on was maybe a metre wide, so he'd only get one step before he'd have to launch himself. He walked to the edge and looked down, sending shivers through his body. He retreated, climbed back inside and said,

"What are we going to find in there anyway? The whole place is being renovated. I think we already know enough to continue our investigation, don't you? And we can ask my dad about the gardener?" She nodded. They retraced their steps to say goodbye to Albert.

DASHA and Aji sat on the sofa. The TV was mumbling in the background as Aji passed over her mobile, saying,

"It's on speaker." Dash held it between them and when Marcus answered said in her strongest accent,

"Marcus Taylor."

He said,

"Who's this?"

"Mystique."

There was silence for a while, before he said,

"Oh, look, I'm sorry about the other night and—"

"Have you told anyone? Made any grand claims? About what you did to Aji?"

"No, absolutely not."

"Good, because if you tried to claim you had sex with her, you'd be admitting to child rape, yes? And if Aji hears even a snicker in the hallway at school, or a giggle behind her back, this picture will be everywhere, understand?"

He agreed.

"And you will wave 'Hi' to Aji every day even if she never waves back, and be friendly when your paths have to cross, and if you behave, it will be like this never happened, yes?"

"Absolutely, yes, thank you, thank you."

They hung up, Aji sighed.

"Now your turn," said Dash, handing her the phone, "call Dora and persuade her to tell her mum that Amber did not stay with them on Friday night."

Aji crinkled her face and said,

"I don't know..."

Dash retrieved her flip-phone from her pocket, scrolled through her contacts and said,

"If you don't, I'll call her mum. Do it. For Amber."

GRODY sat in the Greasy Spoon on Watling Avenue. He was pleased with himself, and with the Roast Beef and Yorkshire pudding he'd just eaten. He was thinking about having ice-cream for dessert when his Motorola buzzed. It was a text:

>*"She knows your name"*

He wasn't sure what to say in reply, but his first thought was something snarky like 'well if you told me what you wanted them for then I would know better than...' but he couldn't be bothered to write that long a sentence, and also this person was paying him handsomely. He decided to write instead,

>*"Sorry, it just*
>*slipped out.*
>*won't do it again"*

EVA looked out of the window at the view of a frozen Hampstead Heath and beyond. She was hugging her hot water bottle inside her big cardigan but couldn't get warm. The living room of the Victorian pile was enormous and almost impossible to heat without a total refit with underfloor heating. Mickey sat at the table on his laptop.

"What do think about Brook Green?" he asked.

"Near Hammersmith?" asked Eva, "I don't really think anything about it. Why?"

"Well there's this amazing property on top of a block by the pub and the tennis courts that I thought we could check out—"

"To move to?"

"Yeah, this place is too big and cold isn't it?"

Eva jumped onto his lap and kissed him.

"I would love to move there. Or anywhere in fact!"

"I'm sorry I made us move here—"

"It's okay. It's what we needed to do at the time, and it was cool and breezy in the summer."

"But now it's just fucking freezing!"

Eva laughed. Mickey rarely swore, so when he did, it had added effect. She said,

"If you feel you're ready to move back then I'm happy for you; and happy to move."

"Well, let's go see it this week. It's empty so if it's warm and secure we can move straight in."

"Secure?"

"Oh yeah, I forgot that doesn't have to be a priority anymore. What a great feeling!"

"So if it's warm—"

"We can move straight in!"

"Exciting!" she said, doing a little dance, "so are you going to drive us all to Wiltshire?" she asked Mickey. He looked up from his laptop and cringed,

"Could you? I've got a meeting later and don't want to risk not being back in time."

Eva nodded,

"Okay, just us girls on the road-trip then," she said, picking up the keys, "I'm gonna collect Hannah then Dash and go. See you tonight."

ART and Lori stood outside the Mansion.

"We have two choices," Art said, "we can go into the park and dig up the Time-Capsule, or go see my father and ask about the Gardener?"

"Neither" replied Lori, "I think I need to go to bed. I shouldn't have drunk that. Stupid. I was just a bit nervous about confronting him."

"Perfectly understandable," said Art, hailing a passing cab, "I'll go see the old man and you can call me whenever, okay?" They hugged and Art could smell her hair. It seemed to be the same smell she had when they were kids. He waved goodbye then headed to his childhood home.

He let himself in through the garage door and wound his way between the motor bikes of various vintage. A Norton Commando rubbed handlebars with a

Honda Fireblade and a Vincent Black Shadow. This was where his own passion for two-wheel travel had been inspired - one of the only things he seemed to have in common with his father. He opened the door to the stairs and heard the old man shouting at the telly. He was in a belligerent mood which made Art stop. He had forgotten it was Sunday. He closed the door, went back outside and called him on his phone instead.

"Hey Dad, it's Art, how are you?"

"Fine."

Art waited for more, but when nothing came, he asked,

"Hey, do you remember our gardener from when I was a kid?"

"Yes I do."

"And did he also do the big house?"

"Yes."

"Would you remember his name?"

"Of course! He is still my gardener now, It's Barry. I'm not totally fucking senile!"

"Okay, sorry. Can you give me his number?"

"Why?"

"Er... because my friend needs a gardener?"

"Oh, okay, wait a minute."

Art stood on the cobbles, with his phone to his ear, looking down the mews. He heard a door open then heard his father's voice behind him. He turned to see him at the top of the steps, holding a business card.

"To save you writing it down," he said, dropping it.

Art picked up the card, feeling a bit foolish. He said,

"Thanks dad. Er... listen, do you—"

But his father just shook his head at him, then motioned for him to go. Art nodded and waved. He could feel his father's eyes on his back as he walked away. Could he also feel his father's sneer, burning into his back?

He felt foolish for the way he'd dealt with Dash earlier. Even though it was a *white* lie, it was still a lie. Could he go back there now? Come clean? Apologize? No, he'd walk back to his bike then do a circuit of his turf.

AJI stared at the T.V. snuggled against Dash.

"Where's Dad?" she asked.

"He said he had to go see his father."

"That's weird, Dad never goes see him on a Sunday cos he starts drinking at breakfast and is angry by lunchtime!"

She then thought for a moment,

"Do you think he's having a mid-life crisis?"

"Your dad? Why would you think that?" asked Dash.

"Because he went to see his dad on a Sunday? Because he seems kind of stupider recently?"

"Really?" smiled Dash, "in the last three or four months maybe?"

"Yeah" agreed Aji, "how'd you know?"

"Because it's the time since your thirteenth birthday?"

Slightly offended, Aji harrumphed.

"You think he's got stupid and he thinks you don't love him anymore."

Aji harrumphed again and said,

"Now that's stupid!

"Which reminds me I texted Dora earlier as you suggested and she has now told her mum. Also about Zorro at the party."

Dash smiled and nodded.

Aji continued,

"She remembers him. She said that he approached her and offered her a funny cigarette, but she told him to eff off and he did, without a second word."

They heard a car honk outside. It was Dash's minicab.

"I'm going to pack a bag for Hannah, and Eva's driving us to the treatment centre. Are you coming?"

"No, I've got homework, but send her my love," said Aji, hugging Dash.

ART fired up his bike and set off on his circuit. This took a route around Kensington and Chelsea which he normally did at least once a day. He headed up to Notting Hill then turned down Kensington Church Street which had a couple of good bends, then at the bottom he turned left along the park, then right down Gloucester Road. The weather meant there weren't many interesting people around, but the air was fresh and blew the memory of his grumpy father from his mind. He turned left and wound his way through to Sloane Square then doubled back west along the King's Road. He was mildly disappointed that fate had not intervened causing him to deviate from his classic route. There were almost always little variations, stop-offs and deviations. Even a red traffic light could alter his course, or a Lamborghini that needed chasing. He decided to stop for a warming hot chocolate at Picasso's, dumping his bike on the pavement. He sat in the window watching the shoppers pass by, then got out his new phone and called Barry the Gardener but it went straight to voicemail:

"Barry, this is Bartholomew here. Son of Frank in Holland Park. How are you? I'm calling because I wanted to pick your brains about something that happened when I was a kid? I'll try you again. Thanks, Bye."

DASHA ran down the stairs of Hannah's mansion block to the waiting car. Eva and Hannah sat in the front. She threw Hannah's bag in the back, including a six-pack of cold beer (on the advice of the nurse who'd said Hannah was shaking). She jumped in and they headed west along the Old Brompton Road.

EVA was not really sure how taking someone to rehab should work. Should it be a celebration? Or a wake? She didn't speak, just navigated the traffic at Hammersmith to get on to the A4.

Hannah sat in the passenger seat and looked out the window saying,

"This is good."

"This is good." repeatedly.

Was she saying it to convince herself or because she really believed that it was good? Eva didn't want to ask. She didn't want to get into it. It had been hard watching Hannah for the last few years slowly destroying herself. She had tried to intervene, but Hannah had just laughed it off.

They'd met in 1999 when Eva had been homeless, and Hannah had offered to help her. She'd given Eva the spare keys to her apartment and Eva had gone there for a shower, but Hannah had never shown up. Eva had lived there alone for a year before Hannah had finally returned with a pint of milk and an ounce of cocaine.

"This is good."

"This is good," Hannah repeated.

She had hardly drunk the beer that Dash had gotten for her, which surprised Eva because Hannah was still shaking. Normally, she'd be desperate for a drink to stop the shaking. But she guessed that there was a difference between physical and mental addiction. So once you made that choice that you needed to stop, the physical withdrawals were just something a seasoned alcoholic would know they would have to go through?

The traffic was light. Sunday afternoon was a good time to get out of town as others were returning from their weekend break. It started raining. Not good weather for a road trip. But they were warm and dry.

"I'm sorry," said Hannah, "I must have caused you a lot of worry."

Eva smiled,

"It doesn't matter. If you get the help you need then it's all been worthwhile."

"So what's been going on for you guys?" Hannah said.

Dash sighed then said,

"Amber left your party with some dude dressed as Zorro and hasn't been seen since."

"Oh my God!" said Hannah, "wasn't she dressed as Catwoman?"

"Yes."

"She's always been a bit flighty hasn't she?"

"Yeah. But normally it's just for a night."

Hannah took a swig of beer and counted:

"Friday, Saturday, Sunday, That is a long time."

DASHA looked out the window.

"I blame myself," she said, "because I was supposed to be looking after Aji and should have been watching her friends, too."

Eva shook her head,

"You can't blame yourself. You couldn't watch all of them all the time. Even Art wouldn't have managed that if he'd been at the party; and they're not children."

"Well, they are children. They pretend not to be children and they get offended when we treat them like children, but they are."

Hannah said,

"So what's being done about it?"

"Nothing, parents are away, housekeeper is drunk and the police said it's not our responsibility when we called them.

"Hopefully she'll turn up," said Eva, "though she left her phone in your bathroom, which isn't a good sign is it?"

They all shook their heads and remained silent.

HANNAH was feeling a little better. She'd drunk one beer but had no desire for another. The D.T.s had settled, and she felt a little perkier,

"And how about you Eva?" said Hannah, "how are you and Mickey?"

"He's the same warm, friendly beautiful man I fell in love with three-and-a-half years ago..."

"But?"

"But in some ways, he's still an enigma to me, still a closed book. He stares over the Heath, and I'm not sure if he's reliving the horrors of his past or thinking about Karen Ford."

"Oh Sweetheart, you've got to stop thinking that you're just a stand-in for the real thing."

"But that's how we met - I *was* a stand-in."

"But now you're not - *you* are the real thing, and he loves you. But that's not what I meant when I asked how you and Mickey are. I meant how's the sex?"

Eva laughed nervously,

"Ooh, big news! We're gonna look for a place near you guys! We're moving out of that draughty haunted house in Hampstead!"

"Hurrah! and how's the sex?"

"You keep asking me that!"

"Because you don't answer!"

Eva blushed,

"It's good."

"That's not an answer."

"He's great!"

"But?"

"No but. It's just different because he doesn't feel horny like a normal person..."

"Yes?"

"It takes a while to get him on the boil..."

"So he's not impotent?"

"No! Once he's up and running it is very very good."

Hannah said,

"Eva, you're blushing!"

"I'm American, and not used to talking about sex the way Europeans are."

"I love to talk about sex," said Hannah, "I had a Red Indian Chief at my party on Halloween." She paused and rephrased:

"I had a Native American Chief at my party, and I mean had! And he was a Big Chief!"

They laughed.

"I do remember it - my party," Hannah said, "at first I didn't and I was thinking I was going out on an anti-climax. That I'd never have anything to remember? But now I remember more. I remember the Big Chief. I remember snorting lines with you Dash. I remember smoking that purple joint. And then waking up in a hospital, and I remember behaving badly to you Dash in there, and I'm sorry. But mostly I remember the Chief. The Big Chief!"

They laughed. Eva said,

"We see the Big Chief every day at work, of course. We're going to have to call him that from now on. His real name is Nigel, so Big Chief is much better."

They laughed again.

"You remember smoking the purple joint?" asked Dash, "so it was purple before you smoked it?"

"Yup, but it had already been lit up before I got to it and the purple seemed to be scorched onto the inside of the skin, and it made me feel woozy, but you know me. I persisted!"

"Then that was the joint Amber was smoking that made her woozy. We looked at the photos on her phone, and the last one was of her in your bathroom mirror and she had that joint in her mouth."

"Shit!" said Hannah, "so we were both victims of this Zorro then?"

"For sure," said Dash, "but what does not make sense is that a homeless man was also poisoned with another purple pre-rolled joint outside Art's flat!"

"Well," said Eva, "there's only one common denominator who was at your party and at Art's—"

"And that's Art himself," they all said together and laughed.

EVA followed the directions down small country lanes and after a couple of mistakes, which led them down paths to other enormous houses in the middle of nowhere, they finally approached at Klaus House. From the side it looked in keeping with its neighbours, but in the car park it turned into a jumble of extensions perching on scaffolding, pre-war nissan huts and breeze-block out-houses. Hannah paid no attention and got out of the car. A nurse was standing in the car park. She was tapping her watch and said,

"You're late. But luckily the doctor is still here. So we can admit you."

She gave Hannah a hug, and started walking towards the door. Eva got her bag out the back and walked after her.

"Oh you can't come in," said the nurse, "you have to say goodbye now."

Dash and Eva ran up and gave Hannah a hug. The nurse took the bag and ushered Hannah inside, who smiled and waved.

"We'll come and see you as soon as we're allowed!" shouted Dash.

"If we can ever find the place again," muttered Eva.

Dash and Eva looked at one another and shrugged.

"Fingers crossed."

They got lost again trying to find their way back to the A303. So many big houses in massive grounds in the middle of nowhere.

"Who lives out here?" said Eva, "who can afford a place like this?"

"They probably cost the same as a two bed in Chelsea! But they can't all have been turned into rehabs and hospitals and conference centres."

They even saw a helicopter in one garden. Finally, they found their way out and headed for home.

"So, now you've left William," said Eva, "you can get it together with Art."

"Yes. I could," said Dash, "but it's a bit soon. We almost kissed after the Halloween party but Aji interrupted us."

Dash smiled,

"But our lips touched—"

"But you've kissed each other many times on the lips."

"Yeah, but this was different. This would have been the kiss."

"So you're moving forward? Do you mind if William finds out?"

"Yes. I do."

"Maybe you should have a secret affair then," suggested Eva, "I won't tell anyone. Neither will Mickey."

"Yeah, maybe," Dash said, then shook her head, "I'm bored of 'A Forest'. I'm not interested in learning new songs."

"Me neither."

"Let's try out for something like Les Miserables."

"Where we don't have to wear a skin-tight, 'naked' costume and a giant blow-up head."

"I like the head though; it makes me feel strangely safe when I'm wearing it."

"I know what you mean," agreed Eva, "it's like wearing your very own air-bag, though the eyes have a very bleak look to them."

"I might keep it, when I quit, as a memento, a keeps sake, a souvenir, a trophy. Where it around the house sometimes."

"So in effect you're saying 'when I quit, I'm keeping the head'," they chuckled, "speaking of which, I thought you came off the best in Art's book."

"Came off best?" asked Dash.

"He portrayed you fairly, and without giving you any embarrassing scenes, unlike myself."

"But you must've told him that, for him to write it, yes? He wasn't hiding in a cupboard in the kitchen while you stood naked on the table, was he?"

"No, you're right there. I guess I mean that he almost made you perfect, which is not surprising, considering the massive crush he'd had on you forever..."

She looked over at Dash, who didn't react, except to smile.

"Yes, a nice peasants' costume would make a change."

"But ones that *don't* push our boobs up and out."

They laughed.

"Let's look in the trades. I'll pick up a copy of The Stage before rehearsals tomorrow."

"Shall I drop you off at Hannah's? Or at Arts?" asked Eva, with a devilish smile. Dash laughed.

"My place please. I don't think we're ready to tell Aji yet anyway. Though, I think she suspects."

ART and Aji ate supper in silence. He knew she was thinking about Amber. He wanted to ask her about the party on Friday night and the boy who might have hurt her, and he wanted to ask her whether she'd done her homework but decided to give her a break.

"Fancy an hour of 'Ico' before bed?" she said.

"You read my mind," he said, getting up and turning on the PlayStation.

Monday - 3rd November

ART was eating breakfast when Aji ran in.

"Why didn't you wake me?"

"Because you have an alarm clock of your own?"

"Then you'll have to give me a lift!"

"Not if you speak to me like that."

Aji stopped.

"Can you give me a lift to school please?" she said, "I can't be late today."

"Sure," he said, "get dressed and we'll go in ten."

Art finished his oats and got ready.

The wind wasn't so freezing outside. Art started the BMW's engine then got on. Aji, wearing the big leather overcoat got on behind him and tucked it over her knees. She asked,

"Who was that woman in Mike's on Saturday? What was her name?"

Art popped the bike into gear and pulled away, while thinking about what to say. The truth or the Slippery Slope?

"Flora, an old schoolfriend; first time I've seen her since then."

"You actually went to Holland Park together all those years ago? So where's she been?"

Art zigzagged the blocks towards her school,

"Tahiti most recently, but all over. She seems to have been on a world tour, and now she's visiting London."

"Visiting London or visiting you because you wrote about her in your book 'You're losing your head'?"

Art didn't want to tell her about Lori's search for her abuser so said,

"Maybe both? And it's 'I'm Keeping the Head'."

"Yeah yeah Dad" she said, patting his shoulder, rather patronizingly, he thought.

They had pulled up at the entrance to the school. Aji got off, gave him the helmet and the coat and said,

"Thanks Dad. See you later." Art watched her go. He'd never thought through the ramifications of writing the truth in such a blasé manner; never thought of humiliating Lori (though she was the one that had brought it up in Mike's) or Mickey, or Hannah; never thought of Aji growing up and reading it; never thought he'd be lying so regularly. He needed a meeting. Maybe there was one at ten in Elgin Avenue?

AJI waved goodbye to her dad and wondered why he'd given the woman a different name. She knew it wasn't Flora because she would've remembered that (there were three Floras in her class!) It had been a uniquely American name like Candy or Britney. Why would he lie? Was it a guilty little secret?

She walked into school with a nervous feeling. Was everyone looking at her? Did they all know about Halloween? That she had got drunk and... There was only one way to find out. She tried to act normally, but wasn't sure what that was? Should she be smiling? Or sad? Or just look at her phone? Yeah, look at the phone. But then she couldn't see if everyone was sniggering? She was almost at her locker. So far, no one was paying her any attention. She opened her locker and hid her face in it. She was bound to bump into Marcus. How would she be able to tell if he had kept the pact? She took the box of photos from her bag and put them in her locker. That fucking shit! She'd get him good and go to the police!

What was she doing? There was Amber to think of: Did they know Amber was missing? Should she tell Miss Pringle? Or would Amber suddenly appear with a great story to amuse everyone? Her name was called on the tannoy. Was she in trouble?

She arrived at the Head Mistress's office to find Dora and Margot looking worried.

"Apparently Amber has gone AWOL again?" said Miss Pringle, without looking up from her laptop, "what do we know?"

Aji looked around at her friends but they cowered at the carpet.

"We were all at a Halloween party on Friday night and she walked out with an older man Miss," she said, "but he was in fancy dress, so no one got a good look at him. But Margot took some pictures which could be useful, and we have her phone and bag that she left behind—"

"Okay, so it's been two whole days. She's not normally gone this long is she?"

The girls all shook their heads.

"Your mother Dora, called me yesterday when she found out about your deceit – pretending Amber had stayed the night with you?" Dora's head bent further towards the carpet.

"And according to Amber's drunken house-keeper both her parents are away?" The girls all nodded their heads, "I've tried calling both of them but no joy so I'm going to call the police. As of eight o'clock she became my responsibility. Thank you girls, you can go."

They filed out and headed for class. Dora said,
"I've been grounded for a month for that." The
other two mumbled commiserations.

Margot said,
"I got two weeks for saying I was staying the
night at Aji's." The other two mumbled
commiserations.

Aji said,
"My dad confiscated my electric blanket." The
other two gasped in horror.

GRODY, wearing his favourite disguise, stared at
the young man on the other side of the desk. He didn't
look like a man, and the way he held the handkerchief
to his nose the whole time made him look like he had
something to hide (it takes one to know one).

"So do you have any previous experience in the
catering trade?"

Grody took a breath. The boy was looking directly
at his CV on the desk in front of him. Could he not
read? Did he need the paper held up to his eyes? Would
that help? Or actually pressing the paper through his
miserable eye sockets? He took another breath then
said,

"I've worked as a barman in pubs, but also in
hotels where I learned to mix cocktails, there," he
said, pointing to his C.V., "and I've bussed a lot of
trays and carried a lot of barrels and like staying up
late—"

"Great! We're near the start of party season so
we're gonna need you almost immediately," he said,
sneezing into his hanky, "in fact, there's a private
Fireworks Night party in Windsor on Wednesday and you
could do the little bar which is in a marquee in the
grounds? Is that good for you?"

"It sounds perfect."

"And you can help erect the marquee?"

Grody shrugged.

"Sure."

"Fantastic! So I need a photo ID and your
National Insurance number and we're good to go."

Grody got out his ID and double-checked he'd
brought the one that matched his disguise. Yes,
handlebar moustache, beard, and bushy eyebrows. He
handed it over.

"You can join us on the mini-bus if you want? We
leave here and meander westward around 2pm, to avoid
traffic."

"No thanks, I think I'll drive myself if it's all
the same to you?"

"Sure, less organization for me."

Grody smiled. That would mean he could be late and miss the erection of the marquee. He left the office, walked down the stairs and went into the toilet on the next floor. There, he removed his disguise and placed it in his messenger bag and took out his red crash helmet and put it on.

ART rode to Elgin Avenue and watched the smokers milling around outside the modern church. He saw a couple of friends and a couple of enemies. Not enemies exactly - strong word - more addicts who rubbed him up the wrong way and vice versa probably: Differences of opinion were fine in the decision-making process, but not accepting that decision was unforgivable to Art. Addicts or alcoholics who resigned from a committee because the vote went the other way were not in *Recovery* in his opinion, thus he wouldn't waste any more time on speaking to them. One such addict was the man who ran the meeting. Art watched him herding the smokers inside, and wondered if there was any point in going in? Would he be able to share in front of him?

Dangerous territory for an addict, thinking of excuses to *not* go to meetings.

DASHA and Eva took the tube into the West End for a rehearsal of some new songs for 'A Forest'. They were reading the sheet music and humming along.

"It's not going to improve the show enough to make me want to stay," said Eva, "unless they're written by..." Dash waited but nothing came,

"Are you trying to think of famous song-writers?"

"Yes, but I've come up blank."

"Me too. That's terrible, considering we're in the trade. Maybe we should try some modern dance, or even modern ballet companies?"

"Sure. We're better than this," Dash said slapping the sheet music, "Forest doesn't deserve us."

"Yeah, I'll get the coffees in and pick up The Stage as well."

Dash nodded then said,

"I hope Hannah is going to be okay."

"I don't get it," Eva said, "why is it so hard for Hannah to stop? Isn't almost dying twice in a weekend message enough?"

"You'd think, wouldn't you?" replied Dash, "but that's the nature of addiction. It seems to be like that classic of good versus evil? Of two personalities fighting for control of the brain, like Gollum and his Precious?"

Eva nodded and they both stood up as they approached their stop.

They emerged on to Charing Cross Road then walked up to Cambridge Circus where they parted company, Eva saying,

"See you in ten."

Eva turned left to go to the theatre, Dash turned right on to Shaftsbury Avenue where the costume hire shop was. She loved Angels. It was the fulfilment of her childhood fantasies of having the greatest dressing up box which never ran out of new costumes. Many of them were from movies and musicals, and before going to the desk she took a turn around the isles to spy new arrivals. A despatch rider was leaving the shop as she approached the counter.

She said 'Hi' to Christine as she laid the costumes next to another return. It was a dark costume, mainly of leather. She looked closer and saw it was 'Zorro'.

"Christine, do you have a record of who hired this costume? I met him at a party on Halloween and quite liked him."

Christine nodded, spinning the ledger around.

"His name was Iain and there's a number."

Dash punched the number into her phone, but it made that awful 'unavailable' sound.

"So how can I find him?"

"Well, he ordered it over the phone and a despatch rider brought in the cash, including the deposit."

"And when was it returned?"

"Just now. The same biker I think, but he must be going back as I refunded the deposit, which reminds me I owe you—"

"What did he look like? The biker?"

"All I saw of him was a red crash helmet and the usual big messenger bag."

"Thanks!" said Dash, running out the door.

"Good luck!" Christine shouted after her.

Outside, on Shaftsbury Avenue Dash looked both ways and saw a red crash helmet 50 metres away on Cambridge Circus turning right. She ran, dodging through the tourists, and there, up Charing Cross Road, was the Despatch Rider, helmet bobbing between the crowds. She ran to catch up and was only a few metres behind him when he veered right and walked up to the entrance of a modern office block with the name Pedant Publishing above the door. He got a clipboard from his bag and entered. Dash waited outside, for only a minute, before he emerged carrying a jiffy bag. She was about to accost him but as she approached, he started tearing the bag open. Were despatch riders meant to do that? Or maybe it was for him? He stopped

at a bin and dropped the bag and a few leaflets in,
then placed a solid looking item in his messenger bag
as he walked on. Dash continued following, pausing to
glance in the bin at the bag. It was addressed to
Samsung.

The Biker stopped outside another office block
labelled Mondo Magazines and seemed to look it up and
down. He got out his clipboard again and seemed to be
copying the name above the entrance into the sheet,
then finally wandered in. Dash waited again, and he
emerged carrying a parcel. He walked north again, then
turned down a little alley towards the Phoenix Garden.
There, he stopped and started to unwrap the parcel.
Dash ran behind a wheelie bin which rolled as she
bumped into it. She pulled it to a halt, hoping the
biker hadn't noticed. She peeked. He was concentrating
on the box. He ripped it open and picked out a small
pamphlet. Then another and another. Seemingly angry,
he threw the box down and was walking away, when he
stopped. Dash ducked down as he turned, walked back,
picked up the pamphlets and the box and carried them
in the direction of the wheelie bin. Dash sunk lower
and held her breath.

GRODY was disappointed. Mondo was normally so
great for gadgets and luxury items, but it was still
the luck of the draw. When he'd walked to the desk
he'd had moments to scan the parcels sitting beside
the receptionist. He'd perfected the reading of
addresses upside-down, and plumped for Sony in
Hounslow. She'd signed his worksheet and given him the
parcel without question and the weight of it made him
think it'd been a Camcorder or Walkman Pro on its
return trip after having been reviewed. But no.
Fucking promo booklets!

He threw the box down and walked away, but then
thought better of it. He was right behind the office
which was a stupid place to open the parcel, but an
even more stupid place to drop the contents. He
retraced his steps while looking for a dumpster. There
was one in the alley. He caught a movement. Behind it,
a little blonde head had ducked as he approached.

Was that the same blonde he'd seen when he left
Pedant, who looked like she was going to say hello? He
picked up the booklets, stuffed them in the box and
walked to the dumpster, pretending not to see the head
sink even further. He popped the box in and shut the
lid, then peered over and saw a girl crouching low,
definitely hiding from him. Should he grab her and
confront her? Or walk away?

DASHA stared at the shadow on the ground as it grew, and the footsteps got closer. She heard the lid lifting and the box drop in. Then there was silence. No movement. From the shadow she knew he was still there. What was he doing? The shadow loomed closer.

GRODY lunged over the dumpster and grabbed the girl's arm.

"Why are you following me?"

She pulled away but he hung on and coasted on the dumpster as it followed her down the alley. She spun around and grabbed his helmet by the chin guard with her free hand then jabbed her fingers towards his eyes. One finger struck his eyeball, making him let go of her. She ran and he chased her, the pain in his blinded eye becoming a violent throb. She crossed the Charing Cross Road by leaping between the busy traffic, whereas he blundered into it with no depth perception and got hit, sending him bouncing into the next lane where he got hit again, depositing him on the pavement outside Foyles. He saw her running down the alley next to the bookshop and followed at a limp. Luckily, the new pain in his hip was taking his mind off the pain in his eye. She went under the arch into Greek Street and left towards Old Compton Street. He'd only made it through the arch in time to see her duck into a doorway. When he got there, he saw the sign above: Stage Door. He hobbled round to the front of the theatre and read the name above the entrance: 'A Forest - The West End's longest running animal-based musical (except for Cats & the Lion King)'. Where had he heard that recently? Oh yes; many of the girls at that Halloween party had been performers from that musical, and the blonde must've been one of them.

DASHA ran through the open stage door and pushed it shut behind her and leant against it. Who was this guy? And why had he ripped up the parcel he collected from the office? The door pushed her in the back, and she leant into it, but then she heard a voice and recognized it as Eva.

"Eva? Are you alone?"

"Who's that? Let me in! It's cold!"

Dash opened the door, ushering in Eva with their coffees, then scanned the street. As she looked right towards Old Compton Street, she saw the red helmet round the corner. She ducked in and leant against the door again.

Eva was staring at her.

"A guy was chasing me, and I just saw him again coming back round the corner."

"Do you know him?" asked Eva.

"I'm not sure. I was taking back the costumes to Angels and he was dropping off the Zorro suit. So he's either Zorro, or a despatch rider who's on his way back to Zorro with his deposit—"

"Then we must follow him!"

"Really?"

"Yes, come on, before he gets away."

GRODY limped towards the Soho Center for Health & Care at the top of Frith Street. He'd say he'd been knocked off his bike, but what could've poked him in his eye, while wearing a full-face helmet? The Winged Lady on a Roller? Unlikely. No, an aerial would do.

Why was the blonde following him? She must've known the girl he'd taken from the party and clocked him at the costume shop. That was sloppy. He can't leave a trace like that. He'd have to deal with her. He was on a roll and didn't need her fucking it up.

EVA opened the door a fraction and peered out. No one was nearby so she they exited. To the left, they saw the red helmet bobbing through the crowd. Eva grabbed Dash's arm and pulled.

"Come on, we've got plenty of time 'til rehearsals," said Eva, "don't worry, the two of us could take anyone, just remain on opposite sides of him and go for the bollocks and the eyes using every we weapon we have - boots, elbows, teeth, nails—"

"You sound like you've done this before?"

"I was homeless remember? Travelling the Night Bus means you need to do anything to protect yourself. So why'd he chase you?"

"He caught me following him."

"Well that's an admission of guilt in itself! No law-abiding citizen would ever worry about a beautiful woman following them."

Up ahead the red helmet turned left into a side street.

"Didn't you speak to Zorro at the party?"

"I did, unfortunately. He was definitely a homophobe, but I got the impression he was a total bigot in every way."

"And what did he look like?"

"Moustache, beard, bushy eyebrows over dark eyes was all I could see under his costume."

"And this guy?" asked Eva.

"No facial hair. Just the same dark eyes."

They followed turning left then right into Frith
street, then he turned right into a doorway crowded
with smokers.

"I'll follow him," said Eva pulling up her
hoodie, "he doesn't know me. If I scream, come
running."

They continued up Frith Street and saw the door
was the entrance to a doctor's surgery. He was talking
to the receptionist. Eva waved to Dash, then wandered
in and took a seat in the back row of the waiting
room. There were maybe ten others waiting, but a
steady stream of people just walking through to a room
behind her. She vaguely recognized a few who were
Mickey's friends and it dawned on her that this was a
venue for N.A. meetings.

The red helmet finished with the receptionist
then went into the adjacent pharmacy. When he exited,
he was tossing back pills and pressing a swab against
his left eye. Holding his right hip, he limped to the
back row of the waiting room and sat down, just four
seats away from Eva. Had Dash just done this to him?
She obviously didn't need any advice about how to look
after herself. Eva watched him through her hair,
protruding from her hoodie. Wasn't he going to take
off his helmet? How was she supposed to find out more
if she didn't get to see his face? Finally, he was
called (Grodenko?) and he limped off.

GRODY's eye was throbbing. He felt like it was
gonna fall out if he didn't hold it in place with the
bit of gauze the pharmacist had given him. He applied
pressure and it hurt. He released pressure and it
hurt. The painkillers were useless. If the Doctor
didn't actually shoot morphine into his eyeball and
his hip, he'd call one of his boys. He'd do that
anyway - get Darren to pick him up outside the
Dominion in twenty minutes with some gear. He fired
off a text:

> "4*2?1%3* 5*4* 2?3? 20
> 1?3!3%2?3?2?3!3?
> 1£4%2?3?2£ 2£1!1*4%"

The Doctor came in and asked him if he could
walk. He did so, with a pronounced limp.

"It's not dislocated, just bruised. I'll
prescribe an anti-inflammatory. Now your eye. Please
take off your helmet."

"I don't think I can Doc. I'm afraid my eye will
pop out."

"Don't worry. I won't let that happen. Would you
like a lollipop?"

"Er - yes - okay."

"I'll give it to you when you've taken it off."

Grody eased the helmet off and the Doctor pushed
the Chuppa-Chup into his mouth.

"Ah yes, it is bruised but it's not punctured.
I'm going to clean it then tape it shut."

It took only a few minutes, then the Doctor said,

"You must try not to move it too much. Try to
stare straight ahead, okay?"

Grody nodded as he put his helmet back on.

EVA went outside and found Dash lurking in a
doorway.

"He's gone in to see the doctor, but he never
took off his helmet so I have no new info, sorry."

"Shit! And time's running out - we have to be
back in ten minutes - no time to follow him even if he
leaves now."

A crowd of people walked out of the entrance and
Eva realized it must be the N.A. meeting finishing. A
boy she recognized saw her and walked over.

"Hey, I'm Dudley. Aren't you my sponsor's
girlfriend?"

"If you're talking about Mickey then I am! Eva,
and this is Dash," she said smiling, "I've seen you at
our place, haven't I? with your identical twin
brother?"

"That's right. My brother Pete, and what are you
doing hanging outside an N.A. meeting."

"We're following someone—"

"Really? Someone from the meeting?"

"No, a guy who attacked Dash, who she beat up,
who then came to see the doctor—"

"I didn't beat him up, I just defended myself—"

"That is so cool!" said Dudley, "what a bastard!
And getting his comeuppance!"

"Comeuppance?" queried Dash.

"Punishment, an eye for an eye," shrugged Dudley.
Dash smiled and nodded, saying,

"Then we need more comeuppance," said Dash, "we
were going to follow him, but we have to get to
rehearsals soon—"

"Oh that's right, you dance don't you?"
Eva picked up on her idea and said,

"So what are you doing right now Dudley?"

"Nothing - going for coffee—"

"Then would you follow him for us?" she said,
trying to emulate Hannah's legendary charm, "he's got

on a red crash helmet and is carrying a big messenger
bag with Hotline written on it—"
      "No way! Follow a psycho? You think I'm crazy?"
he said, "that's my brother's department. He's the
hard man in the family. I'm just his alibi!" he
smirked as he walked away.
      "Well that didn't turn out like we hoped did it?"
said Eva, "listen, you go to rehearsals and I'll
follow him, okay? We've got no choice really have we?"
      "But you might be in danger," protested Dash.
      "Don't worry. I travel prepared for any
eventuality," she said, pulling a short black metal
tube from her bag. She pressed a button and it
expanded into a long rod with a deep metallic thunk. A
couple of passers-by saw and looked shocked, so she
pretended it was a cane and did a dance from a Fred
Astaire movie.
      "Where did you get that?" asked Dash.
      "It was my dad's," she said, pushing the thin end
hard against the wall to collapse it, "it was in a
trunk of stuff he left behind in Cheltenham."
      "Oh sorry - I didn't mean to remind you. Have you
heard anything?"
      "No - he's on the log as 'Missing in Action', but
I realize I've been talking about him the past tense
for a while now..."
      Dash hugged her and said,
      "Let's both go to rehearsals now, forget this?"
      But Eva shook her head and pointed across the
street as their quarry emerged from the building.
      "No, this is for Amber."
      "Then I'm coming with you," said Dash, pulling
off her sweatshirt, "let's swap tops so I can hide my
hair in your hoodie." They did so, then set off after
his limping figure.
      "He's gonna get on a bike pretty soon then we'll
lose him," said Dash.
      "I'll get my scooter and come to you. Text me
your progress, okay?"

      DASHA waved bye and continued following the red
helmet north across Soho Square, then right on to a
crowded Oxford Street. He crossed at the lights then
waited outside the Dominion Theatre. Dash texted Eva
just as a scooter stopped next to the red helmet. Dash
thought they would lose them, but the red helmet was
doing something with a rolled-up fiver. He was
snorting something. He threw his head back and shook
it, then got on behind the rider. Eva pulled up
alongside her. She got off and lifted her seat,
revealing a spare helmet. Dash put it on and sat

behind Eva. A chase ensued, which felt like it might
be exciting but was a slow boring zigzag among the
buses on Tottenham Court Road. They came to a traffic
light and the red helmet disappeared through a tiny
gap between two buses, slowing as the lights turned
red. Eva couldn't squeeze past, and when the lights
turned green, the red helmet was gone.

"Shit. Still, we know he's a despatch rider don't
we. So that's a lead," said Eva, "let's go do these
rehearsals and have a look at The Stage."

ART sat at his drawing board staring out of the
window. He was listening to his new favourite song on
repeat: 'Catalyst' by Oceansize.

He tried calling Lori's hotel, and was told that
she'd left instructions to not be disturbed. Of
course, it would be the middle of the night for her.
She'd only be properly awake for his first thing in
the morning, and last thing at night.

At break, AJI saw Marcus down the hall and her
heart raced. She was about to turn around to avoid
him, but she decided not to. He was with Brandt and as
they saw her Marcus faltered for a moment. Their eyes
locked as they closed the space between them. Brandt
had been at the party as must've known they were in
that bedroom together. With only three metres between
them Marcus smiled and waved. As they crossed Brandt
looked over to her and said to him,

"Hey, isn't that the girl you were with at the
party?"

Aji didn't get to hear his response as they were
too far away, but it didn't seem as if he'd be able to
keep a lid on it. She walked on thinking the worse
when a text pinged.

> *"I said you've dumped me*
> *and I'm upset*
> *cos I liked you. OK?"*

Aji did not reply. Another text arrived for Dash:

> *"Saw a man at Angels taking back the Zorro*
> *costume.*
> *He could be Zorro or a despatch rider?*
> *He had a messenger bag with the name*
> *Hotline on it XXX"*

Aji went to the phone booths which weren't used
much anymore, but they still had a Yellow Pages and a
Thompsons Local which she picked up. She flicked

through looking for Hotline. There is was – a despatch
company with an 0208 960 prefix, meaning it was close.
Dash and William's number had been a 960 and they were
at the north end of Ladbroke Grove. She texted back:

> *"Let's go to Hotline this afternoon.*
> *It's not far from Lisboa!*
> *Shall we say 'Natas' @ 4pm? x"*

She got an immediate reply saying yes.

EVA, Dash and Aji had already had their promised
Natas and were discussing the pros and cons of having
another. Eva was happy in London, with Mickey and her
friends. She'd come to love Dash and Aji who were
chatting:
    "Do you know a woman called Flora?" asked Aji.
Dash thought for a moment then shook her head, and
said,
    "No why?"
    "I met her with dad in Mike's on Saturday. Old
friend? Was in dad's book."
    "Do you mean Frieda?" asked Dash.
    "No, I know Frieda. I met her once in the
bathroom at 4am when we both needed the loo."
    "Recently?" asked Dash, looking slightly
concerned.
    "No, two years ago, when they were having their
fling—"
    "You knew about that?"
    "Duh – of course!" laughed Aji, "everybody knew,
didn't they?"
    "I didn't," said Dash and Eva simultaneously.
    "So he's not quite as inept as I thought. So when
did you find out?" asked Aji.
    "When the book came out. I asked him how he knew
her story and he told me the whole thing then."
    Eva took The Stage from her bag and flicked
through to the ads section. There were a couple that
looked promising. One was for a troupe leader for new
West End show, but no other dancers were needed. That
would mean splitting up the gang. The gang of two. The
other was for a Dance Collective in Camden. No money
but could be fun? She circled it then watched Aji
talking about Amber with Dash. Sometimes Aji seemed so
mature for her age. She remembered herself at thirteen
in Maine, messing around in boats and playing with the
dog; no boy's on her mind, no fashion. Just singing
and dancing in the mirror with a hairbrush. She and
her dad though, had had a similar relationship to Aji
and Art, which she missed every day. Maybe she should

call Cheltenham again? Or the Embassy? No, if they heard anything, they'd be calling her soon enough. Again, she'd been thinking about him in the past tense: "*Had* had a similar relationship..."

She got up.

"Let's walk round there. It's almost at the top of Portobello." They walked out and crossed the road and took the turning by Oporto, then they cut through the park where Aji had spent a lot of her childhood on the swings.

They then made a detour into the fabric shop on Portobello road and all bought some haberdashery.

Finally, they turned the corner into Telford Road. There was a cluster of bikers and their bikes which made it clear where Hotline's base was. As they approached a guy came out of the neighbouring building holding a camera.

"You're late, but it was worth the wait!" he said in a German accent, looking them up and down, "two beanpole chaperones for a schoolgirl! Interesting combination!" He fixed his lens on them and Dash and Aji stopped and posed whereas Eva pulled up her hood to cover her face and walked on by.

"Oh nice," he said, snapping away, "now the young one on her own!"

Dash stopped and pulled Aji behind her and said, "We're not here for your casting."

"But she has potential!"

Eva stood among the despatch riders and bummed a drag off one of their joints, while watching the drama unfold. It looked like Dash was going to knee the man in the balls, much to Aji's amusement, who was alternately egging her on, then saying 'But I have potential'.

"Is your boss inside?" asked Eva of the rider. He had the classic 'panda' eyes bikers get from rubbing the smut out of his eyes, onto the surrounding area. He took his joint back and said,

"Sure, he's the one on the mic. Name's Kevin."

She went inside as Dash was wrenching the camera from the German dude while Aji and the riders laughed. An outer office had three girls on phones, filling in dockets. Past them, Kevin sat in front of an enormous map of Greater London, and two computer monitors, while wearing two headsets.

"Kevin?" said Eva.

He swivelled in his chair, smiled and waved but said nothing. His fringe was covering his eyes.

Eva was about to speak when he said,

"Echo Eight. No, it's wrong on the docket. It's number 77 so it'll be on the other side of the street." Then he swivelled back to the wall, saying, "Echo Two. You're late, they just called again. Echo Two?"

He swivelled back and said Sorry, then nodded.

"Hi, a rider brought a Halloween costume back to Angels in Shaftsbury Avenue this morning. But we didn't give him the deposit to return to the customer—"

"Echo Two! Last chance!" then, "we didn't send anyone to Angels today. We normally get a few at Halloween, but none today."

Noises were coming through the wall: Banging and crashing.

"But he had one of your messenger bags?"

"Doesn't mean he's working for us *now* though," he said sadly, "we lose a few every year to these scumbags, one of which will be Echo Two in five minutes when I sack him. You hear that Echo Two!"

"Do you have a list of these scumbags?"

"Fuck yeah!" he said turning to the monitors, "I can sort ex-riders by that column's property and print out the last two years? Echo Eight. 77! On the opposite side of the road!" He pressed 'Print' and swivelled back to her.

"Thank you," she said.

"Fuck 'em. They all leave me eventually, and normally in the middle of the day with packages on board. Including Major Scumbag Echo Two! You fucking fuck-wit!" He turned back to the wall and Eva tore off the sheet from the printer and left. Outside, Dash was banging on the locked door of the photographer's studio.

"There's a lot of anger in the air today," Eva said to Aji, then went and pulled Dash away and they headed back to Lisboa.

AJI glanced down the list while Eva talked to Dash about her anger issues:

"Seriously darling," she said, "maybe you should see someone?"

"No, that was a one-off because he was a..."

"Photographer?" suggested Eva.

"Speaking of which," said Aji, taking a photo out of her bag. The photo of Dash elongating a schoolboy's penis. Eva burst out laughing.

"I do not have a problem with anger usually, I'm just a little... I don't know the word..."

"Frustrated?" suggested Aji.

"Dissatisfied?" asked Eva.

"Heated?" asked Aji.

"Horny?" asked Eva.

Dash found it very amusing and grabbed the list. Eva said,

"Look for the name Grodenko."

"Grodenko?"

"Oh yeah, sorry, I forgot to tell you that was the name they called him in the Doctor's."

Dash scanned the names, and there he was, with a telephone number and an address in Wembley.

"Shall we go there now?" suggested Aji, excitedly.

"Would love to Darling," said Eva, "but we have to get to work now. We're already in trouble for being late for rehearsals this morning."

"Then let's try the number, at least?"

Dash nodded and said,

"I like when you get excited and go back to being that kid I loved so much."

"Don't you love me anymore Dash?" asked Aji.

"Much more, but in a different way," she said, handing Aji her tiny phone, which was perfect for Aji's tiny thumbs to punch in the numbers.

"Nothing," Aji said, "it just hangs up. Does that mean it's a fake number?"

Eva nodded.

"Probably."

Aji felt very disappointed. They got up and left. Aji hugged them and said Goodbye, then watched them cruise off. She went home to do her homework, wishing she was in a musical in the West End.

MARGOT went home after school and picked out shots of Zorro to give to the police. She decided on six which had him prominently featured. Margot found the negatives and went to work.

ART put the phone down and smiled, but then frowned.

"What?" asked Aji.

"That was Zal, updating me on offers to option my book—"

"What does that mean?"

"According to Zal, a film producer can buy the right (for one year) to develop it; to transform it into a screenplay and attempt to raise money to actually produce it—"

"Wow, that would be awesome!" said Aji, "so are we going to be millionaires?"

"No, sorry," said Art, "an option is only a few thousand, but if they go into production, then we'd get one or two percent of the budget."

"Oh, so it would have to be a hundred-million-dollar budget for us to be millionaires?"

"And that's not likely to happen," said Art, "no special effects, fleets of helicopters or demolishing buildings in my book."

Aji shrugged,

"Then try to write some into the sequel, okay?"

"Sure."

Aji caught his eye, but he looked away.

"What's wrong Dad?"

"Mickey called me at the weekend, said he'd forgiven me for writing about him—"

"That's great!"

"But I didn't dare tell him it might be made into a movie."

They both sat and thought for a moment.

"So what would you choose? Mickey or the money?"

"It would have to be Mickey."

Aji smiled and nodded.

Dash and Lori were also on Art's mind. Having failed to make it that morning, he thought maybe he should go to a meeting to share about his confusion. But Aji was obviously not to be trusted to be left on her own. He tried his list of babysitters, but none were available. He found he was relieved. He hadn't really wanted to go. What was wrong with him? For the first eight years he'd been so keen as he believed it was for his survival, but since then he'd been tailing off, making excuses, disengaging from committees he'd been passionate about, and become cynical about the whole idea. It was weird, because he knew those first five years when he'd been going to a meeting every day had been the happiest of his life, but did it impinge on his creativity like he'd told Lori? How different would the 'Head' book have been if he'd kept up his meeting a day routine? Would it have been all sunshine and positivity? Probably not, as it was based on fact; there wasn't any way of describing intestines flowing from D2's slashed stomach that was joyous and positive...

AJI sat on the sofa and watched him staring out the window. What was he thinking about? Sometimes she didn't want to interrupt his musings, but this time:

"I take it you were making a point?"

His eyes lit up and he turned to her:

"That you can't be trusted on your own? Yes."

"I'm sorry dad, it was stupid of me. I won't lie to you again, I promise."

"Okay, it's really important that we be honest with one another."

"Absolutely," she said, then remembered him lying to her that very morning. Should she bring that up and use it to slap him down? No, she'd put that in the bank for a more important moment when she needed some leverage.

"And by the way," said Aji, "I find the term *babysitter* offensive,"

"I agree," said Art, "though I didn't actually use the term."

"It's written at the top of the list on the fridge," she said.

"It's a very old list. But would you like to rub out the 'baby' then?"

"Abort the 'baby'? Yes - yes I would." She went to his drawing board and retrieved an eraser, while scanning the bookshelves.

"Do you have a copy of your book here?" she said, "I think I might give it a try. See what all the fuss is about."

"Er... I don't think so. You wouldn't enjoy it anyway. It's about certain people you know all having sex with one another—"

"Eurgh" she said, but had the feeling he was exaggerating to put her off the idea. She'd have a look in his bedroom while he was making supper.

ART peered round the corner and watched Aji leave the room, making sure she wasn't just getting something and returning. She looked back but didn't see him, then she went into his room. Fishy. But he was free to call Lori at her hotel. They rang her room and put him through.

"Hi, how are you?" he asked.

"Very groggy. Just waking up. How are you?"

"Fine thanks. Tomorrow morning, if you're feeling up to it, maybe we could go to the London Library? Check on our Conductor neighbour?"

"That sounds good. Call me, okay?"

"Sure, will do."

Tuesday - 4th November

DASHA sat in Lisboa, a coffee, the Guardian and the trade papers on the table before her. She was staring out the window, slightly shocked. She had just read a story in the paper about the inventor of a particularly vicious landmine. He had been the victim of a home invasion, but the perpetrators hadn't stolen anything, except for his legs, that had been neatly amputated at the knee joint.

To distract herself, she picked up "The Stage" and turned to the classified ads, looking for any jobs that might interest her and Eva. She circled a couple, drained her coffee cup then got up to leave.

ART sat in his usual spot, watching the world go by. The usual faces slowly growing older before his eyes: Mothers and children on their way to school; the stall-holders laying out their wares; the bin-men on their loop and the tourists. What made anyone want to come and look at this? But then, why was this his favourite place on earth? Why did he choose to bring up his daughter here? He pulled the stylus from his X.D.A and started writing this observation on the screen. Such a clever device. He could write in one spot on the screen with his left hand, while drinking his coffee with his right hand and still stare out the window!

He wrote about the last day's developments then he called Lori at the hotel.

"Hi, how are you feeling today?"

"Weird Artie, I'm still on Tahiti time, so I've been up all night, and will be getting sleepy again about your 1pm? So I reckon if I keep pushing myself every day to stay up an extra hour, I should be on your time in a couple of weeks?"

"So you're expecting to stay that long?" asked Art.

"I've got nowhere to be, Artie."

"Well, I haven't heard back from the gardener yet, but if you're up for it, let's take a ride to Saint James's this morning; before you feel sleepy?"

"Ready when you are, Artie."

"See you in 20 minutes."

Art put down the phone and Dash jumped into his mind. He felt guilty for not telling her about Lori. Maybe he should call her?

In class 3B, AJI sat at her favourite desk by the radiator, leafing through her journal. She had

119

been given it by Dash for her eleventh birthday and she'd started writing it when she was twelve and had continued sporadically (as long as there was something interesting happening - no point journalising a boring day).

Her pen hovered above the paper, then started writing:

> *"What is Amber doing right now? Is she making love with this older man in between breaks for champagne and caviar? I wouldn't put it past her. She had been gone more than a week in the past, but we covered for her. She was angry with us because she said the whole point of being gone was to get her parents to worry. But what she won't hear is that WE worry too! I hope this is worth it for her. I hope she is having a great time and getting her parent's attention! Or.*
>
> *Or is her body lying in a ditch somewhere?"*

She looked across at Margot. She must've been thinking the same thing - there was a tear in the corner of her eye.

> *"None of us have heard from the police. I wonder whether they are investigating at all?*
>
> *We handed Margot's photos of Zorro in to the Head Mistress's office. So maybe that'll give them the nudge they need?"*

But she was torn:

> *"Though I'm wondering if we should tell them she's been gone much longer than this in the past?"*

This was serious. Probably the most serious subject she'd ever written about. Recently, a lot of it had been about Marcus, including the Halloween finale to their 'relationship'.

But previous entries included a few evenings at group outings to the cinema and visits to friends' homes where they'd eaten pizza and watched a DVD. When she read them back she realized that, alongside the events and the people and the chat, she had actually written reviews of the films as well. Of course, from her perspective her reviews were insightful, funny and she also marked the films out of ten. But she'd never shown her writing to anyone. She needed some feedback. Maybe she should show them to her dad? Absolutely not. Or Dash? Maybe. Or the girls? Or just Margot?

ART asked for Lori at reception, but the guy looked blank.

"Tall strawberry blonde?" Art said, "Latin American?"

"Oh yes, she said you'd be calling for her. Hang on."

He liked the way Lori clung to him on the bike. He wanted to go faster just to make her squeeze him tighter, but she was already a bit hysterical. The sleep deprivation was screwing with her mind. They parked in the motorcycle bay on St James's Square and walked to the London Library.

"Why this one," she asked, "and not the British Library?"

"It's smaller and quieter, but it has what we need."

They entered and bought Day Passes, then walked through the main hall to a spiral staircase at the back. This took them to the Archives Section.

They toiled with the massive shelves, moving them back and forth by turning the big wheels, but had come up with nothing.

After an hour Lori said,

"This Kerkovich dude is an elusive creature. Shall we try Goggling him?"

Art nodded, resisting the urge to correct her,

"There's an internet café on Piccadilly Circus."

They set off.

DASHA and Eva were driving to Wembley in Mickey's luxurious car. Much better than the scooter for such a long journey. They'd met in Camden for a casting which they both felt went well:

"And they needed a few dancers, so hopefully we'll both be offered a part!"

"And I like the way we'd be doing different pieces regularly, so it would never be boring."

Λ song came on the radio; one they both liked (Toxic - Britney Spears) and they sung along.

The address was nearly impossible to get to, as it was off a slip-way between two dual-carriageways and they missed the turning twice and had to circle back to try it again. When they got there though, they were disappointed to find it didn't exist. There was no 11a, Selbourne Gardens. They parked and scanned the area: Dishevelled semis covered in soot from the motorway. There was a lane leading behind the houses and Eva drove the car round the back. A cluster of garages backing onto the M1 were all they found. Abandoned fridges, mattresses and syringes dotted the area.

"It would be a perfect place to hold a kidnap victim don't you think?" suggested Dash, "with the rushing of the traffic drowning out any screams?"

Eva shuddered,

"That's sick Dash, but you have a point."

Dash smiled and they got out and searched. Most of the garages were derelict and the couple that were useable had no hidey-holes. They walked back to the car.

"Have you seen Art?" asked Eva.

"No, it's odd as we've spent years 'bumping into each other' at Lisboa, but now that I've broken up with William, that sync doesn't exist anymore."

"Maybe it's cos you've moved?" suggested Eva, "you can't spend hours hanging around there anymore?"

"I didn't spend hours hanging around there," said Dash, a little offended, "but now you have a point. I hadn't realized what moving would do to our relationship. Maybe I've taken for granted our 'meetings' at Lisboa?"

Eva nodded and started the engine.

ART and Lori walked up to the Internet Café and bought a 30-minute ticket. Lori chose a booth with a view, just as Art would have. He punched 'Albert Kerkovich' into the box and pressed 'enter'. There were lots of results and he clicked on one randomly. Art pulled up another chair, but Lori ignored it and leant over his shoulder; so close, he could smell her choice of soap. She read the entry aloud, and her tick (turning her head to the side at the end of a sentence) seemed more pronounced than usual:

> "Albert Kerkovich (October 16, 1932 –) is a German double-bassist and orchestral conductor whose career has extended over four decades. A child prodigy, he joined the Frankfurt Philharmonie at age 16, becoming the youngest instrumentalist in a major symphony orchestra in Germany. As musical director of the München Symphony Orchestra, he supported the Allies with cultural diplomacy initiatives in Europe after World War II.

Born	October 16, 1932 Frankfurt-am-Main, Germany.

Occupation	Conductor
Known for	Directing and conducting: München Symphony Orchestra; London Philharmonic; Den Haag Symphony Orchestra
Years active	1948-1999
Spouse(s)	Marilyn Manon (m. 1960; div. 1978)

Later life:
The tragic disappearance of his daughter in 1976, while on a touring holiday of Europe, put a self-imposed pause on his career for five years. He came back at the Royal Albert Hall in 1982 with...

Mystery:
There was a long-running rumour about Albert Kerkovich, that he had never dispelled, that he was a cat burglar of exquisite jewellery. According to the legend, he would supplement his busy autumn touring schedule by researching that cities patrons. He would then spend a pleasant evening climbing the rooftops of his ostentatiously wealthy victims and enter through their chimneys. He would then steal a few good pieces, leave his calling card (a 24 carat Clef {musical symbol}) and be back at his hotel before he was missed. It was never proven, as the dates weren't 100%, and he always had an alibi. Apparently, he liked the rumour and was quoted as saying: "The idea that I am agile enough to climb up and over buildings is very flattering and I only wish it were true. Also the wealth that would come with such a career; how I would love to be that rich!"

He lives in London, in a mansion off
Holland Park which can only be afforded by
crooked Hedge Fund operators, Middle Eastern Oil
magnates and U2. This point has never been
addressed by him.

Another tragedy occurred at his home in
1989 when his butler, Silvert Glarium, fell from
the roof of the building during the night. No
one could explain why the butler was up there
and the mystery has never been solved."

Lori looked out the window at Piccadilly Circus
below. The people were running from the lashing rain.

"So that's interesting, that he may also be a
cat-burglar?" said Lori, "it's almost worth revisiting
him just to ask about that, isn't it?"

Art nodded,

"Quite a life he has lead, if this article is to
be believed? It's a bit judgemental for a biography
don't you think?"

"What website is it?" asked Lori.

"Wikipedia?"

"Never heard of it," said Lori, yawning, "I think
I need to go to bed though. I'm gonna get the tube,
okay?"

"Sure. In this weather I'd like to join you."

She kissed him on the cheek, and left. A kiss. On
the cheek, but still a kiss. Art felt he was blushing.

AJI was curious about the girls in Mike's on
Saturday (Flora?), but she knew that her Dad wouldn't
give anything else away.

She wrote in her journal:

*"My dad is weird. Him and Dash have been
circling one another for years. She's been
threatening to leave William for ever, and he
encouraged her. He thinks I didn't know what he
was doing, but he really is an idiot. But now
another girl is on the scene. I saw them in
Mike's. And he's seen her since. I wanted to ask
Dash about her, but I don't think he's told her
she's here. Which is fishy. I know I said I
didn't want anyone to be with my dad, but if it
has to be anyone it's got to be Dash. I need to
get the Flora[?] person out of the picture.
She's in his book, but I haven't read it, and he
won't tell me anything else. I suppose I'll have
to read it! (Apparently, I'm in it though, which
might make up for it!)"*

124

She checked if the school library had a copy of his 'Head' book. It didn't, so at lunch she asked Dora if she'd like to go to Waterstones with her.

"The one on Notting Hill Gate or the one on High Street Ken?" asked Dora.

"High Street Ken," said Aji.

"Really? The other one is closer by thirty-nine steps, you know; and it's on the flat. Whereas you walk downhill to High Street Ken, but then you have to walk uphill on the way back?"

Aji grabbed her hand and they sneaked out to Notting Hill Gate.

Dora, pulled her buttonless coat around her.

"I didn't know your dad was a writer?"

"Neither did I!" joked Aji, "he mainly draws or stares out the window!"

Dora laughed.

"Though he did drag me to a couple of literary festivals over the summer and he read passages of his book to people and they clapped and some even wanted his autograph. Apparently he used to be quite famous before I was born, under his pen name, Artemis Grime."

In the warmth of the bookshop they searched the shelves randomly then asked an assistant. She looked in the database and there it was, in the True Crime section sandwiched between 'For the Parsimonious' by N.S. Grigson and 'Floggerythms' by Merki Grobian.

"But we don't have it, sorry," said the assistant, "we can order it for you?"

Aji thanked her but declined her offer and they left.

"How about the Notting Hill Book Exchange?"

They set off into the wind whipping down the street. The shop wasn't warm but at least it was out of the wind. A lot of the central isles were devoted to Comic Books but the walls were all paperbacks. They found their way to the 'G' section and started scanning. Someone walked behind Aji and stopped (maybe shifting through the comic-books?) but she continued her search. Finally, there it was - the name Artemis Grime on a couple of books. She went to pluck one just as another hand reached over her to do the same. Their hands touched and an electric shock passed between them. She turned and a tall woman loomed over her. For a moment she thought it was Miss Pringle and she was in trouble, but then she realized it was her dad's new friend.

"Hello Aji," she said, "great minds think alike!" she laughed.

Dora peered upward and giggled,

"Fools seldom differ."

Aji smiled, slightly baffled,

"What are you doing in here?"

"Same as you, it would seem," she said holding out the two books, "which one were you after? The long-windedly titled anthology 'He travelled the world looking for trouble and invariably caused it', or the long-windedly titled twisty mystery 'I'm keeping the head', hyphen, brackets, '1999' close brackets?"

"The Head book please," replied Aji.

"That's lucky, as I came for the anthology."

They went to the counter and the woman bought them both and gave Aji the Head book saying,

"On me. Want to get some lunch, or supper in my case?"

"Thank you. Er, we'd love to but we have to get back to school, sorry."

The woman nodded then bent down and hugged Aji and whispered,

"Don't judge me too harshly please?"

"You know he does have a girlfriend?" Aji said, "she is beautiful and her name is Dasha."

"I'm not talking about that," she said, then strode off, Aji looking after her slightly confused.

"Who was that?" asked Dora.

Aji squeezed her eyes shut and gritted her teeth. She'd forgotten to ask her name.

HANNAH woke up and had no idea what day it was. She knew she'd checked in on Sunday and seen a doctor. But then she'd slept on and off ever since. A kindly lady had brought her her medication to her a couple of times, always insisting that it was the last time, and that she must get up. She had been intermittently throwing up and had felt like shit, but she seemed to be feeling better today. She heard laughing below. It sounded aggressive. There was a knock on the door and a girl poked her head round the door.

"Hi, I'm Anne. How are you feeling?" she said, walking over to Hannah .

"Not bad thanks, considering." Anne smiled and sat on Hannah's bed. She was about 30, skinny and ravaged.

"Then can you please get up and come downstairs? I'm feeling totally outnumbered here."

"Why?"

"So it was about 50/50 male/female last week, then three more guys arrived and Eleanor and Jessie got clapped out, then yesterday a couple of girls got thrown out; so that leaves me, Jodi, Chloe, Clementine, Jo-2 and Furgustina, and you're up here."

126

"So it's all men, and us seven? I like those odds," she laughed, "and is anyone using?"

"A couple have been smoking pot, which was fine, but they're planning another delivery of harder stuff. Which me and Jodi are more worried about. Think we might have to report them."

"Shit! But no booze?"

"No, but please come downstairs?"

"Okay, I'll get washed and dressed and come down."

Anne said thanks and left. Hannah got out of bed and went to the basin by the window. She turned on the Hot, then looked at the view. Ugh: Trees; grass; sheep; hills - the countryside.

JOSEPH sat behind his dais in the foyer of Ebury House, leafing through a Blackberry catalogue. He was so engrossed that he missed the door opening.

"Are you the porter?" said a slim silhouetted figure.

"I am Sir," said Joseph, jumping up.

"You're the man to let me in to Karen Ford's apartment?"

"Absolutely, everything is at your disposal," he said, handing him the fat catalogue as he led the way into the lift, "I'll show you up and then you have two hours, in which time you can make yourself at home," he said, closing the grille and punching a button, "eat from Karen's fridge; drink her favourite teas; listen to her favourite music, and marvel at the work of art which is her apartment, just as she left it all those years ago."

Joseph was getting a bit bored of his spiel. He decided to rewrite it. The man was in his forties, oriental, expensively dressed. He said,

"I am a big fan," she is the most beautiful woman who has ever lived."

Joseph smiled,

"You'll get no argument from me Sir. She was even more beautiful in person—"

"You knew her?"

"I was her porter when she lived here—"

"Oh, that is amazing! Once I've finished upstairs I'd like to pick your brains about your memories? Maybe we could go to dinner?"

"Okay, yes," said Joseph, "sometimes I like to reminisce..."

ART needed something for Aji's supper. He'd forgotten as he'd been engrossed in his work all day, while listening to his new favourite song on repeat: 'Catch the Sun', by Doves.

He put on his coat and walked to Tesco's up the Portobello Road. He normally steered clear of certain isles which contained foods and drinks which were to be avoided: Alcohol, obviously; Wheat, which depressed him; and Sugar, meaning the Biscuits and the Cereals and the Sweets and the fucking list was endless! So navigating became like the old PacMan video game with the maze full of munching yellow mouths that you had to avoid by back-tracking and he saw one ahead and turned but his eye was caught by a 'Lion' bar which he hadn't had in years and he remembered it had rice crispies on top and some toffee and wafer or was it something with slightly more body and crunch and he was standing there with one in his hand looking at the picture and reading the description and—

"Fucking Pig!" someone behind him said, then pushed him hard into the racking, causing many Lion bars, and Twix's, and Milky Ways to go tumbling to the floor. He recovered himself then shouted after the figure,

"That was judgey of you! I was only going to have one Lion bar!"

The guy turned and Art realized it was the albino dude who lived opposite. He came right up to him and said,

"I know your game, Pig!"

"What game?"

Other customers were squeezing past them, looking worried.

"You're watching me—"

"Who are you?"

"You're watching me and reporting to your little piggy friends!"

Art smiled,

"Oh! You're calling me 'pig' like in 'policeman' as opposed to a food piggy snuffling at the Lion bars? Cool, I'm not so offended, and thanks for saving me from myself because one Lion bar is too many and a thousand never enough."

"Fuck off!" the dude said, "and stop watching me!"

"Don't flatter yourself—"

"Stop watching me—"

"That is my home asshole! I sit there at my drawing board working all day - every day!"

"You spend far more time looking out the window than you do looking down at your so-called work!"

"Again with the judgey-ness!" said Art, "I may spend some time looking out the window, but it's part of the creative process, and anyway, who the fuck are you and what are you doing in there?" A small crowd had gathered, and the tired old security guard was hovering.

"Only someone with a guilty conscience would think they were being watched! What are you doing in th—"

"Just Fuck Off!" screamed the albino before forcing his way out of the store.

Everyone watched him go, then turned back to look at Art.

"I only wanted a Lion Bar," he said, holding it up as evidence.

JOSEPH scrolled through the cameras and found the man in the black bedroom, dancing slowly in front of the full-length mahogany mirror. He was wearing one of Karen's mini-dresses and her classic bob wig. Something was sticking out the from th—

Joseph turned off the monitor. He decided he'd be unavailable for dinner after all.

HANNAH walked downstairs unsteadily, holding the railing. At the bottom of the steps was a payphone in an alcove. She thought for a moment about calling a cab, then walked on. The place looked familiar: To the left was a massive room with many sofas and tables, populated by other inmates; to the right was an arched hallway with a fountain at its centre. Had she been here before?

Yup, her feet were taking her to a door on the left. In the smoking room, the air was non-existent above five feet. Luckily, Hannah didn't have to duck like everyone else, if she wanted to breathe.

She looked around her: Addicts, the moment you take away their drug of choice they'll just start up on something else. It was pathetic. She took a spare seat at the long table and introduced herself to her peers. She immediately forgot their names but knew their drug of choice without asking: Drink; crack; heroin; drink; speed; crack; heroin; drink; crack; meth; heroin, plus one she wasn't sure of. She may have to ask her later. They were all smoking like their lives depended on it. Maybe it did? Maybe the moment they stopped they wanted crack or smack or... the smell was good. There was a void inside her that could do with filling with this smoke. She bummed a Benny off the guy opposite. Mmmm, she hadn't had one in a while. She'd forgotten how much she liked them. But of course, one really needed a drink to compliment the fag, and you know what would go really well with that? A nice line of coke? Yes, and... oh shit.

ART and Aji had finished their supper and were watching a DVD of 'Down with Love'.

"I thought Rene Zellweger was English?" said Aji.

"Because of Bridget Jones's Diary? Yeah, she did do a great English accent; whereas Ewan McGregor's American accent in patchy, at best."

"This isn't very good is it?"

"It's trying to be like a Doris Day, Rock Hudson romcom from the fifties and failing embarrassingly."

"Shall we eject?" she said, "I'm going to read in bed."

Aji reading? Wonders will nev– His phone vibrated. A London landline. He pressed the green button.

"Artie, Lori here. Awake, showered and ready for breakfast!"

Art smiled and said 'Hi'.

"You want to come over and join me in the restaurant?"

Art smiled and said 'Okay'.

He went to Aji's door and knocked. She said Yup so he entered. She slid her book under her duvet and smiled.

"I thought I might pop out for a while, if I can trust you?"

She smiled and said,

"Yup, I'm not going anywhere."

"Okay then, nighty-night Sweetheart."

Nighty-night Dada."

He put on a coat and grabbed his helmet and bounced down the stairs.

He found Lori at a corner table in the restaurant. She looked beautiful, smiling and waving him over. She pushed her lips towards him, and they kissed briefly.

"I've ordered scrambled eggs and smoked salmon, and a coffee," she said decisively.

"And I shall have Lapsang Souchong Tea and some toast please," he said to the hovering waitress.

"So, I've found Catherine the Cook!" she said, laughing, "I suddenly remembered her family came from Rutland, 'the smallest county in England' she was proud to tell me, so I looked up her surname on Goggles and eventually I spoke to her nephew, who gave me her number in London, and we can see her tomorrow!"

Art was impressed.

"I'm impressed! You're actually very good at this. You don't really need me do you? You and Goggles make a great team."

The song 'My Father's son' by Joe Cocker was playing over the speakers. Lori said,

"This song annoys me."

"Why?" asked Art.

"I suppose, because it's about loving his father?"

Art listened.

"And that annoys you, because?"

"Because I never loved my father."

"Same," said Art, copying his daughter's abbreviation.

"Mine was an arrogant bully and yours was an angry alcoholic."

"True, you're right," he said, "it always surprises me when anyone claims to like their father, let alone love them."

"I know!" agreed Lori, "I wonder what it would be like to have that? To be a small child being protected by god-like presence that instilled you with confidence and made you believe 'men are good'? Do you think we'd be completely different people?"

Art thought for a moment as their food was delivered,

"I don't know. If he'd been loving to me, but the same in every other way, then he'd have still been a bigot, a racist and a misogynist, so even if I'd loved him, I would've still eventually decided that I wanted to be the exact opposite of him."

Lori raised an eyebrow and nodded,

"I remember the way he treated you. Has he mellowed?"

"Not at all. He's more curmudgeonly than ever."

"Do you remember he was always away on Thursday nights, 'entertaining clients'?" she said, "I remember because if your mum babysat us on a Thursday she was always sad."

"Oh yeah. There was a T.V. show on after my bedtime, 'What the Papers Say' and she always expected a call from him before it started. If he called, she was often angry and if he didn't, she was sad."

"The theme song was quite jaunty I recall, but if it came on the radio, she'd come over all melancholy..."

Lori put her hand on Art's and squeezed.

They finished eating in silence.

"So, we have two choices," she said, "we can go round and burn down your father's house, or we can go upstairs and make love?"

Art's heart skipped a beat,

"Well they're both very tempting offers, but I think the second one is more appealing—" She took his hand and led him from the basement. As they walked through Reception his phone vibrated. It was an S.O.S. text from Aji.

> *"Dad, there's a spider in my room*
> *the size of a dog! Please come home now!"*

Art showed it to Lori, who shrugged,

"You go be a good dad," then stuck her tongue out at him, and walked upstairs alone.

Wednesday - 5th November

ART was woken by the phone. He picked up to hear
a voice:
"Bartholomew, it's Barry Gardener here. How are
you?"
Art sat up,
"What time is it?"
"6.30, Sorry, I'm on my way to work and this is
the only moment I'm with my phone. How can I help?"
"Er...well, when I was a kid I got to know our
neighbours in the big house? A pair of twins?" he
would have liked to have a coffee before attempting
this conversation, "anyway one of them has some
questions about that time. Stuff that happened in the
household and they wondered if we could come and see
you today?"
"Could we do it over the phone?"
"Not really. It's a visual thing..." said Art,
not really sure what he was on about.
"Then of course!" said Barry, "I'm in Hampshire
all day but I'll be in Windsor this evening, trying to
protect my favourite garden from a firework display if
you want to come down?"
"That's great Barry, can you give me the address
please?" Art wrote it down then couldn't get back to
sleep. He got up and made coffee.
When he was fully awake he called Lori at the
hotel, and was put through.
"Hey, how are you?" she said.
"Regretful? I got home and she had exaggerated;
the spider was only the size of mouse!"
He heard Lori shudder,
"Still enormous!"
He sat in the window with his coffee,
"So what have you been doing?"
"Went for a walk around Holland Park, did some
window shopping in High Street Ken, did the crossword,
watched some porn on cable—"
"Ooh," he said, "what kind?"
"Hetero, lesbian and threesomes."
"Two guys?" he asked.
"No. Two girls."
"Nice."
"But it's always so unrealistic—"
"Threesomes? Of course they're unrealistic!" he
agreed, "no one has ever actually had a successful
threesome in real life!"
She laughed, then said,
"I meant the hetero, no build up, just straight
in there."

"Sex is never depicted well. It's just as unrealistic in movies, but in a different way."

"Huh?"

"Well, in movies, a man and a woman will often meet in a bar or a club and within a couple of minutes they're in the loo having animalistic sex, that is completely out of character for a normal person."

"True," she agreed.

"It's only sex-addicts who actually behave like that—"

"And you should know!" she said.

"And there's never any foreplay, or lube, or protection and rarely does the woman come and—"

"I see you've put a lot of thought into this," she observed.

"Well, at least in porn, the guy goes down on her first and makes sure she comes many times, and—"

"You make some good points," she said, "I'll re-evaluate my appreciation of porn tonight, or in a moment."

Art's heart skipped another beat.

"So when shall we go and see the Cook?"

"This morning? Before I get sleepy?"

"Okay, where does she live?"

"South Ken? She suggested we meet in Dino's?"

"Perfect. Shall I come and get you in an hour?"

ART dropped Lori off outside Dino's then went to find a bike park. When he came back, Lori was whispering with an elderly woman in a hoodie.

"Artie," said Lori, "this is Catherine; or Cookie, as I used to call her."

He squeezed her hand and said 'Hi', then sat down.

"I can't believe I'm seeing you both again after all these years!" she said, "it's so exciting to see how you've grown up!"

"So what are you doing now, Catherine?"

"Still cooking, just round the corner for a nice family," she said, "and what about you, Artie?"

"I'm an illustrator and—"

"And what about you Lori?"

"I've been travelling mainly and—"

"So what do you want to know? I can't be too long, got lunch to prepare for eight."

"Er, okay," said Lori, "you slept next to the kitchen didn't you in that suite?"

"If you can call it sleep. Mostly I read in bed, by the window—"

"So did you ever notice any comings and goings in the night?"

134

"I remember you used to go visit him, quite regularly," she said, elbowing Art in the ribs, "why do you ask?"

"Someone was coming to my room and molesting me," whispered Lori, "and that's why I was running and hiding at Artie's."

"Oh my God!" hissed Catherine, "of course, now I remember; you were a nervous wreck sometimes," she clasped Lori's hands in hers, "and I asked you what was wrong but you would never tell, oh I'm so sorry Lori."

"It's okay, it's been a long time and I'm healed, but I would like to get some closure—"

"I understand, I understand. Ask me anything, no rush."

"Thanks Cookie," said Lori, "so any other traffic through the kitchen door?"

"Well yes. I'd see you run, then once or twice, someone would follow after you and look around the garden; at first I thought it was your father but he didn't return through the kitchen, he'd search and then disappear."

Art thought for a moment, then asked,

"Did he disappear through the hedge like Lori, or over the wall maybe?"

"I don't know, maybe the hedge? Sorry, it was dark and—"

"So did you know Albert," asked Art, "the conductor, living next door?"

She looked offended and said,

"Yes, as a matter of fact I did."

"Why do you say it like that?" asked Art.

She had been hunched, but she relaxed and smiled at Art,

"Well, I thought you knew and I got all defensive, but I don't suppose it matters after all this time," she drew a breath, "but after his wife left, we had a little fling. He'd climb over the garden wall and spend the night with me. He saw the comings and goings too. Once he actually chased the man around the garden!"

"But he didn't tell us about that?" said Lori, "we questioned him on Sunday."

"Well, he's a gentleman isn't he?" Catherine said, "he wouldn't've wanted to compromise me, would he?"

Art was disappointed, and seemingly, so was Lori.

"He was our prime suspect," she explained, "we thought he was coming in over the roof."

"No, that door was always creaking in the night.
We should've locked the thing, but your father
wouldn't hear of it—"

"So you'd sometimes hear it creak, like someone
was coming in, and then later hear Lori running out?"

"Yes, sometimes."

"Which implies they weren't a member of the
household like the Butler or Johan the Security—"

"Johan was gay. And so was Silvert. And they..."

"Really?" said Lori, "I had no idea."

"How about the Gardener?" asked Art.

"Barrington?" recalled Catherine, "I saw him
talking to you in the garden a couple of times, and
then you ran in and sobbed into my apron. I don't know
what he'd said." She looked at her watch.

"Well, we're going to see him later today," said
Art, reminded of his early morning call.

"Thank you so much Cookie," said Lori, "if you
think of anything, you know where to find me."

Catherine said 'Bye' and left.

"So that eliminates many of our suspects," said
Art, a little bewildered.

"But we're seeing Barry later?"

"Yes, at a Fireworks display tonight."

"Then I'd better get some sleep."

HANNAH didn't feel like going to Group. She lay
in bed, looking out across a valley of bland
countryside when Anne knocked and entered her room.

"Come on, it's time."

Hannah pretended to be asleep, but Anne had been
sent by the counsellor to collect her and wasn't
allowed to take no for an answer.

"It's only one floor above us; perfect for
someone as lazy as you."

"I'm not lazy," said Hannah sitting up, "I just
don't want to go."

"All that money you're spending - you may as well
be at a cheap hotel in Bath for all the use you're
making of the facilities."

Hannah swung her legs off the bed.

"You're right. Sorry. I do want to stay clean.
Let's go."

Once she was there, in an attic room with twelve
others, she didn't feel like joining in, even though
she knew the counsellor would be on her case pretty
soon. He was a bald man with a big head and tiny
features which reminded her of a toy she'd owned as a
kid. His glasses were taped together at the bridge. He
rested his hands on his beer belly and didn't inspire
confidence in her at all.

136

She sat back, gently swinging her legs under her chair, looking at her peers. Out of the twelve sitting in the circle, two were doable. One male, one female. No.1 (as she'd affectionately named him) was an annoying prick who kept trying to drag her into the conversation, but he also looked like he wanted to eat her; which pleased her immensely. Yes, she'd do him, 'if the world depended upon it'. That phrase rang a bell; where was that from? Art! During her previous stint in Recovery when they'd got clean together, he'd told her that he would sit in N.A. meetings deciding who he'd choose to sleep with 'if the world depended upon it', and she had judged him severely for his obsession with sex. Ironic. But what else was there? Her phone - confiscated on arrival; music - not allowed; exercise - yeah, right; food - it was shit! They'd served Lasagne yesterday, but with pork! Not minced. With the rind still on. With hairs sticking out of it!

"What about you, little lady?" asked Mr Potato Head.

"Sorry?"

"Do you know why you're here?"

"Absolutely."

"Why?"

"Because I'm an addict. A full-blown ten-out-of-ten addict."

"But you've been in Recovery before. What happened?"

"It wasn't my fault. I didn't choose to relapse—"

"But you surely put yourself into a situation where you allowed that to happen?"

"I guess so."

"When was that?"

"Two, three years ago?"

"So why didn't you come straight back to meetings afterwards?"

"Er... it was very traumatic, and I guess I was in shock and needed something to calm me and then I was back on the rollercoaster and..."

"So your addiction was strong again, from the moment it happened?"

"Yes, ten-out-of-ten."

"So you know—"

"Yes, I know."

"But it wou—"

"I know."

"But—"

"I know."

"You—"

"I know!"

"Hannah, you have a really bad case of the *I knows*."

"I know!"

AJI was reading her dad's 'Head' book in the library. There were a few others sitting around chatting or reading. It was a kind of journal even with the days of the weeks mentioned. She'd never paid any interest to his work, so never known he had written like this. However subliminal her awareness was, he must have inspired her somehow to start writing a journal. Or maybe it was in their DNA?

She had been disappointed when her 'character' had gone on holiday on the second day of the book, but she didn't mind his depiction of her. Her mum, however, hadn't come off quite as kindly; she felt maybe her dad was still a bit angry at her?

Marcus walked in and saw her. He waved, came over and crouched down to look at the cover of the book. She looked around nervously to see if anyone was watching them. He said,

"What are you reading?"

"What are you doing?"

"Being friendly when our paths cross, as agreed?"

She couldn't argue with that. She held up the book.

"Oh you shouldn't be reading that. It's adults only."

"Have you read it?"

"Yes," he replied, "it's gory and druggy and sexy, so I enjoyed it."

"You're not an adult either," she said, then went back to the book.

"Why are you reading it?" he persisted, sitting opposite her, "it's not on the syllabus is it?"

She laughed,

"No. My dad wrote it and—"

"No way!"

Aji nodded.

"Really?" then said,

"Oh shit yes!" he touched his forehead, "so you're the daughter!"

"I'm only in it at the beginning, but I'm more interested in his friend?" she said, "he wrote about her when they both went to this school - was her name Flora?"

Marcus shrugged,

"Flora? I don't know, but yes, I remember that bit—"

"I met her recently and she seemed pissed off that he wrote about her."

"I'm not surprised if it's a true story," said Marcus, "that would be pretty embarrassing."

"Why, what happened?"

"You should read the whole thing. It's a cracking thriller and the drug-taking and the sex are quite educational."

Aji said thanks (begrudgingly) and continued reading. He stood there for a moment, like he was about to say something then turned away, then,

"Oh shit!" he said, "I just realized who Mystique is! She's your Russian babysitter, isn't she?"

"Doh!" said Aji.

MICKEY and Eva parked outside the pub on Brook Green. The estate agent stood in doorway, sheltering from the wind. They leant forward and peered up at the building. The lower floors just looked like any mansion block but at the top the windows were tall, some arched, some square, jutting out from the steep roof. It was definitely going to be interesting. Eva looked excited,

"Let's go see if the underfloor heating works!"

They greeted the agent then walked over to the entrance.

Mickey liked the lift, but not the agent. But on the top floor the apartment was stunning. The views over the green and the light reminded him of their place in Sloane Square. Eva loved it. It did have efficient underfloor heating and double glazing.

AJI got a text from her dad:

> *'Hi Sweetheart. I've found a sitter for you this evening.*
> *Philippa can help you with your Spanish or there's fireworks in St Mark's XXX'*

She replied:

> *'OK but you know I hate fireworks right? x'*

GRODY was annoyed. He thought he'd arrived late enough so that the marquee would already be erected, but the incompetents had failed. He stood and watched, getting more frustrated by the second until he shouted,

"Stop! You, get off the canvas. You, the poles need to be under the canvas and to point towards the centre. Then you attach the guy-ropes. But first, let's move the whole thing further into that corner on the flowerbed."

They all jumped to it, maybe relieved that someone knew what he was talking about.

AJI and Margot crossed paths with Miss Pringle in the corridor, or Aji would have liked to have crossed paths, but the Headmistress barred their way.

"Oh I passed your photos on to a man from Scotland Yard this morning" she laughed, "I say 'man' but he looked about your age! It's true what they say about growing older: 'You know it's happening to you when the policemen start looking younger than you!'"

Aji and Margot watched her carry on down the corridor.

"Someone from Scotland Yard came here to pick up my photos!" said Margot, "maybe this will be my vocation? Crime Photographer!"

GRODY was content. The floor was down, the canopy was up and the sides were going on, but he hadn't lifted a finger, except to point.

The bar and the lighting were complete when an old bloke came over and started complaining,

"This isn't where the marquee is meant to be. You're on the flowerbeds here. The flowers will be ruined." Grody ignored him and went to stock the bar.

ART rode over to the Portobello Hotel to meet Lori. He asked the Receptionist to call her.

Lori emerged from the restaurant downstairs, dressed in a jumper and jeans.

"I've just had scrambled eggs and a pot of coffee, so feeling wide awake."

"Here," said Art, "We're taking the bike. I've brought you a coat, it's cold out there." He held out the leather overcoat and she pirouetted into it and smiled as she pulled up the collar.

As they set off Lori said,

"I bought your anthology again in the Book Exchange at Notting Hill Gate?"

Art smiled, slightly embarrassed.

"It's strange that I read your articles the first time, without knowing they were written by the boy next door? They so inspired me to revisit the places I'd ignored as a kid; but I wonder if my perspective would've been different if I'd known it was you?"

"So when did you realize?" asked Art.

"The first clue was in that teenage fanzine interview where Artemis Grime said his star sign was

Leo, his favourite colour was black, his favourite pastime was biting his fingernails and his type of girl was petite freckly blondes; it gave me an inkling, as I knew those would've been your answers too."

They carried on in silence for a few minutes until she said,

"Then in other articles more and more clues presented themselves, like your upbringing in Holland Park, in that little mews house full of your dad's motorbikes; I was sure then."

Art smiled and was about to reply when she continued,

"But it was really selfish of you to die on your Book Tour. I was planning on coming to see you in New York, and maybe hook up? And then you were dead! I was devastated, and then a rumour started circulating that you'd been resuscitated, and I wrote to your publishers, but..."

Art was speechless. When he was using, he *had* been selfish, never thinking of the consequences (not that that was a consequence he could have ever foreseen). But what if he hadn't 'died'? What if they had hooked up in New York? His life might have been totally different.

"Lori, I'm so sorry! I was at my worst then, and close to admitting defeat. I came home and laid low, and my publisher did send my mail to the mews, but I'm ashamed to say I never opened any of it."

Lori didn't answer. He could see her in his mirrors, thinking.

"And did you try to get hold of me last year to ask my permission to be in your book?"

"I did. I looked for you on Friends Reunited and you were mentioned as having been to Holland Park school, and then Lima, but then the trail went cold. I also Googled you and I got the impression you'd changed your name, but couldn't find to what?"

"I did. I did it on impulse, thinking it'd help with my abuse issues, and it did... for about a week..."

He squeezed her knee. She hugged him back.

"So we both have aliases."

HANNAH hadn't used a payphone in years, and even picking up the receiver was quite nostalgic. It didn't require coins though, but a phonecard which you pushed into a slot. She called her own landline, in the hope of catching Dash, but she got the answer-phone. After the beep, she said,

"Hi Dash darling... how are you? I'm calling on a pay-phone from Klaus house... I guess I'm almost detoxed and feeling a bit more human... but I really hope you're coming to see me on Sunday... I'm feeling really isolated here. I'm gonna put all you and Eva on the list just in case, okay? I miss you..."

Anne came down the stairs,

"Coming to the meeting in Salisbury with us?"

Hannah cringed and shook her head.

"Please come? It's nice; Viktor plays Radio One in the coach and he's very charming. He's actually a grown-up compared to us lot, stuck in our adolescence."

"Okay, it'll be nice to hear some music."

ART and Lori parked among the cars that lined the road in front of a massive house near Windsor. They walked into the manicured garden and could see there were a lot of workmen around: Technicians setting up the firework display; Caterers preparing a bar in a tent and gardeners laying down matting for guests. Lori spotted who she thought might be Barry and they wandered over. He was having an argument with a barman, but it was over by the time they got to him.

"Hey Barry, I'm Bartholomew, this is Lori." Lori smiled and shook his hand. She didn't seem at all nervous like she had been with her neighbour Albert and they chatted amiably. Art left them to it and explored the garden, which was seemingly big enough to have its own herds of deer roaming elsewhere. It was getting dark and guests were arriving. Art wondered if they should be leaving, but when he returned to Lori, Barry assured them it was fine to stay for the fireworks. When they were alone Art asked,

"Well?"

"It's not him. No vibe. He just felt sorry for me. He said he noticed the change in me, and had an inkling of what was going on but when he tried to approach me about it, I just cried and ran away. Which I vaguely remember, but... it's not him."

ELSIE GREY wasn't sure she felt comfortable amongst such opulence, in her dress from Marks & Spencer's. Elsie had been invited to the fireworks display by her 'friend' Patrice, whose parents were clearly filthy rich.

Elsie and Patrice had nothing in common except they went to the same Sixth Form College and had one class together; but they hardly spoke, so when Patrice had handed her the gold leaf embossed invite, Elsie had asked why her? Because you're so beautiful, she'd

replied. Elsie had been shocked. Was she beautiful?
She had looked at herself in the mirror (something
she'd tried to avoid since succumbing to acne in her
adolescence) and found a different face staring back
at her. Yeah, maybe she was kind of attractive. Did
that mean Patrice was gay? Apparently yes, as Patrice
had tentatively touched her fingers as they'd watched
the fireworks, then, when Elsie hadn't pulled away,
interwoven their fingers into a gentle embrace.
Patrice turned and took her other hand, whispered
something and Elsie moved closer to hear, and she
whispered back, her mouth brushing Patrice's ear. She
felt Patrice's breath on her; her lips brushing her
cheek as she spoke. She whispered back, nuzzling her
as she felt her own heart racing. Patrice pulled back
slightly, but their cheeks never lost contact, so
their lips were almost touching, and then they were
kissing. Gentle pulling and pushing, then stronger and
more passionate as the fireworks exploded above them.

   HANNAH enjoyed her 'night out' in Salisbury. The
meeting wasn't as boring as she had feared as the
inmates spoke about subjects they didn't dare speak of
in Klaus house (and some of the locals were cute).
But, best of all was the music. Viktor had fitted a
fine sound system into his coach and the songs made
her feel quite emotional. This was nothing compared to
some of the junkies though: Grown men weeping to
Busted's 'Sleeping with the light on'.

   ELSIE's head was in a spin. One moment she was
kissing a girl, and the next, Patrice had been called
away by her father to meet a Duke of Somewhere. Elsie
was left on the lawn, frozen to the spot (Patrice had
said 'Stay right here'), as the other guest retreated
into the warm. She heard music and turned to find its
source. A marquee, lit with fairy lights and warmed by
space heaters drew her over. Inside, a few tables were
taken by couples and groups while a barman with a
dashing moustache and an eyepatch mixed cocktails for
an already drunken man in a top hat.
   She sat at the bar where she could watch for
Patrice. Maybe, come to think of it, she was a lesbian
too? She'd never had a crush on a boy at any of her
schools. But then she'd never had a crush on a girl
either. Until this moment.
   "What can I get you?" the barman said, smiling.
   "What do lesbians drink?"
   His face lit up as he said,

"Brandy Alexander," without hesitation. She
nodded then watched as he found the ingredients and
mixed her drink.

"My, that is delicious," she said, "what are the
crystals you sprinkled on top?"

"Nutmeg," he replied, "you like it?"

"Purple nutmeg?" She nodded and smiled.

"Purple nutmeg?" said a South American voice
beside her. She turned to see a tall blonde in a cool
old leather coat examining her drink.

The Barman leant in and said,

"No, sorry, the nutmeg isn't purple, it's brown;
the purple crystals are just for decoration—"

"What's it made of?" said the blonde.

"Er... Beetroot."

"It looks delicious! One of these please Barman!
and a pot of Lapsang Souchong for my friend," she said
then turned to Elsie, "are you alone here? coz you can
come sit with us if you want? Oh, I'm Lori and this is
Art"

"Hi, I'm Elsie, thanks but my friend has just
gone to say Hi to someone."

"Oh okay, so he's coming back soon?"

Elsie watched the tall guy go to get a table.

"She," she whispered.

"Oh yeah, I noticed the lipstick on your cheek
and your ear."

Elsie touched her cheek and smiled.

"Don't let your parents see that!" laughed Lori.

"God, my dad doesn't even know I'm here! He
thinks very badly of Patrice's dad. Called him an
asset stripper - whatever that is." The barman laid
the tray with the teapot next to them.

"Patrice's dad?" asked Lori.

"Oh, he's the host."

"Lucky Patrice!"

The barman put the Brandy Alexander on the tray
and asked,

"Shall I carry it over for you?"

"No thanks," said the blonde, "I'll take it
thanks. But first I'm gonna need more purple please;
you've hardly given me any and it's sooo pretty."

Elsie saw a slight eye-rolling from the barman as
he sprinkled more on.

"That's better! Thank you!" she said, winking at
Elsie as she carried the tray to Art's table.

ART sat with Lori in the corner of the marquee
near a space-heater. It had been a good evening. Lori
sipped her Brandy Alexander and said,

"Mmm, it's delicious and the purple makes it look so special."

They sat and watched the people, then Lori said,

"So you didn't stay at Holland Park for Secondary?"

"No, my dad just suddenly announced that I was going to his old boarding school instead," he said, "and you'd left, so in a way I didn't mind."

"Really?" said Lori, "from your article entitled 'Bartholomew Mistletoe's Schooldays', (3) it sounded like a bit of a nightmare?"

"Well yes," agreed Art, "but I had no idea then, that the school was so far away in the middle of endless forests and farmland and that it was going to be run on the Laws of the Jungle."

"Why would a man send his son to a school in the sticks," mused Lori, turning her head away and looking at him out the corner of her eyes, "which he himself had hated, that he knew was nick-named 'Bummers' by the other schools, and which also had a terrible academic record?"

"Maybe he thought it was like a 'Right of Passage?" suggested Art.

"Or maybe he was the kind of guy who thought, as he'd had to go through it and had been broken, his son would have to go through it and be broken as well?"

"That sounds more likely."

She sat in silence, watching his face, then gave him a hug and said,

"If the title of your book is so hard to remember, and it is, just rename it something snappier like a well-known idiom, like all novelists do—"

"Like 'Speak of the Devil'?"

"Yeah, or 'Cut to the Chase'," she said, "that's a good one, especially with all the drug taking."

"Or half an idiom like 'Or Die Trying!'"

"Or 'Two wrongs'."

"What?"

"'Two wrongs don't make a right'?"

"That's a proverb, not an—"

"And you're still a pedant."

"Sorry, I'm trying not to do that."

"It's okay," she said, "I'd run out of idioms anyway."

They both sipped their drinks. He said,

"I'm not sure you can do that with a book."

"What? Republish it under a different title? Sure you can. One of my favourite books was called Addie Pray until the movie adaptation came out, called Paper Moon. Then the book was republished with the new title."

"But that was probably only because the movie was such a success."

"Okay, then you could just call it 1999 (I'm Keeping the Head)."

"Swap the title and the subtitle around?" asked Art, "now that's quite a good idea."

"And at the same time you can cut out the part about me. After all, it didn't actually affect the plot at all."

"But it did. It brought you here to me—"

"But it didn't affect the plot—"

"Not of that book, but the next one—"

"You fucker—" she said,

"But you knew that's what I do! I've always documented my life, I'm a journalist—"

"You're a 'Gonzo' journalist! And Gonzo is the name of a Muppet!"

"But—"

She put one hand over Art's mouth and with the other waved at a Security Guard and asked for a local taxi number.

"There's a few outside in the lane," he said as he helped a drunken man to his feet.

She turned back to Art and poked his face,

"I didn't come here sho you could write more about me!" she said as she tried to stand.

"I know you didn't, but—"

He helped her and she put her arms round his shoulders saying,

"I hate you, but I want you so bad right now."

She kissed him, then said,

"Get off me!" loud enough for everyone to look.

He said, 'Sorry!' and held her at arm's length but then she pulled him to her and kissed him again.

"You are a very shelfish man!" she hissed as she staggered out of the tent. Art knew, in his heart, he'd been really stupid but wasn't sure he wanted to back down. She staggered and he caught her.

"I think we should fuck right here..."

Could he do that? He really wanted to. He might be feeling bloody-minded about his next book, but was he that selfish that he could take advantage of a drunken—

"You've got a shock coming to you, ash-hole..."

Art steered her to the lane, helped her into a minicab, told the driver the address and gave him two twenties. He took the driver's photo on his X.D.A and another one of the car's number plate as he drove away. Art sighed, then went to his bike.

Was there any feeling more powerful than first love? Totally all consuming? Can one ever feel that again? Does one want to feel it again? Is it too over-powering? Some people will chase Love for the rest of their lives but never feel it like the first time. Like that first hit of crack? If you're unlucky, it can flick a switch in your brain and you can spend the rest of your life trying to recreate that first buzz, but it's never the same. Was that what he was chasing? Was it mad? Only a couple of days ago he was all set to embark on a relationship which he'd thought could last for the rest of his life, and instead he was trying to catch hold of something that didn't exist anymore. And really was it that great? He'd loved her but could never say it; she'd punished him daily for being her brother's friend; she'd lured him in with a carrot then given him the stick instead; then when she came to his bed for refuge and he'd loved her all the more, she'd shunned him at school and at play. Then she was gone, leaving a massive hole inside him for years to come.

That had been his template for relationships from then on. Being needed but getting nothing in return; being offered a carrot that turned into a stick; followed by loss.

But had it been insensitive to write about her and Mickey and Eva and Hannah, in the name of documenting the truth? Duh! Obviously. That's why they'd all been so pissed off with him. It *was* selfish of him, but it had been such a cracking story. So what was it to be? Lori or the story? He got on the bike and pressed 'start' but nothing happened.

ELSIE looked around her and wondered how long she'd been sitting there. The Brandy Alexander had made her feel woozy, but it was a nice buzz and she thought she'd order another. The man in the top hat had passed out on the bar and was being carried away by a big man in a black bomber jacket. The tables were emptying, but she liked it there, even while the tall couple had a hissy drunken argument and they staggered out. The barman shrugged and winked. Still, the music was good and hopefully Patrice would be back soon and they could share a Brandy Alexander and kiss some more. She wondered if she should call her dad.

GRODY mixed another Brandy Alexander for the girl. He'd only sprinkled some of the Purple on top of the first one, as an experiment. He hadn't wanted her passing out and being rescued by security like the oldie in the top hat. But it seemed to have worked fine on the tall blonde. Where had he seen her before? Only recently?

147

He placed the glass in front of the girl and said,

"On the house."

She looked at him and smiled, saying,

"All the drinks are on the house," then looked at the drink,

"Not many purple crystals?"

He smiled and sprinkled some more on,

"I saved it just for you."

She picked up the glass and took a sip.

ART couldn't get the bike to run. The starter motor was turning over, but the engine wasn't catching. He checked the air and fuel lines for blockages, but they were fine so he figured it must be a fuse. He opened the seat unit and found the fuse box, but there were no spare fuses. Cursing himself, he called the Breakdown Service.

HANNAH resented being told when to go to bed. She had been sitting in the main hall, watching the fish swimming round the fountain; daydreaming about her new crush (Viktor the coach driver), when the burly Nurse had appeared and announced it was bedtime. If they were going to treat her like a child, then she'd behave like one:

"I haven't got the energy to walk up three flights Nursie. Will you please carry me?"

The Nurse smiled down on Hannah then scooped her up.

"Only because you're so tiny."

Still got it. She really didn't need drugs to be able to manipulate anyone; it was just a gift she'd been bestowed, like Art's drawing, and Dash's and Eva's dancing. Maybe she could use it more for good in the future? Instead of just to make pots of money?

She shut her eyes and imagined Viktor was carrying her to their bed-chamber.

"I was going this way anyway," Nursie said, slowing noticeably on the second flight of stairs.

"Nursie, I think I need to see a dentist in Salisbury? Would I get a cab there or..."

"No, Viktor would drive you."

On the top step Hannah wriggled from her arms, gave her a peck on the cheek and said,

"Then could you arrange an appointment for me please? Thank you Nursie. Nighty night." then skipped down the landing to her room.

ART had been waiting a while and was very cold. People, as they were leaving the party, had offered him lifts back to town but he didn't want to leave his bike there, so he hugged himself and waited in the dark lane among the cars parked on the kerbs. A couple staggered out of the gate. She was laughing and stumbling while he supported her. He looked like the barman from the marquee, and maybe that was the girl who'd been sitting at the bar? Art felt like he might have seen him somewhere before. Jumping out of a car? Yeah, but that car had been white. The guy opened the rear door of an estate car and almost poured her onto the back seat, then got in and drove off.

GRODY rolled the sleeping figure into the boot and set off. There was another of those BMW dirt bikes he wanted. The tall bloke was standing next to it. No tall girls though. She must've been pissed off!

He was on the M4, heading back into town when he realized he hadn't sent the text. He retrieved the Motorola and sent a text saying,

> "*30 mins*"

Five minutes later, he saw a Police car following him. He slowed to 70mph and crossed his fingers. They remained behind him as other cars overtook doing well over the speed limit. He grabbed the Motorola and typed another text saying,

> "*May be late.*
> *police tailing*
> *me on M4*"

It felt like they were crawling along. Maybe he should run for it? This car was actually built for such an occasion. Yeah, there was a junction in half a mile...

The blue light went on followed by a couple of 'whoop's. Grody pulled over onto the hard shoulder. The traffic cop took ages to leave his vehicle, and walk over. Grody was ready with his license and insurance but he was shaking slightly and he was holding his breath. The cop bent down and said:

"Naughty Naughty."

Grody tried to look bemused and innocent,

"Sorry?"

"Texting and driving! It might not be illegal yet, but I can still lock you up for the night."

"I wasn't—"

"Hand me your phone please sir."

Grody gave him the Nokia, which he examined, "What's this? Some sort of code? What does it say?

'2£4%3!1?5! something something'? What's it mean?"

"I've no idea sir," shrugged Grody, "I think it was a butt text?"

"A butt text?"

"A text sent by your butt."

"Where's the other phone? You had another. I saw it."

"No - I—"

"We can stand here all-night sir," said the cop, "or on second thoughts, we can search your car, and strip-search you here on the hard shoulder—"

"Okay! I'm sorry," he said handing over the Motorola.

"There, you sent a text saying '30 mins' exactly when I logged you and another saying 'I may be late, police tailing me on M4'."

"Yes, I'm sorry, I..."

Another car pulled in front of Grody's with its blue light flashing. His heart sank. It was over. A plainclothes officer approached and pulled the cop round to the grassy verge. They spoke for a few minutes, occasionally looking at him. The plainclothes was small, wearing a trench-coat three sizes too big for him. He shook hands with the cop then came and got in the passenger seat. He smiled and showed his warrant card:

"Inspector Gâjhette?" Grody asked.

"It's French," he said, "pronounced Gâjhette." Grody could see the beginnings of a wispy moustache. It was true what they said about growing older.

"That's all sorted. Here's your phone," he said, dropping it in the cup holder, "best send the text before you set off?"

He smiled again, nodded, then was out the car and back in his own and gone moments later. He'd had no idea they had such backup. Had he been alerted by his text, or was he already tailing him?

Grody had only been driving for five minutes when he hit queues caused by an accident ahead. Sally Traffic had said it was on the out-bound lanes but that there were queues in-bound because everyone was slowing down to have a look. Bullshit. It was the blue lights ahead that made them all slow down, creating a concertina. Did Sally have a morbid streak that made her slow down, hoping to see a severed head in the road or a burning body screaming inside a caravan?

Ten minutes late, Grody was just arriving at Berkeley Square. He drove along the west side and found a good spot near the center. The spaces all pointed outwards from the curb, and he followed protocol and backed in. As instructed, he turned off the engine, left the car in neutral with the handbrake off. Then he got out, locked the doors and opened the bonnet. He jumped the gate into the garden and walked away as quickly as he could. He had made it all the way to the other side of the square, by the Rolls Royce dealer, when he saw a breakdown truck pull up by his car. He then realized why Berkeley Square was the drop site: The parking spaces jutting out at a perpendicular and the slight incline (so the rear wheels would lean safely against the curb) made it easy for the truck to winch it on to its flatbed. He wondered where it was going? And for what purpose? Maybe next time he should have a car parked nearby so he could follow and find out.

Thursday - 6th November

LORI sat in her hotel room reading a book. It was Art's anthology which had been published and sold very well some ten years earlier when he still had cult status. The chapter she was reading was about his time at Secondary school entitled "Bartholomew Mistletoe's Schooldays". (4)

She smiled as she reached the end of the chapter and put the book back in her rucksack. Then she took out her digital camera and had a look at the photo of Art's map of Holland Park. She grabbed her bag and went downstairs to reception.

"Hi, are you okay?" said the pretty night porter, beaming at her, "need a Hair of the Dog?"

"I'm fine, why?" asked Lori.

"Er - you came in slightly worse for wear—"

"Oh yeah! And I only had one drink, can you believe it?"

"No," she said, "I had to carry you to your room!"

"Really?"

"Yes, and then put up quite a struggle when I undressed you," she beamed again, "plus when you wanted to undress me!"

Lori wasn't sure what to make of that.

"Well I woke up at 3am as fresh as a daisy!" she laughed, "which is my 3pm of course..."

The girl smiled,

"How can I help you?"

"Is the kitchen open? I really need some lunch? Or supper? I don't know."

"I can make you something. Let's go down and see what there is." She put her arm around Lori's waist as she led her to the stairs.

DASHA and Eva sat drinking coffee in Lisboa. Dash was reading the Guardian; Eva was looking at an IKEA catalogue for ideas to decorate her and Mickey's new apartment.

Dash was more shocked by the news every day. The coverage of the War on Terror was frightening. It seemed to make no sense.

"I don't get it," she said to Eva, "After 9/11, the 'allies' began by targeting Afghanistan, even though the attacks were mainly by Saudi Arabians?"

Eva nodded.

"Me and Art watched live as the World Trade Centre buildings fell in on themselves, just as if they'd been demolished; we watched as the BBC reporter claimed building Seven had fallen, even though it stood right behind her; We heard an intercepted message from Larry Silverstein instructing building Seven to be 'pulled', and then it had fallen."

"I know. I was with Mickey and said the very same thing: How stupid do you have to be to believe anything about this was the truth?"

Dash nodded, saying,

"But then I saw an interview with David Lynch, the creator of Twin Peaks, being asked if he thought it was an inside job by Cheney, Bush etc, and he'd just said 'It is unthinkable'; and that was from a man with a massive imagination."

"That's what it was," said Eva, "unthinkable. That's how they'd got away with it. Still conning everyone into believing the USA is always on the side of good."

Dash looked out of the window. Art wasn't coming.

ART sat at his board, drawing boxes. He often drew boxes when he felt confused. And he was; about his argument with Lori the previous night. He'd handled it badly. He should never have mentioned writing a sequel to Lori. It was insensitive. And insensitive to have written about her without her consent in the first place. He had a choice: Lori, or the story.

He also felt torn between Lori and Dash, and guilty about the way he'd treated the Russian. It was a continuation of the slippery slope. Was it a sign? Was it bad karma to go after his friend William's ex? Maybe he'd been saved for doing the wrong thing? He tried to call Lori but she wasn't in her room.

AJI had been reading her dad's book, since the previous night. Philippa had brought a boyfriend with her and told Aji to go to her room, which she'd found incredibly offensive, considering the girl was only three years older than her.

The book charged along at quite a pace. Of course, her dad's sex addiction was gross, and the sex scenes which took place between him and Hannah were disgusting so obviously she glossed over them, but the part with Lori (not Flora!) was actually quite touching. She felt sorry for both of them. No wonder he started drinking. Had she become a drinker too? Had they? Were they? Ugh, she couldn't even think the

words. Anyway, she couldn't let it happen. If her
father had to have a partner, then it had to be Dash.

At breakfast she said,

"So, I'm reading your book—"

"You are? Where did you get it?"

"Er... from a bookshop?" she said, "and I see I'm
in it and you gave me an alias, just like everyone
including yourself."

"Yes, I changed all the names."

"So what made you choose Aji [5] for me, and Art [6]
for you?"

"It's too convoluted to tell you now."

"Okay, another time. So answer this: When our
'characters' speak in the book 'you' called 'me' by
the alias, Aji."

"Yes."

"So if you say my name now, it'll be my real
name."

"Of course."

"Say it."

He said it.

"But if you transcribe this conversation and put
it in your next book, when you say my name, it'll be
Aji again."

"Sure."

"Okay, so on the way to school on Monday, I asked
you the name of the woman in Mike's (because I'd
forgotten) and you said Flora, even though you
introduced her as Lori in Mike's (I am now reminded
from reading your book). Why was that?"

"Because in Mike's, after I told you she was
Lori, she mentioned she was featured in my book and
had been humiliated by it."

"Yes," said Aji, "that intrigued me."

"Well it surprised me that she told you at all,
but she was jet-lagged; and then she said it was
humiliating, which made me question my decision to
write about her, and in fact, the whole book."

"So?"

"So, stupidly, I thought I was doing her a
favour; that if you ever did read it, you wouldn't
associate her with the character."

"I am reading it, and I'm very sad for her."

"Yes, I am too, and I'm sorry I wrote it. I
really didn't think it through. Need a lift to
school?"

"No thanks, see you later." She picked up her
keys by the door and considered whether she needed a
coat. There was her puffer, but where was the leather
coat? She pushed a light waterproof jacket into her
bag and left.

GRODY sat on the edge of his camp-bed
contemplating life. On the one hand it wasn't good.
His eye ached a little but he could move it without
the sharp pain, even before he'd had his hit. But he
didn't have any gear left! Again, he'd promised
himself he'd keep some for the morning but had failed;
and he could feel the sickness upon him: The mild
sweats; his sense of smell returning; his bowels
liquifying. He texted Darren asking for some gear and
to be picked up.
      On the other hand, the boys were doing well so
he'd need to see Revox again this morning. The girls
were also doing well. He was on a roll. He was
interested to see how much he'd get for last night's
bar girl - more or less than Catwoman?
      As if on cue, his Motorola buzzed:

            "Nice job!
            R reg vauxhall
            450 watling lane"

      That was interesting. Actual affirmation! So what
was it? Age before Beauty? Or visa-versa? Or some
other criteria? He tried sending a text asking for
clarification. They seemed to be more open to
answering questions when they knew the sim card was
about to be fragged. But there was no reply. Never
mind. If the money was good, maybe he should look for
the BMW dirt bike he wanted? He'd buy copies of Loot
and Auto Trader and check out second-hand prices. He
found his Nokia and sent a text to Revox asking for a
visit just as he heard Darren approaching. He smiled.
Life, on reflection, was good.

      LORI walked through the park looking for the
Frog Ponds, as they had called them. She held her
digital camera (with Art's map on the screen) and
occasionally referred to it. She found the statue with
the ducks, then hopped a barrier and headed into the
undergrowth. There they were. Three brick squares
about knee height, full of slimy water, which when
they were kids had fresh running water and tons of
wildlife. The undergrowth was thicker than she
remembered but she headed off down the hill counting
her (small) paces as best she could, then stopped and
recited the poem again. It took her a while to find
what she hoped was the 'spot' (as there was no
sycamore tree), then, from her rucksack she took a
carrier bag from the camping shop on Kensington High

Street. Inside was a collapsible spade. She unfolded it and started digging.

ART sat at his drawing board, watching the world go by. He was listening to his new favourite song on repeat: 'Miss Parker' by Morgan.

The doorbell rang. It was Dash. He dropped the keys and automatically counted 'One Elephant, Two Elephant, Three Elephant...' and sat back at his drawing board.

Art had kept meaning to tell her about Lori, but every day he failed, the more guilty he felt and the harder it got to say anything. But here was his chance.

Dash came and stood behind him, looking at what he was drawing. He liked that she never judged him for the subject matter.

"Where've you been?" he asked.

"Lisboa," she said.

"You were in Lisboa?"

"Yes, well I thought maybe—"

"Oh I wish I'd known," he said, "I wanted to talk—"

"Yes, but why don't you come to Lisboa anymore? Or are we just missing one another?"

"Because I didn't think you'd be there, now you live in Earl's Court?"

"Oh, is that all it is? Then shall I call you to arrange to meet? Instead of our old system of relying on Fate?"

"That's a good idea. I did think of that last week but I thought calling you would be a bit presumptuous—"

"Really? After all these years?"

"But I did want to tell you—"

"Fuck!" shouted Dash.

GRODY was riding pillion on Darren's scooter. He'd only had a little gear left, but it had been enough to hold him, stop the genie from escaping the bottle, though he could feel a chuckle growing in his throat at the size of his payment for Elsie. He had texted, asking how the payment was calculated but had got no reply so decided to leave it and frag the phone and sim. They swung into Elgin crescent and then crossed the Portobello Road and stopped. He got off and Darren zipped away. Once he was out of sight Grody walked up the side street, into the 'garden' of Revox's block (full of bins and broken bicycles) and climbed the stairs.

DASHA shouted "Fuck!" and moved closer to the window. She was peering down at the street. He followed her gaze and saw a scooter parked on the corner of Portobello Road with a guy getting off the back. He was wearing a red helmet. He walked up the street towards them then turned left through the entrance to the block opposite.

"That's him!" said Dash, "that's the Zorro guy. I saw him taking back the Zorro costume on Monday and followed him. Then me and Eva followed him on her scooter but we lost him—"

"Oh yeah, Aji told me. Are you sure that's him?"

"Yes! That's him! I recognize the helmet and the stickers."

Dash got out her phone and called Eva,

"I've just spotted Zorro in Portobello! Can you turn around and come to Art's right now? Okay, don't come right to his door though. Park by the little playground. Thanks."

She hung up and moved back into the shadows of the kitchen area.

"What can you see?" asked Dash.

"Nothing," said Art, "why are you hiding?"

"In case he looks out. He knows my face." Dash started to explain their history...

GRODY's eye started throbbing so he stopped and sat down on the steps until it subsided. Darren had had only enough smack to delay the sickness, but he would have a lot more inside him soon, then everything would be alright. He definitely had a habit again, which was annoying, but he still got high when he took it so he wasn't in too deep. But he knew he'd have to take a holiday soon. He took out the envelope and counted the money again. Slightly less than last time (age before beauty then?) but still a fortune. Enough for him to buy truly in bulk and get the price down even more. Enough for him to expand his network. He climbed the rest of the stairs slowly then did the knock.

Maurice let Grody in and ushered him through. Revox grunted at him from his chair by the window. As arranged, his purchase was waiting: Three Ziploc bags full of various pills and two bigger bags full of heroin and cocaine ready for him to weigh. He did so, then asked to test the quality of the smack.

Revox, looking slightly offended nodded then swung away.

"There's some guy over the road watching me," he said, "he's been there ever since I moved in. He just sits in the window the whole time."

Grody, a straw hanging from his lips, poured a pile of the brown powder onto a square of foil and used a lighter melt it into a sickly smelling puddle. He then upped the heat, and the smack ran down the foil, letting off a trail of smoke which he hoovered through the straw. It didn't give the instant numb you got from jacking it, but he could already feel less throbbing in his eye. Though he didn't want to engage with Revox, he felt he should say something as he was starting to feel more benevolent:

"Maybe he was there before you moved in?" It did seem likely to Grody and Maurice looked up from the game on his phone and nodded in agreement. Through the heavy netting, he could just see a guy, staring out at them. There was something familiar about him. Grody got up and joined Revox at the window. He put his good eye to the crack and parted the curtains an inch. There, across the road was the tall bloke...

"I saw him at a party last night."

"You? At a party?"

"I ran the bar, but it's still a great place to sell drugs and get girls."

Revox looked at him, surprised,

"Get girls?"

"He had an argument with his and she walked out. And he followed, like a pussy-whipped gay-boy."

"Slightly mixing your metaphors there," said Revox, looking shocked, "and I had no idea you were so bigoted?"

"I'm not really - I just hate everyone equally."

"Well, just because you've suddenly got lots of money, doesn't mean I have to put up with it. You can go now."

Maurice ushered him to the door. He walked downstairs then looked up at the tall bloke's window. Had he been following him? Had he been watching him the whole time? Now he thought about it, he'd seen them both on Saturday on the street when he'd been carrying in the sound gear. Was it just a coincidence? Or could the cops have known where Revox was moving? But what was the point? What's the point in continually watching and bugging a drug-dealer, but never busting him? Was it all in Revox's head?

LORI was digging yet another hole in the undergrowth. It hadn't been as straightforward as she'd hoped. She should've bought a metal detector! Why hadn't she thought of that before? She'd give it another five minutes then go buy one. She was beginning to sweat so took off the coat Art had lent her. She took a deep breath, then once again rammed

the spade into the ground. A hollow metallic ding made
her smile. She uncovered a biscuit tin and lifted it
out, brushing the dirt from it. She lifted the lid a
little, peeked inside, smiled then decanted the
contents into her rucksack. At the same time, she took
out Art's book, opened it to the chapter she'd been
reading, and laid it in the tin. She then placed the
tin back in the hole and covered it over. She was
sleepy so headed back to the hotel.

ART was trying to pretend not to be looking out
his window (even though that was pretty much what he
spent his entire time doing), while listening to
Dash's news:

"...from a picture on Amber's phone we know she
smoked the purple joint and disappeared from the party
with Zorro, then Hannah smoked it and ended up in
hospital; and Zorro had a little vial of purple powder
which he said was a sedative so it all fitted together
very well. But then God almost died from the same kind
of purple joint, which made no sense until now, when
Zorro just ended up here, so it all ties together!"
she said, without taking a breath.

Art's ears had pricked up at the mention of
purple. He thought of the previous night; Lori being
overcome by the purple crystals (maybe), and the girl
drinking it and leaving with the barman. He was about
to tell Dash his news when he realized it included
Lori. He wanted to tell her about Lori first, *then*
tell her about the purple crystals.

He saw Eva pull up just round the corner by the
playground.

"Eva's here. What are you going to do?"

"Wait for him to come out? Then follow him."

Dash went to get her usual helmet and leather
overcoat, but the coat wasn't there. Art realized he'd
lent it to Lori and ran to offer her a puffer jacket
of Aji's.

"Listen Dash, I have news too. I need to—"

"Can it wait Arthur? I don't want to miss him."

"Okay, sure, but let's make time... to..."

She waved and ran out to the stairs. He went back
to the window. The girls stood there shivering in the
wind. He was thinking about making a thermos of tea
for them when he saw the red helmet walk out of the
block and down to the Portobello Road. A scooter
pulled up and waited for him to get on then they were
gone, with Eva and Dash not far behind.

Art called Barry the gardener and got his
voicemail:

"Barry. Bartholomew here. Good to see you last
night. Er, a strange thing happened. I think the
barman in the marquee spiked Lori's drink? She was
falling all over the place. And I think he also spiked
a girl sitting at the bar. She left with him. I didn't
think much about it at the time, but, er, more info
has come to light. The girl's name was Elsie, and she
was a friend of Patrice, who is the host's daughter. I
think you should follow this up with him please.
Another girl went missing in the same circumstances at
the weekend. Thanks. Oh, and whoever employed the
staff? An agency maybe? We need their name and number
too please. Thanks. Bye."

He put the phone on the table, then picked it up
again and tried calling Lori at her hotel. The
receptionist said that she'd gone out. Art left his
number and hung up.

HANNAH was starting to feel a little better:
Less shaking and sweating which surprised her. The
medication was flattening the curve; maybe she was in
for a protracted, but painless withdrawal? She must
remember to ask Nursie what they were giving her.

She stayed in bed until it was time for Group.
That way, she only had one flight of stairs to climb
to the top floor.

The annoying Mr Potato Head was running the
group.

"Miss Samuelson, how are you feeling?"

"Good, thanks."

"That isn't a feeling sweetheart. Could you be
more expansive about your actual feelings?"

Hannah riled at being called sweetheart by the
oaf, but chose to remain silent. She shook her head.

"What happened to bring you here?"

"I overdosed at my Halloween party."

"What had you taken?"

"Oh, everything; it was one of those nights when
you needed to keep tweaking the cocktail to keep in
the zone, you know—"

"I don't know. Please explain."

"You know, some booze to lower your inhibitions,
then some coke to keep you straight, but maybe an 'E'
to add to the buzz, and then a blue or two to keep you
from cuddling on the sofa too long, and then another
drink—"

"Okay, little lady, We get the picture."

Some of her peers were nodding and smiling
nostalgically.

Little lady? Sweetheart? Who was this patronizing asshole?

"Why don't you know?"

"Know what?"

"Know what it's like to be tweaking the cocktail to keep you in the zone?"

"Because I'm not an addict—"

"Then what the fuck are you doing here?"

"I'm—"

"If you aren't an addict you can't understand how our brains work. We're hard-wired differently to you, so you can't help us."

A few others nodded. No 1 said,

"That's why they say N.A. works, because it's addicts helping addicts."

"I know what I'm doing," Mr Potato Head objected, "I come from a family of addicts and alcoholics and my wife was an addict too."

"So you know how to respond in certain situations?" asked Anne.

He nodded.

"So it's like painting by numbers to you?" suggested Hannah, "no intuition, no instinct?" The others all joined in at once and it was chaos. Mr PT tried to regain control but they were up in arms. Hannah hopped off her chair and went to lunch, or in her case, breakfast.

EVA and Dash were far from home. Neither of them had even heard of Burnt Oak before. The red helmet was dropped off on the High Street then he walked down a side road. Eva parked the scooter and they followed on foot. The side road led to him taking another turn and they stopped on the corner and watched. The lane ran behind the shops on the High Street and was mainly populated with garages. He opened one and went in. They advanced along the lane, taking cover behind parked cars, until they were close enough to see. It seemed as if he was living in there, as they could see an armchair, a make-shift sink and a day-bed that he was folding.

"So this is his lair." whispered Eva.

"Lair?" asked Dash.

"Hideout?" suggested Eva.

"Or his home? He's putting away his bed isn't he?"

GRODY opened his messenger bag and took out the drugs and laid them next to the scales. The boys were due any minute, so he folded the camp-bed and put it under the tarpaulin. He sprayed some air freshener around, picked up the Shitty Bucket and was walking out of the garage when he spied someone ducked down behind a car.

"What the fuck are you doing?" he shouted, running round the car. The blonde again, trying to disguise herself in a hoodie and another skinny girl with a mop of black wavy hair.

"Why are you following me?" he said, "this is harassment! You attacked me!"

The blonde advanced, while the other started to flank him. He held out the Shitty Bucket in defence.

"You took my friend from the Halloween party!" shouted the blonde, "have you got her in there—"

"There's no one here but me! You can check! And I didn't go to a Halloween party. I was in hospital on Friday."

He saw them falter, doubt their convictions. He pointed at his bandaged eye and shouted,

"You did this to me for no reason!"

"I had a reason - you grabbed me and I defended myself!"

"You were following me!"

"Which proves you were guilty!" shouted the other one, "no one would object to being followed by a beautiful woman unless they were guilty of something!"

"Why were you following me then?" countered Grody.

"Because you took the Zorro costume back to Angel's."

"So? That's what despatch riders do! We collect things and transport them to other places!"

"We went to Hotline and Kevin says you don't work there!"

"You mean my bag?" said Grody, "I use the Hotline bag because it's waterproof! I work for Mercury! You can call them and ask!"

"So where did you collect the Zorro costume from?" asked the brunette.

"From a bloke in Chelsea. By the river."

"What's his name and full address?"

"I can't give you that. It's against my solemn oath as a—"

"Let's blind him in the other eye—" said the blonde.

"Wait! Wait! His name is Ian Waverly. He's at 46, Blood Street. Between the King's Road and the Embankment. It's a whole house on the left as you're going to the river. It's posh."

"Okay," said the blonde, "let's hog-tie him then go check—"

162

"Don't come any closer!" he said, threatening them again with the Shitty Bucket.

They were pincering him when he heard the sound of scooters. His crew was turning the corner. He shouted to them and pointed at the girls, who saw the reinforcements and ran.

"We know where you live!" shouted the blonde.

"I know where you work," he muttered as his boys arrived. One continued to chase the girls but he waved him back to the garage.

The four boys parked their scooters then lined up in the entrance, as if on parade. He walked down the line taking their money.

"Stand easy, boys," he said. They relaxed.

"Who were they, Sir?"

"Feminists," spat Grody as he checked their money, "now boys, we're upping our game. I've invested in more product so we can drop the price and double your quota." They looked surprised, but happy.

"Shut the door Darren, then I'll show you how I divide the powders into your quota without any waste. So you'll be able to split yours into your usual end-user amounts okay? Oh and don't forget to take a set of scales and a load of baggies when you go, okay?"

"So we're doing our own weighing now?" asked the short one. Darren nudged him and whispered 'Sir'.

"Sir," said the short one.

"Yes, but only cuz I've got other work to do, and it gives you more chance of making your quota for charity."

Darren raised his hand.

"Yes Darren?"

"Sir, also if we're raising our game don't you think we should start selling crack? Coke is great but it doesn't appeal to a lot of our customers, who are always asking for crack, sir."

"Interesting idea, do you know how to make it?"

"No sir, but I know someone who does."

"Excellent." he said, "give him a call," rubbing his hands together.

He was impressed by their initiative. Was there a badge for that? He looked at them and wondered if they hated him as much as he hated Revox? Were they just waiting for their chance to usurp him?

EVA laughed as she fired up her scooter,

"So now we know what he looks like! Ugly fucker!" she said, "and why were you talking in that fake American accent?"

Dash got on behind her,

"Because I didn't want him to recognize my voice. We spoke at the party and he knew I was the host."

"Oh, good thinking! Don't want him turning up at your home," said Eva as they put on their helmets, "so, where to? Rehearsals? Or shall we go straight to Blood Street?"

"Fuck rehearsals! Let's go to Blood Street and then arrive in time for the evening performance as if nothing has happened."

Dash laughed, and hugged Eva who said,

"Now how do we get back to London?"

"Well it's the afternoon so the sun is south and west of us," mused Dash "so it's got to be that way." Eva nodded and followed her direction. Soon she saw signs for Central London and relaxed.

Eva had been excited by the adventure, but the adrenaline was wearing off. They were still ages away from central London and then Chelsea was another long journey in the cold. Where were they? North west London? And Chelsea was south west? That meant that they could cut the corner by taking the north circular road? But she hated that road: It was filthy and more dangerous than some actual motorways, and did it cut the corner? Maybe it bulged out so far it didn't cut the corner at all—

"Hey, let's stop somewhere for a coffee," said Dash, "and we could call Directory Enquiries for Ian Waverly's number."

"Nice idea," said Eva, "it's too cold to ride all that way right now."

ART was considering going out when his phone rang. A local landline number. He picked up and said 'Hello'.

"Art, it's Lori."

"Hi. I'm so sorry about last night."

"Okay, though you are a total jerk."

"Yes" he said, "I am, but listen, I think you might've been drugged last night? That purple powder on your cocktail?"

"Really? No wonder I slept so well! But I feel fine now."

"You remember the girl Elsie at the bar? I think she was drugged and taken by the barman," he said, "and it's bizarre, a friend of my daughter's went missing on Halloween after smoking a purple joint given her by a guy dressed as Zorro, and Dash just saw him out of my window and is following him—"

"Dash?" she asked, "it seems you have more than one mystery on the go? This isn't going to detract from mine is it?"

164

"I don't think so," he said, "I'm just worried
about the Elsie girl we met last night and—"
  The phone went dead.

DASHA and Eva looked out on an anonymous street
from the warmth of the Café. They were drinking sweet
tea while they waited for their bacon sandwiches.
  Dash called Directory Enquiries. There were a
couple of Ian Waverleys in Chelsea. She wrote down the
numbers.
  "You'll have to call them," she said to Eva,
punching in the first number.
  "Why?"
  "Because I can't imitate the girl from Angels."
Eva nodded and took the phone.
  "Oh hello Ian, it's Angels here. Had the despatch
rider brought your deposit back yet?"
  "Angels?"
  "Costume Hire Shop. You rented Zorro for
Halloween?"
  "Not me. Sorry." he said.
Eva hung up and rang the other Ian Waverly. Same
answer. She put the phone on the table just as their
sandwiches arrived.
  "Let's go to the Police, It's obviously him,"
suggested Eva. Dash nodded as she took her first bite.

HANNAH was supposed to be writing her life story
and was looking for somewhere to work. The Living room
was quite spectacular with its high ceilings and tall
windows looking out on meadows and trees. A stream ran
across her view at the bottom of the valley,
surrounded by grazing animals. She walked around the
room and surveyed her non-smoking peers. Some fit
young men; some not so fit men, some not so young men;
and some cute, and not so cute girls. A few of them
were doable, though; at a push. She chose the table
with the highest cute/fit ratio, and introduced
herself.
  After a brief conversation about why there was a
condom machine in the loo by the back door, she was in
there with No.2 (as she'd affectionately named him)
about to try one on for size. After a brief snog and a
feel-up, she'd invested her cash while he dropped his
trousers. He had a big one, but she probably should've
asked him what he was in for, before grabbing it and
rolling the rubber down his hard-on quite so
vigorously. At least he didn't ruin her pretty dress.
Lesson learnt: Heroin addicts, who previously had no
sensations, and couldn't ejaculate; get a week's
cleantime and suddenly feel every sensation and can't

do anything *but* ejaculate. Slightly disappointed, she started on her life story.

ART was staring out the window, thinking about Lori when his doorbell rang. He looked out and there she was, smiling up at him. He dropped the tennis ball to her and put on the kettle.

When she arrived, she collapsed onto the sofa, wrapped in the leather coat, a pair of Ugg boots on her feet.

"I'm sorry for last night Lori. I won't write about you again," he said, "I can be a selfish cunt sometimes and I know I was just gratifying my own ego by writing about you. I will take it out when we reprint it."

She nodded, then said,

"It's okay Artie. I think you might have done me a favour actually."

"How's that?"

Lori smiled but shook her head,

"I was so mired in my swamp of *isms*, so entrenched in the support groups and therapy, still looking at myself as the victim; that reading your book galvanised me into action, coz I suddenly knew what I had to do. This will be cathartic, and then I'll be able to let go and live happily ever after. I love you Artie."

"I love you too Lori," he said.

"Though," she qualified, "I think I might have had lesbian sex last night," and shut her eyes, pulled the coat over her knees and fell asleep.

AJI headed home, deciding to go via Blockbuster's. She texted Dash to ask if it was okay to use her account. Dash replied saying,

> *"Of course! Same password.*
> *We're in the area.*
> *See you there xxx"*

That was good news. Hopefully she'd get her to come home with her so she could get the lovebirds back on track.

DASHA and Eva parked outside the video shop and went in. She saw Aji by the New Releases. They hugged and perused the boxes. Dash picked up Finding Nemo (which she hadn't seen), Eva looked at Charlie's Angels: Full Throttle (which she hadn't seen), and Aji held Legally Blonde 2 (which she hadn't seen).

"We've just come from the police station," said Dash, "we saw Zorro this morning and followed him, so we could tell them where he lives."

"Wow!" said Aji, "Well done! How exciting! So are they going to bust him?"

"We don't know," said Eva, "they're not that convinced."

"Yes it's all circum... circum..." Dash tried.

"Sized?" suggested Aji.

"Circumstantial," laughed Eva, "circumstantial evidence."

"Then we must take matters into our own hands," said Dash, "for Amber."

"For Amber!" they all said together, like a scene out of The Lord of the Rings, (which they had all seen).

ART sat at his drawing board staring out the window. He occasionally glanced over his shoulder at Lori. Lesbian sex. He'd like to have seen that. Why did he like the idea of lesbian sex?

Because there were no dangling participles? He always found those displeasing. Just the female form... He was—
The doorbell rang, saving him from his reverie. He got up to see who was at the door.

Below stood Aji, Dash and Eva. His heart missed a beat.

"Sorry!" shouted Aji, "I thought I'd lost my keys, but I haven't!"

He looked behind him to check to see if Lori was still there, and of course she was, sleeping deeply. Could he quickly usher her into his bedroom, like in an episode of Frazier. No; he hadn't done anything wrong. He tried to decide how to play it, but came up with nothing.

AJI loved coming home with the girls because they still did the same thing every time since she was little: Lifting an arm each and flying her upstairs at break-neck speed! They were all laughing when they tumbled into the flat.

Her dad stood by the table with a blank expression, and someone, wrapped in Aji's very own leather coat, lay asleep on the sofa. No wonder she was freezing when he kept giving away all her warm clothing! Dash bent over the sofa:

"Who's this pretty thing?" she asked.

"And why's she wearing my coat?" said Aji.

"That's Fl—"

"Lori!" corrected Aji.

167

"Lori from your book?" asked Dash.

"Yes."

"Ooh! You're first love!" said Eva, prodding him; then she looked at Dash and said 'Oh'.

"No, it's nothing like that. I'm just helping her with an investigation, that's all—"

"But you just told me that you loved me Artie," said Lori, sitting up. "Sorry Aji, do you want your coat back," she said, allowing it to fall open to reveal she was only wearing a man's shirt (that looked suspiciously similar to one of her dad's) and a pair of Uggs.

Aji was shocked, and turned to look at her dad, who also looked shocked. Dash seemed more angry, as she punched him in the jaw, sending him spinning into the table.

"I, I," stuttered her dad.

"We should go," said Eva, putting an arm around Dash and ushering her away, "we don't want to be late." Aji followed as they walked out on to the landing.

"Sorry," she said, her heart sinking, "I didn't know she'd be here."

"Where did she come from?" asked Eva.

"Er, Tahiti?"

"When?"

"The weekend?"

"And you didn't tell me?" asked Dash.

"He said her name was Flora and I had no idea..." But they were gone. Aji's heart sank even further. She went to her room and slammed the door.

EVA rode sedately into the West End trying to think of something comforting to say to Dash, who remained silent. What could she say? Dash had been dithering with William for years, which had been quite frustrating to watch. How Art had managed was a mystery to her; and his first love coming back! Was that like a fairy tale? Had he summoned her with magic? Finally, she thought of the right thing to say:

"Let's get drunk tonight."

Dash hugged her and nodded, making their helmets bump together.

ART knocked on Aji's door. She said 'Yup' so he went in.

"Are you okay?" he asked, "I'm sorry about all this, I didn't—"

"Can I go stay at Mum's tonight?"

"Sure. I'll call you a cab."

DASHA's inflatable head had a leak, which was tickling her nose as it slowly deflated while she danced, but she didn't care. She was over 'A Forest'. She was just 'going through the motions', 'phoning it in', 'uninspired'. Valerie even picked up on her lacklustre performance and made a comment while they passed one another onstage. Jerry, a stagehand waved at her from the wings, holding up a bicycle pump. On her next break she trotted over to him and he helped her out of the slightly flabby tiger head and put some gaffer tape over the puncture.

"It should be fine for the rest of the show," he said, as he reflated it, "and I'll do a proper repair tomorrow before the show okay Dash?"

She smiled and nodded but she didn't care. She was over it. She was over Art too. And maybe over London. She just didn't care anymore about anything or anyone. Except Eva and Aji. And Hannah. And Amber. No one in Amber's own family seemed to care for her, but that's what made her do the things she did. Maybe Eva was right. They should go back to Zorro's garage tonight and block the door, then smoke him. Smoke him 'til he confessed. Once she'd got Amber back, she'd fuck off, maybe to Paris or Tokyo?

ART and Lori sat and ate together: Art, his supper; Lori, her breakfast. She had buttoned the coat, explaining away her shirt as confusion from the jetlag.

"So who was that beautiful girl with the fists?"

"She's Dash, my friend; or she was..."

"So why was she so pissed at you then?"

"Because we were on the verge of something just before you appeared, and she obviously thought we'd just had sex."

"On the verge of getting it together?"

"Yeah, we almost kissed on Friday night. I was thinking she's the one. That I could spent the rest of my life with; and then I met you on Saturday..."

"Really?" she said, going to change the record, "that was unfortunate timing."

She went to the CD player and put on 'Hayling', by FC Kahuna.

Lori took Art's hand, pulled him to his feet,

"Dance with me." It was a slow song and they swayed together. He could smell her hair. She raised her head and rested her cheek against his.

"This is nice," she said, and he nodded and smiled. But Dash was still on his mind, taunting him for his dishonesty.

"I remember this coat," said Lori, "I always coveted it, even though it was way too big for me then."

"Really? I don't remember that."

"Yeah, I used to wear it a lot when we were exploring in Holland Park. Your mum never minded."

"Oh, of course, it was hers. I'd forgotten."

"It's weird what we remember isn't it? Like you remember me hurting you, which I'd blanked; and I remember that your mum was sad on Thursdays which you'd forgotten."

"So much I've forgotten. I don't remember you spending so much time with her?"

"Yeah, she watched me and Richard a lot when my parents went to functions. You, of course spent more time in your room playing boyish games with my brother, so I was more inclined to be with her. She taught me how to play Go—"

"Me too! We should have a game sometime."

They swayed together for a few minutes.

"So why did you write about me Artie? Were you just bragging?"

"Bragging about losing my virginity at such an early age? No, at the time, I thought I was illustrating a moment in my life which changed everything for me, certainly changed my relationship with my peers later in life..."

Lori stared at him like she was trying to read his face.

"But my friend Mickey suggested it was an unconscious attempt to bring you to me, but I'm not sure... I shouldn't have mentioned you. I'm sorry."

"But then I wouldn't be dancing with you right here and now."

She raised her head and kissed him gently on the cheek, then again on his mouth, slowly pushing her tongue between his lips.

REVOX peered out of the crack in his curtain.

"Holy shit! The cops are snogging. Dancing and snogging!"

DASHA, and the rest of the girls congregated in their dressing room after the show. There was a lot of laughing but Dash didn't find anything funny. She had a pain in her heart. *And* she couldn't get her fucking inflatable head off!

"The padlock on the collar is broken! Help!"

Eva and Valerie came to help.

"It just needs a little jiggle darling," said Valerie, "there, here you go."

170

Valerie and Eva lifted it off her head and gave her a hug. Dash punched the thing then undid the bung so it slowly deflated. She was just out her latex bodysuit when her troop leader started to give her a hard time about her commitment to the musical and Dash agreed with her:

"For sure, you're right," she said, "I quit!" The troop leader blustered for a minute until she realized Dash was serious, then ran to tell the producer. Dash pulled her jeans on, put on her sweatshirt and coat, then grabbed her deflated head and shoved it in her pocket. She blew a kiss to the shocked and silent girls, waved goodbye then started the long meandering walk up to the street. Eva caught her up and put her arm around her. Once they were at ground level, both their phones buzzed as they got signal. They stopped and retrieved them. Dash's was a rambling apology from Aji. Eva's was from Mickey,

"He's in Bristol on business," she said, turning back, "he needs a number from his other phone, which is in my locker, so I'm gonna run back and get it. I'll just be a minute. See you there?"

Dash nodded okay, though the dressing rooms were a few minutes away, or more, she didn't care. She just needed a drink. Two drinks. She headed for the stage door. Outside, there were no Japanese salarymen like usual, but a hairy European stood waiting with a bunch of flowers. He was well dressed with a mop of curly black hair, a beard and moustache, and expensive looking spectacles.

"My dear," he said, in a fruity upper class accent, "I have seen you dance in 'A Forest' maybe a hundred times and you put the 'so called' star to shame! I've come here to the Stage Door before, but never dared to speak to you. But I have summoned all my courage to say you are talented and beautiful and I would be honoured if you would join me for dinner." He bowed and held out the bouquet. Dash took it and said,

"Are you very rich?" in an American accent.

"I am, my dear."

"Then shall we start with a drink at Blacks and see what happens?"

She took his arm and they walked into the wind.

ART became aware the music had stopped. The magical moment was broken. He smiled and pulled Lori over to the sofa. His phone pinged. He hoped it was Aji saying she was safely at her mums, but it was spam. He laid it beside him.

"So how did our sleeping together change everything?" she asked, "with your peers in later life?"

"Oh, you know..."

"No, I don't."

"The girls I slept with. I was a bit intimidated..."

"By what?"

"They seemed..."

"Seemed what?"

"They seemed a bit hairy and lumpen?"

Lori laughed,

"Oh yeah," she said cupping her breasts through the coat, "these lumpens can be rather intimidating."

He smiled,

"And you? How did it impact on you?"

"It?" she asked, "you mean my frequent rape? To me, sex was about being taken; being an object to be penetrated; having no say; being in pain..."

Art waited, there was obviously more to come.

"But that last night with you went a long way to resetting those feelings. So thanks Artie. I wish I'd come back here sooner. You're the only boy I've ever trusted."

"For years I thought I'd never get over you."

"But I read lots of your exploits, so you clearly did."

"But if you'd paid close attention you'd have noticed that my 'exploits' were often 'petite freckly blondes'."

"So you were looking for me (subliminally), or something close to me?"

"Yeah."

"Dasha almost fits the description. She's blonde, but more willowy than petite and she doesn't have freckles on her face, but she does have them on her temples—"

"You noticed that? Yes, freckly temples; and those eyes—"

"So really, you didn't want someone like me," she said, unbuttoning the coat, "you wanted me." She stood up.

"Do you still want me? Or am I too hairy and lumpen for you?" she said, dropping the coat and undoing the bottom buttons of her shirt to reveal her surfer's tanned and toned body.

REVOX's face was glued to the curtains.

"Oh shit! She's just taken off the coat, she's unbuttoning her shirt and moving towards him!"

172

"Fuck, I should be filming this! Maurice! Where's the video camera? The expensive one Jonno gave us, for this month's interest?"

DASHA sat at a corner table with the man and sipped her drink. His disguise was quite convincing, but his eye was weeping slightly, like someone might have poked it a while back.
She wanted to appear unsuspecting, so listened to his stories and questions, and replied with enthusiasm, but it didn't seem to be going anywhere.
"Got anything to smoke?" she asked.
They went on to the street and he lit up a joint. She pretended not to notice that he didn't inhale and she took a couple of drags. She could've pretended too, but what difference would it make? She wanted to know what had happened to Amber and this was the only way to find out. Nothing else mattered to her anymore. They went back inside and she ordered another vodka and tried to flirt with him. She could feel the effect of the joint, making everything a little hazy. Her eyes were drooping. He whispered,
"I want to fuck you." She opened her eyes, smiled and nodded.
"If we're gonna screw, I should buy some condoms," she said, standing up shakily. He grabbed her arm.
"Here, let me help you," he said, "I need the toilet too."
In the 'Ladies', she went into a cubicle and fired off a text to Eva then started rifling through her bag.

REVOX watched the action on the screen of the video-camera, zooming in and out on the girl's tanned body-parts. The bay window had been great for when they'd been dancing and snogging, but the French windows gave him ceiling to floor view. The girl walked towards him, and the cop leant forward and kissed her tanned tummy, gently nudging her breasts with his forehead. She hugged his head and tousled his hair, but her face took on a faraway look.

ART smiled and leant forward saying,
"You're not *hairy* or *lumpen*," as she advanced on him until her tummy was brushing the tip of his nose. He took a deep breath and inhaled her freckly freshness, just like all those years ago. She pulled his head to her and massaged his neck as he kissed her tummy. He ran his hands over her back and her skin was smooth and taut.

173

She crouched slightly and lifted his face to her breasts. Her nipples were hard, and he kissed one and sucked it between his lips, squeezing it gently. She gasped and whispered,

"Harder." He squeezed harder, but still only with his lips.

"Harder." He used his top teeth with his bottom lip, and she squealed in delight, pulling him closer, digging her fingernails into the back of his head.

She broke away for a moment and knelt down, straddling him on the sofa.

"Now the other one," she said, "or she'll be jealous."

Her wish was his command.

REVOX chuckled as he zoomed in on her breasts. This was going to look great on the big telly, but he really needed a tripod as he wasn't managing to hold steady.

GRODY locked himself in a cubicle then took off his shoe. Under the insole was his gear. He opened a sachet and used a key to shovel some of the brown powder up his nose. His eye started to water. It stung, but he didn't have time for the whole rigmarole, and it was better than nothing. When he emerged he saw her waiting by the phone.

"All sorted," she said, winking at him; or was that the powder taking effect? Her eyelids had become independent of one another.

"Shall we go to your hotel?" she asked.

"Yes, my dear," he said, "I've got my car outside."

She stumbled and took his arm then he led her outside and up the street.

"This car is shit!" she said.

"It doesn't matter," he said, opening the door, "lie down in the back."

She nodded.

"It doesn't matter," she said, lying down in the back.

He was amazed by the Purple. It was almost as if it gave him hypnotic powers. Maybe he should just take her to a hotel and fuck her? She didn't quite fit into the age bracket he was instructed to provide, but she was hot. Yeah, he hadn't tried out the Purple for his own amusement yet. On the other hand, he needed the money and needed to dispose of her.

ART counted the freckles on Lori's chest as he nibbled her nipple and she hummed a middle 'C' at the ceiling. He wondered why there were so few words for pleasurable sounds. There were plenty of words for sounds, but you always had to add a modifier ('with delight'; 'in ecstasy'). Cats 'purred'; Pigeons 'cooed', but they were the only verbs he could think of that stood alone. He should try to correct this omission. They needed to be onomatopoeic, but also sexy. How about Bubbling? The sound of a gurgling exhalation during the act? or Moooning? A slow, on/off inhalation as the female experiences orgasm?

EVA's phone bleeped as she came back to ground level. It was a text from Dash:

> *"In the club with Zorro.*
> *I smoked the purple.*
> *Come now and tail us*
> *when we leave."*

"O.M. Fucking G!" she shouted and headed for the Stage Door. It was only a couple of blocks to the club, but she ran, pulling up her hoodie as she went. Outside were the usual smokers and a couple of mini-cabs. She jumped in the back of the first one and watched the door of the club, while she texted Art:

> *"Dash drugged by Zorro at club*
> *& he's taking her away.*
> *I will follow. Come now.*
> *Call me from the bike so*
> *I can update you. Eva."*

"Where to?" asked the driver, holding his cigarette out the window.
"I'm waiting for someone," she said, "but start the clock."
"I don't have a clock," he said, turning to her, but she ignored him and watched the door.
"I could have a clock if I wanted," said the driver, "I could pass the fucking Knowledge if I wanted."
Eva zoned him out and concentrated on the door of the club. But how long ago had Dash sent the text? Eva had been in the bowels of the theatre where there was no signal and she'd only got it when she'd emerged. She sent a text to Dash then told the driver to wait, jumped out, ran over the road and into the club. She

searched the rooms, but Dash was not there. She called
her phone but got no answer. She started to panic.

ART looked up at the pretty face that he'd been
imagining as they'd grown up so far apart. She held
his face in her hands and gently disengaged her
nipple, then slowly came in for a kiss. She smiled and
moved closer and brushed her mouth against his lip;
then she bit it.
    Her tongue was hot, and aggressive, as were the
hands that were kneading his hard-on through his
pants.
    "So you can get it up for this old heffalump,"
she said, then, "got any lube?"
    He reached over the arm of the sofa, pulled open
a drawer and retrieved a little pot of Aqueous Cream.
    "Purely coincidental," he said.
    She kissed him again. Hard. Then trapped his
tongue between her teeth and tightened until it hurt.
He liked it. The Carrot and the Stick.

EVA saw Dash emerging from the loos and exhaled.
She was on the arm of a bushy haired and bearded
hipster dude. Was that Zorro? He was good at
disguises. She hid and they passed, fighting every
instinct to intervene. They walked out, Dash stumbling
a bit, him propping her up. They walked twenty yards
to a grey station-wagon where he opened a rear
passenger door and Dash got in, with his help. Was she
faking it? Eva ran to her mini-cab.

    As they kissed, ART's hands moved up her smooth,
tanned legs until his thumbs rested in those sexy
clefts between the thigh muscles and the hips, as she
nibbled on his ear lobe. Waiting excitedly for the
bite, he moved his hands round behind and under her
knickers and massaged her tight buttocks.
    "M-m-m-m," she mewed, "an artist's hands. No
rough callouses," she chuckled, and squirmed against
his touch, then kissed him again, her tongue becoming
even more probing.

    REVOX couldn't believe two cops could be so
sexy,
    "These two should be porn-stars, not coppers. In
fact, I'm gonna make them porn-stars!"
He zoomed in on their faces to get a close-up, then
down to his hand on her butt.

EVA watched as Zorro got in the front and drove north.

"Follow that car." she said, pointing at the old grey station-wagon.

"Awesome!" said the driver, putting on Firestarter by the Prodigy. They zigzagged through the back streets of Soho's one-way system so she couldn't predict where they'd end up.

GRODY was in two minds. Horny? or Greedy? - Sex? or Money? Wait. Was he being followed? He took a right towards Soho Square. Maybe he was being paranoid. It was all one-way, so processions occurred frequently, but he would just make sure.

ART's phone pinged. He glanced at the screen thinking it would be Aji, but it was Eva. Her message popped onto the screen.

EVA saw they'd rounded Soho square more than once. She saw a black cab behind them, shouted 'stop!' and jumped out, as did her driver, protesting about something. She was in the black cab before the grey station-wagon had made another circuit. She then realized she hadn't paid for the mini-cab and threw a tenner out the window. When the station-wagon passed by she said,

"Follow that car."

GRODY saw the mini-cab had pulled over and the driver was shouting at a black cab. Maybe they'd had a prang? He smiled, retraced his steps, and headed west.

Out of the corner of his eye ART read Eva's text, then tried to ignore it. Ten minutes! Lori was just about to free his erection from– Five minutes!

"Oh shit!" he said, sitting up abruptly.

"Fuck Artie!" screamed Lori, "what's going on?"

"I'm sorry," he said, "I can't ignore that text!"

"But we're literally about to–"

"I'm sorry," he said, as he lifted her off him and pulled up his jeans, "so, so sorry."

"What's happened?" she asked, as he put on his boots.

"I have to go. Dasha's in trouble," he said as he plugged his earbuds into his phone.

"But Artie, I need you!" she said, still almost naked on the sofa.

He shook his head in regret as he pulled on his leather jacket.

"You can't go!"

But he was putting on his helmet.
"Artie, if you leave now I'll..."
But her voice faded out as he bounded down the
stairs.

LORI looked out the window and watched him speed
away, then said 'Fuck!' very loudly.

REVOX looked out the window and watched him
speed away, then said 'Fuck!' very loudly.

EVA got a call from Art, saying he was about to
hit Marble Arch so could go down Park Lane or straight
along Oxford Street.
"So we're just on Regent Street by Liberty?
Heading south-ish?. Now he's going down Conduit
Street."
"Okay, I'll go down Park Lane, turn left and
hopefully we'll converge."
"Who are we following?" said the cabbie
excitedly, "some evil-doer? A criminal mastermind? No,
not likely in a Vauxhall."
"We've crossed Bond street heading straight,"
said Eva, "where are you?"
"I'm coming towards Berkeley Square too, from the
other side. What car is he in?"
"Grey station-wagon; I mean estate car, sorry.
It's a Vauxhall apparently. Okay, we're on the square
I see you on the other side by Annabel's, and he's
going round your way; and he's slowing down. Shit,
he's looking for a space! And he's parking!"

LORI got dressed and walked back to her hotel.
The night porter she called Honey was behind the desk;
her face lit up when she saw Lori,
"Good evening Miss Shapiro."
"Good evening Honey," she said, leaning on the
counter and beaming a wide smile at her.

GRODY followed protocol, but then realized he
hadn't sent the text. He fired off '10 mins', even
though he knew 30 was the minimum, in the hope that
the tow-truck was parked close by. He got out, opened
the bonnet, and walked away.

EVA said,
"Stop here please Cabbie," then to Art, "Zorro's
got out and he's opening the hood! Maybe he's broken
down, what a stroke of luck! and now he's walking
away!"

"Yeah, I see him," said Art, "I'll stick with him as he's coming my way. You check on Dash."
Eva jumped out and ran to the car, ducking down when she saw Zorro look back. But when she got there, Dash was not in the car.
"She's not here Artie!" she said, trying the doors, "she got in the back but now she's not here!"
"Don't worry, I've got him," said Art.

ART ran at Zorro and barged him against the garden's low, spiked railings which stabbed him in his chest. Zorro tried the reverse head-butt, probably not realizing his assailant was wearing a crash helmet.
"Where's the girl?" Art said quite calmly, considering how he felt, "if she's not in the car, where is she?"
"She isn't in the car?" asked Zorro, whimpering as the spikes found the gaps between his ribs.
"He must have the keys?" Eva said through his earbuds, "I'll come get the keys."
Art was trying his pockets when some drunken toffs came out of Annabel's and looked over their way. To them, it looked like someone was being mugged. They approached, shouting. Art flipped Zorro over the railings then jumped after him. Zorro rolled like a parachutist and ran. Art followed, but weighed down by his winter biking gear, he couldn't zigzag like Zorro.
Eva ran into the square on the west side as Zorro sprinted out the east side. They followed up Bruton Street and then left into New Bond Street. Art gave up when he got to Oxford Street. He had lost them both.

EVA ran fast, gaining on Zorro easily and caught him halfway up New Bond Street. He must've heard her, because he turned and punched her in the stomach. She collapsed and he ran on. She pulled herself up and ran on. When she got to Oxford Street she couldn't spot him, so randomly took a left and then a right. He grabbed her, gagging her mouth with his hand.
"The other American!" he hissed as she struggled, "the other thorn in my side. Why didn't you come to the club earlier? I could've killed two birds with—"
She bit his hand, twisted and rammed her knee into his groin. He fell to the floor, curling into a ball, his hands cupping his testicles.
"Where is Dash! She got in the back but I didn't see her there!" she said, getting down behind him, "tell me, or it's another in your balls or a maybe my thumb in your good eye."
"She's in the boot!"

"Why did you park there? You lifted the hood. Did
you break down?"

"No, that's just for show, but a tow-truck does
come and pick up the car."

She reached for her phone but it wasn't in her pocket.
He tried to elbow her, so she kneed him in the balls
and he screeched in agony.

"Where does it take the car?"

"I've no idea," he whimpered, "I swear! I just
drop them there and that's it!

"When will the tow-truck come?"

"Soon!"

Eva wanted to take him to a Police station, but she
couldn't call Art. He might've already freed Dash, but
she couldn't take the chance. She kneed Zorro one more
time and started running, all the time looking for her
phone.

ART ran back to Berkeley Square, planning to
break a window and search the Vauxhall. He saw a phone
lying on the pavement and it looked like Eva's Nokia,
so he popped it in his pocket, then ran on. When he
got to Berkeley Square, he looked for the Vauxhall but
couldn't find it.

He fired off a text to Dash while he waited for Eva.
When she appeared, he watched the awful realization
cloud her expression,

"The car's gone!" Eva cried, then burst into
tears. Art hugged her while she sobbed. He felt on the
verge of doing the same. Dash would never had done
this if he hadn't have been with Lori when they'd come
round; if Lori hadn't have been dressed so bizarrely;
if she hadn't said 'but you just told me you loved
me'. It was Lori's fault. She planned the whole thing.

"I'm going to the police," said Eva, hailing a
cab. Art gave her back her phone and said bye. He was
torn between chasing after a tow-truck he hadn't seen,
on a route he didn't know; or going to Lori and
venting his rage.

LORI lay on her four-poster bed, snogging with
Honey, just as if she was a horny college girl. Maybe
Honey *was* a college girl? What was the English
equivalent of College? University? She slipped her
hand under Honey's shirt and felt her smooth skin and
tiny boobs. Had she been here before? She had a vague
memory of tiny boobs with erect nipples like the
erasers on pencils. She kissed her and gently massaged
her nipple, and lo and behold it grew and grew and
just begged to be sucked on—

A hard knock at the door. Lori stood and approached
the door. The girl gasped and covered herself with the
duvet

"Who is it?" asked Lori.

"It's Art."

"What are you doing here?" she said.

"I came to..."

Lori opened the door and let him in. Art saw the
girl's eyes peeping over the duvet and stopped.

"Sorry..." said Art, but Lori pushed him past the
bed and sat him down on the sofa.

The look on their faces when they'd seen one
another made her smile. They were both embarrassed and
Lori giggled, before realizing she'd maybe gone too
far.

Art seemed to be looking at the T.V, even though it
wasn't on.

"I came to..."

Lori walked round in front of him and saw he was
crying, clutching his heart.

"They've taken Dash; drugged in the boot of a
car, just like Amber and Elsie..."

Lori sat next to him and put an arm over his
shoulders. On the table in front of them was her
'minibar'. She popped some ice in the cut-glass
tumbler, poured a very generous measure of single Malt
from the decanter, then slugged half of it back and
put it on the table.

The girl had dressed and was leaving, still blushing.

"Can you bring another bottle when you get a
chance please Honey?" asked Lori, then turned to Art,
"don't worry, you'll get her back soon," she said,
hugging him.

ART had wanted to shout at Lori, to tell her he
was on to her, that he wouldn't be manipulated any
longer, but when he'd walked in and found Lori with
the receptionist in her bed all the anger bled out of
him. For a millisecond he imagined Lori had arranged a
threesome for him after their chat the other day, then
he came to his senses and the pain resurfaced more
savage than ever. He just wanted it to go away. He saw
Lori pick up the decanter and through his tears the
lights flashed prismatically through the cut-glass and
then the whiskey and she poured it over ice and it
splashed in slo-mo like an advert and the ice cracked
and she lifted it to her beautiful freckly face and
sunk it back as a girl wiggled into her knickers in
the background and he'd never wanted a drink more and
she put it on the table with the light glinting and

dancing on the ice cubes and he picked it up and drank
it and for a moment the pain in his heart was gone.
     For a moment.

     GRODY limped towards his home in Burnt Oak. Or
more accurately, walked like a very bow-legged cowboy.
He rounded the corner into his lane and saw a Police
car stopped by his garage. There, stood the American
bitch who'd crippled him, talking with an officer.
Grody crept closer until he could hear the officer
say:
     "But maybe she got out of the car while it was
out of sight; on the other side of Soho Square? You
said yourself she wasn't in the car when you looked—"
     "Then where the fuck is she ass-wipe?"
     "No need for that kind of language pretty lady—"
     "So are you going to break down this door?"
Grody backed away from the scene. He thought for a
moment, checked his keys, then limped away.

     LORI was bored of whiskey. It was clouding her
brain. Maybe some grass would lift the mist? She got
her stash (provided by Honey) and skinned up. Art's
eyes lit up,
     "Grass was always my drug of choice. Before N.A,
I tried to abstain hundreds of times and it was always
the grass that pulled me back."
     "So what's wrong with a bit of grass?" asked
Lori.
     "For most people, nothing. For me, it always led
me back to the smack."
     Lori lit up and inhaled, then held it between
them.

     ART's phone bleeped. A text had arrived from
Eva:

          *"Took the police to Zorro's garage
          but they found no leads."*

He replied with a sad face. Then he put his phone away
and tried to forget again. He looked at the joint for
a few seconds before taking it from Lori and inhaling
deeply.
     "Can you still put both your thumbs up your
nostril?" asked Lori.
     "I can, but my skins not so elastic so it takes a
week to—"
     "Do it!" she cried, "do it!" He did it and she
laughed.

182

"Let's play *Do you remember?*" she said, "if you
fail, I get a point."
Art nodded so she said,
    "Do you remember when we met?"
    "I do, you had crawled through the hedge to
retrieve a ball from my garden and I jumped on you for
trespassing—"
    "Then followed me back through the hedge to join
our game and fell in love with my brother."
    "I may have given you that impression..."
She smiles and said,
    "Your turn."
    "Shall we walk down to Shepherd's Bush?"
    "Why?"
    "Because there's a kebab shop on the green that
might sell us something stronger? I need to feel
brittle."
    "Okay!" she laughed.
They put their coats on then walked downstairs.

    LORI smiled at the night porter,
    "Sorry about that Honey," she said, "I acted
selfishly, and I wasn't thinking when I opened the
door."
Honey eyed her suspiciously.
    "This is my old school-friend Artie."
Art, swaying benevolently, said 'Hi'. Honey smiled and
blushed.
    "He's just had an upset so we're going to the
chemist but will be back in an hour."
They walked out into the cold. Lori pulled the leather
coat tighter and put on her gloves.
    "Do you remember the first time our lips
touched?"
Art looked at the clouds, low lit by the city lights.
    "I think we were playing Cowboys and Indians and
Richard had tied you to a tree in Holland Park—"
    "And you wouldn't release me until I kissed you!
Yes, well remembered."
    "Except you bit my lip and it bled for a week
inside my mouth."
Lori laughed and smiled nostalgically,
    "But do you remember our *second* kiss?"
    "That was when we were playing hide and seek in
the park. It was after you'd started coming to my room
and you seemed to like me on that day. I was crouching
in the bushes and you followed me and sat on my lap
and wriggled as Richard walked right past us without
noticing, and I must admit I did get a bit turned on."
    "Yes, I was feeling very grateful to you that
day; and I wriggled on you on purpose, because I'd

183

noticed the same thing happen to you sometimes when I wriggled against you in the night, even though you were asleep."

"And then you put your arms around my neck and kissed me."

"Yes, I did. I kissed you good. And that was my *first proper* kiss—"

"Mine too—"

They looked at each other and smiled. She was happy. They were having fun. She was distracting him from his guilt and pain and he was rising to the occasion, and for the first night since she'd got to London she wasn't alone.

"Do you remember the name of our Art teacher?" asked Art.

"Mr Hart-Dyke? Yes! He'd throw paint-pots at everyone except you because he loved your talent, and he'd buy you lollies in the summer!"

ART nodded,

"It was my first inkling that outside of the sheer pleasure of drawing, there could be material rewards as well."

They'd walked over the hill on Ladbroke Grove and were approaching Holland Park Avenue and their old homes.

"Do you remember our first drink?" he asked.

"It was my dad's Cinzano wasn't it? We'd seen the advert on the telly with the racing boats and the pretty girls and the stupid slogan 'anytime, any place, anywhere'."

"Wrong! One point to me," he said, "it was Martini who had the redundant slogan."

"Oh yeah, you, me and Richard drank Martini and lemonade in a bush in the park during lunch-break and then I fell asleep in class and got sent home."

"That's funny; I don't remember Richard being there in that bush?"

"You seem to have airbrushed him from a lot of your memories."

"Well, he was actually a bit of a wanker, wasn't he? He was cruel to you and he also led me astray on many occasions, turning me on to stealing from school, shop-lifting and maybe even instrumental in me becoming a pornographer."(7)

LORI hugged her coat around her and looked in the shop windows on Holland Park Avenue. It felt like it might snow.

"He was a wanker, and you wrote about that in your 'Head' book, but also I remember you telling me a story from when you were four or five? About your

184

first theft, way before you met us. You'd seen a toy, a yellow Matchbox bulldozer sitting on the counter by the till in a shoe shop. It'd been accidentally left behind by its owner and the next time you went there with your mum it was still there and you snagged it as you were walking out!"

ART smiled shamefacedly,
     "Yeah, okay, it wasn't Richard, I was always like that. It wasn't that I didn't know right from wrong, it was that I didn't care; that 'my need was greater'. It escalated after I got expelled and came back to London. My dad told me to get a part-time job to pay my way and I came across a "Help Wanted" sign in a petrol station on St Mark's Road."
     "I know the one. With the car wash?"
     "Yeah, nestled next to the railway lines and the Westway Flyover, opposite a newly built estate of houses?"
Lori nodded.
     "Little known fact? The estate where once stood the notorious Rillington Place? Where Christie buried many of his victims in his basement. There's a gap left in the new houses where his house had stood with a nice silver birch growing on it, and next to that was the home of the manager of the petrol station."
     "Creepy, I could never live there."
     "Indeed, and he thought he was cursed, but really I think he just made bad choices, like employing a teenage stoner to run his business Monday to Friday afternoons."
     "So you stole?"
     "Nothing as stupid as that. As an attendant, my job was to serve the customers their petrol. The pump's display was mechanical, with the cost and gallons rotating in their windows like a fruit machine."
     "Actual wheels turning?"
     "Yeah, and after filling a car, I was supposed to turn off the pump using a big handle then zero the clocks with a small handle; but if someone only bought a gallon I could loiter by the pump and wait for another customer who wanted filling up. Thus, I made two customers pay for the same gallon."
     "That is very sneaky."
     "And exciting, I loved the danger, the adrenaline. But it also became a game to me: How many times could I do it in a day? How many twenty-pound-notes could I accrue in a week? I got my friends gigs there too: Billy, Simon and Hew all ran the same scam—"

185

"So actually, you were leading *others* astray?"
Art smiled and nodded,
"And it went on a long time and I had a lot of
twenties in a box under my bed, and I think this is
when I started buying drugs in bulk, just to get them
cheaper, honest; not to deal them."
Lori shrugged and shook her head.
"Then one day a nice woman came in and said
'Phew, I made it!' then 'Fill her up'. I was holding
the nozzle already on a quid and popped it in and
squeezed."
"Oh no, I can feel this is going to end badly."
"'Stop!' she shouted, 'I forgot my purse.' I
should have continued, but stupidly I did stop. She
looked at the clock, on £1.05 and promised to return
with the money. I said okay and watched her drive off
and immediately run out of petrol."
Lori cringed, then laughed.
"And that was the end of my career in the Petro-
Chemical industry."
They walked in silence for a moment before he said,
"What about you? Where were you when you were a
teenager and what were you doing?"
"Nothing," she said, turning her head away and
looking at him out the corner of her eyes.

LORI put her arm through his, then buried her
hand deep in her pocket. It was getting colder.
"I was in Tokyo. Going to the American School,
being a fucked-up teenager, but nothing ever happened
to me of any note, no stories to tell, sorry. Let's
continue playing... Do you remember..." but she
couldn't think of another shared experience to test
him on, "what do you remember...from your early
childhood?"
Art looked at the sky for a moment then said,
"My earliest memory is being cuddled on my
Mother's lap while she read to me. Our books of choice
were the 'Just William' stories about a ten-year-old
boy who was always in trouble. I can't remember if we
had no kid's books, or whether I refused them, but I
loved William."
"I remember those. They were set in the 1930's.
Very English."
"Yeah, even at that pre-school age I wanted to be
like William, though he lived in the countryside
surrounded by angry farmers, irate bobbies, amiable
tramps and filthy chimneysweeps. Not many of any of
those in Kensington, but probably for the best as I
was a bit of a scaredy-cat."
"So you *wanted* to be as brave as William but?"

186

"But my imagination over-ruled reality a lot of the time: I was convinced there were ruffians in the tree outside my window at night who were plotting heinous crimes. I was sure that if I peeked through the curtains and saw them, and *they saw me*, a witness, that they would burst through the window to kill me."

"So you never looked out?"

"Never. But there were also dangers inside my room; faces in the Rambling Rose wallpaper waiting for me to go to sleep so they could ramble over me and have their way; my remedy for that was

drawing the wallpaper repeatedly, but each time making the faces slightly less demonic."

"You really were a little bundle of neuroses, weren't you?"

"Absolutely! Drawing was my saving grace. As long as I was drawing, I was fine. I'd started early with Knights in Shining Armour. Filling a page with them calmed me. I would enter the page to be with them. The certainty of their actions was far preferable to the nasty, smelly kids I was surrounded by at school."

"Any other weird obsessions?"

"The spikey chandelier in the living room?"

"I remember it."

"It was waiting to unscrew itself and impale me as I lay on the carpet beneath, trying to concentrate on the television (but really waiting for any sound from the chandelier)."

'Why didn't you just move, you idiot?'

"I did. I went to sit on the sofa with my dad, but every time, I got this awful feeling that he was going to reach out and grab my leg so I started sitting on a step-ladder instead."

"I'm not surprised; your dad was a meany. Do you remember he used to ignore your mum for days at a time?"

Art looked at the pavement,

"No, I don't remember that."

"One point to me then. Classic withholder your dad. A right cunt."

Art raised his eyebrows.

"Another thing you've airbrushed?" suggested Lori, "but surely it'd be in your journals, wouldn't it?"

ART pondered this for a moment then nodded. They had left the glamorous surrounds of Holland Park, and crossed over to the filthy pox-ridden quagmire that was Shepherd's Bush. Ahead, he could see the welcoming lights of the 24hour kebab shop.

187

Friday - 7th November

AJI was late. She was always late when she stayed south of the river. She ran down the halls to get to her class, turned a corner to see Marcus and her on a collision course. There was nothing she could do to avoid him. He went one way but she dodged the same way and they bumped into one another, books falling to the floor. They knelt to pick them up. Marcus whispered,

"I'm so sorry about Halloween Aji, I was drunk."

Aji hissed,

"I was drunk too. You got me drunk. You probably even spiked me."

"I didn't spike you," he winced, "I think we were both drinking the punch without realizing how much effect it was going to have on us and suddenly we were drunk and doing things that we weren't supposed to, maybe things that we didn't even want to do, if we had been sober."

Aji thought for a moment and then said,

"Yeah, I guess that might be true."

"I didn't spike you Aji, I'm not like that, and," he whispered, looking over both shoulders, "I'm still a virgin, okay? I have no idea what I'm doing."

Aji chuckled and said,

"Me neither."

"I'm so sorry. I meant what I said."

Aji raised an eyebrow.

"Not to get you into bed. But because it's true." Aji wasn't sure what he'd said. The whole evening was a little fuzzy. And she didn't know if he was trying the same thing on again or whether he was sincere. She nodded her head and ran. She was confused. Maybe she still had feelings for him, even if he turned into an asshole when drunk. She should talk to her Mum; alcohol had also made her turn nasty (enough for her to abstain), so maybe Marcus was the same? A chemical thing?

ART awoke to the sound of his phone vibrating. He opened his eyes and found himself lying next to Lori in his own bed. His head ached and his mouth tasted like he'd eaten a parakeet. He sat up and looked at his phone with Mickey's face smiling at him. Aw, Mickey... Art smiled back and picked up the phone, but it stopped vibrating and his friend's face disappeared. Why would he be ringing so early? And why was Lori in his bed? Then he was reminded of everything that had happened the night before. Dash had been taken and he had relapsed. He got up and went through to the living room, cursing himself while he turned on the kettle. Was he still drunk? He tried talking and found he was able, without slurring his words; he tried walking in a straight line and found he was able. It was just his brain that wasn't quite able. He'd turned on the kettle but hadn't put any water in it. How many hours sleep had he had? None? Ugh, he was too old for this. He saw some coke on the table and some bits of foil. Oh shit. They'd gone to the kebab shop and...

He went to the mirror and his pupils were like pin-pricks. He was still pinned. Fuck! How could he tell Aji? and Mickey! and Dash, if he ever saw her again... Was that why Mickey had called? Was there news? Other than his own? Maybe don't tell them? He found his shades and popped them on, snorted the rest of the coke, smoked some smack off a piece of foil and then filled the kettle again *and* switched it on.

Could he have a conversation with Mickey? Maybe after a pot of coffee. Could he tell the truth immediately? Come clean to Mickey straight away?

He sat at his board and stared out the window, while the coffee slowly woke him up.

The phone buzzed again, Mickey's face popping up on the screen. He took a deep breath and answered:

"Hi Mickey. Any news on Dash?"

"No. Eva took the police to Zorro's lock-up last night and they searched it but found nothing."

"Shit, so he won't be going back there anytime soon. And that was our only lead," Art said, but stopped as a thought came to him, "except for the party on Wednesday night. He was the barman, so he must've been employed by someone—"

"An agency maybe?"

"Yeah, that's something to tell the police—"

"Well we're at Scotland Yard now, waiting to speak to someone, so yeah, that is something."

"And they must be able to catch that tow-truck on CCTV, don't you think?"

"I hope so. There's enough of those cameras around!"

"But even then, we're going to have to wait for them to..."
Staring out of the window, Art had an idea.

"The dealer over the road knows Zorro. I think it might be worth paying him a visit—"

"No, that'd be crazy. The guy who attacked you in Tesco? That guy is a psycho and a drug dealer!"

"Yeah! So Zorro is one of his minions. He'll know
where to find him. We can't waste any more time
sitting around. I'm going over—"
"You idiot! Wait! I'm coming too! Wait for me!"
But Art was already putting on his jeans.

GRODY unlocked the door and entered the
building. Inside, he hung his jacket in the lobby. The
main hall was spacious with the tables and chairs
stacked in the corner, with other gear leaning against
the walls. The notice board held messages for upcoming
events. He crossed to the changing room and started to
remove his disguise. Wig, moustache, sideburns and
goatee were placed on the sink's counter then he took
his shirt off and examined the wounds on his chest.
Three or four broken ribs, but no actual punctures,
just severe purple bruising which was painful to the
touch. Then he examined his testicles, which were the
same colour and even more painful. He got out his
works and prepared a hit.

REVOX was woken by the doorbell.
"Who the fuck would dare visit at this hour?"
He got his forty-five then looked out the peephole.
"That fucking sexy pig from opposite!" he
whispered, then called,
"What do you want pig?"
"I need to talk to you!"
"At this ungodly hour?"
"It's 10am! and what's so godly about you?"
"Are you armed? Because I am!"
"I am not, and I don't care if you are. Open the
door!" he banged both fists on it until Revox cracked.
"Stop! You'll wake the neighbours! Okay!" he
opened the door and waved the gun in his face.
"Come in for fuck's sake!"

GRODY, feeling much better, washed and changed.
Returning to the hall, he took a camp-bed from the
stack, and carried it into his office, where he
unfolded it, and gently lowered himself on to the thin
mattress. He looked at the ceiling and wondered if
he'd blown it. Ten seconds later, he was asleep.

JOSEPH sat at his desk watching the monitor.
Natalie, the attractive American woman he'd let in
earlier was not behaving like the previous visitors to
Karen Ford's apartment. She had done a quick circuit
of the apartment then started rifling through the 12"
record sleeves in the music room, picking them up and

letting the contents fall onto the table. What was she looking for? Was there something of value hidden in there? And how would she know that? She'd gone straight to the double albums section and—

She'd found something. She was examining a catalogue, was it? Flicking through the pages. Lithographs? She put it in her bag and ran from the room.

Joseph switched views and found her in the kitchen, heading for the utility room and its exit. But the door to the lightwell was locked for that very reason: No one could leave with valuables that way. He waited for her to reappear, but she didn't, and he started to doubt himself. Had he left it unlocked? He walked to the lift, then up one flight of stairs and peered out of the window into the lightwell, but the fire escape was on his side so he wouldn't be able to see her anyway. Should he go down and out into the lightwell, or up to the apartment? Up. He was sure the doors were locked and she would still be in the apartment. He called the lift, scanned the monitor again, picked up his hefty torch and headed up. Unlocking the door, Joseph called out that he was coming in, then he opened it a crack and peered through. The door swung away from him and she swerved past him and down the stairs before he even realized what had happened. He didn't bother to chase her but went to the music room and looked at the albums and sleeves lying in disarray on the table.

He cleared up the room, putting as many of the records back in their sleeves, as best he could. Some of the covers had such byzantine artwork that he couldn't make out the name or title to match them up with the discs. He'd have to get his reading glasses from downstairs. In the past fans had pocketed trinkets or ornaments or stuffed a framed photo under their coat which had been embarrassing for all concerned, but this had been quite traumatic. What could she have taken? How could a few sheets of paper be so valuable that she'd do that?

She clearly knew what she was looking for and where to look, so how did she find such information? Should he tell Mickey and Eva about this? If he did, he might get sacked.

ART stood while the albino sat by the window, gun pointing at Art's crotch.

"You have a fucking nerve coming here, pig."

"I know, but 'needs must' as they say—"

"As who say?"

"They."

192

"They?" said the albino turning to the window, then quickly back, his eyebrows raised, "yesterday I *was* thinking I'm gonna kill you just so's I don't have to see you staring at me anymore. Then last night went a long way to making up for everything."

"What happened last night?"

"You got it on with your blonde partner, dancing and kissing and disrobing and sucking and it was all very sexy—"

"You saw us?"

"Yeah, but then you ran away just before the finale! Where did you go?"

"Shit! That's really embarrassing!"

"But it was really hot, so..." Revox smiled, "so I forgive you."

Art looked at the floor.

"Did you come to ask if I videotaped it? Cos I did."

Art shook his head and said,

"I just wanted to tell you about the guy with the eye-patch, who helped you move in on Saturday?"

"What about him?"

"He drugs and abducts young girls. Last Friday at a Halloween party in Earl's Court, then again on Wednesday at a Fireworks Night party in Windsor, and again last night in Soho. I don't know what he does with them, whether he buries them alive, or sells them to a dogfood factory or whatever, but they must be terrified, and you are my only lead to him."

He had the guy's attention.

"What do I care? I care more about your porno tape than I care about that!"

"No, I saw it in your eyes. You have a little girl in your life and you just thought of her, frightened and helpless."

They looked at each other for a moment.

"Listen, I've met the 'dead-eyed' of the world. I used to seek them out to write about them: Despots, Slavers, Arms dealers, Torturers who thought nothing of human life, because they weren't human themselves, and I don't see that in you—"

"Artemis Grime?," he asked, his eyebrows rising in awe, "*King of Drug-Pigs*? I thought you were dead!"

"I was!"

The albino cleared an armchair of newspapers,

"Sit down; so, can I get you anything? Brown? White? Blues? Reds? All the colours of the rainbows!"

Art rubbed his hands together in glee.

JOSEPH trawled through his emails for Eva's letter regarding Natalie Anderson. There was so much

junk-mail from people offering him Viagra. How did
they know he needed it? He didn't even know he needed
it, as he hadn't had sex in eight years. It dawned on
him that he could have more than one email. It wasn't
like a house address which was fixed. It was more like
mailboxes which you could visit. So he could use
different ones for different facets of his life.

He found the email and tried the number, but it
was unobtainable. But below, among other probably fake
details was her reference which was an Agency called
Models One. That rang a bell with him, he guessed,
because a lot of Karen Ford's fans were models?

He called the number. A pleasant sounding man
answered, saying his name was Jeff, then asked how he
could help.

"Hello, my name is Mr Joseph, a Natalie Anderson
gave you as a reference to visit our museum, and she's
run off with a valuable artefact."

"Oh, I'm so sorry, but I don't know a Natalie
Anderson. She's not one of my clients here. They're
the only people I'd be giving out a reference... Oh
wait. I remember. Kirsten said Natalie was her good
friend and asked me to write her a reference and okay
her if...wait...just checking...if *Eva* called. So
sorry."

"Kirsten?" Joseph asked, "who is she?"

"So, she is one of my models here, and she did
originally ask me to be her referee if Eva called.
You're at Karen Ford's, aren't you? The best kept
secret in fashion? I must admit I have been thinking
of coming to view the wonderous apartment myself; just
to look through those wardrobes if nothing else."

"You're welcome anytime, but could I get
Kirsten's number please? I need to find this Natalie
Anderson as soon as possible."

"I can't give her number out, but I can ask her
to call you?"

"Please do, thank you. And come see us soon. Bye"

Joseph went back to trawling his emails. Maybe
she was the model who'd visited last Saturday with her
photographer boyfriend? He finally found the email and
it was Kirsten and there was a number. He dialled it.

When she answered and he introduced himself she
hung up. He called twice more before she chose to
speak to him,

"Jeff called and told me. I'm sorry but this is
not my fault."

"How so?"

"I didn't know she was going to do that."

"That's not an excuse."

"You can't blame me for her actions—"

"But we can sue you and Models One for giving a false reference."

"Then I'll tell the neighbour what you're doing. The creepy old man you said would stop you if he found out."

Joseph was impressed. Quick thinking on her part.

"Okay, you have information that I need. What do you want in return?"

"To be able to publish the pictures we shot in Karen Ford's apartment?" she pleaded, "it'd be great for both me and my boyfriend's careers, and the neighbour need never find out."

"You signed a contract agreeing not to do that. We'd both need to sign a new one nullifying that one. Why don't you pop over as soon as you can?"

She laughed and said,

"I'm only in the King's Road at a casting. I can be round in an hour or so."

Joseph put down the phone and wondered if he should give up, and tell them what happened. Not yet. He'd have this meeting with her and if it didn't lead anywhere, he'd have a rethink.

GRODY sat on a bench in the changing room, hair still wet from the shower, a towel over his shoulders. He was looking at his Motorola. No light flashed, meaning no text had arrived. Maybe they weren't happy with his latest choice? Maybe the police had stopped the tow-truck and found the girl? Maybe he'd been cut loose? Should he text and ask what was going on? A phone chirped! He looked at the Motorola, but it was the Nokia ringing:

"Grody! Revox. I hear you're in trouble?"

"No, no, why would you think that?"

"Because your 'home', that pigsty lock-up was busted last night?"

"Oh, yeah, that's not my home. It's just where I based my operations, but there were no drugs there, or anything to lead to me so—"

"So where are you?"

"At home. Why?"

"Because I have a friend with me, who needs your help. Come over now. I'll make it worth your while."

Grody shrugged. If he had no more income from the girls, he'd have to keep Revox sweet.

"Okay, but it'll be about an hour."

He sent a text to Darren, summoning him, then stood (carefully) and got ready to go.

HANNAH called Dash from the payphone on the stairs. It rang but she didn't pick up. She'd wanted

to tell her about visiting times so after the beep,
she left a message. She was feeling disconnected from
the world, isolated from everything she loved. She
needed a connection. But no one was answering.

DASHA dreamt there was a vibration deep within
her. Maybe it was her ovaries? Her body-clock
reminding her that time was marching on ?
It started vibrating again. It was very pleasant.
She felt groggy, like she'd had too much sleep; but
also like she hadn't had enough. She awoke in the
dark.
Just one sliver of light above her stopped it
from being pitch black. She wasn't bound or gagged.
She was still in her own clothes, lying on a bed,
covered in a duvet. She felt around her, and
everything was soft and padded. She wasn't in a bed;
she was lying on the floor of a padded cell. She stood
up and felt along the walls. Each one was about three
metres. In one corner she found a loo with styrofoam
covering everything but the ceramic bowl. Above it was
a sink in an alcove with soap, a plastic cup and a
toothbrush. In another corner was a pile of clothes:
Pyjamas; leggings; tops and a towel.
She reached up and touched the ceiling which was
also padded. She squeezed her fingers into the slot
where the light was coming from, hooked her fingers
over an edge, then pulled herself up, so her nose and
one eye were in line with the slot. A beam of light
streamed across her view, illuminating the dust
hanging in the still, musty air outside. Then
everything dimmed as the sun maybe went behind a
cloud? She could see the ceiling above: An old-style
vaulted stone (covered in cobwebs) like a cellar or a
crypt would have. When she lowered herself, she
realized she'd got a splinter in her finger from the
un-sanded wood the cell had been constructed from. She
guessed it had been built in the larger room next to a
window? Maybe there were other cells, holding Amber
and Elsie nearby?
She wondered if there were cameras in her cell?
There were types that could film in complete darkness.
What were they? Infrared? There didn't seem to be, but
they could be easily recessed. But they worked on heat
anyway so it wouldn't be a problem.
"Who are you?" said a voice.
Dash jumped thinking there was someone else in the
cell with her. But then she realized it was a tinny
voice from a speaker.
"Who are you?"
"I'm Dasha Petrova. Where am I?"

"Why are you here?"

"I don't know."

"How did you get here?"

"Some guy, he must've drugged me?"

"Where were you?"

"In a club in Soho. Can you please let me go now please?"

"What were you doing just now? You were making a noise."

"Can't you see me?"

"I ask the questions."

"Can you see what I'm doing now?" she asked, while giving every wall the finger.

"Oh, we've got a feisty one. Then you can just stay in there, in the dark. We don't need you—"

"No, no, I'm sorry. I was trying to see out the light slot. But I can't. All I've got was a splinter in my finger."

"You sit still and be quiet, ànd we'll see how good a girl you can be."

Then there was no more from the tinny voice. It was good they couldn't see her, but they *could* hear her. She took her overcoat off, her sweatshirt and jeans, her one-piece stage costume then got under the duvet.

She licked two fingers, reached around her knickers and slowly pushed them inside herself. She felt the rolled edge of the condom and hooked a finger over it, then pulled on it, slowly easing her phone out of its hiding place. Curling into a ball, she unwrapped it and looked at the little screen. Latest call was the payphone at Hannah's rehab; missed calls from Eva, Valerie, Aji and Mickey; and lots of texts. She didn't want to waste the battery reading them all so she composed a text message and sent it to Hannah, Eva and Mickey, then turned off the phone and returned it to its hiding place.

She stayed under her duvet and tried to collect her thoughts. She had wanted to find out what had happened to Amber and if this was it, then there was hope she could find her and free them both. She must bind her time. No, that didn't sound right. Bite her time? No. Bide? Yes, bide her time.

MICKEY was waiting in his car outside Art's flat. He had tried calling him but got no reply. His gaze swapped between the two sides of the street, trying to figure out which window would be the dealer's. Probably the third of forth? If Art didn't show in another five, he'd start knocking on doors.

He popped the boot. Under the spare wheel was a heavy steel box welded to the car. He unlocked it and took out his automatic pistol and a loaded magazine. His heart ached at the thought of Dash going missing. Art couldn't go too.

A scooter stopped on the corner of Portobello Road and a guy in a red helmet got off. The Zorro that Eva had been talking about. The dealer must have called for reinforcements.

GRODY was limping towards Revox's block when he saw the bloke jogging towards him smiling. Dark guy; floppy hair; smart suit and glasses. It never crossed his mind that he was going to do anything, then, once he was at the bottom of the stairs he felt something sticking in his back, and an arm around his neck.

"Which flat is it?"

"Who's flat?"

"The one you were going to?"

"Revox's? 3b."

"Then let's go." he said, loosening his grip around Grody's neck, "but remember I still have this." He waved the pistol in Grody's face, then shoved it hard into his back. They walked up, Grody wondering why bad things always happened to him.

Outside Revox's door, the bloke hung back while he pressed the bell.

"Finally!" said Revox, opening the door.
The bloke struck Grody on the head and he blacked out.

Ten minutes later: When he came to, Grody was wet, lying on a rubber sheet on Revox's floor with three men looking down at him. An empty water jug sat on his stomach.

"Well Grody! You missed quite a Mexican Standoff there," said Revox, holding his forty-five in one hand and a cleaver in the other, "we nearly blew each other's heads off!"

Revox and Mickey re-enacted the scene holding their guns to each other's heads and twitching their fingers on the trigger, gritting their teeth and pushing the barrel aggressively. Everyone laughed, except Grody. His head ached, his eye ached, his ribs ached, and his balls ached.

"Let me introduce these two reprobates to you. The bloke who coshed you so efficiently used to run *all* drug imports and deals in the entire city of Milan; can you imagine Grody? Puts our little enterprises to shame doesn't it? And you won't believe it but the bloke from over the road wasn't watching me," laughed Revox, "he really was there before I

moved in, and he is none other than the infamous
Artemis Grime!"

"Really," said Grody, looking at the tall bloke
who'd impaled him on those railings, "never heard of
him."

"What? The 'King of Drug-Pigs'? Inventor of the
'Flyaway Stag-night'?"

"Nope."

"I'm not exactly proud of either of those—"

"Well he knows you." interrupted Revox, "he knows
you drugged and abducted a schoolgirl from a Halloween
party; that you were running the bar at a Fireworks do
on Wednesday where you abducted a sixth-form girl, and
that you did the same to his friend at Blacks last
night."

"Shit."

"Yes Shit! Grody, you shit! What kind of
perverted shit are you into? Artie here, thinks you're
burying them alive—"

"No, I was just imagining—"

"No!" shouted Grody, "I'm just finding them! I
don't touch them—"

"So you're being paid to do this? I wondered
where all your extra cash was coming from. What the
fuck have you got yourself mixed up in?"

"I only did it cuz I owed you so many thousands
of—"

"Don't you dare blame me! No one asked you to go
double or quits—"

"You did as a matter of fa—"

"Don't change the subject! So what can you say to
stop me slicing and dicing you right here?"
Revox swung the cleaver through the air above his
head.

"Okay! They've cut me loose anyway. I'm out, so I
don't care. He already knows this," he pointed at the
tall impaler, "I drive the car to Berkeley Square and
a tow-truck comes to collect it. But what he doesn't
know is I'm not the only one doing this. There's
others, and they park in the same spot."

MICKEY turned to Art and whispered,

"So we could stake out Berkley Square if nothing
else."
He texted Eva, telling her about Zorro/Grody and
Berkeley Square.

"And what happens to the girls?" asked Revox,
"where are they taken?"

"I don't know, no one tells me anything, sorry."

Revox ran the cleaver down Grody's sternum, adding pressure as he ran it back up again, slicing his shirt.

"But I do know that there's a cop involved in the team. I got stopped the other day and was about to be searched and this plainclothes just popped up and spoke with the traffic cops and they went away. He was a tiny fella, looked about twelve in a trench-coat way too big for him. Name was Inspector Gâjhette."

"Inspector Gadget?"

"Gâjhette," he corrected, "pronounced Gâjhette." Mickey texted Eva again at Scotland Yard. Could she rat this cop out to them, right there and then?

EVA had written a statement, then been waiting hours to speak to anyone. Maybe it was a test? Maybe they got lots of hoaxers in everyday and this was their way of filtering the bullshit? Seemed reasonable. Finally she was called by the Desk Sergeant and she approached the counter:

"I have read your statement; three abductions in the past week by the same man)? Extraordinary. Though this is the first we've heard of the Windsor one? No one has reported anyone going missing at that party." Eva fired off a text to Art:

> *"Windsor Girl not reported missing to police."*

"How about a girl called Elsie? That's her name, she might be around sixteen?"

"I can look into that," he said, writing on a pad.

A text arrived from Mickey saying,

> *"With Art and ZORRO/Grody who says others like him are dropping their 'cars' in same location. Berkeley Square is the place to be this evening!"*

"But," said the Desk Sergeant, "we've already found CCTV of your escapade in the West End last night, and hopefully soon we will also find the recovery vehicle which took away your friend."

Her phone vibrated. A text from Dash!

> *"Hi! I'm alive!*
> *In a small dark padded cell.*
> *Can you trace my phone?*
> *Sorry, was really stupid idea.*
> *Acted on impulse.*

Text again when I know more X"

Eva's heart leapt! There was hope!

"Can you track a mobile phone these days?" she asked excitedly.

"Oh yes, through the transmission masts. It's quite accurate if there's enough masts around because then you can triangulate the distances..." he tailed off as he looked up. Eva turned as a small man entered carrying a briefcase, but it looked like a suitcase next to his miniature body.

"Ah, here's the man who will know more about this whole thing. May I introduce Inspector Gâjhette."

Another text arrived from Mickey:

"Also there's a cop involved
called Inspector Gadget!"

"Inspector Gadget?" said Eva out loud, then laughed.

The Inspector squinted at her and said:

"Actually it's Gâjhette," he corrected, "pronounced Gâjhette." He placed his briefcase on the counter and said,

"Bad news I'm afraid; there's some footage of the recovery vehicle, but then it just disappears, sorry. We've scoured the area, so maybe it went into an underground car-park? We're going to search all those next."

Eva looked up, then down again at her phone, then up again. She was elated and devastated simultaneously. Eva was alive, but the police wouldn't be any help in finding her.

"Oh, okay," she said as she stood, "will you keep me informed of any developments?"

"Absolutely," he said, "and if you think of anything you know where to find us."

She opened the door and said 'Bye'. They both looked at her, and in unison, gave her a little wave.

MICKEY's phone pinged. He showed Art the text from Dash and they both smiled. At least she was alive, and they had a lead, however tenuous.

"How were you recruited?"

"I don't know. I was approached by a man who said he'd been watching me and thought I'd be perfect for the job. He called me a sociopath, which I didn't understand at the time. He told me a car would be provided, along with the purple powder, a disposable phone and instructions on best practices. I've never spoken to him or seen him again."

"So how did he know you were the perfect sociopath for the job?"

"He must've had some prior knowledge?"

"I'm not a sociopath, I'm an—"

"Access to your data? Do you have a criminal record?"

Grody nodded.

"For?"

"Breaking and entering; mugging; kiting; sexual assault; affray..."

"And you don't think you're a sociopath?"

"You kidnap girls for money."

"But I could be just snatching them off the street but I do it in a stylish way—"

"And that makes you *not* a sociopath?"

"So it must've been another cop?"

"Maybe."

"What do you mean when you say they've cut you loose?" asked Art.

Grody shrugged,

"I think they might've disapproved of my choice last night? She was probably twice the age of—"

Art trod on his ribs and he screamed. Mickey pulled Art off and told Grody to continue.

"Normally, I would've received a text by now on this Motorola, but..." he examined the phone; the tiny clock on the front was wrong. He flipped it open and the screen was blank, with some jagged green lines and patches across it,

"But it's broken!"

Grody held it up exultantly, as if he was a hero, instead of what they all thought he was.

Mickey said,

"We can swap the SIM into another phone, can't we?"

Revox smiled and held up a spare phone. Grody handed the SIM to Revox who inserted it.

"Maybe I haven't been cut loose? Maybe I can carry on wi—"

"Maybe I'll kill you with my bare hands here and now."

The phone pinged. Revox opened it and said,

"It says, '*Strange choice. no car for you today*'."

"So they haven't cut you loose," said Art, "but they are punishing you for... what?"

Grody looked nervous about saying anything:

"No offence but she probably wasn't a virgin?"

"Then why did you take her?"

"She wanted to be taken! I waited for her at the stage door of her theatre to ask her out, just to find

out how much she knew. I was in disguise but she
must've realized it was me. She wanted to be taken!"
    "And you wanted to dispose of her!"
    "She asked if I had anything to smoke, so I gave
it to her."
Art nodded to Mickey and seemed to accept that.
    "She wanted to find out what had happened to
Amber, but that was an extreme way of going about it."

    DASHA had an idea. With the phone flipped (or
was it unflipped?), it would fit into the light slot
and she'd be able to take a photo, like a periscope on
a submarine. She stood, took the photo (coughing to
cover the click), then dropped and rolled under the
duvet. On the screen, she was surprised to see
(through a grimy window) a cloudy sky over a horizon
of rolling hills. One large Georgian house was visible
across a valley, surrounded by trees, and farmland
where cows(?) or sheep(?) were grazing. So she wasn't
in London; maybe not even in England? No, her phone
would have alerted her with messages about roaming
charges, and anyway it looked like the English
countryside.
    A few messages had arrived from Eva (I'm at
Scotland Yard. We will get you back), Aji (Sorry for
Flora/Lori mix up, Marcus's attentions, etc), and
Mickey (we have Zorro. We have a lead. We will find
you); nothing from Art though, which was surprising,
or maybe not, considering she'd punched him.
    To save battery, she sent the same message to
Eva, Mickey and Hannah describing the photo, including
details of the house, the poplar trees, and the river
running across the valley.
    She then took a photo in the opposite direction
(coughing to cover the click): The roof of her cell
covered in cobwebs, plumbing and wiring, beyond which
were more roofs with wiring, all enclosed in a large
musty cellar. She could just make out six tiny windows
in the background, each with a cell roof below it.
    She sent another text to Eva describing the
photo, then read back over Eva's unread texts from the
previous night:

            "*No Dash! Don't be stupid!
            Don't get in that car!*"

            "*Please! I can't get hold
            of Mickey to follow you.
            Getting a cab. Are you
            100% sure about this?!*

*"Art is coming. We cannot
lose you! We're gonna
capture Zorro and free you
from the car which has
broken down in West End."*

*"We chased Zorro. I caught him.
He told us a tow truck was coming.
When we got back, the car was gone.
So sorry. We will find you. Xxx"*

*"So relieved you're alive.
And we will find you.
We have leads! Xxx"*

*"Sorry Darling -
we can't trace your phone.
The police are in on it. Xxx"*

So Art had come to her rescue; that was interesting.
It had looked like he was in for the night with that
girl from his past.

"So let me get this straight," said ART, "is
such a fucking lazy way to start a scene. Oh yeah,
he's just explained it all to me, and now I'm gonna
repeat it back because I'm so thick that—"
       "No, it's not that he's thick—"
       "If he isn't thick, why does he have to get it
straight?"
       "It's shorthand—"
       "Because the writer is so lazy, he can't think of
an original line to start a summary? How many actors
have had to say those words without rolling their
eyes?"
       Revox laughed and nodded his head. Art felt his
nose dribbling and turned away from Mickey, who so
far, hadn't noticed anything odd, fingers crossed. He
wiped his nose and winked at Revox.
       "So, to summarize, we're gonna stake out Berkeley
Square nightly, until maybe Grody is forgiven by his
paymasters, when he'll get a text on this phone
detailing what type of car and where it is?"
       "Yes, with more purple powder, another Motorola,
and the cash for..." Grody looked at the carpet.
       "Why *can't you* text them, asking for a meet?"
asked Mickey.
       "They don't answer any texts," explained Grody,
"I only ever text '30 mins' or 'Running late'. That's
it."

Mickey nodded.

"So I will keep this SIM," said Revox, "and tell you all when the text arrives."
Art paced the room,

"Which means we don't even need this scummy little shit, at all, for anything, do we?"

"Unless Berkeley Square is being watched?" suggested Revox.

"I think it is!" said Grody, "I should at least drive the car to the square—"

"But I so want to hurt you slowly and completely, you pathetic little cunt!"

"And you will Artie!" said Revox, "just not yet."

"So how are we gonna ensure he doesn't just fuck off?"

"Good point," said Mickey, "can he stay here with you?"

"No way, I've got clients in and out all day, what about you guys?"

"I'll gladly take him," said Art, "but I can't guarantee he'll be alive for long."

"Same for me," said Mickey.

"Then I'll ask Maurice to babysit him."
Grody did not look happy,

"But, but—"

"No buts! You truly are a cunt Grody," said Revox, "You know what the definition of a cunt is Grody? A cunt is someone who, when you point out an obvious failing, defect or crime, cannot understand your point. They still can't even countenance the idea that they are wrong, but even if they do, they don't care."

Art nodded and advanced on Grody. Mickey steered Art towards the door, nodding over his shoulder.

ART and Mickey left Revox's flat, and walked downstairs, Art cradling the little baggies that Revox had given him, in his pocket.

"Revox is actually a reasonable fellow when you get to know him, isn't he?"

"Or he gets to know *you*." smiled Mickey, "always handy to be famous amongst the low-lifes."
They crossed the street.

"So it looks like we'll be spending more time in the car again. I'll get the mini-fridge put back in the boot, and you'll need to have a shower."
Art shrank away from him,

"Sorry, what do I smell of?" he said, fearing the worst.

"Sex mainly, and smoke" said Mickey.

Art was relieved that he hadn't smelt whiskey on his
breath, or any of the other substances, but had he had
sex? He had no recollection of that.
Art said,
    "Well, I'll go have a shower and we'll talk in a
bit, yeah?"
But Mickey kept following him up the stoop.
    "Are you alright?" he asked, "you were behaving
very strangely up there."
    "Strangely?"
    "Walking into a gunman's flat like the Artemis
Grime of old, kicking Grody, threatening to torture
and kill him—."
    "Sorry, this whole thing's been very stressful. I
should go lie down with a damp flannel over my
face..." But Mickey was following him up the stairs.
    "Oh shit! I think I left the grill on!" said Art,
running ahead. He bounced upstairs and checked round
the flat for drug paraphernalia, then peeped round the
door to his bedroom as Mickey entered. Lori was not
there.
    "We're meant to be moving to Brook Green
tomorrow," announced Mickey, "somewhere warm and cozy,
but big windows for flinging wide in the summer."
    "Sounds great! It'll be nice to have you back in
the area."
    "Yeah. I've missed it: they've been moving our
stuff in over the last few days."

    MICKEY sat down, took his automatic from his
pocket and placed it on a pile of papers on the table.
    "I dread telling Aji about Dash," said Art,
"unless Eva's already texted her?"
    "If she did, she would've also told her that she
is alive," said Mickey, "speaking of which, she told
me you were caught with your trousers down by all the
girls, and Dash punched you!"
Art laughed,
    "It was ludicrous as I was entirely innocent at
the time, and was fully clothed! It was Lori who had
disrobed, and I did feel kind of entrapped by her?" He
scowled at the memory and held his bruised jaw. Then
he smiled sheepishly and said,
    "But then we did end up making out after they'd
all left, so I don't have a leg to stand on."
They both laughed.
    "She *Femme Fatale*'d you."
    "Yup. We were snogging and disrobing, when Eva
texted me the S.O.S—"
    "And you left?"

"I ummed and ahhed for 30 seconds, but yes; I was out of here—"

"So, when it came to the crunch," said Mickey, "you chose Dash over Lori?"

ART thought for a moment, then smiled,

"I guess I did," then a shadow passed over his face, "but Lori *has* bewitched me Mickey; my first love all grown up. In a way it's been very—"

He heard the loo flush and turned to see Lori walk in. She was just wearing the man's shirt with her long brown legs exposed to the cold. She hugged herself and said,

"Can I put the heating on?" then noticed Mickey who stood and smiled. They introduced themselves and Mickey offered her coffee,

"...as Art's obviously not in a fit state to handle a kettle at the moment."

Lori looked at him standing there and said,

"I think I've broken him."

Mickey laughed and filled the kettle.

"So you're another victim of this author's desire for his book to be in the *True Crime* section?" said Mickey.

"Yeah, but I could just deny it when anyone asked. I imagine that was impossible for you?"

"Yes."

They both looked at Art, who ran from the room saying,

"I'll put on the heating and get you my dressing gown."

He heard her saying 'So where have you two come from...' as he went into the bathroom and locked the door. He leant over the sink and examined himself in the mirror. He was so obviously pinned – the curse of having blue eyes – but also he had some soot on his nose from chasing the dragon at Revox's and his nostrils looked a bit crusty. Shit, Mickey was bound to notice, if he hadn't already. They'd used together a lot a decade earlier before they both got clean, and Mickey knew all his peccadillos. He washed his face then tried to have a pee, but couldn't. The smack had strangled his prostate. He sat down and tickled his tailbone (an old junkie trick), and his pee started flowing.

When he emerged, Lori was wearing the leather overcoat, drinking coffee and sitting at the table chatting amiably with Mickey,

"...so we're gonna stake out the square until we spot another tow-truck, then follow it."

Lori nodded and smiled at Art as he joined them. She didn't seem fazed by the automatic pistol sitting next to her coffee cup. She said "May I?" to Mickey, who nodded, so she picked it up and ran her fingers over its contours. Art poured some coffee and joined them.

MICKEY nodded to Lori and she picked the gun up, revealing the paper it was sitting on. It looked like a contract for something to do with the Head book.
"What's that?" he asked.
Art looked and there was a pause before he spoke,
"It's a contract I've been sent by Zal. Someone would like to develop the book to turn it into—"
Lori squinted at him, saying,
"But you'd leave me out of it completely, right?"
Art nodded vigorously at the girl with the gun,
"Anyway, I haven't signed it."
Mickey looked more closely at the papers.
"I told Aji, if it's between Mickey or the money, then I choose Mickey."
Mickey put the papers down and said,
"It's fine, it makes it so much easier to sit down," then asked, "so who could play me? Ben Affleck? Or Keanu Reeves?"
"I was thinking Rowan Atkinson?"
"Vin Diesel?"
"Rupert Grint?"
"Matt Damon?"
"Keira Knightley?"

HANNAH found climbing the stairs easier; less exhausting. And she wasn't late for Group; things were improving. But Mr Potato Head was no different. He seemed to take great pleasure in 'digging people out', which in some cases meant making people cry. When he focussed on her, she said,
"Could I be assigned to a different group with a female counsellor?"
"Why?"
"Because I find you offensive in so many ways."
"Why? What have I done?"
"You seem to take pleasure in bullying us, and you're very patronizing to the females in the room."
"Ah now *Little Lady*, hold your horses—"
"You see? You just called me *little lady*."
"But that doesn't mean I'm patronizing you; I'm just giving you a nick-name, you are indeed *little*, and a *lady*," he air-quoted.
She air-quoted too as she said,
"Okay, *beer-bellied, baldy*—"
"How dare you call me that!"

"I'm just giving you a nick-name, you are indeed *bald*, and you have a *beer-belly*."
The others laughed as he shook his head.
"Okay," said Hannah, "how about Mr Potato Head?"
"Get out of here!" he shouted, pointing at the door.
"Oh, no! Your bullying patronisations are the only thing keeping me clean!" she said as she exited. This wasn't working. If she didn't get assigned to a different group, then she'd re-evaluate. She felt detoxed which was great, so maybe she could just go to lots of meetings to rebuild her cleantime? She'd done it before.

EVA was on her scooter, cruising back from Scotland Yard, when Mickey called.
"Art's relapsed."
"Shit! Must've happened after he left me last night at Berkeley Square, I'm guessing with Lori?"
"Yeah, he smelt of sex... or maybe it was smack?"
"I never knew they smelled similar?"
"Only if you've done anal!"
Eva laughed and almost crashed her scooter, then asked,
"You gonna take him to a meeting?"
"Not today, just going to watch for now," said Mickey, then he changed the subject, "so we'll stake out the square this evening? Come join me when you finish—"
"I don't want to go to work tonight."
"So they'll be two down?"
"Shit, yes! I'll have to go. Fuck! Are you coming back to Hampstead? We need to check on the removal men."
He said yes and they hung up. Could she go to another police station and report Inspector Gadget? No, they might all be in on it. Maybe the papers?

JOSEPH ushered Kirsten into the lobby and pushed the door shut.
"I'm just drafting it, but it says we agree to a one-time usage in one publication—"
"And I can use them in my book?"
"What book?"
"My portfolio that I show around to clients?"
"Okay, sounds reasonable," he said typing on the old electric machine that had been there forever, "now tell me where you met Natalie Anderson."
"Right outside that door, when we were leaving on Saturday? She must've been waiting for us? She pushed a fifty pound note into my hand and asked if we'd been

in Karen Ford's place and I said yes and she gave my
boyfriend a fifty. Then she asked about my reference
and I said I'd used Models One and she gave me another
fifty. Then she said could she use Models One too and
held out a more fifties! I mean, what was I expected
to do? There seemed no harm in it?"

Joseph raised his eyebrows and took a long look
at her. She clearly didn't understand the definition
of the word reference.

"So she gave me two hundred in advance for Jeff
to type another letter and we arranged to meet once it
was done for the final payment. To make the swap like
some cold-war spies—"

"So where did you meet?"

"I would've liked to have done it in some
glamorous bar like Harry's or the Connaught, but she
was unwell so I delivered it to her flat."
Joseph smiled. It was his day off tomorrow.

AJI sat with Art at their table while he told
her about Dash. It took her a while to accept the
news, and then she was heartbroken.

"But we have something to give us hope: Staking
out the square tonight, so we will find her, and
rescue her."
His dad sounded adamant, but she wasn't convinced,

"But anything could happen in the meantime! She
might be in a container on her way to Rotherham right
now"

"You are right, but don't allow your imagination
to go there. You could go crazy very quickly. Why
don't you go to your mum's and—"

"No way! I'm coming with you tonight."

"It'll be late and—"

"I'm always up until one anyway!"

DASHA wasn't sure how long she'd been in pitch
black darkness as she kept dozing off. She sat up and
found her clothes. Her coat still had the inflatable
head in the big pocket and some tube tickets and cash
in the smaller ones. The makeup and mirror were
missing though. It was too hot for her sweatshirt and
jeans so she felt for the pile of clothes and put on a
tank-top and yoga pants.

The darkness and silence was weighing on her but
she resisted the urge to get out her phone for some
connection to the outside world. The others must have
had their phones taken when they arrived, and how long
had they been in the silent dark?

She heard a click. Another crack of light
appeared, but this one was vertical. A door? She

crawled over and it was: A heavy padded door. She
pulled on it gently then peered through the crack. A
well-lit room with pot plants, a T.V. and modern soft
furnishings in muted colours. No one else was around,
so she opened the door enough for her to squeeze
through on all fours. She hid behind a chaise longue
and looked again. It was a glass walled box maybe
two/three metres wide and six metres long, little
spotlights in the ceiling. To either side were
identical rooms, and in front was a hall with a table
and sofa, then other identical rooms opposite.

Dash crawled along the left side. There, in the
next room, a girl lay on her chaise watching T.V.,
maybe about seventeen? Very pretty; dark shoulder-
length hair; thick eyelashes. She was wearing the same
shirt and yoga pants as Dash, but also what looked
like her own coat on top.

Dash knocked on the glass, but it was so soft her
knock made no sound; maybe it wasn't glass? She got up
and walked nearer the front, into the girl's field of
vision. The girl jumped up, startled; then smiled and
came nearer, saying something Dash couldn't hear,
pointing to some holes drilled in the glass.

The girl asked,
"Who are you?"
"I'm Dasha. I arrived... was it last night?"
"Yes, it was. I'm Elsie."
"Hello Elsie. How did you end up here?"
"I was kidnapped from a Fireworks night party."
"In that coat?"
"Yeah, I've still got everything I had on me
except my phone."
"Same with me. Is there a girl called Amber
here?"
"Yeah, she's right next to me," said Elsie
pointing over her shoulder, "she got taken at a
Halloween party so all she's got is her Catwoman
costume—"
"I know Amber, I was at that party."
Elsie just nodded and said,
"And the other side of Amber there's Jenny. She
got drugged by the river in Richmond when she'd run
away from home, so she's got loads of stuff with her,
including her teddy, but her parents won't even be
looking for her," she said, shaking her head, "we
think it was the same man who brought us here."
"Bushy moustache? Dark, dark eyes? Bad teeth?"
"That's him. Amber said he called himself Grody."
"So why were we taken?"
"Apparently, Amber and Jenny attended a dinner
party upstairs last week and rich old perverts came

and looked everyone over, then a few girls left with them in helicopters. Though if you mention it to Jenny she can't even remember a week ago."

"You seem very calm about this?"

"Oh, we're all being gassed. I can smell it: My one's a relaxant."

"I do feel quite loose too," said Dash, "considering our situation."
Elsie nodded,

"Seems like sometimes it's oxygen, as a reward or a pick-me-up; sometimes it's laughing gas for someone who's sad; sometimes it's painful, if someone's been bad, but most times it just makes us sleep and forget," she shrugged, "I may seem calm on the outside but I'm spazzing out on the inside. There's another dinner party tomorrow night but I don't want to go."

"You don't have to worry about that now. Please tell Amber that Dasha is here when she wakes up. Tell her to keep quiet about knowing me please?"
Elsie nodded and sat back down. She seemed drained.

Dash looked in the room on the other side of hers, but it was empty, meaning this side had Grody's collection in chronological order? Maybe the other side held another 'collector's' victims? She looked across the hall at the others. They were all good-looking tweens and teenagers taking up all six rooms. So that was ten in all, out of twelve.

The lights got brighter in the rooms and the hall went dark. Elsie backed away, as did many of the others but Dash moved to the front of her box, shading her eyes with her hands. Three figures, all in silhouette, entered the hall from the left: Two women (one small, one enormous) and a man, who was saying,

"...so I won't be able to make it unfortunately, so shall we say two mill flat? Then you know you're not losing out by me missing the auction tomorrow?"

"Sounds reasonable," said a female voice, "depending on which you choose of course."
Dash wasn't sure of his accent - somewhere in the middle-east?
He scanned the rooms and walked up and down, Dash following him. He stopped and watched her,

"She is magnificent," he said, "the way she moves, like a cheetah."

"She's brand new, hasn't even started the process," said a woman's voice, "none of these on this side are ready, except Jenny there on the far-right. She's willing."

"It's not exactly a priority for me," he said, laughing.
The woman laughed too,

"And on the other side," she said, turning, "the
blonde girl on the far-right has been here the
longest, so is the most pliant."
He turned back and pointed at Dash,
    "She looks gutsy, but she's not a youth, is she?"
    "Not quite, but our scouts are hand-picking these
fruits for your delectation and they are instructed to
provide a wide range of—"
    "And certainly not a virgin!" he laughed,
"Anyway, I've already made up my mind. From all the
videos I chose..." he span around like a game-show
host, "this one!" stopping and pointing to a dark girl
opposite Dash. She screamed and sobbed. The two women
opened the door and went in. The girl ran into her
cell and tried to shut the door but the burly one
extracted her and carried her out.
    "Be careful! Don't hurt her!" exclaimed the man,
who turned to Dash and brought his face so close to
the glass, it became lit by her room;
    "That's my job," he smirked.

MICKEY scanned the square for CCTV and decided
on a spot which wasn't under surveillance, then
parked.
Art and Aji sat in the back.
    "Are we okay here?" asked Aji.
    "Yeah. I look like just another Limo Driver
waiting for their master. I even put this hat on the
dashboard." Aji nodded.
Nothing. No tow truck. Eva arrived, got in the back
too. Nothing. No tow truck. Aji fell asleep on Eva.
Nothing. No tow truck. Eva fell asleep. Art yawned and
farted. Nothing. No tow truck. At 1am they went home
to bed.

DASHA, assured by Elsie that everyone slept in
their cells, crawled into hers, lay down and pulled
the duvet around her; but she felt claustrophobic so
took her duvet into her room and lay on the chaise
longue. The dinner party tomorrow night sounded like
the perfect time to stage an escape.

ART felt terrible. All the drugs had left his
system and he was yawning and farting and his eyes
were weeping. So far though, no one had clocked him.
Mickey dropped them off and he and Aji walked
upstairs. His knees felt like buckling and he had to
use the bannisters for the first time to make it to
the top. Aji went straight to bed while he went and
sat at his board. There was Revox's one eye peeping

213

out through his curtains, scanning the street. When he
saw Art he opened the curtains and waved. Then
beckoned him over...

DASHA awoke and looked around her. It hadn't
been a bad dream - it was her reality; or was she
still dreaming? She was lying on the chaise in her
room, surrounded by other identical rooms. The lights
were dimmed but she could see two other girls also
sleeping on their chaise. The girl opposite Dash on
the far-right got up. She looked around her, walked
back to her cell then charged towards the front,
headbutting a steel door-hinge with such ferocity she
bounced backwards onto the floor. Dash got up and
waved frantically, trying to catch her eye. The girl
did see her, but just held her finger to her lips and
solemnly shook her head, which was bleeding badly. She
got up and did it again, like a footballer running and
heading the ball into the net, except there was no
celebration. Dash watched her crawl back again, blood
pouring on the carpet. Should she scream? Bring
someone? Or watch this silent snuff movie play out?
The girl clearly wanted to die as she ran at the door-
hinge again and bounced off; but this time she didn't
get up. A smear of blood ran down the glass. Three
women entered from the left and the smaller one
examined the girl's bleeding head, opening a first aid
kit. The other two, who were much bigger, just carried
the girl out to a door on the right, bickering about
which one of them hadn't been watching the monitor.
The small woman shook her head, then saw Dash watching
her and ran through the door on the left.
    Dash was groggy, and not sure if it was a
nightmare or a horror movie. She heard the hissing of
gas...

Saturday - 8th November

DASHA awoke in her dark cell, milky light seeping in the slot above her, but no light from the door which was closed. She lay there dozing for maybe an hour, her dreams spiralling down into horror shows. Finally, she decided she must at least sit up and when she did the lights came on, for which she was grateful. Already, she was grateful for small mercies, in only one day. Was that how it worked? How they broke you? In the corner by the loo, she saw a drain in the floor; above it was a shower head recessed in the ceiling. She smelt her armpits and thought she'd take advantage of that. She sat on the loo and peed, then brushed her teeth in the tiny basin. The shower controls were also in the sink's alcove. She turned the water on and stripped off. It was a good shower and the padding shrugged it off well.

There was a towel along with the clothes, so she dried off then put on a T-shirt and leggings. It made her feel better for a while.

She checked her phone. Messages of love and support from everyone, including Art:

> *"Dash, my love,*
> *I'm so sorry I couldn't save you.*
> *I have fucked up severely.*
> *I will rescue you.*
> *Then you can rescue me.*
> *I love you XXX*
> *PS, is Amber there?*
> *& a girl called Elsie?*
> *XXX"*

It was very unlike Art. Very gushy and he'd sent it at 4.30am. What was he doing up at that time? Was it the guilt? She heard her door unlock and a bell ring, so she concealed her phone then went out.

GRODY heard sounds in the hall. The boys were there. A teenager knocked on the office door and popped his head round.

"Thanks boy. I'll be five minutes."
He opened his locker and reached in for his outfit. Maurice sat at the desk, watching him.
"Would you excuse me while I change?"
"Change?"
"Into my uniform?"

Maurice didn't move. Just smiled, then went back
to playing 'Bejewelled' on his phone.
     "Look, there's no way I could squeeze through
that tiny window is there? So why don't you join the
others in the hall and I'll be out in five minutes,
okay?"
Maurice carried on playing until he reached the end of
the level, then got up and left.

     In Mike's Café, ART and Aji ate their breakfast
in silence, both pondering the fate of the three girls
who had been taken by Zorro.
     "At least we know Dash is alive," said Art.
     "In a locked room with a view of the
countryside," said Aji, "so maybe the others are too?"
Art held up his crossed fingers,
     "I felt bad that the last time I'd seen her was
when she'd just punched me. The look of hatred on her
face as she'd walked away..."
Was that the last time he'd ever see her?
     "I got the cold shoulder on the landing for not
telling her that Flora/Lori was in London. Which was
totally your fault for lying to me!"
Art lowered his head and said 'Sorry'.
They both kept checking their phones for news from Eva
or Mickey. Nothing.
     "Good Morning!"
Lori stood smiling down at them, then slid into the
booth beside Art.
     "So what's happening? Any news of Dash?"
     "This is something to do with you isn't it?"
blurted Aji.
     "What? No, of course not—"
     "You arrive and then all this happens—"
     "Aji," said Art, "that really doesn't add up—"
     "Well you would take her side wouldn't you?" she
said, getting up and crashing between the other diners
to the door, "I'm going to my mum's!"
     "Sorry," said Art, "she loves Dash, as do we all;
and now she's gone."
Lori put her arm around Art's shoulders and squeezed,
     "Don't worry, you'll get her back."
He nodded, then shook his head, then nodded,
     "I'm concerned for the girl at the Fireworks; I
left Barry a message, but I don't think he uses his
phone much, which was why he took so long to return my
call originally."
Lori looked confused.
     "Sorry," he said, "meaning he may not have
listened to my one I left on Thursday about—"

"Elsie, right. Maybe we should go back there and talk to Patrice, was it?"

"Good idea."

They sat for a while, watching the other diners and the tourists outside the Travel Bookshop.

"Then, after that maybe we could think about my thing for a bit?"

"Oh sure; sorry Lori. I have been a bit obsessed with this."

"I was thinking we should go round to my house again; stand by Cookie's window to see her field of vision?"

"That's a good idea," said Art.

They got up and left.

JOSEPH got off the tube as Chalk Farm and walked over the railway bridge into Primrose Hill. Carrying straight on, he found the address on the right. Directly opposite was a Café so he went in and ordered a tea and sat in the window. Natalie's flat was on the first floor. He wasn't sure what his plan was, other than to watch, but his new Blackberry phone was distracting him. He'd bought it earlier and loved the QWERTY keyboard. He was practicing using his thumbs the way Eva did, while trying to keep one eye on the door of her place.

GRODY opened the door and peeked out. There were his boys, his Seniors in their uniforms, looking after the younger ones, while being proudly watched over by their parents.

The whole scene made him very proud too. They had set up the tables and retrieved the gear from the lockers, as instructed.

Then he saw Maurice standing by the door with his wraparound shades on, looking like a bouncer, and he remembered.

He shook his head to rid himself of those thoughts, looked in the mirror and straightened his neckerchief, then walked out,

"Welcome Parents to the Boy Scouts annual Winter Sports Weekend! For those that don't know me, I am your Scoutmaster, Gordon Grodenko!"

MAURICE was surprised. Really surprised. He'd thought it weird when they'd come here, but then lots of events happen in Boy Scout huts: Jumble sales; A.A. meetings; Voting; Knitting circles and Fight clubs. He texted Revox the news.

217

DASHA left her cell and walked to the glass door, scanning the cellar: Opposite her, were only four girls: On the far-left, a pretty girl was brushing her long red hair, counting each stroke almost normally but for the tears streaming down her cheeks.

"Hi," shouted Dash, "I love your hair!"
The girl looked up, saw Dash and smiled while wiping away the tears.

"I'm Dasha," she said, waving.
The girl answered but nothing seemed to come out of her mouth. She shook her head and held her throat. She'd lost her voice. Hardly surprising. She blew her a kiss, which made her smile, but also start crying again.

The two next to her looked like identical twins in their mid/late teens? Both skinny, they leant against the glass like perfect mirror images of each other. They were chatting (or plotting?) like normal neighbours over a garden fence. Dash waved at them and they both waved back in unison.

Next to them, a pretty tweenage blonde looked like she was dancing, repeating the same move on a perpetual loop. It reminded Dash of a news report she'd seen about a zoo where they kept the animals in tiny pens no bigger than her own. They filmed a bear repeat a similar action ad infinitum.

That's what this was: A zoo where they were all in pens to be viewed by visitors, except in a zoo the visitors couldn't take the animals home and screw them. Dash turned away to her own side of the hall. Elsie was lying in her same spot watching T.V. and beyond her, there was Amber, who saw her and burst into hysterical tears.

"It's going to be okay Sweetheart, I promise," she shouted, though she didn't know how... yet. Dash held up her hands and placed them on the glass, and Amber did the same, Elsie between them, smiling at the T.V.

The door in the hall opened and the three maids brought breakfast on trolleys. Trays were passed through letterboxes in the glass and the girls took them gratefully, whether they ate anything or not. One asked Dash,

"What would you like for breakfast, Miss?"
Dash looked around and saw everyone had got something different, so she thought of her favourite breakfast from when she was a kid in St Petersburg:

"Two slices of deep-fried bread and a pot of orange marmalade please? And a glass of cold milk?"
The maid nodded,

"Would you like a magazine? We've got Seventeen, Heat, Teen Vogue—"

"Is that the Guardian at the bottom?"

"Yes, probably more appropriate for your age," she said as she passed the newspaper through the letterbox.

"I'm younger than you," she murmured as the maid exited with her trolley. Dash sat at her stylish (but plastic) table with the newspaper and tried to distract herself from her own terrifying circumstance, with the awful reality of war and SARS and drone killings and rendition and famine...

HANNAH inserted her phonecard into the slot and tried calling Eva and Mickey on their landline. Eva answered so she told her about visiting times over the weekend, but Eva seemed distracted.

Hannah asked, "Are you okay?"

"No, Dash's been taken by the same man who took Amber—"

"Oh shit!"

"She let herself be taken, so she could find Amber, and she's in a padded cell—"

"How do you know that?"

"She texted me; her cell is in a building on one side of a valley in the countryside; there's a river running across her view and on the other side is a big house with six tall windows wide, three or four floors high, surrounded by trees and—"

"But there could be any number of houses like that in England."

"Yeah, we don't have a lot to go on—"

"I'll come home and help—"

"No, no. You stay there and help yourself okay?"

"Only if you promise to visit me on Sunday, okay?"

"Okay, we'll drive down, promise."

They hung up and Hannah went to the smoking room. She was back on thirty a day.

DASHA couldn't eat her breakfast when it had arrived, but she had taken it in the same grateful fashion as everyone else. Again with the small mercies. She lay on her chaise longue and turned on her T.V. She needed to turn her mind off for a while, to recover some blind faith. An advert was playing:

Blue sky filled the screen, then the camera panned down to blue sea, with a shoal of fish swimming through the shot. A cute girl and her friends jumped off the side of a big yacht, laughing. A handsome man held his champagne aloft and smiled at them. They all

ate a picnic on the beach, smiling and laughing. The
cute girl and the handsome man played tennis. An
elderly woman waved and smiled. A glamorous wedding.
Many smiling guests. The happy couple cut the cake.
The girl threw her bouquet and laughed. An open-top
Bentley drove them away. Palm trees. A palatial home.
The family ran into shot and chased each other,
laughing. A chef made delicious dishes. The girl took
a shower and dressed in designer couture. Her friends
greeted her and some toddlers scampered through the
shot. She picked one up and hugged him, then kissed
her husband. They all sat down to eat. They laughed
and drank and smiled and laughed. They danced and
laughed and smiled and danced. The girl went to bed
and was cuddled by her handsome man. Blue sky filled
the screen, then the camera panned down to blue sea,
with a shoal of fish swimming through the shot. A cute
girl and her friends jumped off the side of a big
yacht, laughing. A handsome man...

It was looping. Dash tried to change the channel
but that's all there was. She looked over at Elsie,
who was still watching her T.V. A smile kept
flickering across her face.

JOSEPH, two more cups of tea and a sandwich
later, saw Natalie exit the front door pulling a large
suitcase. He guessed she was in her forties, middle-
eastern, good looking and well dressed. He followed
her to Chalk Farm tube and then into a busy southbound
train where they got the last two neighbouring seats.
He turned and looked at her and noticed a scar on her
face, cleanly running straight from her nose to her
right ear. Not the jagged kind you get from going
through a windscreen in a crash.

"Where are you going?" he asked, pointing at the
big suitcase in front of her.

"Sorry," she said without looking at him.

"Now that you got what you came for?"
She turned and looked at him, but there was no
reaction on her face. Joseph was aware that old people
were invisible to the younger. But maybe when they are
seen, they still all look alike?

"Pardon?" she said.

"Now you've acquired the papers from Karen Ford's
apartment?"
Her face changed as she realized who he was.

"Mr Joseph?"

DASHA realized she hadn't told her friends her
news. She went into her cell and got under the duvet

then fired off the same text to Hannah, Eva, Mickey
and also Art:

> *"Still alive! We are on display for sale.*
> *There are eight girls in other cells.*
> *Amber is here & is okay.*
> *Some are a bit brainwashed.*
> *Others are even worse, kind of lobotomized.*
> *Find me! Find us! X"*

JOSEPH said,
"What are the papers you stole from that album
sleeve?"
She looked around her as if to check that there was no
one listening then said,
"It was a letter Karen wrote in the margins of
the insert."
"Who to?"
"To Michelangelo. It said she was leaving him."
"When did Karen write this letter?"
"On the day of the home invasion? She was locked
in the Music Room and could hear her partner being
tortured next door. She wrote that she was gonna run
because couldn't handle the monsters in her home, but
also that she realized she didn't love him enough to
want to stay and suffer alongside him. She was going
to climb out the window of the music room and knock on
the window of her neighbour, Mr Gustav."
Joseph was speechless. It was shocking. But it
sounded true. She'd known where to look, and it
mentioned the name of their neighbour.
"And how do you know this? How did you know where
to look?"
"Because I met Karen and she told me she
regretted the letter and her greatest wish was for
someone to retrieve it."
"When did you meet her?" asked Joseph, "and
where?"
"A few months after her disappearance, in a
helicopter, when we were both being taken out of
England."

ART and Lori rode west to Windsor, her gripping
him tightly.
"So what do you think? Should I stay in London?"
Art's heart skipped a beat. Him and his first
love together again.
"Don't you have anything to get back to?"
She shook her head and their helmets bumped.

"I haven't been able to settle with anyone; I've
been in Tahiti for six months; before that Tokyo..."
Art thought she'd told him she'd been in Tahiti for a
couple of years? He didn't want to interrupt her with
his pedanticism, so remained silent.
    "I've never trusted anyone but you Artie. I wish
we had met on your Book Tour, or even before that. I
should've come back fifteen years ago."
    "You wouldn't've liked me; I was at my worse
then."
    "But I loved your writing, why wouldn't I have
loved you too?"
    "Because Artemis Grime was my alter-ego; a
character I inhabited when I was high; when I wrote my
articles high; when I appeared at Conventions high;
when I... the rest of the time I was low."
    "You were fucked up Artie; I was fucked up. We
would've made the perfect couple."
He watched her in the wing mirror,
    "And you're fucked up now Artie and I find you
much more interesting."
He started to protest then decided against it...

    JOSEPH followed the woman off the train.
    "Where is the insert?" he asked, "I want to see
it."
    "I destroyed it just like she asked," she
replied, "and you can stop following me now, or I'll
call for a guard!"
    "Maybe *I* should call a guard; you are in
possession of something that belongs to the museum I
curate—"
    "I destroyed it!"
He watched her go. Where was he? Leicester Square, and
she was heading for the westbound Piccadilly Line. He
allowed a gap to grow between them then continued
following.

    HANNAH stood in her bedroom and looked wistfully
at the house on the other side of the valley. She
could just make out figures moving in the tall
windows. What were they doing? Probably having more
fun that she was.
    It seemed familiar? The river, the big house with
six tall windows wide, three or four floors high,
surrounded by trees. Wasn't that what Dash had
described as her view? She raced downstairs to the
basement, where the 'so called' counsellors skulked
like troglodytes in their caves; just the kind of
assholes who'd lock up beautiful girls for their own
gratification. She tried all the doors but they all

222

just opened onto the little windowless offices and none showed any sign of a trapdoor to a sub-basement. She was disappointed.

Then she remembered the crypt. The crypt where the godly sheep went to sing Halleluiah of an evening. She ran back up, then out through the smoking room and down the stone steps, below which was the door to the crypt. She turned the big wrought iron handle, but the door was locked.

ART parked in the same spot, outside the mansion. The gates were ajar, so he and Lori walked up the drive and was met by a burly man who seemed to appear from nowhere. He asked if they could help them. Art explained about the Fireworks night party and the man kept repeating what he said into a microphone, but not quite accurately enough for Art's precise nature. Finally, Lori interrupted proceedings by shouting 'Patrice!' repeatedly. The guard asked her to stop, then tried to put his hand over her mouth so she ran, in circles, still shouting, literally running rings around him.

A girl emerged for the house answering to the name of Patrice.

Lori asked her one question:

"Have you seen or heard from Elsie since the party?"

Patrice said no, so Art and Lori told their story. Patrice, once she'd recovered, promised to call the school and find Elsie's parents details.

JOSEPH boarded the Heathrow Express two carriages behind Natalie. He'd been surfing the internet on and off on his new toy, had taken some pictures of Natalie, created a new email address and actually used his Blackberry as a phone! He sent a text stating where he was and where he predicted Natalie would disembark. At Heathrow, he watched as she exited the train and walked to the lifts. He followed at a distance. The platform wasn't very busy and she was the only one who entered the lift, until just as the doors were closing, a tall man leapt round the corner and joined her.

ART and Lori stood in the mews looking up at the house he'd grown up in. It was already dark and Christmas lights were illuminating inside and outside of some houses.

"For fuck's sake, we've only just had Fireworks!" he grouched, "it gets earlier every year!"

223

Lori mimed fanning him with a wet towel.

"Shall we climb over again?" asked Art.

Lori looked pensive,

"No. Let's go in."

They walked up the steps and Art used his key, calling out as they went in. His father was watching the telly as usual, a Rothmans in one hand, a gin and tonic in the other. He actually turned and smiled, so Art smiled back.

"How are you Dad?"

"Still alive."

"I have an old friend with me," Art said, turning to find no one behind him, "but she... seems to..."

His father had already turned back to his program, so Art went downstairs to the kitchen. The back door was open and Lori was crawling through the gap in the hedge. Art decided, this once, to not follow their tradition, and use the gate. Albert's house was covered in flashing lights much to Art's annoyance; making Lori all the more difficult to see in the shadows of the scaffolding. She was standing by Cookie's window, just to the left of the kitchen door. Art joined her. There was a clear view of the garden wall and the trees peering down from Albert's garden; the lawn as it sloped away from the mansion; the shrubbery and the hole in the hedge; but not the gate.

"Do you think someone could've been coming in from my garden?" suggested Art. Lori's eyebrows perked up and her head turned to the side.

"Maybe they climbed over my house, using the wisteria on the outside and the tree on the inside? Just like we did?"

Lori nodded,

"That is definitely possible. Everyone thought this was a sealed area so left their doors open, but it's easy to breach it."

NATALIE was surprised, but not scared. She looked at the tall man with a scarf wrapped round his face and wondered if he was armed.

He held the doors for Mr Joseph, then let them close. The lift stopped at the Terminal, but Natalie's exit was barred. Mr Joseph pressed the button for the Car Park and the doors closed.

"Well, Miss, you have caused a lot of trouble for us and you must now give us the papers and tell the truth. This gentleman has a knife and has assured me, much to my horror, that he has been instructed to stab you ruthlessly, if you attempt to shout or run when we exit the lift, understood?"

DASHA woke up to see three women in the hall
with clothes rails. They were displaying the dresses
to some of the girls who'd been let out of their pens.
It was the ones who'd been there the longest: Jenny
from Dash's side and the three on the right from the
other side: The skinny Twins and the pretty Blonde.
They were looking at dresses and trying them on. The
chatter pleased Dash; more like normality; a bunch of
stoned teenagers in Top Shop. A small woman, who was
clearly once beautiful, dressed in black, stopped with
a rail outside her pen. Dash thought she looked like
the one with the first aid kit from last night. She
half-heartedly looked at the dresses, but then became
impressed by the designer names and that they were all
in her size, and the latest collections. She chose two
and the woman passed them through the letterbox. It
was fun trying them on in the mirror. The girls were
parading for each other, then commenting, and Dash
found she was joining in, even though she knew what
the dresses were for. The woman in black went to help
Elsie with her choices.
When she returned, Dash asked her about the girl who
had hurt herself.
    "What girl?"
    "The girl who head-butted the door?"
    "I'm surprised you remember that."
    "Is she okay?"
The woman looked her in the eye and just shook her
head, whispering,
    "Net."
'Net' was Russian for 'no'. Did the woman know Dash
was Russian?
    "Vy Russkiy?"
The woman nodded, then looked over her shoulder. She
took another dress from her rail and passed it through
to Dash, whispering (in Russian),
    "The girl is dead. Sorry. She was disposed of."
    "Disposed of? In there?" said Dash, looking
towards the door on the right. The woman nodded.
    "What's in there?"
She didn't answer; just shook her head.
    "What's your name?" asked Dash.
    "Olga."
    "Hi Olga, I'm Dash. So meeting a man here is my
only chance of ever seeing the sun again?"
Olga nodded,
    "Unless you become a maid like myself. But I see
little of the sun and have no prospect of release;
security is tight here."
    "So you do get to go outside?"

"Yes, for one hour I'm allowed to run round the compound. In my fantasy, I'm training for a marathon. It is my escape, when I feel free..."

"So what happens if I don't get picked?"

"Well this is the *Dog's* home, and it's run like the one in Battersea," she said, "you get a month, maybe more depending on your attitude, then..."

Dash's heart sank, but she tried to seem positive,

"Well then, I'd better look my best!" she said, holding up her two favourite dresses, "which do you think?"

The woman pointed at the left one, a Roberto Cavalli mini-*cheongsam* in red.

"Very sexy."

"Thank you."

She watched her go. '*This is the Dog's home*', she'd said. Was that her boss? She'd almost spat the word out of her mouth. For a moment, Dash felt there might be hope. Maybe Olga might want in on an escape plan? Why was she feeling so perky? Was there oxygen in the air? She went into her cell and saw her inflatable head, which gave her an idea. She picked it up, took deep breaths of the oxygenated air and blew it into the nozzle.

ART watched Lori contemplating the garden. She was taking deep breaths like she was meditating. Another few minutes passed then she said,

"Is your room the same as when we slept there?"

"Yeah, I still sleep there occasionally, when the old man is unwell."

"Can I see it? And the view from the window?"

Art nodded and they walked down the path to the gate. Lori raised her eyebrows as if questioning whether she could pass through like a grown-up. He held the gate open and she jumped over the threshold. They walked upstairs and Art took her hand, pulling her into his father's room.

"Dad, remember Lori? Richard's twin? She's all grown up!"

His father turned and looked Lori up and down. A smile crept across his lips,

"Hello Lori."

Lori said,

"Hi," and waved, "what are you watching?"

"Oh, don't ask; it's all rubbish."

"So why do you watch it?"

His father stayed silent for a moment, then said,

"I don't know?" he shrugged, "because anything's better than reality?"

Art looked at Lori and whispered,

"Bleak".

DASHA was pleasantly surprised that her phone
hadn't been discovered, guessing that as the others
had all been taken by surprise, there was little
chance of them carrying a concealed weapon, or tiny
phone.
    When she emerged from her cell, there was big
excitement outside in the hall: The doors opposite
were open and the four girls were sitting on the sofas
and trying on shoes, or having their makeup done at
the table. Dash felt excited and maybe slightly
euphoric; was this the oxygen? The T.V. on the end
wall was playing the advert for their new life on
repeat. Some seemed seduced by it. The Blonde was
having her hair brushed by Olga, as it was knotted and
unkempt. Olga was saying something to her and she was
trying to smile. Dash curled up on her chaise and shut
her eyes. The stress was exhausting. Just a catnap.

NATALIE was led to a people-carrier parked in
an under-populated corner of level 5. Mr Joseph got in
the front while the masked man helped her into the
back; then got in himself with her suitcase, throwing
it down in the luggage area. Natalie sat down and
tried to remain calm, refusing when they asked for the
keys to her suitcase. The man shrugged then produced a
knife and proceeded to force the locks.
    "Tell us where you hid it," implored Mr Joseph,
"and you can catch your flight."
But she said nothing, so the man started taking
everything out. She felt agitated but remained silent,
until he took the knife and started cutting into the
lining and ripping it open:
    "Okay! It's in a hidden pocket in the bottom of
the suitcase. I can open it okay?"
Joseph and the man nodded, so she knelt down and felt
for a button in the lining. They heard a click and she
pushed her hand into a cavity.

ART said,
    "We're going to my room dad, don't worry, we'll
leave the door open!"
Art sat on his bed and checked his phone. Lori came
in, shut the door and looked around her. The lights
from Albert's house lit the room. Primary colours
flashed and splashed across the walls. When he looked
up, Lori had a tear in her eye.
    "Aw, is this too much for you? I'm sorry," he
said, holding out his arms to her. She came to him and

227

they lay down and spooned, just like they did all those years ago.

NATALIE pulled out the papers which she handed to Mr Joseph. It was a soft binder with Bearer Bonds inside. He flicked through them and said,
"Maybe two million Eurodollars?" He handed them to the other one, who examined them and nodded.
"So it wasn't a letter?" asked Mr Joseph.
Natalie shook her head and said,
"No, sorry, it was the first thing that I thought of when you asked."
"So none of what you told me was true?"
"Oh no, she did escape through the window, and we were trafficked to Saudi Arabia—"
"When did she die?" asked Mr Joseph.
"She's not dead. I saw her last week. This money is to buy her freedom. So you must let me go. Her life depends on it."

ART woke up and felt for Lori, but she'd gone, just like so many times when they were kids. He opened his eyes and saw her sitting at his desk reading. She turned and smiled at him.
"What are you reading?" he asked.
"Fan mail sent to you all those years ago; the letters you never opened. I found them in the garage; two sacks. They're gushing!"
"Of course they are - that's what fan mail is. Did you find yours? I really want to read yours."
"I'll recognize it when I see it, but then I'll burn it. Very embarrassing! But probably not as embarrassing as the ones I sent you from Lima!"
Art sat up,
"You wrote me letters from Lima?"
"Yes, of course."
"But I never got any letters?"
Lori looked at him quizzically,
"Seriously?"
Art shook his head sadly. His heart ached. He needed more smack.
"You carry on," he said, "I'm gonna smoke in the garden."
"What kind of smoke?"
"The disgusting, stinking kind that temporarily numbs you while also stealing your soul chunk by chunk."
She followed him down,
"I had no idea souls came in chunks."
They walked up into Lori's old garden and sat on the bench. Art retrieved a tin from his pocket. Inside

were some baggies from Revox, squares of tin-foil, a short 3B pencil and a lighter. He made a smoking tube by wrapping some foil around the pencil, which he put in his mouth. Then he fired up the lighter and melted some of the smack onto another piece of foil. He upped the heat and the angle of the foil, so the smack ran downwards with his tube sucking in the resulting fumes. He finally exhaled and passed it all over to Lori who followed suit. They sat there, watching the Christmas lights blinking and pulsating.

"You know what would make this even better?" She pulled an envelope from her pocket. It was one of the fan mail letters.

"You remember in your piece on Tokyo, [8] where you said people used to send you tabs of acid stuck underneath the stamp? Well, I think this is one of them!"

He took the envelope and examined the stamp. There was definitely a bulge in the paper, which was even more pronounced from the inside.

"Go on," said Lori, excitedly. Art peeled back the Dutch stamp and there were two tiny blotters, a star printed on each of them. They laughed and Lori said,

"Well - it is Christmas!" Art prised one tiny square of paper off the stamp, then handed it to Lori. He popped the other one in his mouth, but didn't hold out much hope that it would dull the pain in his brain, the way the smack had dulled the pain in his heart.

Lori took the tin and poured some coke onto the lid and snorted it. She offered some to Art but he declined,

"I was always disappointed by coke. It never lived up to the hype."

"Well I like it."

"Chasing the Dragon, on the other hand, did to me what I always hoped coke would do—"

"Whereas injecting?"

"Made me fall asleep." They walked back inside and up to his room. She sat at his desk and sifted through the mail. Her face looked childlike in the lightshow and it reminded him of those days and of something in particular:

"That last morning? Before you left for the airport? I woke up and you had gone."

"Oh yeah, sorry, I went downstairs to get a drink and ran into your dad who'd returned, so I fled."

"He'd been staying in Smithfield that night?"

"Yeah. It was Friday morning. You remember he was always away on Thursday nights?"

229

"Oh yeah; you said the other day."

"Yeah, he caught me, but it didn't matter anymore, so I just ran*."

"I wish I could remember more."

"Isn't it all in these?" she said, passing her hand across the shelf of ring-bound books,

"Yes, of course; the musings of a Kensington schoolboy, they were very deep."
He joined Lori at the table and rifled through them until he came across the one he was looking for. He plucked it and they moved back to the bed.

NATALIE explained:

"Karen and I were sold to a Saudi Arabian prince, but a year later he'd become bored with us both, so sold her on. I was worn out and worthless by then so became her maid and companion. These men like owning 'the most beautiful girl in the world' for a while, but even though she is still stunning, she has not been broken like me. She still kicks and bites and they all think they'll be the one she falls in love with, but it never happens; and their egos get bruised and they sell us on, for less than they paid. So now she's in the Swiss mountains. She told him about the bonds and he's willing to trade. So I must get back there as soon as possible so we can do the swap."

"No," said the other one "this is bullshit." He opened the back door and got out, taking the binder with him.

JOSEPH sat in the van with Natalie, watching Mickey walk away. He asked:

"Why didn't you just go to the Police?"

"Because if the Police came to his door, he could flick a switch and our bunker would fill with gravel and she'd be buried alive. There would be no evidence of anything."

"That would take ages, they'd have time to save her—"

"The steps fill first. They'd open the hatch and all they'd see would be pebbles and they could dig them out, but more would take their place. I've seen it happen elsewhere. They've all had fiendish devices to dispose of people like us: Shredders, incinerators, crushers, sink holes, you name it."

"Why didn't she call me?" asked Joseph.

"She didn't have your number, nor access to a phone, nor pencil and paper. Every day she tried to instil some courage into me, to help her, but they broke me. Coming to London has been difficult for me, but he gave me permission, so I could do it."

"Is it that powerful?"

"I was chained, deprived of sound, vision, comfort, sleep and food for so long I would've done anything for the merest kindness; said anything for a drink of water; done anything to see the sky again. Then, as meek as a mouse I was trafficked abroad and met Karen Ford on the way. She'd been in the same facility as me all along and yet hadn't been broken. But her buyer was so desperate to have her, he took responsibility for the outcome; as have all the men she's been passed between ever since. They all have the scars."

"So what are you going to do now?"

"Can you persuade him to bring the bonds back?"

"I can try, but I doubt it."

"Then I guess I'll get on that plane."

ART leafed through the pages looking for the entry for that day. There were lots of writing between the cartoons and diagrams, making each page into a mini comic-book.

"The dates just seem to be random," said Lori, "I can't get my head round it."

"They're just in reverse order," explained Art, "I start at the back and work forward, because I'm left-handed—"

"And that's also the reason you write backwards, weirdo?"

"Yes, but also to make it harder for people to read over my shoulder."

He read it aloud:

> *"Lori came to say goodbye as she was leaving forever the next day. She got into bed with me and said she wanted to reset the past. To 'choose' to invite me inside her, out of her own desire*. It was beautiful and I loved her even more if that's possible? And the bittersweet sensation of knowing that she'd be gone from my life in the morning made it all the more powerful. I woke up alone, and that's how I'll always be from now on. She'd left me her teddy in return for my knife. The Knife and the Teddy Bear – that's what I'll call my band."*

"Bit melodramatic," said Art, "but I was only twelve."

"Wait! You thought she was a teddy bear?"

"Yeah, why?"

"She was pink, had green eyes and pointy ears. She was obviously a cat!"

"Oh, that's so weird. I always thought of him as a bear. Now I'm gonna have to re-evaluate everything!"

"You are, but not because of that. Carry on reading."

> *"Dad was up when I went downstairs. He gave*
> *me a strange look and said that I wasn't going*
> *to stay at Holland Park for Secondary, but was*
> *going to Badfield, the same public school that*
> *he had been to, in Wiltshire. I don't even know*
> *where that is!"*
> *   *(Just realized, if she wanted to 'reset'*
> *she knew it was going to end! Let me hang on to*
> *that. Knowing she's safe should be enough)."*

Art said,

"I didn't remember that happening on the same day. I get it now."

"What do you get?"

"He saw you leaving and disapproved, so wanted to split us up, not knowing you were about to leave for good."

Lori squinted at him then nodded slightly. Art hugged her and she raised her head to him, looking at his mouth,

"Want to *reset* again?"

"Here? In my room?"

"Where else?"

She moved towards him and kissed him. She was more beautiful than then, when she'd just been cute, pulling her nighty over her head to reveal, well, nothing really; but this time, when she pulled her shirt over her head, she revealed her perfect breasts, with their delightfully erect nipples surrounded by those white triangles where her bikini had protected them from the sun.

Where before their kisses had been experimental and all the more exciting for it, her kisses were experienced and in sync with his own desires: Coy and defensive, then welcoming and voluptuous, then aggressive and probing.

Last time, their love-making had come with some awkwardness and embarrassment, but there was none of that this time. They joyously undressed one another while making animalistic grunts and squeals, then fell back onto the bed. They hadn't known of lube then, but this time, with no shyness, Art opened the drawer in his bedside table and produced a little pot of Aqueous Cream,

"Purely coincidental," he said, to which she giggled then took some and worked it into his hard-on, and then into herself. She was kneeling over him and slowly lowered herself, with many 'Ow's and 'Aah's, onto him. She sat there with a knowing smile on her face, then started moving, backwards and forwards, then up and down, then swivelling her hips as she moved him out of her and then into her. He watched her in amazement, her perfect body lit from the Christmas lights outside his window, the little honey-coloured arrow on her groin pointing down to his cock as she buried it into her.

Last time he'd been so afraid of hurting her, but this time he knew she liked it.

Last time, he had come in a minute or two (but was ready to do it again five minutes later) but this time he wanted to savour every moment, to wait 'til he was on the verge, then pull back, then go to the verge again, just like she was when she was almost pulling him out all the way so she could use him to hit that g-spot only an inch or two inside her. She came and he was tempted to as well, but really, he didn't want this to end, ever. He loved her more in that moment - even more than he had loved her the first time.

"Is it better? Better than the first time?" she asked, pumping him faster.

He nodded and laughed.

"Good, I owed you that," she said, swivelling on his hard-on, "the first time in this bedroom; and the last time in this bedroom."

"The last time?" he said. She was looking towards the door, but put her hands over his eyes and said,

"Come in me now; come in me," she said swivelling rapidly.

He wanted to resist, but her wish was his command. He let go and allowed for the shuddering electrics which pulsated through his body and became fireworks when they reached his eyeballs.

She bent down and kissed him, her hair falling over his face, but suddenly she was gone, torn away from him; his father pulling her by the hair onto the carpet.

"What the fuck are you doing in my house?! Under my roof?!"

Lori was grabbing his hand to try to ease the pain of her scalp.

Art jumped up and tried to push him off her,

"Dad, let go of her! I've had many girls in this room!"

"You defile the memory!"

Lori wrenched herself free and covered herself.

"How dare you!" he screamed.

"Dad! I'm sorry I didn—"

But he was gone; slamming the door after him.

Lori and Art got dressed in silence, shocked by the violence. Lori clutched her bag to her chest.

Art picked up his journal and went next door to where his father was watching T.V. with the volume up loud: Some soap with an ongoing domestic dispute. Art blocked his view and waved the journal in his face.

"I know why you told me I was going to boarding school the same day you saw Lori leaving my bedroom!" His father said nothing; just stared at him, breathing fast and shallow like a hamster.

"What you didn't know was she was leaving the country that very day!"
The doorbell rang.

"Saved by the bell," said Art, as he answered it.

"Hi Artie, could you move your bike please?"

"Of course Mary, sorry, I wasn't thinking."
Still carrying his notebook, he put the door on the latch and went down to move his bike. He dragged it in front of their own garage doors then had a thought. He sat on his bike and flicked through his journal, stopping to look at the drawings sometime, as they danced on the page. He'd rarely written explicitly about Lori's visits but instead used little graphic doodles of spoons spooning to mark them. He went through the weeks looking for patterns. The spoons blew him kisses and raspberries but nothing else popped out at him, except that they never happened on a Thursday.

The voices were getting more heated above. Other nights were marked with the sad telephone doodles (which cried real tears) for when his mum was upset that his dad was staying out. They never coincided with a visit from Lori either.

He looked up as he heard shouting from above and realized that no one could have been climbing over his roof, he would've heard them, and seen them in the tree.

So that only left one person who could have had such easy access, once he'd installed a gate.

His father hadn't wanted to break them up; he'd wanted her all to himself.
He ran up the steps but the door was locked. He looked in the window to find Lori pointing a revolver at his father who was up and screaming 'It wasn't me!'. His father saw him and shouted 'She's lying!'. Lori turned and saw Art, giving his father the chance to swing at her, knocking the pistol from her hand. They both scrambled for the gun and struggled for control, but his father was too strong for her, rolling her over then lying on her, the pistol pointed at her head. Art expected him to get off her, but he didn't. He saw him whispering to her, and her crying. He went back to the door and kicked it hard near the lock. It didn't budge

234

but it complained bitterly. He did it again and heard
the fracturing (and whimpering) of wood. Again and the
door opened slightly (pleading). Once more and it
swung free. He ran in and tried to pull him off her,
but his father swung the gun upwards and caught Art on
the temple.

When he awoke, Art's face was mashed into the
threadbare carpet. He looked up and saw Lori pushed
over the sofa, her skirt pulled up and her knickers
being slowly pulled down by a gigantic monster
kneeling behind her. Her ankles were bound and her
wrists were tied in front of her and she was looking
at Art, almost calmly. The monster was looking at him
too, but not calmly. More excitedly, defiantly, with a
lascivious grin and its tongue lolling on his brown
teeth. Art, feeling six inches tall with his hands and
feet also tied, managed to jump at it, trying to push
it away from her, but the monster's bulk meant he
almost bounced off. Art grabbed for the gun and they
struggled for it, falling onto the carpet, rolling
away from Lori. The monster was stronger than Art and
bent the gun towards him, until it touched his head
just behind his ear. Art turned his head away as it
fired, *only* shooting his ear. Blood poured onto the
carpet as they fought.

"He's gonna kill you Artie, and then me!" shouted
Lori who crouched on the sofa, mirroring his actions
with her tethered fists like someone at a boxing
match.

Art knew he should attack. But the monster was
his father. But Lori was right. But his dad? But then
the monster punched Art and went to push the pistol
into his neck. Art thought of Dash's defence and poked
the monster in the eye, making it drop the gun; then
he rolled away from it as Lori grabbed the gun and
shot the monster in the stomach. It screamed, falling
into a sitting position, holding the wound as blood
poured between its fingers.

"You realize it was talking to me just now?" she
said, motioning towards Art's bedroom.
Art looked from her to it, and back.

"Defile the memory?"

Oh shit! It was dawning on him. His greatest fear
- the idea he couldn't think - was true. The acid
though? Why did he take the acid?

She shot it in the crotch. It bellowed, holding
its arms out in defence as another circle of blood
spread across the carpet. Art untied his feet and
tried to intervene but she pointed the gun at him and
he stopped, then she shot the monster in the knee. It
cried and whimpered, blood spurting from its wounds.

"You're crying," she said, standing over it, shaking the gun, "do you know how many nights you made a little girl cry? and how many nights I've dreamt of this moment ever since?"

Art was frozen, torn between their filial history and the grim truth of what this monster had done.

"Only two more bullets," said Lori, calmly, "what a shame." She aimed at its head and it ducked; she aimed at its other knee and it tried to—
She fired into its chest, an explosion of blood flooding its shirt.

"One more bullet," she said, looking at Art, "shall I put it out of its misery; or let it die slowly in excruciating pain, or..." She lifted the gun to her mouth. Art said 'No', carefully took the gun from her and sat them both on the sofa. The monster was weeping, reaching out its hands for... what? Mercy? Supplication? Redemption? Heroin? They watched it, lit by the cold blue of the T.V.

"Have you come up?" asked Art.

"No, I didn't take mine," she replied.
Art couldn't help but laugh. Laugh hysterically. So none of this was real. It was all his fertile imagination's creation. In fact, he was probably still in the garden, looking at the twinkly lights, and holding Lori's hand. So he could do anything he wanted... anything... for so long... he'd wanted...to...

He lifted the revolver, and shot the monster in the head.

Still sitting, held aloft by the mass of his midriff, his father looked at him, sneered, and died. The blood bubbling from every wound, slowed to a cascade, still expanding across the floor.

"You would never've believed me if I'd just told you," she said.
She took the revolver from Art, caressed it lovingly, then pointed it at the ceiling and squeezed on the trigger until it went click. She patted his knee and smiled, dropping the gun and kicking it under the sofa.

They untied each other's wrists. He winced, suddenly aware of the pain in his ear. She took a bunch of gauze swabs from her bag, unwrapped one and applied it.

"Hold that in place, and here are some more," she said, "along with some antiseptic wet-wipes."

Art was speechless, but had a thousand questions running through his head. He could only watch as she checked herself in the mirror, straightening her clothes, cleaning blood from her cheek, pulling her ponytail tight.

"You know? I really do feel a weight off?" she said, applying some makeup.

"There," she said, smiling widely at her reflection, "all better. And I think my tick has gone!" she said, *not* turning her head away and looking at him out the corner of her eyes.

"Now I realize I should've come back years ago... but thanks Artie; thanks for inspiring me."

She unwrapped another swab and carefully took Art's hand from his ear. There was blood running down his forearm.

"Drop that. Take this. But apply more pressure this time." She smiled and touched his face affectionately.

She picked up the receiver on the landline and dialled 999.
He heard them answer, then she put the phone back down.

"Now I really must go," she said, putting on his mother's overcoat, "if I'm to catch the nine o'clock." She stood in the doorway and looked from father to son and smiled,

"Now you *can* write about this if you want. Keep me as a surfer yeah? I like the idea of surfing."
Then she was gone.

ART was still sitting in the same spot, staring at his father when the landline rang.

"Hello?"

"Hello, did you call 999?"

"Er...yes...no..."

"Can you talk?"

"Hardly."

"Are you alright?"

"No."

"Which service do you require?"

"Ambulance and police please. I've killed my father."

237

HANNAH had found the janitor and was frog-marching him back to the crypt. He had soap in his hair and a look of annoyance on his wrinkled face. He unlocked the door and let it swing open. Then he was gone. The steps were dark and she couldn't find a light switch, but she continued down. The steps were steep and she was relieved when she reached the bottom. She heard a creaking from above as the door swung shut, leaving her in total darkness.

DASHA awoke on her chaise, being shaken by Amber,
    "Dash! Thank God you've come! I knew you would!"
Dash hugged her and whispered,
    "How did you get into my pen?"
    "Oh, we're all outside getting ready for the party. The old lady asked me to wake you."
    "Don't let on that we know each other. They'll think that's fishy."
Amber nodded and hugged her again. Over her shoulder Dash could see Elsie and Jenny were in the hall, being tended to by the women. Amber ran out and sat on the sofa, waiting her turn.
    Dash followed Amber and sat next to her.
    "How are my parents?" she whispered, "are they freaking out?"
Dash nodded, then asked,
    "What was the party like last week? It must've been your first night?"
    "Oh, I was still groggy so wasn't really sure what was happening, but I was sitting between two old men and was telling them about my boyfriends and they got up and moved. Then it happened again?"
    "So they all want virgins?"
    "Maybe?"
    "Sounds like a good defence for now, while we work out what to do."
    "You don't have a plan?"
    "It's almost there..."
Amber was called to have her makeup done, and Jenny sat with Dash. She seemed very docile, almost unable to speak. Dash gave her a cuddle and said it was going to be okay, before she got called by Olga. Dash sat in the chair and Olga examined her face for blemishes.
    "So, is the one in the red the Dog?" she murmured in Russian.
    Olga chuckled,
    "Heavens no! She's the same as me, just thinks she's more powerful because she looks like a weight lifter!"
Dash chuckled too,

"So who is the Dog?"
Olga applied some foundation to Dash's skin,
    "He's an American. He helicopters in for the
parties; sometimes tries the merchandise beforehand.
Came down here earlier as a matter of fact."
    "Really? When?"
    "When you were all sleeping. He gassed the whole
cellar. Then he fucked the pretty blonde."
Dash was shocked, but tried not to show it.
    "That's why we call him the Dog."
    "Because he behaves like one?"
    "Exactly," she said as she applied some eye
shadow, "but he won't fuck you in your sleep; you're
ten year's too old for his taste."
    "That's another small mercy to be grateful for,"
said Dash, "so what's his name?"
    "Something German/Jewish? Ends in stein? Can't
remember. There! You're all done. Don't mess it up
when you take off that T-shirt!"
Dash looked in the mirror and smiled. It was very
subtle, just like if she'd done it herself. She
thanked Olga and went back to the sofa.
Elsie, all made up, came and sat with Dash and they
tried on shoes.
    "Amber said that at last week's party she told
the men all about sleeping with her boyfriend and they
stopped being interested in her—"
    "That was stupid, doesn't she want the fabulous
lifestyle?"
    "You believe the video?"
    "If he's handsome and kind, I could go for it.
And I am a virgin."
Dash was stunned. Elsie really had been seduced by it.
It was the carrot and the stick, and the carrot was
doing fine on Elsie.
    "Where were you taken?" asked Dash.
    "I was at a friend's Guy Fawkes party. The barman
spiked me—"
    "Oh yes. Your friend. Was he your boyfriend?"
Elsie looked wistful and said,
    "Girlfriend actually."
    "And do you love her?"
    "We'd literally *just* kissed and I haven't seen
her since."
    "So we need to get you out of here. We need to
get *us all* out of here."
    "What are you two whispering about?" said the
burly one in red, "you're not plotting some idiotic—"
    "We both really like the video," said Dash
excitedly, "when are the men arriving?"
Elsie nodded and smiled, genuinely.

239

The red one shook her head,

"I don't know what he was thinking, choosing you. He's an idiot. I'm not sure you should even come upstairs. You might be a disruptive influence." She grabbed Dash's arm, threw her back into her pen, and locked her door. Dash went to her cell and sent a text about Jenny going missing in Richmond, Elsie in Windsor, and the Boss's name ending in 'stein'.

MICKEY sat outside Bar Italia drinking a coffee while Eva cleared her locker in the theatre beneath him. She'd quit and the matinée had been her final performance. The crowds were rushing by, dressed in their winter coats, on the hunt for some Christmas gift for a loved one? Or a loathed one? Almost more important to get a good present for a loathed one.

His phone buzzed. A text from Dash.

"Stein?" he said.

He used his new WAP enabled Sony Ericsson P900 to try googling for names ending in stein: Bernstein; Einstein; Epstein; Eisenstein; Frankenstein; Weinstein, but no infamous perverts became apparent.

AJI was at her mum's watching a Jennifer Aniston movie called 'The Good Girl' which was depressing her, and not taking her mind off her troubles. She'd wanted to go on the stake out later, but she didn't want to see her dad. So she was here, with Jennifer Aniston, and a tub of Ben and Jerry's.

Her mother was on a date, and unlike her weirdo father, trusted her to behave when left alone. Between spoons of Cookie Dough she was taking notes about the film so she could write up a proper critique later.

The doorbell rang. She went to the window and pulled back the curtain. Marcus stood there, holding a bunch of flowers that looked like they came from someone's garden. She wasn't sure what to do. He had redeemed himself over the past week but she still felt shocked by his behaviour on Halloween. She'd spoken to her mum who had agreed that he might suffer from the same allergy that she did. An allergy to alcohol that turned her into a 'beast' (her own words). Marcus hadn't become a beast, but by not taking no for an answer, he had been halfway there. She opened the door,

"Have you been drinking?" she asked in as gentle a fashion as she could muster.

"Not at all," he said.

"Drink doesn't agree with you."

"I have realized that," he said, "do you want me to take a sobriety test?" He walked along the line

240

(marking the space between her mum's car and their neighbour's) as if he was on a tightrope, while touching his nose and reciting the alphabet backwards.

"Very impressive," she said waving him in. He gave her the flowers and she thanked him (even though they were pretty manky) then went to the kitchen and put them in a vase of water. He followed her in.

"How did you know I'd be here?"

"I didn't, I just took a gamble. What's the worst that could happen?"

"You could've been dragged in by my mother, and forcibly regaled with stories about her youth and the punk movement and Uni and..."

"Hmmm, I get your point," he said, "maybe I'll call next time, if you give me your number?"

Aji nodded.

"What's up? You look sad."

He looked genuinely concerned so she told him about her dad's new girlfriend and them all coming in and finding them, and Dash punching him and storming out, and then her going missing in the same way Amber had.

"Wow!" said Marcus, "that's crazy. No wonder you're sad."

"I just want to take my mind off it by watching a movie, okay?"

"Okay, what are we watching?" he said, flopping onto the sofa. She decided against subjecting him to The Good Girl and picked up another box at random:

"Femme Fatale," she said, popping the DVD into the player and handing him the box, "starring the Dirty Girl from 'Friends' Season Four, Episode Six."

"And, ironically, the same girl who played Mystique in...the...X-Men..." He tailed off when he saw the look on her face. Bad choice. Not his fault. She sat down and tried to get caught up in it.

It started well, the setup seemed promising, maybe exciting stuff was coming, and Marcus seemed to be engrossed, and then there was a film premiere and a sex scene in the Ladies loo and Aji didn't want to watch anymore and she went to the kitchen to make popcorn.

MICKEY and Eva sat in his car on Berkley Square listening to Spartacus by Khachaturian.

"So glad I quit," said Eva, "Dash not being there. Just can't do it..."

"I'm not surprised Evie, but we'll get her back. Maybe tonight, and then you can both look for another musical."

241

Eva nodded, continuing to scan the square. Mickey took the binder off his lap and passed it to Eva. She opened it and asked,

"What are these?"

"Bonds, issued by the Bank of England, worth one-hundred-thousand Eurodollars each."

Eva looked pleasantly surprised,

"So we're going shopping tomorrow?"

Mickey smiled and nodded,

"Why not?"

"So where did they come from?"

"Does it matter?"

"Kinda."

"The woman, Natalie, who visited Sloane Square on Thursday found them in the Music Room."

"Seriously? She found them?"

"She knew where to look. She claimed Karen told her where to look."

"O.M.G!"

"And that she was collecting them to buy Karen's freedom."

"Freedom?"

"Natalie claimed that during... on that day... of my torture... Karen climbed out the window and along the ledge to Mr Gustav's to escape."

Eva was speechless.

"But that instead of escaping she ended up being captured and trafficked."

"By Mr Gustav?"

"She didn't say."

"Then you should go with her. Keep these bonds on you. Then if it's bullshit, come home."

"Yeah, maybe. But I think the moment I say I'm going with her she'll go off the idea anyway."

"So what have you got to lose?"

HANNAH was locked in the crypt. She had climbed back up the stairs to find no handle on the inside. She sat there, looking at the sliver of light on the floor, but even that would be gone soon when everyone went to bed. She bumped back down the steps on her bottom, then crawled along the edge of the wall until she hit a table leg. She was alone in the pitch blackness. She hated the dark almost as much as she hated being alone.

EVA swallowed and stared out the window. What was she doing? What had she done? She should say she's changed her mind. Stupid, dangerous idea. He might get hurt; he might get killed; he might fall back in love with Karen Ford again.

"Mickey, I, I—"

"Wait! Look!"

A station wagon was reversing into a spot outside Annabel's. The driver then opened the hood and walked away. They got out and jogged over, Eva heading for the car and Mickey to the driver who was crossing the square.

He caught him near the east-side entrance and shot him, then bundled him into the bushes. Eva was shocked. She stood by the station wagon and watched him approach,

"You killed him?"

"No, tranquilizer dart. I'm gonna come back for him later."

Mickey ducked behind the station wagon and looked in the window.

"There's a bicycle and luggage in the boot; there's no room for anyone in there."

Eva shrugged,

"Pop it anyway."

He used a tool to unlock the trunk. Eva was always proud of him - ever prepared - even if he was such an enigma to her in so many other ways.

As Mickey lifted the tailgate, the bicycle and luggage lifted too. They'd been sawn in half and stuck to a plastic panel.

Below it, was a girl, about Aji's age wrapped in a fleecy blanket. She was asleep, so Mickey scooped her into his arms and started walking back to his car. Eva watched him for a moment then climbed into the trunk. Mickey turned and saw her and ran back,

"What are you doing?"

"I'm gonna find Dash!"

"No! We can just follow the tow-truck. You don't need to be in there."

"But I do. What if the truck driver checks?"

Mickey wasn't convinced but Eva implored him,

"Quick! Before the tow-truck comes!"

She pulled the tailgate shut.

MICKEY stood there for a moment, then started back to his car. He was almost there when he saw a Police car. It whooped its siren once and pulled up alongside him.

EVA pushed her head up, forcing the plastic panel to bend enough for her to see Mickey in a struggle with a Policeman. She needed to get over there and corroborate his story. She tried to open the trunk, but the latch was firmly back in the locked position.

MICKEY had his hands above his head. The girl was in the back of the Police car. He was trying to explain but was distracted by the sight of a tow-truck loading a car onto its back.

EVA got out her phone. She tried calling Mickey but there was no answer. Then she tried Art, but there was no answer. Who else could she call? Dash and Hannah were both unavailable.

AJI sat on the sofa with Marcus, sharing the popcorn, and sharing her thoughts about Femme Fatale on her laptop. The film wasn't very good. She was gorgeous obviously, which was keeping the boy engrossed, but the plot wasn't that exciting and the romance was lacking. Then she was in a bar, getting sexually assaulted by some thug and Aji wanted to flee to the kitchen again.
Her phone rang and she was so grateful to answer it and run out of the room. She saw it was Eva calling and answered brightly.
    "Aji, I'm in the trunk, I mean the boot of a car, on the back of a tow-truck."
    "Oh my god, he got you too?"
    "No, I climbed in—"
    "Why?"
    "Because it seemed like a good idea at the time. Mickey was going to follow but he's been arrested, and I can't get hold of your dad—"
    "So you need to be followed, to the place where they've got Dash?"
    "Exactly! I can see where I'm going, so can direct you and your mum to—"
    "Oh, my mum's not here. I'm here with Marcus—"
    "Can he drive?"
    "Can you drive?"
    "Er - a moped, yes - but not a car"
    "Yes, he can."
    "Great, well it looks like we're heading out of town past the Natural History Museum so—"
    "On the A4 west."
    "Exactly."
    "We're on it."
Aji hung up, got her bag and phone charger and wrote a note to her mum. Then she put on her stacked platform sneakers, grabbed two cushions from the dining table chairs and said,
    "Want to come for a drive?"

EVA popped her head up again and saw they were passing that weird boat-shaped building next to the Hammersmith Flyover. She texted Aji, then lay down. What was she doing? She was acting crazy. Very unlike her; was a collective madness overtaking them all one-by-one?

AJI unlocked the car, put the cushions on the seat and got in. Marcus opened the passenger door and bent down,
        "Are you sure about this?"
        "Yes, what's so hard about it? There's a foot thingy to 'Go', and one to stop—"
        "Peddle!" said Marcus, "you calling it a thingy is not inspiring confidence."
        "And this round thingy is for... just kidding!" She had to pull the seat forward a lot, so she could put her foot on the brake to start the engine. Marcus sat down beside her and put on his seatbelt.
        "Lucky it's an automatic," he said.
She only dinged their neighbours' cars once or twice during the process of reversing, which she was pretty happy with. Then they were off. A discussion was had about the benefits of the South Circular over the Fulham Palace Road and then they were onto the A4. Eva had reported that she was on the M3, so they took a left at the stinky brewery and headed for Richmond.

DASHA and the girls, all dressed up, waited by their doors as the burly one in red made her speech:
        "Now this is an opportunity for you. These men are extremely rich and can offer you a lifestyle beyond your wildest dreams, so follow these simple suggestions: Don't cry or you'll smudge your makeup and no one likes that; be nice, good manners cost nothing; and smile, or you'll miss your chance and be left behind."
She looked at the ceiling, then said,
        "And finally, remember the boss will be sitting at the head of the table. Be respectful, he really does hold your life in his hands. Now let's go, and don't try to run; the house is all locked up and the windows are made of the same stuff as your walls."

HANNAH felt something run over her hand and she screamed. She had never been to one of the religious 'celebrations' before, so had no idea of the layout of the room she was in. The floor was cold and sucking the warmth from her hands and knees as she crawled. She found a large straight-backed armchair and climbed

245

onto it. She wondered if she should go back up the stairs and bang on the door again, but feared everyone was out at the A.A. meeting anyway.

EVA poked her head up and looked out at the dark, empty motorway. There were very few cars behind her. She sent a text to Aji saying they'd just crossed Junction Three, then lay back down.

AJI heard her phone buzz and passed it to Marcus.
"Eva says there's no lighting on the M3 where she is."
"We're just entering that area, can't be far behind."
Aji saw a tow-truck ahead. She slowed and drew in behind it, a hundred metres back. Marcus called Eva and put her on speakerphone.
"We've got you, Eva."
She sounded happy,
"Don't come too close, or they might be suspicious."
"Don't worry. Speak later?"

EVA lay down and tried to remain calm. She was an idiot to get in the trunk. This whole thing was stupid. And boring. How long could she endure this? How long could Dash? How long her dad? A small dark cell was what she'd always imagined him in, after he first disappeared. They really hated all Americans, and who could blame them? He'd told her that they didn't want to kill them so much as grind them slowly down, until they weren't human anymore. Thanks for that Dad! Three weeks before he went back there and she never saw him again. She couldn't breathe. The box was closing in. A vacuum was sucking in the walls. The darkness was hungry and eating her layer by layer, she curled into a ball and wept for her Daddy.

HANNAH awoke in the armchair with a cricked neck. She was cold and in pitch black darkness. She hugged her legs and rocked. Was this her fault? She hadn't been at all charming to the janitor, like she would have been normally. The stress had got to her and she'd behaved badly and ended up locked in the cold, dank and dark crypt. Maybe she'd apologize to him tomorrow, if she didn't kill him.

AJI answered Eva's call:

"Aji, I'm freaking out here. I don't think I can do it."

"I don't blame you!"

"I'm not brave, Aji."

"Can you open the boot?"

"No, it's locked."

"Can you climb out onto the back seats?"

"No, there's a panel above me with a bicycle and luggage on top. I can only just squeeze my head up to see you guys."

"So how about the back seats? They must fold down. Look for a latch at the sides, maybe?"

"O.M.G! Yes! Here it is! Yes! I'm out!"

"Okay, if you want out I'm going to overtake the truck then slow down. I'll block it 'til we're stopped, then you can jump off, okay?"

"Look at me! I'm free!"

Aji couldn't see anything in the back of the car.

"I don't see you."

Marcus shook his head,

"Me neither."

EVA looked back at the car,

"Put your indicator on."

"Okay," said Aji.

"Is it on?" asked Eva, "because I don't see anything flashing."

"Oh shit! Have we got the wrong tow-truck?"

"What colour's your car?"

"White."

Eva's heart sank.

AJI panicked,

"We haven't passed any other tow-trucks, have we?"

Marcus shrugged,

"I wasn't really paying attention, once we'd locked on to this one."

"We're not sure if we're ahead of you, or behind you, Eva."

"Can you see anything?" asked Marcus, "anything that will pin-point your location?"

They waited...

"Oh, one thing I hadn't noticed, but it's gone down to two lanes from three."

"That's ahead of us," said Marcus, "put your foot down!"

"We're coming Eva, sit tight."

EVA felt relieved, but also a bit of a chicken. It was weird being so high and pointing uphill while driving along in the darkness, with no one in the driver's seat. She tried Mickey again, but got no answer.

DASHA watched the blue and red women whispering by the door, shrugging and shaking their heads. The red one picked her walkie-talkie from her belt and called Olga,
"I'm sorry, I've forgotten the code for the doors again. Can't I write it on a post-it?"
"I'll come down. One minute."
Dash heard a click as their doors were unlocked. The blue one led them through the left-hand door, past Olga and the red one sitting at some monitors, then up a stone staircase.
They emerged through a door guarded by two armed men, into a corridor that led to large hallway with a flagstone floor. Arches gave it an eastern feel. In the centre was a shallow pond. Carp swam as a fountain burbled on the lily pads. A man, his face hidden in shadows, stood on the mezzanine above, looking down on them. Under an arch, they walked through double doors into a large dining room with tall ceilings. The velvet curtains were closed and the lighting was subtle. A long table was set for dinner with twenty-something placings. Red and Blue grabbed Dash's arms and carried her to the centre of the table,
"Here's your place," Blue said, dropping her onto the seat, then chaining her ankles to the chair legs.

AJI and Marcus saw a tow-truck ahead. When they got close enough they could see Eva sitting in the back. She was crouching behind the driver's seat, but waved surreptitiously. They pulled back a bit to a safe distance then called her. Eva was frightened,
"What if it never stops? I can't jump off at 70 MPH!"
"It has to stop eventually Eva. There will be plenty of chances to get off."
"Or," suggested Marcus, "we could pull up really close and you could jump on to our bonnet?"
"Like in a movie?" asked Eva.
"But we could be so close it'd be more like stepping than jumping, and I could be out the sun-roof ready to grab you, and then we just slow down really gently?"
"Let's file that under 'last resort' okay?"
Marcus looked disappointed.

DASHA wondered where her anger had gone.
Wouldn't having your ankles chained to a chair make
her angry? She'd been expressing her anger a lot
lately. But now she just understood. Compared to the
others she was strong and fighting fit, though she
didn't feel any fight in her.

The others looked shocked but Red barked and they
all found their place-cards and sat down, a few spaces
between each of them. One of the twins sat two places
to Dash's left. Which one was she Emma or Ava? They
were identical until you got up close and saw they had
beauty spots on opposite cheeks, like they were a
mirror image of each other.

Everyone seemed more docile than usual, including
herself. Had they had an extra dose of tranquilizer
gas before the came upstairs? Or was it also added to
their food? A cocktail ever in need of tweaking, as
Hannah would say.

Classical music played, but didn't quite drown
out the sound of helicopters landing close by.

HANNAH sat in the dark, on one of the armchairs
she'd found. She kept telling herself that it would be
over soon, even if soon was tomorrow morning. What if
Dash was in that little dark box for the rest of her
life? She heard a helicopter approaching and landing
close-by. Then another and another. What was going on?

DASHA heard noises behind her and she turned to
see the doors opening and another group of six girls
walk in with Red. They took their places at the table
still leaving a free chair between all the girls. To
her right, one of the girls was also being chained to
her chair by Red and Blue. She struggled a bit and
Dash saw a kindred spirit in her. She rattled her own
leg-irons and the girl saw and chuckled, then winked
at her. She was beautiful when she smiled, her black
bob framing her face perfectly.

"So are you all from downstairs too?" asked Dash.
The girl nodded,
"I'm CC."
"I'm Dash."
"I don't understand what's going on," said CC,
"one minute I'm so sleepy and happy, then the next I
realize those are the last feelings I should be having
and try to fight against it."
Dash nodded and said,
"It's the gas."

"Every day I feel a little less like me," CC
said, "but I'm not going down without a fight."
"Me too. We can beat this."
A waitress (pretty, but for a scar running from her
ear to the corner of her mouth) interrupted them,
asking Dash what she wanted to drink. She asked for a
whiskey. The others ordered various cocktails and Dash
watched the waitress at the bar. She mixed their
drinks, but Dash could tell they were very small
measures, she supposed so none of them would get too
'emotional'.

EVA sat up a bit and looked out. She called Aji,
"Wait, are we slowing down?"
"We're pulling into a Service Station," said Aji,
"now's your chance!"
Eva watched as the truck pulled into the parking area,
near the loos, and slowed to a stop. She hunkered down
as the driver got out. Eva was surprised to see it was
a woman, who was obviously desperate as she ran to the
Ladies. Eva, so relieved, pulled the door handle.

AJI and Marcus watched the woman run to the loo,
and expected Eva to make her escape.
"What's going on?"
"I can't open the door!" said Eva, "maybe child-
locks?"
"Try the driver's in the front. Marcus is going
to come help!"
"I am?" said Marcus faintly, "I am!" he said more
bravely and jumped out the car. Aji also got out and
headed for the Ladies.

EVA got in the front and tried the door, but it
wouldn't open. Marcus jumped on the truck and tried
the door but no luck. He mouthed something to her and
then jumped off. Eva's heart sank.

AJI went into the Ladies and saw only one door
was locked. She went into the next cubicle and
listened. She'd finished peeing and was wiping
herself, then she was pulling her boiler suit back up
and was leaving.

EVA accepted she wasn't getting out, climbed
back into the back and dropped into the footwell. One
tear dripped onto her knee and then the dam burst.

AJI heard the woman leaving (without washing her
hands!)

250

"Excuse me!" cried Aji "could you pass me some loo-roll please?"
She heard the woman walk on.
"Please!"
The woman stopped, retraced her steps, and then a loo-roll flew over the door. Aji caught it, hearing the woman leaving.
"Wait!" she shouted, "you didn't wash your hands!"
But the room was empty. Aji ran after her.

EVA felt the truck rock slightly and guessed it was the woman getting back into her cab. She had missed her chance.

AJI followed the woman out of the Ladies. The truck was to the right, looking very much the same. She called to the woman who turned her head, but carried on walking.
"Thanks!" said Aji, running up to her on her left side, hopefully diverting her gaze from any Marcus/Eva action, "that was very kind of you; so many people don't care about others, don't you think?," she noticed a scar on her face running all the way from her ear to the corner of her mouth, "this world is really turning to shit don't you think?" The woman kept on walking.

EVA felt the truck rock slightly then a crash as the opposite window was smashed and Marcus leant in and grabbed her arm and pulled her up and through the broken glass and down and off running to the car as the woman walked towards the front of the truck with Aji in tow, talking bollocks. Eva fell into the back seats.
"It's okay," said Marcus, "she didn't notice anything; Aji did a great job; she's driving off."

AJI smiled and waved at the woman as she got into the tow-truck and pulled away.
Running back to the car, she opened the back door and hugged Eva, who had a few cuts from the glass, as did Marcus, who was shaking in his seat, still clutching the rock in his hand.
"You're safe now Eva! So...shall we follow?" she asked.
They both looked at her with wide eyes and then at each other. Aji took that as a yes. She started the engine, saying,
"This has got to be the best night of my life!"

MICKEY sat in the interview room, praying that
Eva was okay. They'd taken his phone, his belt and his
shoe laces. So far he'd remained silent. But that
meant he might never see Eva again. Could he sit and
say nothing, knowing that she might not have been able
to find anyone to tail the tow-truck? That she was
just going to disappear into the same black hole that
Dash did? He'd all but given up hope when he had a
thought. But would it put Eva in more danger? He had
to take the chance:
        "Inspector Gadget will know about these
abductions."
        "Inspector Gadget?" asked the Detective.
        "Or the French equivalent?"
        "Oh, you mean Inspector Gâjhette, pronounced
'Gâjhette'."
        "Exactly. He will know the situation."

    DASHA heard noise behind her again. Around
twelve masked men entered. Most in suits and a couple
in Arabic thawbs. An American, who Dash guessed was
the Dog, did most of the talking as they
circumnavigated the table, oohing and ahhing at the
merchandise. One man in a thawb came close to the
pretty blonde and she instinctively shied away. He
laughed and pulled her by the hair.
        "No touching Gentlemen," said the Dog, "yet!
Maybe someone else has their eye on her too? We'll get
to the auction after dinner."
The men mostly seemed to be from the east, judging by
their skin colour and accents, except for two plump
Englishmen: One, with floppy blonde hair and a fruity
accent, the other younger, slicked-back hair with
shaved temples and a manicured beard. He didn't sit at
the table, but hung back in the shadows with the
maids, occasionally chatting to Olga.
        The rest were all old, with paunches and none of
them were handsome; but Elsie was smiling away like
her life depended upon it. Which it did, unless Dash
could find a way to stop this? She saw Olga watching
her, slowly shaking her head.
        Drinks were served. A chubby little man, mid-
sixties, brought Dash another whiskey and sat beside
her. His mask hardly hid his features which were
classically Korean. He introduced himself as Kim then
said,
        "Your eyes are extraordinary, like a Husky."
She smiled involuntarily. What was she on? Had she
been roofied?
        "And your body! Are you an athlete?"

"Dancer."

"I would love to see you dance," he said, "we must arrange that for after supper."

"And I would love to dance, but..." she motioned to her feet, "I'm a bit tied up at the moment."
He laughed, and she did too, weirdly.

"Oh. You're one of the 'feisty' ones, of course!" he said, turning to the Dog, who winked, "he already has plans for you, so I look forward to getting to know you better, later."

He got up and moved on to the twins. The other men were doing a similar circuit, except for the Dog, who sat imperiously with his fat cigar clenched in his big jaw, smiling and watching developments.

AJI kept a discreet distance behind the tow-truck as it left the motorway and wound its way onto a smaller road towards Salisbury. She suddenly thought of her mum and asked Marcus to compose a text.

"Mum, sorry I forgot to say I've gone over to
Margot's. It's so late now, may I stay please?
Love you xx"

"Perfect," said Aji, "that'll buy us some time. You'd better do the same."
Marcus found his phone and did so. They had turned on to an even smaller road. While the truck was out of sight, Aji turned off the headlights and turned on the fog lights.
Marcus, still a bit speechless looked said 'Huh?'.

"Oh, it'll make it look like a different car is behind them now."

MICKEY waited alone, watching the second hand of the clock circle again and again, praying that Eva was okay. Finally the door opened and a little chap walked in, saying,

"Who are you?"

"An innocent bystander," said Mickey.

"I don't seem to be able to find anything but the most rudimentary records for you. I think you've given us an alias."

"Not at all. I just lead a very quiet life."

"So why did you ask for me?"

"My girlfriend came to see you yesterday, concerned about her friend going missing. We thought maybe Berkeley Square was a pick-up point for this gang, so we all staked it out, and we were right. We saw a car park on the west side of the square, then the driver opened the bonnet and walked away, just like my girlfriend reported to you at Scotland Yard on

253

Friday morning. We suspected that the same thing was
happening again so I popped the lock and found the
girl in the boot, drugged. How is she?"
    "She is reunited with her parents."
    "That's good. So now I really need to get out of
here and check my phone. Please."
    "Why?"
    "Because the tow-truck is being followed by the
rest of my friends in another car. They will have
texted me updates."
Mickey tried to look innocent. Maybe Gadget was trying
to look innocent too? They looked at each other;
stared, without blinking; a game Mickey had played
hundreds of times in his previous life then Gadget
cracked.
He pressed the intercom,
    "This man's story checks out, please bring his
belongings and the *Release*."
A sergeant opened the door,
    "Are you sure, Sir?"
    "Yes, he may have important information being
relayed to his phone and we need to be tracking these
miscreants immediately!"
The sergeant nodded and left.

    DASHA felt drowsy, happy, hungry, and shit-
scared all at once. The first course was brought out:
Finger food, appropriate as there were no knives or
forks available. The men sat down between the girls
and they all ate. A dark-skinned man in his fifties
introduced himself as Mahammad. He ate heartily and
pronounced that he was searching for a wife, the
younger the better as was the custom in his country.
To bear him many sons and carry on his dynasty by the
Silver Lake. He somehow made it sound romantic (or was
that the roofie talking?) His eyes flitted between the
Blonde, Amber and the Redhead as he spoke about his
palace and the jewels and the oil and the cars... None
of them looked keen, but Elsie and one of the twins
nodded and smiled at his every word. Brin, the big man
sitting next to Dash, twirled his spring roll between
his fingers and muttered something under his breath: a
disparaging remark in Russian (roughly translated as
'baby fucker'). Dash replied in Russian, agreeing with
his comment. He turned to her, smiled, then whispered
in Russian,
    "Well, I thought you were all meant to be
virginal English Roses, but you could never have been
sired from such an insipid race—"
    "Virginal?" she murmured, "not after our host has
had his way with them."

"Really? That is interesting. I had heard rumours along those lines. Him, and his house have lost credibility recently."

"Who would you hear something like that from?"

"Oh you know, with friends; or acquaintances at conventions; summits; parties: They talk about their art collections, their jets, their yachts, their houses, their mistresses and also their 'basement girls'."

He said it without irony, sending a shiver up Dash's spine, even in her drugged-up state.

"Speak American!" shouted the Dog, "only American here!"

"You mean English?" snorted Brin.

The two men clearly didn't like one another. They stared at each other until Olga broke the stand-off with by calling the Dog aside,

"Emergency situation sir."

The Dog followed her out of the room.

EVA tried Mickey again but got no answer. She tried Art, but his phone was switched off. She texted them both an update. The road was narrowing and Aji was staying even further back, swapping her lights.

MICKEY and Inspector Gadget stood outside the Police station. Mickey unlocked his phone. There were a number of texts from Eva, including one saying she was on the M3.

"Okay, tell me," said the Inspector.

"They were on the M3."

Then the one saying she was free. He smiled. What else did he need to tell him? He was getting impatient.

"Let me see!" he said, trying to grab Mickey's phone.

Mickey held it higher and the little man tried jumping to grab it.

"I'll arrest you again!"

"It was on the A303 and now it's on a 'B' road somewhere near Salisbury."

Mickey showed him that text and the Inspector took out his phone and walked away.

OLGA and the Dog walked to the fountain in the hall.

"What the fuck is Brin doing here?"

"He was nominated by Prince Ali—"

"Don't let him in here again. You know he's a potential rival, yeah?"

Olga nodded then said,

255

"There's been—"

"And you've overdone it on the girls. Some of them are asleep on the table!"

"Sorry Sir," she said, "a miscalculation after your unscheduled visit this afternoon—"

"Are you trying to blame me?"

"No Sir."

"Good!" he took a deep breathe and asked,

"What were you saying?"

"There's been a security breech. The tow-truck is being followed. They are close."

"Who's on the back?"

"It's Coburn's car. It was followed from Berkeley Square."

"Get the boys out. Road-blocks; uniforms; pistols only," he said, turning to go back to the dinner party, "Let's dump Coburn and change the drop-point to St James's Square."

"That means we only have a couple in the field, as we've suspended Grodenko?"

The Dog thought for a moment, then said,

"Okay, get him back. He *had* been on such a roll until this latest aberration."

Olga nodded.

"Maybe point out the requirements to him again? He seems to have forgotten?"

Olga nodded.

"And this bunch aren't very good, are they?"

"Well we had such a turnover this month that most of them are new so—"

"Not much positive feedback so far except for the twins and the pretty blonde. Let's see what sells tonight, then we clean house tomorrow, except for the youngest..."

Olga watched him depart, then spat. He was right, but she still spat.

MICKEY hailed a cab and asked the driver to take him to Berkeley Square.

His phone rang. It was Eva. He said,

"Oh, thank fuck you're okay?"

Eva laughed,

"Mickey, you just said Fuck!"

Mickey laughed too.

"So we're both free?"

"Yeah, I couldn't go through with it. Aji and Marcus got me out."

"Aji? Well done Aji!"

"So the police released you?"

"Yes," he said, "I just rolled the dice with
Inspector Gadget and luckily it turned out alright.
Are you on your way home?"

"No, we're following the tow-truck down some
narrow country lanes—"

"No! You should stop! I just told him that the
truck was being followed so that—"

"Oh, wait," said Eva, "there's a road block
ahead. Blue flashing lights. Stop the car Aji."

Mickey said,
"Is Aji driving?"

"Yes, but it's the least remarkable thing about
this evening. We've stopped. They're looking in the
trunk of the car. Nothing. They're coming towards us!
Aji, back up!"

AJI reversed fast up the narrow lane, careering
off the banked sides like a bobsleigh on the Cresta
run, then bouncing off the hedges and tree roots on
either side, as it flattened out. The men stopped
running and went back for their car. She continued
speeding up saying,

"This is quite fun!" as she ricocheted from side
to side. The last bounce was too strong and there was
nothing to stop the car on the other side and it
rolled down a hill, into (then onto) a cluster of
large bushes.

"Turn off your lights!" whispered Marcus. Aji did
so then said,

"Why are you whispering?"

"Shhhh!"
Above, the lights of a car sped past them. Then
circled behind them, slowly descending then fading
away. Marcus got out and, using his phone as a torch,
clambered up the slope. He returned saying,

"They've left the roadblock but the truck has
carried on."

"Is the car stuck here?" asked Aji, getting out
and seeing it squatting on the Rhododendrons.
Eva got out too,

"No. I reckon we can just push it downhill.
Gravity will do most of the work. The road's just
below us."
They all pushed the car, which was looking really
tatty, and it slid off the bushes and rolled on down
to the flat field below.

MICKEY sat in his car on Berkeley Square
watching the *sleeping* figure in the bushes. There was
no one around so he moved his car to the east-side

gate and opened the back door. In the bushes he found
the man snoring loudly and laughed. These were slow-
release tranquilizers that lasted until the dark was
removed. He picked up the man and put him in the back
of his car.

DASHA said, in Russian,
"So this isn't a pedo ring," asked Dash, "where
you come to fuck all the kids in an orgy?"
"These men don't want to share!" laughed Brin,
"they are connoisseurs, and billionaires! They can
afford any price to satisfy their warped desires."
He retrieved a case from his pocket. Inside was
three fat Cuban cigars, a lock-knife and a lighter. He
unfolded the short but chubby knife, pushed the cigar
through a hole in its body, then closed the razor-
sharp blade, snipping off the end of the cigar. He
punctured a hole in the other end, put it in his mouth
and lit it, saying,
"This is like an art lover owning a Monet, a
music lover owning a Stradivarius, or a movie buff
owning Rosebud, except of course, they're stolen so
have to be hidden away and visited when desired."
"You keep saying they, as if you're not also
sitting at this table?" observed Dash.
"Anyone in the know can buy a seat at this table.
It doesn't mean I'm a *baby fucker*. But I might be
thinking of starting a rival house, for girls of legal
age—"
"Hardly an improvement."
"Come work with me. You can help me procure."
Dash shook her head.
"Better to be predator," he said, pointing at
himself, "than a victim," pointing at her, "I'll buy
you and we'll walk out of here—"
"Speak American!" shouted the Dog, slamming his
fist on the table, "only American here!"
"American?" said Brin in English, "you mean the
language of the Native American? Which tribe?" The men
laughed, except for the Dog, who slammed *both* fists on
the table.
"What the fuck are you doing here Brin? You've
shown nothing but contempt for our services!"
Brin looked at the Dog but said nothing, then turned
to the rest of the table, and said in Arabic,
"Apparently, my beautiful friend here, says he's
been fucking the merchandise? That none of these
pretty things are virgins."

Everyone looked outraged, except for the Dog and the girls. Olga whispered in the Dog's ear and his reaction was so explosive that it was obvious to Dash what Brin had said.

"You fucker!" said the Dog, producing an automatic pistol and pointing it at Brin. A few of the men and all the girls jumped up and backed away from the table, except for Brin who remained frozen and Dash who hopped her chair sideways and some of the other men who also produced guns, pointing them at the Dog or randomly at one another.

The Dog pulled back the gun's hammer, making that little clickety-click that was so recognizable. Dash hopped further away from Brin - she didn't want brains on her Cavalli. Then she heard a similar clickety-click from under the table. Brin said,

"I have my forty-five pointing at your balls. Even if you shoot me in the brain, I will already have shot."

The Dog was gritting his teeth and sweating profusely and shaking and pulling the trigger and blood sprayed Brin's face and Dash's and the Dog's face was hanging off, blood overflowing onto the table.

Behind him stood Olga; a smoking gun in her hand.

"Couldn't have him shooting our precious clients, could we?" she said to everyone, "Gentlemen, please excuse us, tonight's party must end here, but we will continue providing our unique service, only from now on it will be run by women so no fear of the merchandise being tainted. And, just for today, do take anyone with you, on the house. Normal terms and conditions apply."

Three men walked, or ran out empty-handed, with Red following them to unlock the door; the forth in the thawb dragged the little blonde behind him. Dash's heart leapt and she tried to grab her as they passed but... they were gone, with Blue following. Dash heard the helicopters starting.

Wiping his face with a napkin, Brin got up, put his lighter back in his pocket and held out a hand to Dash. She had her chance of escape; she could get up and leave with him. But what about the others? She turned and looked at their little faces watching her. She couldn't leave them. Brin still held his hand out, a wicked grin exposing his whitened teeth. But then she realized what he was doing. She placed her hand in his. He raised his eyebrows and she did too as though she was thinking about his proposal.

She smiled, retracted her hand and shook her head. He shrugged and bowed to everyone, then exited. Olga followed him out. The girls slowly emerged from their

corner. Dash used a napkin to wipe the blood from her
face then sat back and waited to be unchained.
    The sound of helicopters grew louder, then faded
away.

    EVA, Aji and Marcus followed the car into the
field. They got in and Aji drove to the gate. Marcus
said,
    "What shall we do? The trails gone cold, hasn't
it?"
    "Yeah," said Eva, "the house could be anywhere;
these roads wind around and around and we could drive
past it in the dark and never even know it."
They heard a noise and Eva wound down her window.
    "It's a helicopter."
    "Two helicopters!" said Aji.
    "Three!" said Marcus, examining the horizon,
"more!".
Far off, lights blinked as they took to the skies in a
swarm.
    "You think that's the place?"
    "Absolutely!"
    "We'll never find it, will we?"
    "It's a mile off as the crow flies, but these
roads are so kinky..."
They all felt defeated, and sat there for a while,
before Eva said,
    "I'd better drive. Don't want to get into any
more trouble tonight."
Aji agreed and they swapped seats,
    "I'm going to take notes, so we can retrace our
steps with reinforcements tomorrow."
    "I'll help," said Marcus, joining her in the
back.
Eva drove on, listening to them chuckling behind her.
The roads reminded her of something, but she couldn't
think what. She guessed she was still in shock from
her earlier scare.

    DASHA went meekly back to her pen. She was far
too doped up to make a snap decision on an escape
plan, let alone enact it. Safely in her cell, she took
the cigar cutter from her mouth and smiled. When
folded, it was only the length of her index finger,
but that meant the blade was also that long. Of
course, having a weapon was one thing; being able to
use it was another.
She took a shower, dried herself then got under the
duvet and opened her phone. There were texts from Aji
telling the story of following the tow-truck to
somewhere near Salisbury and promising to return the

next day. Salisbury? Wasn't that where Hannah was in rehab? Was her prison also in Salisbury?

Sunday - 9th November

EVA, exhausted and still quite shocked, dropped
Marcus off at his friend's house then took Aji to
Margot's. Next, she drove to Aji's mum's house. Mickey
was waiting for her at the end of the street. They
wound their windows down:
"Good to see you."
They leant out of their cars and kissed.
"There are no lights on at the house, so maybe
Nina is still out, or in bed?"
"Hopefully she hadn't noticed it's missing and
called the police."
She pulled away, then turned off the car's engine and
lights and coasted into the drive. The car was a wreck
and she felt bad about abandoning it, but still, she
giggled as she ran and jumped into Mickey's car as he
said,
"Shall we stay at Brook Green tonight? Most of
our stuff has been moved in and it's so much closer
that Hampstead."
Eva nodded.
"Is that because you've stashed the driver
there?"
Mickey smiled,
"Oh you know me so well."

ART looked at the Detective's mouth as he spoke,
which was distracting him from what the man was
saying. Maybe he should look at his eyes instead? Or
his ears!
"So she definitely said she wanted to catch the
nine o'clock?"
Art nodded.
"Train? Bus? Plane?"
Art nodded. He was feeling better; clearer; the acid
was backing off; only coming in waves every ten
minutes or so. This one was receding... His father had
been removed, leaving a big dark circle on the carpet.
He wondered if the blood had been dropping on the
motorbikes below and tried to calculate which one
would've been effected.
Detective Doobry had obviously found Art to be a
frustrating interviewee as he was going through the
same questions one more time, while others searched
the property. They'd found the pistol under the sofa
so the CSI guy dusted it for prints, then asked if he
could take Art's to 'eliminate him from enquiries'.
Art panicked, until he remembered Lori taking the
revolver from him, and he realized what she had been

doing. He agreed and while he pressed his fingers onto the sheet, the interview continued:

"So you think she's changed her name since she lived here as a child?"

"Maybe? but maybe she just got married? She definitely booked into the hotel under a different name though."

"The Portobello Hotel?" he said, checking his notes.

"Yeah," said Art, his eyelids drooping.

"It seems she wanted you to find out for yourself before she took action? Why do you think that is?"

"So it would cushion the blow, I guess?"

"An act of kindness? Or maybe the opposite and she wanted you to discover exactly what he'd done and what he was," suggested Doobry, "otherwise she could've just come here and shot him, leaving no trace and you would've never known why."

"I guess," said Art, needing sleep.

"And you say your book detailing your relationship inspired her to come here?"

"Er, yeah," he said, suddenly realizing the implications, "oh shit, I kind of brought this on him, didn't I?"

"Is that what you meant when you called 999?"

"What?"

"You said 'I've killed my father'."

"Did I?" said Art, his heart beating a little faster, "then I must've meant that; sorry, I'm in shock and very tired."
Doobry nodded.
The CSI guy came over, holding some sheets of film:

"Just looking at these, it's obvious he hasn't touched this gun, except maybe on the barrel."

"That was when I was struggling with my father," said Art, "when he shot my ear."

"Ah, that would account for the powder burns we found on his shirt."

"Thanks Jimmy. Would you say that it was a small hand, maybe a woman's hand that used the gun?"

"Definitely."

"Speaking of which Art, have you seen this gun before? A Webley Service Revolver from World War Two?"
Art shook his head, even though it did look familiar.

"Then we should get you to hospital," said the detective, "you need some serious stitches in that ear."
Art nodded and walked down to the car with a constable. He saw his bike then thought of all the other bikes in the garage. Were they his? Or had his father bequeathed them to the R.N.L.I. like he'd

263

threatened on so many occasions? What would they do
with a Laverda Jota?

DASHA lay in her cell trying to remember the
night before. The only clue was the dress she was
still wearing, and something pressing on her cervix.
She retrieved her phone and found along with it a
knife, no bigger than the phone, but with a sturdy,
razor-sharp blade. Then she remembered Brin, and the
Dog being shot by Olga, and everything else.

ART had fallen asleep in the waiting room after
he'd had what was left of his ear stitched and
bandaged.
It was light when he awoke, so he called Aji.
    "Dad, where were you last night? I tried calling
you?"
    "I was at the mews with my father," was all he
could muster.
    "Are you alright? You sound terrible."
    "Well, I'm at the hospital—"
    "Oh no, is he dead?"
    "Er, well, yes," he said, "yes, he is."
    Aji didn't sound that surprised or upset. They
had never been close, except when she was tiny, and
they'd watch shit television together.
    "Aw, I'm sorry Dad. Are you okay?"
He said yeah.
    "Would you like me to come there?"
    "No, thanks Sweetheart. But I'll see you later
yeah?"
She agreed and they hung up.
    Well, that was easier than he thought it would
be...

MICKEY and Eva woke in their new bed in their
new gabled picture window overlooking the Green. It
wasn't such an expansive view as Hampstead Heath, nor
as cosmopolitan as Sloane Square, but it felt like
home. A family were playing tennis below. Kids played
on the swings. The coffee was fresh ground and perked
them up.
    "So today, me and Aji thought we'd retrace our
steps from last night, hunt around the area in the
daylight? Want to come?"
    "I'm not sure. We might be driving in circles all
day and never find it; and hopefully we'll have
Grody's car soon, which must give us our best chance."
    "Sure, but I still want to go."
    "Then you'd better take the 101."

Eva nodded,

"Can you drive me up to Ladbroke Grove in twenty minutes then?"

"Yeah, and I'll pop in on Art once I've dropped you. He's not answering his phone."

Eva sent Aji a text, saying where to meet, then went to have a shower.

DASHA opened her phone and wrote a text to Eva, Mickey, Art, Aji and Hannah:

> *"Still alive! There was going to be*
> *an auction of the girls last night.*
> *Bidders arrived in helicopters,*
> *but it got disrupted. X"*

ART was back home. Considering what had happened he didn't feel too bad. Was he suffering any grief for his father? He could muster a bit if he reminded himself of his dad helping him with the tappet adjustment on his Honda CB750, or swapping out the engine block of his Ford Escort, but otherwise all he remembered was the sneer.

Art thought of the five stages of grief, as relayed to him in a Simpsons episode (like so much of his adult education) when Homey thought he was dying: Denial; anger; bargaining; depression and acceptance.

Denial? Definitely, unable to comprehend what had happened, hoping Lori was about to walk back through the door; Anger? Yes, as the full impact of what his father had done to Lori dawned on him; Bargaining? Sure, he'd considered calling the hotel and pleading with Lori (as she packed her bags) to take him with her on the nine o'clock, wherever she was going; Depression? Yeah, still in it; Acceptance? Begrudgingly, he knew she wasn't coming back, that she'd done what was needed for her own sanity and that she—

Hang on. His grief was about Lori, not his father.

But he wasn't ready to accept that Lori was gone. The acceptance he felt was around his father, as she'd slowly led him to the answer which he had feared for a number of days. Had she been trying to spare his feelings, or was it all one big fuck-you? Why bother to pretend to be wanting to stay here and get together with him, if all she ever planned was to kill his dad and fuck off? It made no sense, but then maybe the whole thing never made sense to her either? She was just winging it all along? Would she not have seduced him if Dash hadn't've been in the picture? Was she as alone as she'd made out, or had she gone back to her loving family in Lima/Rio/Quito/wherever? Fuck, he was going round in circles...

REVOX turned on his phones. There was a message to Grody:

> *"S reg Nissan.*
> *10 Gervase Road.*
> *New location for drops:*
> *North side of St James Square W1.*
> *Sorry for the delay.*
> *If you have anyone*
> *waiting, drop off*
> *any time after 12noon"*

He called both Mickey and Art but got no answer.

EVA and Aji had met at Mike's on Blenheim Crescent. They'd had a bacon sandwich and a coffee then had walked round to the underground garage where Mickey kept his collection.

There was a line of low-slung cars under covers. Aji lifted a few to get a glimpse and found a Ford GT40, a Ferrari Boxer 512 and a Porsche Turbo.

"Why don't we take one of these? It'd be much cooler burning down the motorway in one of these."

"It would. But what if we find Dash, Amber and any others? They're gonna want lifts home too won't they?"

"Good point," agreed Aji, "plus Marcus wants to come."

"So we need this," said Eva pointing at a big yellow boxy 4x4, "it's a Land Rover 101 'forward control', meaning we sit above the engine. It's water-proof, gas-proof, bullet-proof and bomb-proof, and has various James Bondy gadgets, in case of emergency."

"Cool! Custom-built for Mickey during his former life, I'm guessing? Can I drive?"

"Maybe later," said Eva, reaching up to unlock the door, "now let's go get Marcus."

They climbed in and Eva fired it up. Its 3.5 V8 burbled bass notes and gently shook the cabin. Eva's phone vibrated: A text from Dash. She showed Aji Dash's text saying she was still alive, then replied:

> *"Hi Darling! Glad to hear it!*
> *Followed another tow-truck last night.*
> *Went to Wiltshire, near Salisbury,*
> *but we got ambushed. All OK. Gonna retrace*
> *our steps today with reinforcements*

and find you.
Love you xxx"

She put the Land Rover in gear and trundled forwards, before remembering they'd have to let some air out of the tyres to squeeze it under the exit...

DASHA, showered and dressed, finally heard the door unlock and she exited her cell. The other girls seemed even more passive than before. Could they remember anything from last night? The waitresses were buzzing around, more excited than usual, arguing and shouting about last night. Dash smiled and pretended she didn't understand what they were talking about, like all the other girls. She ate her breakfast and read the newspaper. She wondered if the American Black Sites that were rumoured to exist were anything like her own cell? Without the nicely-lit pen and the breakfast service? Did they use chemicals, or the traditional methods of inflicting pain to break their victims?

ART lay on the sofa and felt sorry for himself. Lori; Dash; his dad; his ear... self-pity, manna to an addict. He checked his phone to find missed calls and a text from Dash saying about the auction.
An auction? So not a pedo-ring but a real slave-trade operation. He had a moment of inspiration and dragged himself up from the sofa, found a number in an old notepad and dialled. It rang four times before a familiar voice answered 'Hello'.
"Milo, it's Artemis Grime here, how are you?"
"Who?"
"Artemis Grime? I wrote that exposé of you in—"
"ohhhh yes; I remember now. And I swore to kill you in a fashion befitting an arrogant, drug-addled little prick such as yourself—"
"But Milo, I made you a celebrity! You seemed to be loving the attention whenever I saw you in the gossip columns?"
"Okay! I did, but it was not good for business!"
"But you released that range of pasta sauces?"
"Yeah, admittedly, that is good business."
"The Puttanesca is my favourite!"
Silence.
"So bygones are bygones?" asked Art.
"You still stole my girl!" (9)
"We fell in love Milo—"
"I was in love with her too!"
"How could you be? You were about to sell her to an Arab sheik for a million dollars—"

267

"That cannot be proven!"
Art heard a low growling then,
"Where are you?" asked Milo.
"At home," replied Art.
"In that same little flat off Portobello? Shall I come round and kill you?"
Art heard a little humour creeping into his voice.
"Sure, why not, and I can pick your brains about a problem I have at the moment too—"
"What kind of problem could I possibly help you with?"
"Unless it's pasta related?" Art joked, but Milo didn't laugh, "my daughter's best friend has been abducted by a gang who run a secret house somewhere in the country where the kids are sold at auction—"
"I've heard of these pedo cunts. I'll make a call and get back to you."

MICKEY had dropped Eva at Mike's then drove round to Art's. He'd had a bad feeling about him but was relieved when Art threw him down the keys. Art was lying on the sofa. He looked terrible: Blood on his shirt; a bandage around his head and ear; sooty face from chasing the dragon, but enormous saucer-like pupils unlike any junkie.
"Are you alright?" asked Mickey.
"Not too bad, considering..."
"Considering what?"
"Er... Mickey, I'm sorry to say...that... I've had a drink."
"A drink?"
Mickey tried to look surprised and keep from laughing.
"And a joint..."
Mickey sat down at the table and waited...
"And some coke..."
Mickey nodded...
"And some smack..."
Mickey raised his eyebrows...
"And then some acid last night."
Mickey nodded and said,
"So that accounts for your massive pupils. You must still be tripping?"
"A little. It's calmed down a lot."
"And what happened to your head?"
"My dad shot my ear off."

REVOX saw Art and Mickey across the street and tried to attract their attention. Neither of them were picking up their phones. He tried shouting one more time, then thought of shooting out their window, then

resigned himself to getting dressed and going
downstairs...

ART continued with his summary of the last
twenty-four hours.
"She screwed you good, boy."
"She did, in both senses," Art agreed, "but did
she want me, or was it just another chess move to
her?"
"She wouldn't've done it if she hadn't wanted
you, would she? More importantly, you're in the clear,
yeah?"
"Yeah, there were none of my prints on the gun
because she took it from me and smothered it in her
own, which makes me think she must be—"
"Forget her Artie! We've got Dash to think about
now."
Art nodded...
The doorbell rang. Mickey looked out, said 'it's
Revox' and dropped the tennis ball down to him. Revox
let himself in and gave them the news:
"So new location and we can be there anytime from
midday!"
Mickey wrote a text to Eva:

> *"Revox got the text.*
> *We can drop off at midday.*
> *Keep in touch*
> *XXX"*

He got one back immediately:

> *"Hi Mickey, Aji texting for Eva.*
> *Great news! But we're gonna*
> *continue as we've also promised*
> *to visit Hannah. Xxx"*

Revox looked disappointed that no one was cheering
him. He said,
"You look awful Art! Who died?"
"My dad."
"Aw, sorry. Cancer?"
"I shot him."
Revox looked blank for a moment, his gaze switching
between Art and Mickey, but they both remained stony-
faced.
"In the head."
Revox squinted. Finally, he laughed,
"Oh, you got me there! Funny! Very funny!"
Art had met a lot of fans over the years and they all
fell into four distinct categories. Revox was in the

269

Licky Puppy camp, who always wanted to please, but
after five minutes, invariably ended up doing the
opposite; but of course, Revox had a secret superpower
which Art wanted to exploit.
Revox said,
　　　"So I'll go get Grody and Maurice, pick up the
car from Burnt Oak, then pass by here on our way to St
James's, okay?"
They both nodded and he ambled towards the door. Art
jumped up and followed him out on to the landing,
　　　"Hey, you don't happen to—"
　　　"Have a little Ziploc bag in my pocket, just for
you? I thought you might be in need," he said, handing
it over.

　　　DASHA watched the maids come in with their
trollies followed by Olga, and then Red (where was
Blue?). Olga had clearly won control of the house and
was lording over the others. Olga nodded to Dash and
asked her how she was.
　　　"Quite bored really, after last night's
excitement."
　　　"You can remember that?" asked Olga, looking
disappointed.
　　　"Yes, I've never been splattered with blood and
brains before."
　　　"It was exciting wasn't it?"
　　　"Is that the first person you've killed?"
　　　"With a gun, at so close quarters, yes."
　　　"So specific! And now you're in command?"
　　　"I am."
　　　"Congratulations. How are you celebrating?"
　　　"With a spring clean."
　　　"Sounds ominous."
　　　"Well, it's one way of curing boredom," she said.
Dash's heart sank as Olga walked away to the door on
the right. The door that led to the 'disposal room'.
Was she part of the 'spring clean'? This could not be
it. She had a weapon, but could she use it?
　　　She went into her cell and retrieved her phone.
There was a text from Mickey saying they had Grody and
his car so would be with her later that afternoon. She
replied with many a smiley face.

　　　ART smoked some smack in the bathroom with the
window open and the ventilator going but he knew
Mickey would know exactly what he was doing. Then he
changed his clothes and went to re-join Mickey, but he
wasn't there.
　　　A note on his board said:
　　　　　　"Gone to the meeting at the Tabernacle.

                    See you at the meeting?
                    Or I'll come by after."
Art felt guilty about Mickey. He'd been his closest
friend for ten years and he'd betrayed him by
relapsing, though of course Mickey would never see it
that way; Mickey knew that no addict ever thought
about someone else when they chose to pick up; they
just thought of themselves. But having only just
reunited with him, Art knew exactly how he must've
felt: Worried about his old friend, but also
threatened by the allure of using with his old using
buddy. Maybe that meeting was where he should be going
too, instead of getting his little tin from the
bathroom... and opening it... and...

     EVA drove west out of London after having picked
up Marcus. Aji and Marcus explored the open-plan rear:
Amongst toolboxes; cooking and camping gear; weaponry;
hazmat suits; and other apocalyptic sundries, there
were netting hammocks that could hang on carabiners in
the back. Aji and Marcus tried them while wearing
gasmasks and using the periscope.
     "The periscope has a cross in the centre of the
lens. Do you think it is also a sight for some
weapon?"
Aji examined the controls on the handles and nodded,
     "You know, I think it must be..."
     GRODY, Revox and Maurice found the estate car
in Gervase road. It was a spacious Volvo Estate with
the same bicycle/luggage panel covering the boot.
Revox opened the hatch which revealed the large
compartment,
     "Easily fit us both in there," he said.
Grody sat in the driver's seat and opened the glove
box saying,
     "One envelope stuffed with... oh, not so much
cash as usual."
     "I'll take that." said Revox, sitting next to
him.
     "One vial of purple powder."
     "I'll take that." said Revox
     "And a Motorola with one text saying, 'Who is
this?'."
     "I'll take that." said Revox, "sorted. Maurice?"
He passed the money and the vial back to him and
Maurice passed a bag forward. Inside was a long chain
which Revox wound around Grody's ankle.
     "So you're a Boy Scout," laughed Revox.
     "I'm Scout Leader, yes."
     "So what's the scam you're running?"
     "What do you mean?"

"Grody, you're not doing it out of the goodness of your heart; there's no good in you; you're pure Cunt through and through. What's your angle?" he said, padlocking the chain in place.

"I don't have an angle."

Revox passed the length of chain to Maurice in the back who, while playing Bejewelled, was smiling enigmatically. He glanced at Revox and raised one eyebrow.

"Oh no!" he laughed, "you can't be!"

Maurice nodded and grinned.

"The Boy Scouts! They're your crew!"

Revox couldn't stop laughing.

Maurice locked the chain onto the back of the driver's seat then left them and returned to his own car, while Grody set off for central London with Revox still cackling beside him.

DASHA lay under her duvet practicing holding the knife in her mouth without gagging, but the most she could manage was about ten seconds. Last night it seemed to be quite easy to hide it there, but she had been heavily sedated. She tries again - twelve seconds. She needed it on her if they came for her. But last night she'd *had* to put it in her mouth as her dress couldn't have hidden it. She found the yoga pants with the big waistband and pulled them on. The knife fit snugly in there. She put on a baggy sweatshirt which easily covered her waist, and for a moment she felt more hopeful.

Then the dread took hold again. She sent a text to Eva:

"Please hurry xxx"

GRODY followed Revox's directions and found himself back in Portobello, parking next to the yellow, squint-eyed BMW he'd been lusting after.

"Just gonna ring Art's bell then pop upstairs to get the guns. All shapes and sizes," said Revox, opening the door. Grody leant his head on the steering wheel. He'd just realized who the BMW belonged to: The bloke who wasn't a cop: the bloke at the party in Windsor who's girl had humiliated him; the bloke who'd written some book, and could buy the bike, but not Grody. He'd never have one now. He was going to lead these scumbags to the doors of his employers who had treated him well and paid him generously for something he enjoyed doing and then it would be over. He'd either be dead or in jail or penniless living hand-to-mouth in that stinking lock-up in Burnt Oak. He needed

to warn them, but Revox had the phone, there, in the
top pocket of his 'leisure suit'. Revox was getting
out:
"Can I come up with you? I need the toilet and
also a hit if I'm to survive the journey in the
boot..."
Revox looked at him and nodded,
"I'm feeling benevolent today," he said, getting
in the back and unlocking the chain, "you'll have to
carry that as unobtrusively as possible—"
Grody snatched the phone from Revox's pocket, jumped
out the car and ran, the chain unravelling and
jangling on the pavement behind him. Maurice got out
of his car and tried to step on the chain but missed
as it snaked past. Grody turned right on to the
Portobello road and sprinted between the Market Stall
holders and the sleepy tourists as Maurice and Revox
followed, less willing to dodge the pedestrians, so
sending them scattering like pins at the bowling
alley. Maurice got to almost stamp on the chain while
it was momentarily still, but then it jerked and
unbalanced him. Maurice fell and Revox tripped over
him and Grody turned the right-hand corner before the
flyover and ran and ran...

MICKEY sat in the N.A. meeting in the
Tabernacle, five minutes' walk from Art's place. He
hardly recognized anyone which he was grateful for,
but worried at the turnover in members in only eight
months since he last sat there.
When it was his turn, he shared about the madness
that was surrounding him (in very vague, generalized
terms): His dear friend going missing; moving house;
his girlfriend quitting her job; his old friend, who
he'd just got back in his life, relapsing...
After he'd finished, everyone said, 'Thanks
Mickey', then one guy said,
"Moving is one of the most stressful activities
of all."
Mickey stared across at the idiot, back-lit by
the little arched window, but then his eye was caught
by movement below. Someone was running into the
grounds of the Tabernacle with a chain dragging behind
them...

ART's doorbell rang, startling him from a
pleasant doze. His ear was aching. Sitting up and
walking to the window made it throb. Below stood Milo,
Pasta Sauce Magnet! He dropped the ball and went to
tidy up the foil and paraphernalia from the table.

273

Milo wheezed as he entered, then laughed at the state of Art. Milo had aged considerably and put on a lot of weight (from trying all his pasta recipes maybe?) but he still had that evil twinkle in his eye.

"What the fuck's happened to you?"

"My dad shot my ear off."

"Because you're such an annoying prick?"

"Yeah, but then I shot him in the head; just to annoy him some more."

"And then did you fuck your mum?"

Art wondered where this was going but didn't really care, as they'd got Grody's car, but his ear was throbbing and he decided he didn't need to worry about what Milo thought of anything so got out his little tin and prepared himself a smoke. Milo sat and watched him.

"Did you find out anything?" asked Art.

Milo said nothing, then,

"What do you know?"

Art shook his head,

"Nothing much..."

"So not nothing?"

Art ran the smack down the foil and sucked its dark fumes into his lungs. He held it, exhaled, then said,

"My daughter's friend was taken from a Halloween party last weekend—"

"What's she like?"

"Er... Thirteen, five foot tall, long dark hair, cute kid."

"Okay, go on."

"Er, then at a Firework night party which I was attending, another girl was taken by the barman—"

"And what's she like?"

"Sixteen? Pale. Beautiful. Black shoulder length hair?"

"And you witnessed this? And saw the barman?"

"Yeah, and then my best friend was taken by the same man?"

"Seriously? And what's she like?"

"Late twenties, stunning, platinum crop, eyes like a galaxy being sucked into a black hole—"

"Oh yeah, I remember her. She was the trouble-maker—"

"What are you talking about?"

"Don't worry about it," said Milo standing up and reaching into his jacket.

HANNAH was finally released from the crypt by the janitor, who laughed and laughed. She kicked him on the shins then went upstairs for a shower. She never wanted to go down there again, though she knew

274

she must if she was to make sure there wasn't a
dungeon next to the crypt. What had been all those
helicopters in the night? Was she confused by her
withdrawals about the house? Maybe there were many
houses in the countryside that looked like that one?
She wanted to call Eva but was so sleepy. She'd lie
down for just ten minutes...

DASHA sat on her chaise and weighed up her
chances of escape, now that she had a weapon. First
she had to be sure she would use it if the opportunity
arose; otherwise it was useless. She envisioned
herself stabbing Red, Blue and Olga repeatedly in
various body-parts until she became less squeamish.
She imagined blood spurting from arteries, showering
her all over, but her continuing to stab. She imagined
Olga, all innocence and 'I'm one of you really',
pleading for her life, but still the knife went into
her soft parts or slashed the skin on her hard parts.
She had to be able to do it, otherwise she might as
well cut her own wrists instead.

It would be helpful if she could get the oxygen
turned on too - that'd hype her up; get her adrenaline
flowing. How could she do that?

MICKEY searched the ground floor of the
Tabernacle and found Grody in the loo, trying to pick
the lock on the padlock, the Motorola sitting next to
him. Grody saw Mickey, grabbed the phone and tried to
send a text, but Mickey batted it from his hands and
punched him in the stomach. Grody crumpled to the
floor.

"How did you get here?" said Mickey, as if
talking to a toddler or a puppy.

He picked up the phone and checked the texts.
Nothing sent. Taking out a small wallet, he chose a
tool then preceded to pick the padlock in... twelve
seconds. While Grody got his breath back, he gathered
up the chain and draped it over his shoulder.

"You have to do this Grody, even if you have no
conscience; the alternative is more painful and
permanent."

ART watched Milo, through his smack haze,
stretch out a cheese wire between his fists.

"Are we having cheese with our pasta?"
But then Milo was rounding the table and Art freaked
out and jumped up.

"What are you doing?"
Milo was a big man and lumbered around the table as
Art skipped away from him.

"Listen, I'm sorry about Miriam, I didn't know you felt so strongly about her!"
Three laps later, Milo tossed the table aside and charged directly at Art, who dodged him as he rammed the drawing board, sending it into the window and breaking the glass, pencils flying everywhere...

HANNAH woke up and saw she'd been asleep for ages. She cursed herself then got dressed. She went down to the phone and called Eva...

EVA was getting petrol at a service station on the M3, when she heard her phone vibrating. It was the landline at Klaus House:
"Hi Eva, Are you coming today?"
"Yes, me and Aji are on the road now, how are you?"
"I'm okay, feeling almost normal now, except for being locked in the crypt all night in pitch black—"
"How did that happen?"
"Oh, I'll tell you later - it's pretty embarrassing..."
Aji and Marcus were in the back, investigating a mechanism that was part of the periscope on the ceiling. It seemed to open like the breach of a gun.
"Maybe we slide something in there then close it?" said Aji.
"Er, don't..." said Eva, her attention split between Hannah, the pump and Marcus opening an ammo box with the words 'Flash Bang' stencilled on it.
"I just thought it might be where Dash was being held," said Hannah.
Aji inserted a cannister into the mechanism. Eva held up a finger and shook her head.
"So you think she might be in Klaus House? That would be ironic, wouldn't it?"
A voice came over the tannoy telling her to get off her phone.
"Yup."
"But maybe correct, because we followed a tow-truck last night to Wiltshire and I thought the roads looked familiar. Your rehab is near Salisbury isn't it?"
The pump clicked off. Aji swung the periscope around. Eva hung the pump on its cradle. Aji pressed a little red button. There was a P-TONK sound.
Something flew through the air above them. Eva followed its trajectory as Aji scrambled out saying 'Uh-oh!"
It flew over the shop, and over the line of trees into a field, where it exploded with such ear-splitting

276

volume that other customers ducked, screamed, or
fainted. Eva carried on walking to the counter.
        "Well we can combine visiting you with our search
for Dash."
        "That's great! Your names are on the list."
Back on the road, after bollocking them for their
irresponsibility she told them about Hannah. Aji
looked sceptical,
        "That can't be possible, can it? Running a rehab
with all those mad-as-a-brush patients running around
above ground, and a prison below?"
        "It does sound unfeasible," said Eva.
        "We'll soon see," said Marcus, "by following our
notes we might end up there..."

        HANNAH hung up, then went round the corner to
the hall. The fountain in the pond made a relaxing
sound and she sat on a bench and tried to remember...
what? Something? She looked around at the arches; the
flagstone floor; the ornate door with the angels
carved in the frame, which apparently had had a song
written about them; two paintings of her view on
opposite walls, kind of mirror images of each other;
the little hatch where you could buy sweets and
ciggies; the door to the smoking room where a heated
discussion was kicking off; the main staircase which
you weren't supposed to use; and the loo with the
condom machine. What was she forgetting?

        MICKEY led Grody back to Revox's, to where they
and the car were waiting. He saw someone ringing Art's
bell and thought he vaguely recognized him.
        "Maurice, I'll follow with Art in my car, okay?"
Maurice nodded,
        "I'll call you with our location later."
        Mickey turned back to see Art dropping the tennis
ball.
        The convoy pulled away and Mickey remained,
looking up at Art's window.

        GRODY was led back to Revox's by Mickey and
found himself chained behind the wheel again. This
time though, Revox swung down one of the back seats
and locked the other end to the spare wheel. He drove
in silence with Revox behind him.
        "If we text '30mins' now," said Revox, "that'll
give us enough time to park won't it?"
        "As long as the traffic doesn't get worse."
        "Okay, I'm sending it. Then I'm getting in the
boot."

ART was bemused by Milo's over-reaction; and to
hold a grudge for so long seemed quite petty, and to
be chasing him around his own flat? Milo lunged at him
again, but he dodged, and Milo fell but grabbed his
ankle and felled him and started pulling him in. Art
held on to the table leg, but the table just slid
along the floor with him. His pencils were all around
him and all Art could think of was that their leads
would be shattered and how heart-breaking that was.

MICKEY watched the drawing board come through
the window and saw that as his cue. He climbed the
stoop as he withdrew the little wallet from his
pocket.

ART stabbed a pencil into Milo's calf which
momentarily released him, and he managed to retreat a
few feet before Milo grabbed his ankle again. Art saw
Mickey in the doorway behind him, smiling, hands on
his hips. Art took another of his beloved 3Bs and
stabbed it into Milo's thigh making him scream and
release Art, who got up and ran to Mickey saying,
    "Shall we go? Bit of a hostile atmosphere in here
don't you think?"
    "You're really getting the hang of this," said
Mickey in a congratulatory way as they descended the
stairs.
    "Aji's with Eva, right?"
    "Yeah, they're on their way to see Hannah."

MAURICE watched Grody reverse the car into the
space on St James's Square, then get out and lift the
bonnet. He then tried to walk away until the chain
pulled taut. Then it jerked and pirouetted him around,
pulling his leg up and straight out from his body. It
then forced him to hop back to the car like a scene
from the Ministry of Silly Walks. Luckily the square
was empty.

From the boot, REVOX yanked on the chain again
and Grody's leg appeared by the steering wheel.
    "Get in, or I'm gonna shoot you!"
But Grody persisted in fighting against the chain, so
Revox put all his strength into one last heave which
pulled Grody's leg through the gap between the seats,
while his other leg was still on the ground. Grody
shrieked in agony, having probably not done the splits
since he was seven. Revox heaved again, pulling

Grody's other leg into the car and allowing him to un-
scissor himself.
    "Shut the door you fucker!"
Grody did so.
    "Now get in the back!"
Grody did not do so. Revox heaved again and Grody's
other leg appeared over the driver's seat then Revox
slowly reeled him in, still fighting like a thousand-
kilo Marlin.

MAURICE saw a tow-truck enter the square and
make its way around to the north side. Grody was still
visible, his head wedged between the two front seats.
The truck rounded the corner.

REVOX had Grody by the legs and then his belt,
tugging him into the boot, but then Grody's head
slipped between the seats. The more he pulled, the
more he strangled the little weasel, which he had no
objection to but he could hear a truck nearby. He
crawled out and grabbed Grody by the hair, extracting
his head from its vice. Then threw him in the footwell
and ducked. The truck trundled past then did a sharp
left so it could load the car. The perfect moment to
grab Grody by his scruff and bundle him into the boot.

MAURICE watched the truck manoeuvring itself as
Revox stuffed Grody into the boot. The driver got out
and walked to the car just as the back seats return to
their normal position.
    She extended the ramps, chained the wheels, then
dragged it onto the back.

DASHA watched the maids come in from the left
with a trolley. Was it lunchtime? But wait, it wasn't
the maids. It was Olga and Red and it wasn't a
trolley, but a gurney with a sheet over it. As they
passed her, Dash saw a few strands of black hair poked
out from under the sheet. Was that her new friend from
last night? The feisty one who also got chained to her
seat? The girl with the beautiful smile?
    Dash's heart sank: So they were killing the girls
in their cells *before* taking them for disposal...

REVOX and Grody lay in the darkness of the boot
in silence; except for the noise of gas expelling from
Grody's bottom - each one smellier than the last.
    "For fuck's sake Grody, you are disgusting!" he
said, unclipping the back seat and folding it down for
fresh air, "they're getting worse!"

"It's because I haven't had any gear! I told you
I needed to come upstairs with you—"
"And then you ran away like a little girl!"
Revox checked the tow-truck driver couldn't see them,
then stuck his arm out and wound down the back window
an inch or two.
"Oh yeah, but I can't help it. My stomach's
turning over and my eyes are watering, I really need a
hit, or I might shit myself."
"Oh, for christ's sake!"
Grody fished an almost empty baggie from his pocket
and threw it at Grody, who opened it and stuck his
nose in it, inhaling deeply. Revox pushed himself
through the gap and sucked in some lungsful of
untainted air.

MICKEY and Art got into the car. Art looked up
at the broken window and shook his head.
"What the fuck?"
Milo was looking down at them.
"I recognized him from somewhere," said Mickey
"remind me?"
"I infiltrated a slaver gang, running out of the
Conservative Party Headquarters?"
Mickey shook his head. Didn't ring any bells.
"He always had beautiful girls with him, who he
was about to 'introduce' to some billionaire, and I
stole Miriam off him and ran to Berlin with her for
six months?"
Mickey shrugged, some of that sounded familiar.
"He's on those awful telly adverts for Milo
Pucini's Puttanesca Pasta sauces?"
"Ah, yes! Of course!"

DASHA saw Olga enter from the room on the right,
dropping thick arm-length gloves on the floor. There
was an acrid smell wafting through the holes in the
glass.
"I'm going to miss talking to you in Russian,"
Olga said as she approached, "these kids don't have a
lot to say for themselves in any language, do they?"
They both scanned the room,
"That was one reason I kept you. They wanted to
dispose of you the moment you arrived, but I also knew
I'd find a use for you, and you did well last night."
"You manipulated me well," said Dash, "you knew
what I would do."
"With the right cocktail and the right prompting
I can make most people do what I want."
"So you're the chemist, not some minion."
Olga nodded,

"I have perfected my cocktail now. Ten days down here and then it's permanent."

"What is?"

"The effect. It never will wear off. You'll become pliant and eager and able to put up with the most awful abuse and never cry."

Dash felt like she was about to throw up. She should've gone last night when she had the chance. But then she looked around at the helpless children in their pens and knew she'd made the right choice.

OLGA said,

"We used to have to subject you to months of torture to get the same result... which was really tiring... and quite boring once the novelty had worn off... and of course a lot of you didn't survive..." Olga looked up and saw Dash was crying,

"Oh, my dear, don't worry, it'll all be over in another week and you won't have a care in the world." She walked away then stopped and turned,

"But what am I saying?" she said, slapping her forehead, "you're slated for disposal, now you've served your purpose."

She came close to the glass and whispered,

"Don't bother to say goodbye to anyone. You'll be forgotten in a day."

MAURICE called Mickey and told him they were on the M3. Mickey thanked him and told him they'd catch him up as soon as possible.

GRODY felt much better once the smack took effect. It had neatly stamped on his emotions and brought back his mindless courage. Maybe, he could get the Motorola off Revox and warn them that the truck was being followed. Or if he killed Revox, that would show his loyalty to his 'bosses' when the tow-truck arrived at its destination. Yes, the gun case was right there in the boot with him, but he must've locked it? He shunted over and his chain jangled. His chain...

ART and Mickey were also on the M3, going twice the speed of any of their procession. Art's ear was throbbing, but he resolved not to take any 'pain killers' while in close proximity to his friend.

"Why was Milo at your flat?" asked Mickey.

"Oh, I called him and asked him about slavers. Whether he might know where that house might be."

"And why did you imagine that would be a good idea?"

"I'm sorry, I wasn't thinking. Might he be part of this setup?"

"He could be. What did you tell him?"

"Nothing, other than I knew what Grody looked like."

"So nothing that might mean they're shutting up shop as we speak?"

"Nothing. Nothing about Grody's car and the tow-truck, which I didn't even know was happening today when I called him."

"Good."

"Sorry Mickey. You're always having to bale me out or save the day aren't you?"

"Well, I was ready to jump in, but I didn't have to today. Who knew a pencil could actually have a practical use in life?"

EVA followed Marcus's instructions and took the turning off the A303. She saw signs for Salisbury. Marcus and Aji were getting on very well. He was doing a great job of distracting her whenever she fell into a depression about Amber and Dash and her mum's car and her dad and... most everything.

MAURICE stayed well back from the tow-truck. He had a serious desire to play Bejewelled. He could actually see the jewels falling before his eyes. He called Mickey and Art. They were only a few miles behind him. He told them they had just got off the M3 and were now on the A303 heading for Salisbury.

GRODY slowly pulled his chain, link by link, into the boot. Most of the spare was in the footwell of the back seats, right by Revox who was saying,

"We've turned off the motorway, maybe another half-an-hour?"
Did that mean Revox knew where they were going? If so, why were they going through with this charade? Jeez, he so wanted to kill the albino creep. He pulled another link into the boot. It occasionally clinked but nothing to alert the idiot to his plan. He judged he needed another foot maybe, before he could make his move.

EVA stopped the Land Rover. They were lost.

"Well no, we're not lost," said Marcus, "we just
haven't found ourselves right back at the field with
the curving road."
Aji nodded,
       "This is the right area, let's keep going."
Eva pulled away and carried on for a mile or so before
coming to a junction. There, before them, was a road
sign saying:
            'East Noyle - 1½ miles'.
       "That's where Hannah is. Let's go there."
Eva turned right.

       GRODY slowly arranged the chain, then moved
forward into position - his head and shoulders almost
protruding from the boot, his legs coiled and feet on
the wheel arch. Revox was asleep. Perfect. Grody
sprung from the boot, curled the chain around Revox's
neck and pulled hard. Revox awoke, his eyes bulging
from their sockets. Grody tightened his grip as he saw
Revox take a pistol from his pocket and hold it
against Grody's temple.
       "You're the idiot," was all Revox said.
Grody retreated back into the darkness of the boot
like the hermit crab he was.

       DASHA, heart sinking, watched Olga walk back to
the left door. She heard gas hissing into her pen.
This couldn't be the end. This couldn't. She held her
breath then ran into her cell and grabbed her giant
inflatable head. She pulled the gaffer tape off the
puncture then put on the head and felt the clean air
tickling her nose. She fastened the neck strap, closed
the padlock, then lay on the floor of her cell. She
felt for the knife in her waistband. It was closed.
She opened it and hid it again, as she heard Red
approaching. It pressed into her tummy, stabbing her,
cutting her, but maybe that was a good thing? It might
keep her alert.
Red stood over her and said,
       "What the fuck?"
       "What?" said Olga's voice over the tannoy.
       "Her head has blown up like a balloon, or she's
wearing a balloon or-"
       "Is she dead?"
Red poked her with her foot.
       "Yeah."
       "Then proceed."
Red leant down and tried to pull the 'balloon' off
Dash's head but failed, so picked her up, put her on
the gurney and rolled her out of her pen. Was this the

283

moment to stab Red? Maybe not in front of all the girls? Maybe in the 'disposal' room?

Dash's head was translucent so she could see the lights in the ceiling, and it reminded her of being wheeled into surgery, when she had her tonsils out, counting back from ten...

Red wheeled her through the door on the right into the dark. Something stank. A walkie-talkie crackled. Olga's voice:

"Have you remembered to put on the gloves this time?" Red grunted and she heard that rubbery slapping sound ringing out in the echoey room...

Confident that Red couldn't see her face, Dash opened her eyes and saw she was parked next to a vat? A tank? A giant bath? A bath of bubbling, stinking liquid. Even protected by the giant head and the oxygen blowing in her face, the fumes we're getting in and making her eyes water. Red leaned over her and touched her balloon face.

"So weird," she murmured to herself. She put an arm under Dash's shoulders, and another under her knees and effortlessly lifted and...

Dash shut her eyes and stabbed the knife into Red's stomach with all the strength she could muster. Red doubled up, dropping Dash back onto the gurney, where she was in the perfect position to look away while stabbing the knife into Red's back. Red bellowed and straightened up, making Dash lose her grip on her weapon. Red tried to reach it in vain, her hands scrabbling behind her, knocking the gurney, making it roll away.

"Take it out!" screamed Red, "it's excruciating!" Dash crouched on the gurney,

"You were about to kill me! Why would I take it out?"

"I'll let you go, if you take it out!" she said, motioning towards a spiral staircase in the corner.

"I don't need you to let me go."

Red charged the gurney, belly-flopping on to it to grab Dash, who somersaulted, her feet landing on Red's back, pushing the knife in further and severing her spine. Red screamed and thrashed her arms, pushing the gurney off from the wall and back towards the vat. Dash retrieved her knife just as the gurney hit the vat and Red rolled into the bubbling liquid face first, but she reached out as she fell, grabbing Dash's foot. Dash fell onto the gurney and kicked at the hand with her other foot but she was getting pulled closer to the burning acid and Red kept writhing and every time she surfaced more of her flesh was missing and bones were becoming visible and Dash

could feel the heat and she couldn't fight it and she
realized the easiest thing would be to let go. She
did...

....and fell...

....off the gurney towards the floor. Red lost her
grip.

Dash hit the floor face first, luckily protected
by the inflatable head, but then the gurney toppled,
and the bed struck her on her neck and everything went
black...

HANNAH watched as friends and family were
starting to arrive. Nursie and her cohorts opened the
front door and checked their names off their list.
They smiled at Hannah as they passed through to the
main room where most of their addicts were waiting.
She could feel the emotion charging the air. Ugh, it
was unbearable. She went into the smoking room and lit
up, then went out on to the balcony. To the left was
the stairs down to the gardens which sloped away down
to the river, and to her right was the car park where
families were arriving.

She'd only been there for a few moments when she
saw an enormous yellow truck pulling to a halt, Aji
waving from the window.

AJI recognized the place as she walked through
the hall with the pond and into the big room with the
six tall windows. Her dad had been in here when Aji
was tiny. It brought back what must've been one of her
earliest memories: They'd sat in an armchair by the
door and her dad had read her the Velveteen Rabbit,
with tears streaming down his face.

After lots of hugging and introducing Marcus,
they sat around a breakfast table and Hannah pointed
out the window,

"Doesn't *that* look like Dash's description of her
view?"

They all peered out and nodded.

"That is eerily exact," said Aji, and last night
we followed another tow-truck like Amber's and Dash's
and we ended up half a mile from here, so this must be
the place don't you think?"

"I guess, but there doesn't seem to be anything
under the house, other than my prison for last night."

"Where's that?"

Hannah led them through the smoking room and down the
steps. Below was the open door to the Crypt.

"Unfortunately, the lights aren't—"

Aji tried the switch and they came on.

HANNAH was shocked, but then thinking about the
hateful janitor she wasn't so surprised. She followed
the rest of them down. There was the spot she'd laid
on the floor, until she felt something crawl over her;
there was the armchair she'd tried to sleep in until
she feared she'd crick her neck; and there was the
table she'd lain on and the ancient tapestry she'd
wrapped herself in to keep warm. But there were no
other doors, no hidden panels, no flagstones big
enough to hide a staircase. Nothing.
    "Where's Art? Didn't he want to come?" asked
Hannah.
Aji looked sad and said,
    "Oh yes he did but he was at the hospital last
time we spoke. His dad died in the night."
    "Oh shit. I wonder how he feels about that?"
They walked outside then looked down the lawns to the
river, then up the other side of the valley to the
house
    "That is the very same view that Dash described."
Other patients and their guests dotted the lawn,
casting long shadows as the sun moved closer to the
rolling hills on the horizon. They walked down the
hill to the river to get a closer look.

    DASHA lay on the floor of the 'Disposal room' as
Red's walkie-talkie barked into life:
    "Can you hurry up? We've got a lot to get through
today."
Olga waited for a reply, then,
    "What's going on? Why aren't you out yet?"
Dash was appalled, but she had done it. She'd imagined
it and then she'd done it. She felt sick, but she was
still alive. Still clutching her knife, she pulled
herself out from under the gurney, only then realizing
she'd twisted her ankle. She heard footsteps so hopped
behind the tubs of chemicals piled in the corner, then
tried to take off the giant head, but the padlock was
stuck. Olga entered, carrying a cattle-prod,
    "Are you okay?" she said, "where are you?" and
froze.
Dash, trying to hide her enormous carbuncle in the
shadows, could see Olga peering into the acid bath,
which was still fuming, scum bubbling on the top. A
skeletal hand broke the surface still enveloped in red
polyester and Olga stifled a scream. Her eyes were
watering, or was she crying? Then she clenched her jaw
and looked about her. Dash was amazed that Olga
couldn't spot her; the Tiger camouflage was clearly
working. Olga went over to the spiral staircase and

looked up into the light, then ran her fingers across
a step and saw her finger was covered in dust.

"So you're still in here, my dear," she said,
peering into the shadows, "show yourself now and I
promise it will be painless."

She started searching the room, wielding the prod
before her, pressing the button so it made the
crackling BZZZT! sound. Dash whimpered at the noise
and Olga homed in on her,

"Aha!" she cried but then saw the giant head and
seemed confused.

Olga headed round the tank, so Dash limped from
her hiding place to keep it between them. Dash, her
vision compromised, blundered into some drums and
fell. Olga almost got her with the prod, but Dash
recovered then hopped into the hall. Olga wasn't far
behind and caught her with the prod - BZZZT! She fell
and Olga tripped over her and they both tumbled across
the floor. Olga ended up on top of Dash, head-to-chest
pinning Dash's arms under her. The girls watched on,

"Dash?" said one, "is that you?"

She nodded but they probably didn't see that. She
was frozen in horror, knowing what had happened. Blood
started seeping from Olga's mouth, which she opened,
and Dash could see her knife protruding from the tip
of Olga's tongue. She moved her fist under Olga's chin
and saw the knife move too. Olga didn't scream, but
some of the girls did.

"I'm... I'm so..."

"You're not apologizing to her are you?" said one
of the twins, Halsie or Eislah? Which was which?

Olga tried raising her head to stop the blade
from piercing the top of her mouth, giving everyone a
horrifying sight...

MAURICE called Mickey and relayed directions.
They were now on 'B' roads and Mickey was close
behind. Finally Maurice saw Mickey's car in his mirror
and hung up. They must be close.

REVOX got back into the boot, kicking Grody
'accidentally' a lot, then pulled the seat back up.
The tow-truck slowed to a crawl and then stopped. They
heard voices and then a heavy gate opening. This was
Maurice's moment. The tow-truck moved forward, then
stopped, then moved off again.

MAURICE hung back and watched the tow-truck
stop near the entrance. He had Mickey on speakerphone.

"There's just one guy at the gate. Not armed."

"Good. This is our chance."
It had to be timed perfectly. He was ready.
"Oh shit!"
"What?"
"There's two armed guards coming over, and they've got the wrong kind of gate," sighed Maurice, "it's a fuck-off steel girder meant to defend against exactly our kind of attack."
The guy used all his weight to swing the ram-bar open, then the truck pulled up to the chain-link gate, and the bar was locked back in place.
"Do we have a Plan B?"
"I saw a Mr Kiplings van turn off about a mile back."

MICKEY smiled and turned to Art to say... but Art was asleep.

REVOX got his guns ready and peeked through the crack.
"The car's being unloaded into a small garage," he said and then it all went dark.
"They must've shut the doors."
Revox pushed the seat back up and crouched down in the footwell, just in time to hear a hissing sound.
"Do you smell gas?"

DASHA lifted Olga's head and slowly pulled the knife out. Olga spat blood then tried to stand.
"Get the prod!"
Olga was in no state to fight. Dash picked her up.
"Get us out of here Dash," pleaded Amber, "get these doors open please."
"I will. We're all getting out of here today. Put some clothes on and get ready to run."
Dash got behind Olga and put an arm around her neck, almost carrying her. In her other hand she held the knife and the prod under her arm. She walked Olga out the left door into a dark hall. On the right was the service elevator and on the left the stone steps leading upstairs, under which was the door to the Control Room. She pushed Olga in and sat her on a swivel chair. A bank of monitors showed various views including the girls in the cellar getting dressed; another identical cellar where the girls were moping around their pens; upstairs where a guard sat eating popcorn, and a perimeter fence among trees. Below the monitors was a microphone for the tannoy and an old PC with a keyboard but no mouse. A few floppy disks lay on the console.

GRODY woke up as a guard with a gun opened the
boot. The guard seemed surprised to see an ugly man
instead of a beautiful girl and immediately zapped him
with his prod,
BZZZRRRKKK!
    "Ack! No! Wait, I'm Grody your collector!"
BZZZRRRKKK!
    "Gurk! Grodenko? I was hijacked by a group of..."

REVOX awoke to the pleasing smell of Grody being
electrocuted, wafting through the gap beside him,
where the seat was folded flat. The lights were on in
the garage and he sat up without thinking. Luckily the
boot was open so the bicycle/luggage combo was
shielding him from the person behind. Grody was zapped
again while he tried to explain. Revox took out his
guns then knelt in the footwell so he could look back
into the boot. He saw the man with the prod and shot
him immediately, spinning him around until he fell.
    Grody was gone, jumping from the car during the
shooting. Revox squeezed through into the boot and
then clambered out but Grody was nowhere to be seen.
He rubbed his temples and breathed deeply. Had they
been gassed in this airtight garage, full of cleaning
equipment and tool benches?
    Stepping over the body, he slowly crept into the
house. A red light flashed on the wall of the
corridor. To his left looked like a kitchen, to his
right a hall with a fountain. No one was around. He
heard noises below from a stairwell, shouting and
footsteps, so he ran into the kitchen and hid behind
some stainless-steel fittings.
    A few guards ran up and out, then all was quiet.
He walked back to the stairs and crept down. There
were a couple of guards still below, one of them
trying to break down a locked door.

DASHA said,
    "How do you open the doors to the pens?"
Olga reached forward and stabbed a little red button
by the microphone. On the monitor, the girls continued
to prepare themselves as if nothing had happened. The
only difference was a red light flashing on the wall.
Upstairs, another red light flashed, and the guard
sprang into action, unlocking a cupboard and reaching
for a gun. Dash cursed herself, then pulled the heavy
door shut and bolted it. She saw another guard run
across a car park. She took Olga's belt and strapped
her hands to the chair behind her back. Then she

jiggled the padlock on her neck until she finally
heard a click, and she could take her head off.
    "How many guards are there?"
Olga said nothing and didn't move. Dash heard
footsteps then saw guards in the cellar. The walkie-
talkie squawked:
        "Blood! There's blood here. But whose?
    Everyone's in their pens."
        "Maybe the Bosses? Where is she?"
        "No sign of her on the monitors."
        "I've found Bluto!"
        "Who?"
        "The one who always wears red. She's fallen
    in the vat of lye."
        "Shit, you don't think the boss is in there
    too, do you?"
        "Who would have done such a thing?"
        "This door is open, according to this map
    it's the feisty one!"
The guards finished their search then looked the girls
up and down while waiting for orders.
Dash noticed another door to the left of the monitors.
She listened for noises then said,
    "Where does this door go?"
But Olga remained silent.
    Dash unbolted the door and pushed it open a
crack. There was the other cellar, identical but for
being a mirror image of her own prison. She saw all
the girls who'd come to the 'party', including the
dark-haired girl.
    "I'm getting us all out today girls! Get dressed
and ready!"
They smiled and waved, then a guard entered from the
far end so she shut and bolted the door. She turned to
Olga,
    "It's your last chance to tell me, then I will be
forced to hurt you."
There was a knock on the door.
    "Miss Olga? This is Robbie and Churchill. Are you
in there? Did you sound the alarm?"
    "I did!" she croaked, impeded by her wound, "I'm
being held hostage by the feisty one, but she doesn't
have the balls to hurt me so go ahead and break down
the door."
Dash was speechless; saying she didn't have the balls;
she'd already stabbed her in the throat.
    "I've already stabbed you in the throat, and I
can hurt you some more whenever I want—"
    "That, my dear, was purely accidental. You can't
hurt me. It's not in your nature. Now unlock the door
and go back to your room."

Dash almost did so. What was the point? The door was being hit with something heavy. They'd be through soon. Olga sat there smiling victoriously. Smugly. But wait; she'd *pulled* the solid oak door shut, against an oak frame, set in a thick stone wall.

Dash scrolled through the cameras until she found two guards by the steps - one black, one white. She watched the white guard on the screen. The moron could hit it all day with a fire extinguisher and it wouldn't give. Dash grabbed Olga by the hair and spun her round.

"Two things I want. To know how to control the gas, so I can sedate the moron outside this door, and to open the girl's doors."

Olga had been momentarily shocked by the hair-pulling but looked composed again. She shook her head.

Dash raised the knife to Olga's face and tried to press it against her cheek, but she couldn't make her hand turn the knife so that the blade...

"Fuck!!!" is all she could yell.

HANNAH, Eva, Aji and Marcus stood by the riverbank looking up at the house. Six tall windows across with double doors and a balcony in the centre; six smaller arches below; two more floors above.

"How many houses could there be that look exactly like that?" asked Aji.

Dave, a counsellor from the rehab sat by the river birdwatching. He laughed and pointed over his shoulder. Aji turned and looked back at Klaus House and said,

"Er, guys..."

They all turned and looked back up the hill. It was the mirror image of the one opposite.

"Didn't you know Hannah?" asked Dave, "haven't you been outside at all?"

He handed her his binoculars and said,

"Two identical houses were built by identical twin brothers, Luka and Klaus, who decided they needed to be independent of one another to find wives, but still wanted to be within semaphore range—"

"And what is that place used for now?" asked Hannah, scanning the property.

"Dunno, but the locals think it's a high-roller casino/brothel, judging by all the helicopters that fly in on Saturday night—"

"So that's where she is, looking back at your house!" shouted Eva. Hannah handed her the binoculars, and said,

"There's a tall fence all around and guys patrolling the grounds with bears."

291

"Bears?" enquired Aji, "you really do need an eye test!"

"So there's no point in arriving at the drive and ringing the bell," said Marcus, "our best bet is ramming the fence with the 101, but who'd be crazy enough to..."
One-by-one they all turned their eyes on to Aji, who smiled and started running back up the hill towards the bright yellow truck.

"Come on!" she shouted. The others ran after her.

AJI fired up the engine while the others jumped in. There weren't enough seatbelts for them all so Hannah and Marcus climbed into the hammocks. The Land Rover was looking directly down the hill but there was a small wall that they'd have to circumnavigate. Aji struggled with the clutch and the gear lever.

"You'll have to back up a bit," said Eva as she sent Dash a text.

Aji got it in gear, checked her mirrors, let out the clutch and the 101 lurched forward, through the wall, dropped the four feet onto the grass and bounced across the lawn, flinging everyone around inside.

"Oops!" laughed Aji, as she put her foot down and accelerated towards the river, scattering onlookers. She didn't slow down as she approached the river and Hannah started screaming.

"Don't worry, it's watertight," she cried, "and if it's so deep we even have a periscope!"
The others shut their eyes as the birdwatcher ran for his life and the truck jumped off the riverbank...

into two feet of water.

"Bit of an anti-climax," she said as she gunned the 101 up the hill, the immense tyres carving a path through the scrub. They sped past a man tending a large bonfire. 40mph had seemed so slow on the motorway but now it seemed momentous. The fence loomed above them.

She aimed for the space between two posts and put her foot down, crashing the truck into the fence which stretched dramatically but didn't break. Everyone got thrown forward as they slowed to a halt a few yards past the posts. Aji revved the engine and tried to continue to plough the fence below them but the wheels slid, so she backed up to try again. The fence contracted back into (almost) its original position, but she wasn't giving up. When she stopped reversing Hannah said,

"Can you drop me here please Sweetheart? Not sure my body can take a lot more of this."

"Me too," said Eva. They got out by the bonfire and Marcus strapped himself into the other front seat and they were off again.

HANNAH and Eva dodged as the 101 sprayed mud everywhere as it accelerated. The man by the bonfire said,
"What's going on?"
Hannah smiled and moved towards him,
"Do you work in there?"
"No, I'm a crofter."
Hannah moved closer. In the twilight he could see he was handsome. She whispered so he had to bend down to hear,
"Our friends are being held captive in there—"
"Really? Then we should call the police?"
"Not yet. We think the police may be in on it."
He looked up at the truck charging the fence and shook his head.
"What's the bonfire for?"
"Having my family over in a while for fireworks...brothers and sisters and all their sprogs—"
"And your wife and kids?"
"Single."
Eva rolled her eyes and laughed, saying,
"I'm gonna jog up and see if I can help, okay?"
"Yup, I'll hold the fort here," she said then turned back to the crofter, "and do you have supplies for your guests?"
"I have a box of fireworks, six sausages and lots of beers, but they're not chilled."
He looked a bit ashamed of himself.
"I can get you ice and food," she murmured.
He leant in to hear her and his rugged face was half-lit by the flames.
"Maybe some cutlets and some more sausages?"
He smiled.
"How can I ever thank you?" he said, offering her his hip-flask. She could smell it om his delicious breath and her hand automatically reached out for it, but then she stopped herself.
"Better not, I'm an inmate at Klaus house on the other side of the river," she whispered.
"Also, against your will?"
"No, I really do need to stay stopped this time, but I'm realizing that I'm just transferring my addiction on to..."
"On to what?"
"Sex?" was her last word before their lips touched.

DASHA wished she'd taken her phone out as well as the knife, but she hadn't been thinking straight. Could she retrieve it in front of Olga? Maybe that was just the visual that would make her talk? She looked around her, as the banging continued. On the table were some floppy disks. Who still used floppy disks? This antiquated computer, clearly. She picked one up. Written on the label was 'Gate'. Another was labelled 'Lift'. Another was labelled 'Water'.

"What are these?" But Olga said nothing, just sat there smiling that smug smile.

"These may be programs for your computer? Maybe this one can control the water; this one the lift?" She flipped through the others and found 'Gas' and finally 'Doors' and popped it into the slot on the front of the computer.
Nothing happened.

"So there's a code to get them working. What is it?"
Olga said nothing. She tapped the PC's keyboard and the screen lit up. A cursor blinked at the top-left corner. She tapped a few keys and the letters appeared, so she pressed 'enter'. But it replied:
> *"Bad command or file name*
> *C:\>_ "*
She said,

"Your burly assistant in red mentioned the code yesterday when she was trying to open the doors. She'd forgotten the code. What is the code?"
Olga looked as though she were at a tea party listening to an amusing tale told by a vicar.

"I'm serious!"

"You do *look* it, my dear, but can you *be* it?"
Dash turned away, disgusted with herself. She saw the cattle prod and picked it up. She pressed the button and it crackled. Without turning back to Olga, she swung her arm and the prod connected with Olga's leg, making her scream. Then laugh. Dash turned back to her, surprised.

"That's more like it! Even if you had to look away to do it."
The fire extinguisher stopped slamming on the door:

"Are you alright Miss Olga?"

"Yes Robbie. Less disappointed in my Russian compatriot than I was, though it'll take a lot more that an electric shock to make me talk."
Dash gritted her teeth, but then saw on a monitor a top-down view of a yellow tank, firing bombs while ramming the perimeter fence. Could that be one she'd seen Mickey driving in the past?

There was shouting outside the door and
footsteps. The guards who had been leering at the
girls were leaving the cellar by the stone steps and
the spiral staircase. The black and white ones outside
her door remained, the white one trying to persuade
the black one to take over the battering of the door.
Dash heard him say 'That door is solid oak Robbie, you
ain't getting through that with a fire extinguisher'.

AJI rammed the fence again and then reversed up.
"Maybe it sagged a bit more and sprang back a
little less?" said Marcus.
"But at this rate it might take all day."
Eva lurked behind a bush nearby. She waved and pointed
at the house. There were armed guards running down the
hill through the ornamental garden. Eva ran up to the
truck and Marcus let her in. Shots grazed the bodywork
reverberating inside like a drum.
"Fire one of those Flash Bangs at them," shouted
Eva over the ringing, holding her ears, "this is why
armoured cars should have soft furnishings and padded
linings on the interior!"
"Maybe a nice Paisley?" suggested Aji.
Marcus loaded the cannister then used the periscope to
aim and fire. It landed close to them and they ran,
but then they realized they hadn't been injured and
regrouped.

DASHA held the prod against Olga's leg.
"Tell me the code."
Olga said nothing. Dash tried to press the button. Why
couldn't she? Wasn't there enough urgency? Enough
danger to these girl's lives? Did she expect her
friends to pit themselves against armed guards and
win? Were they going to die too? How come she could be
cruel to Marcus when she found him trying to assault
Aji? Because she loved Aji with her every atom? Didn't
she love Amber and Elsie and the others, who she'd
promised she would free? She turned her head away and
pressed the button; and held it. Olga screamed. Dash
tried to distract herself. Mmm - the smell of burning
flesh reminded her of a barbeque she'd attended in the
summer with Art. Where was Art? Was he in that yellow
tank, still ramming the fence, but now with guards
shooting at it. Olga screamed. Robbie yelled,
"Open that door, or I'll start killing the girls
one-by-one!"
Dash watched the two guards walk into the cellar.
"Wow, I've never been down here before," said
Churchill, "but what the fuck? What is this?"

Robbie ignored him and shot directly at Elsie who
screamed... but was unhurt. The bullet was embedded in
the 'glass'.

"What the fuck are you doing?" said Churchill.
Robbie held the muzzle of his pistol against one of
the holes drilled in the glass and fired, but Elsie
had already moved close to the door so he couldn't aim
anywhere near her. He looked around the cellar and saw
Jenny sitting near the rear of her pen, daydreaming.
The other girls shouted at her to move and she looked
at Amber banging on the wall, but didn't seem to
register the danger. Churchill held his head in his
hands. Robbie positioned his pistol, then looked at
the camera.

"Okay! I'm unlocking the door!"
Dash pulled back one of the bolts noisily. He lowered
his gun and walked to the control room. Then she
quietly bolted it again.

"Jenny! Jenny!" she shouted repeatedly over the
tannoy, then she jammed the prod between Olga's legs,
shut her eyes and pressed the button. Olga's screams
rang out through the cellar and Jenny flinched, then
put her hands over her ears. Robbie ran back,
Churchill grabbing at him. Dash pressed and held the
button and Olga's scream was louder and more
horrifying. Jenny curled into a ball. Robbie tried to
line up his gun with the hole, fighting off Churchill.
The scream was shriller. Still covering her ears,
Jenny scurried into her cell as Robbie fired.
Did he hit her? She wasn't making any noise. Robbie
pushed Churchill and they tussled until Robbie ran
away, up the stone steps. Churchill stood there and
shrugged at the camera, then walked out of the cellar
towards the spiral staircase.

"We're alone now," said Dash, "you can tell me
now..."
But then Robbie ran back down and banged on the door,

"I've texted for back-up Miss Olga. They will be
here in fifteen minutes."
Dash grabbed Olga's ears and shook her,

"Tell me how to gas that fucker!"
Olga swallowed, no longer smiling, no longer
confident.

Dash pushed the prod between her legs and shut
her eyes and--

"Wait!"

MICKEY crouched in the bushes close to the
guardhouse by the main gate. The guard was on his
walkie-talkie. Things were kicking off on the
perimeter and he was missing out.

"Can I go help out?" he was saying.

A yellow tank was ramming the fencing? That must be the 101. Mickey realized he hadn't spoken to Eva in ages and got out his phone, but then a Mr Kiplings van appeared in the lane. The guard noticed it too and hung up. The van stopped near the ram-bar and honked. The guard shook his head and waved it away. The van honked. The guard got out his phone. The van honked. The guard threw down his phone, exasperated. The van honked. The guard picked up his pistol, exited the guardhouse, unlocked the man-sized gate within a gate, then pointed the gun at the van and let loose six shots into the rear storage compartment.

Mickey took out his gun and shot him in the butt. He looked surprised, turned and tried to remove the dart from... fell forward... then passed out. Mickey came out of hiding and retrieved his dart from the guard's butt as Maurice climbed down from the van, still wearing the white coat and stupid hat he'd stolen from the original driver. He went to the guard, found a bunch of keys, and relocked the man-sized gate.

"I've brought another dart-gun for you, if you like?" said Mickey while he hog-tied the guard.

"What do you mean?" asked Maurice.

"So you don't have to kill?"

"Yeah, that's the bit I don't get."

"The *not* killing bit?"

"Yeah, it's really the only reason I came along; to legitimately kill people—"

"Legitimately?"

"Yeah, we're in a life or death situation; I want to be on the side of the living. You may jeopardize that by not killing this guy now, and he might get released by his buddies and end up killing you, and then you'd feel stupid, wouldn't you?"

This sentence was the most Mickey had ever heard Maurice speak. More than all the other words combined.

"You have a point Maurice. I *would* feel stupid if I was dead."

Then,

"You don't have a twin, do you?" Maurice shook his head.

The guard was waking up.

"How many guards on duty?" asked Maurice.

"On a Sunday? Maybe eight or nine including me."

"What is this place?"

"It's a repatriation centre for abducted girls," he said while rubbing his butt where the dart went in.

"And how many girls are there here?"

"Er well I'm just a gate-keeper. I've never seen them. Even the senior guards rarely get to see the girls except on Saturday nights at 'repatriation'. Last time, apparently, there were about twelve I think?"
Mickey and Maurice carried him into the guardhouse and gagged him, then walked up the drive...

DASHA pushed the prod between Olga's legs then shut her eyes—
"Wait!" shouted Olga.
Dash waited.
"I just wanted to say, one torturer to another, that I have no respect—"
Dash turned away and pressed the button. Olga screamed.
"You fucker!" shouted Dash, "you're making me do this!"
"That's what all torturers say," said Olga, between retching and shuddering.
"I am not a torturer!"
"That's what all torturers say," said Olga.
"Let me remind you of what you said to me earlier today, when the roles were reversed: *'The effect will never wear off. You'll become pliant and eager and able to put up with the most awful abuse and never cry.'* You are not some innocent Muslim snitched on by a neighbour for the bounty from the C.I.A. You are a monster with information I need and that's what makes me able to do this."
She jammed the prod against Olga's ear, and without looking away, pressed the button. Olga's eyes bulged as she jerked and shuddered and frothed at the mouth.
"Tell me the code!"
Olga, tears in her eyes, looked up at her torturer and said,
"I've survived this before, and now I only need to survive for another ten minutes, and you'll be gone; then I can return to my life's work—"
"Of breaking children."
Tears were also in her own eyes as she pressed the button and shouted,
"Now tell me!"

EVA called Mickey:
"We've found the place. It's directly opposite Hannah's rehab. We're ramming the fence."
"We're round the other side. There's maybe nine guards in all. How many have you got with you?"
"Five, yeah, four or five."

"Great. Keep it up. We're gonna sneak in and find Dasha."

Eva relayed her conversation to the others. Aji drove the 101 up to one of the fence posts and slowly rocked the truck against it. It swayed with the truck and on each forward motion, Aji pushed it a little harder.

Marcus loaded a tear gas cannister into the breach and aimed high to clear the fence. It exploded near one guard who ran blindly into a rhododendron bush.

GRODY lay on the floor and spied the main hall through the bannisters. First, guards had run out shouting something about a yellow tank, then he'd seen Revox skulking around. He didn't want to be seen by any of them, so lay back and listened to the sound of the fountain below. Maybe he could escape them all? Stay free, at least? Better than facing Revox or that psycho with the motorbike. And his lock-up wasn't too bad. And his boys would have some money for him. As long as he didn't get caught. He decided to find a better hiding place upstairs.

MARCUS felt sea sick. Aji had been pushing the truck against the fence post for so long he thought he might throw up. The post was swaying dramatically though. The 101 had slowly loosened its deep concrete foundations and its neighbours on either side. Finally, it fell and they drove into the compound, scattering the surviving guards on their way up the hill to the house.

EVA called Mickey:

"We're through! The fence at the bottom of the hill is down. Shall we come and meet up?"

"I think you're doing a good job diverting the guards for now."

Eva said to Aji,

"Mickey is about to search the house so thinks we're better off down here creating a diversion."

"Good point," said Aji, "let's cruise around the ornamental gardens tear-gassing as many guards as possible, plus the occasional flash-bang to bring more guards."

"Aye aye Captain!" said Marcus, loading another cannister into the breach.

"So, where are you now?" asked Eva of Mickey.

"We're in the garage where they stashed Grody's car. The boot is empty except for Revox's guns, so

they must be inside I guess, and there's one wounded
guard on the floor. We're going in."
    "Good luck."
Eva crossed her fingers and said a little prayer for
Mickey.

    REVOX slowly descended the stone steps and
peeked the corner. There was the guard pacing up and
down in a dark corridor; the guard who'd been shooting
something in that cellar through the other door. Revox
backed up, then waited for the guard to approach and
coshed him. He crumpled to the floor. Revox took the
guard's belt and hog-tied him. He cautiously stuck his
head round the cellar door. There were girls in glass
cases looking nervous, but no other guards. He put his
gun in his pocket and entered. He heard some gasps and
some of them scurried into a room at the back of their
cases.
    "Hey, I'm Revox; I'm here to help."
A beautiful kid came forward, dark hair, older than
his own daughter by a few years, and spoke through
some holes in her glass case,
    "I think Dash has locked herself in the control
room under the stairs," she nodded towards the way
he'd come in, "she's trying to get the bitch to open
these doors."
He pushed on the glass and realized how thick and
flexible it was.
    "It looks like some kind of special perspex
maybe?" then he saw the bullet embedded in the panel,
"shit."
He nodded at the girl then ran back to where the guard
was.
    "Dash?" he said, knocking on the door, "I'm
Revox, Art's neighbour? We're here to save you all."
    "Who's here with you?" he heard a voice say
through the door.
    "Er, well I came in the boot of the car, like you
did? And Mickey and Art followed me here. And I
believe Mickey's girlfriend might be around here
somewhere too?"
    "Sounds right, there's a big yellow tank in the
garden that's punched a useful hole in the fence, but
I'm still not opening this door."
    "Understood. So what can I do?"
    "Well there's reinforcements coming in five
minutes, so unless I can get this monster to open the
girls' doors it'll all be for nothing."
    "You've tried hurting her, obviously, from those
horrendous screams?"
    "Yes."

"So does she have anything here you can use as leverage? Someone she loves that I can find for you?"

"I don't think so."

"How about her passions?"

"She has a passion for breaking little girls."

"Shit. Anything else?"

There was silence for a while...

"Maybe," she said, "now you come to ask."

"Okay. You get the doors open, then head for the hole in the fence, anywhere *other* than the main gates. That's where I'll be waiting for the reinforcements."

He ran upstairs, straight into Mickey and Maurice.

"Who's downstairs?" asked Mickey.

"The girls, locked in bullet-proof glass cases, and your friend Dash, who's trying to get the boss to unlock the girls' doors, and one hog-tied guard."

"So that's one, plus five with Eva and the truck, the gate-keeper makes seven—"

"That's irrelevant now," said Revox pointing across the car park, "the reinforcements have arrived."

"Shit," said Mickey, taking cover behind the Mr Kiplings van.

Three cars pulled up in the lane near the ram-bar. Armed men got out and unloaded guns from the boots. One ran forward and took out a bunch of keys, so Maurice took aim with his rifle and shot him in the arm.

"Nice shooting," said Revox, as the guards scattered.

"I was aiming between his eyes," said Maurice, shaking his head in shame. They took cover as the guards returned fire.

CHURCHILL sat on the spiral staircase in the dark room that stank of evil. Whatever the chemicals were, they were making his skin prickle and crawl, but he didn't care. He'd been at this job for a year and hadn't had any idea what was going on in the basement. But now it was obvious. This wasn't a repatriation centre. Was that why he'd never been promoted and allowed downstairs? He'd thought it'd been because he was black, but maybe it was because he was too principled compared to Robbie and the other thickos?

Miss Olga and the scumbag American weren't the innocents they led everyone to believe. And even Robbie and some of the other guards knew what was going on. Had Robbie shot that kid? Had he allowed Robbie to shoot that kid? Had he not put up enough of a fight because he didn't believe Robbie was serious? How many girls had passed through this place? How many

had been 'repatriated'? He should have known. That
night when he'd been having a crafty fag by the poplar
trees, that's when he should have known. The guys were
all foreigners and the girls he had seen being dragged
aboard the helicopters had not looked like their
daughters. He thought it weird, and wondered what was
really going on, but his imagination had never come up
with something like that - it was unthinkable. But
should he have voiced his doubts to his mum? Even if
she would have made him quit? They'd needed the money
though. But now he was... what was the word for being
guilty by association? Complicit. He was complicit and
even if he didn't end up in jail, his family would
never forgive him, and Jeanie would never speak to him
again. There was no way out for him...

   DASHA pulled Olga off the chair and laid her on
the floor, face down. Then she grabbed one foot and
sat on her back saying,
   "Being a dancer, I've met so many athletes who've
had to give up their passion because of injury. The
worst one for a dancer, or a runner is the Achilles
heel, as it never recovers totally. Muscles
regenerate, but tendons can't, and the poor souls are
left heartbroken, never able to follow their passion
again."
   Olga wriggled and screamed beneath her, but was
no match for Dash, who held her foot and slowly pushed
the tip of her blade into the space between her ankle
bone and the tendon.
   "Okay! Stop, I'll do it."
   "Tell me the code."
   "It's *not the* code, *it's computer* code: DOS, a
computer language. So when she said 'what's the code',
she meant she's forgotten the command line for opening
the doors."
   "Okay then," said Dash, picking her up and
putting her back on the chair, "I'm going to untie
your hands and tie your ankles to the chair instead.
Then I'm going to re-insert my blade into your ankle
until the job is done."
   Olga looked broken, but maybe she was playing for
time? She looked at the monitor; the reinforcements
had arrived. They were trying to open the gates.
   "First, stop any sedative gasses in both cellars
and pump in oxygen instead," she said holding the
blade against Olga's ankle. Olga inserted the floppy
disk marked 'gas', then started typing what looked
like random letters to Dash, but then she could smell
that slightly metallic fragrance.
She put on the microphone and spoke over the tannoy:

"Breathe deeply girls, get that oxygen in you! Do some star jumps and get your adrenaline flowing! When you hear the door click, meet me by the control room!" She saw the girls in both cellars laughing and jumping and dancing, so she ejected the 'gas' disk and popped in the 'door' one.

"Now do it!"

But Olga hesitated. Was she buying time until the new guards arrived? Dash knelt down and stabbed the knife into her ankle.

"I haven't cut the tendon yet, but—"

"Okay!" She started typing and then pressed 'enter' then typed some more and pressed 'enter' but nothing happened. Dash twisted the knife blade towards the tendon. Olga screamed, but typed again,

"It's not working! I'm writing the code, but it's not working!"

ART had woken alone in Mickey's car. He felt like shit. He had been dreaming about Lori and his dad; less a dream, more of a nightmare. His eyes and nose were running and the pain in his ear (or where it had been) was throbbing. He looked outside. The car was parked among some rhododendrons across the road from the venue? The place where Dash and Amber were? No Mickey nearby. He got out his tin and had a smoke and the throbbing in his head eased; his nose stopped dribbling and he started to feel better. He heard cars approaching and ducked down. The cars stopped and men with guns got out, maybe twelve of them. Through the foliage Art could see them preparing for a fight, then a shot rang out and they all took cover. His phone rang. It was Mickey:

"Are you safe?"

"Yeah, you hid the car well. Are you inside?"

"Yes, it's the right place but we need more time to free Dash and the girls and now a new bunch has turned up at the gate—"

"I can see them. I'm in the perfect position. Weapons?"

"On the back seat. Good luck!"

Art looked behind him. On the back seat was a pair of weird pistols. When he examined them, he realized they were air-pistols, and he was disappointed until he saw their ammo: Tranquilizer darts. He loaded them both, put the other darts in his pocket, opened the door, then dropped to the ground and crawled beneath a thick rhododendron bush. His first shot sailed past the guard closest to him but as the gun made almost no noise it didn't matter. He reloaded, fired again, and hit the guard in the leg; moments later he slumped

303

over the log he was using for cover. The next closest was a hefty fella toting two sub-machine guns that he fired over the heads of his allies. Art couldn't miss, hitting the big man in the back, who turned and looked behind him, then started walking towards the rhododendron...

DASHA pushed the blade into Olga's achilleas heel making her scream,
"I'm sorry, I'm nervous! I..."
She typed again. Nothing. Dash twisted the knife and started sawing. Olga screamed and started crying,
"I'm sorry Mistress! I'll do it! Please! I'll get it right this time Mistress!"
She typed once more and pressed 'enter'. Dash saw the girls swing open their doors and run out. She unbolted her own doors to both cellars and saw the girls running towards them. There was some laughing and hugging and a couple used the cattle prod on Olga, while Dash checked the monitors for guards upstairs. It all seemed clear, so she said,
"Feeling good? Breathe deeply. Escape route is through a hole in the fence," she saw CC, the dark-haired girl from the other cellar, "will you lead them, and I'll bring up the rear?"
CC nodded and flashed that beautiful smile. She looked bright-eyed and brim-full of oxygen. Dash unstrapped Olga's legs and swapped the belt onto her hands.
"Be stealthy, CC," said Dash, "I'm guessing from these cameras that you're gonna have to turn right out of the door then go round the house and down the hill to the hole, okay?"
CC nodded and led the girls up the stone steps.
"Oh," said Dash, "and don't mind the yellow tank, it's on our side,"
She watched them go, with some pride, then joined the back of the queue pushing Olga before her, when Amber said,
"We forgot Jenny!"

REVOX saw the girls emerging from the house. Luckily their exit was hidden from the reinforcements. He was using the classic sniper technique of shooting through foreground objects (into a nissan hut through a tiny loo window, through a hallway and out another window) so as not to be spotted by the background targets. It restricted his choices, but guards kept running from side-to-side, like ducks at the fun-fair, and he'd got a few so far. By the house the flow of girls slowed then stopped as some of them were looking behind them as if expecting more to come. He waved them on but they didn't move, so he ran over and shooed them downhill. But he'd forgotten he was exposed and was shot. He fell over in a pool of his own blood.

DASHA pulled Olga back down the stairs and into the cellar, Amber following. There, before them, stood the black guard with Jenny in his arms. He was crying.
"Churchill! Help me!" shrieked Olga, until Dash pressed a thumb under her chin.
"Is she okay?" asked Dash, "has she been shot?"
"No, but she's unresponsive."
"Get this oxygen into her. Take a deep breath then quickly pump it into her lungs."
He did so, through her nose repeatedly.
"She's been drugged by this monster—"
"I'm sorry, I had no idea—"
"We were all drugged, but Jenny was here the longest, so it's had the greatest effect."
Jenny started to respond, her eyes flickering open.
"Let's get out of here—"
"No, I'm staying. I can't live with myself. I should've known."
"No, how could you if you'd never been down here?"
"I should've known. Give me Miss Olga and take Jenny and run."
"But I want to bring Olga to justice—"
"Don't worry. She'll get hers."
Dash wasn't convinced but she wanted Jenny more than she wanted Olga.
"Okay," said Dash, and they swapped their charges.
She put Jenny on her back and got her to cling on around her neck then grabbed Amber's hand and ran.

ART watched the big man approach the rhododendron bush. Was that why he hadn't fallen immediately? Art took aim from inside the bush but his choice of targets were diminishing with every step. Finally, when the guard stopped, the only target left was his penis. He fired and the man screamed, then fell over. Art liked shooting men in the penis; this wasn't his first time. He rolled the sleeping man under the bush, reloaded and shot the next nearest. No one noticed him fall.

AJI had ploughed the entire ornamental gardens into a quagmire, knocked out four guards with tear gas, and was frankly getting a little bored when she

saw the girls; a whole flock of beautiful young things
charging down the hill. The remaining guards saw them
too and made chase. One stood directly in their path,
dodging from side to side like a goalkeeper. The lead
girl, athletic with a black bob, karate kicked him in
the chest, and he went down into the brown sludge, the
other girls trampling him underfoot. Aji bore down on
another and he took the full force of the 101's
bumper, throwing him onto his front as Aji drove over
him.

EVA looked out the back window. He had fallen
between the wheel tracks and was trying to extricate
his face from the foot-thick mud.
"Did you notice the gardeners had recently put
down horse manure? Lucky our air is filtered eh?"
The front girl was half-way to the hole in the fence,
but a guard was waiting to intercept her. Aji put her
foot down and charged straight at him. He dodged at
the last second but got hit by the wheel which ground
him into the mud. He lay on his back, glued into the
sticky brown substance as the girls hopped over him
towards freedom. They all headed for a welcoming
looking bonfire further down the hill.

DASHA stopped at the door when she heard
gunfire. She saw Mickey and another guy shooting at
the reinforcements and then she saw the white-haired
guy who'd helped her on the ground in a pool of blood.
As Mickey fired a burst of shots, she and Amber
dragged him out of danger then checked his wound. The
bullet had gone straight through his shoulder. He
opened his eyes and saw Dash and smiled, then opened
his eyes wider and smiled wider,
"Jenny?"
"Dad?"
Dash lowered Jenny on her dad's chest, and she nuzzled
into him.

GRODY explored the top floor of the house and
found storage cupboards, bedrooms or small flats. The
flats had kitchens and he searched for something to
eat but the first one had nothing he fancied so he
moved on to the next one. This was more like it, with
cold cuts and beer which he brought to the small table
and started to prepare. Outside the little window was
a view of another similar house on the other side of
the valley. From below came the sounds of war. He made
himself a ham sandwich and walked over to the window.
Below, in the garden was a yellow vehicle charging

around while being attacked by troops. He watched
while he ate until he heard a noise behind him. He
turned to see an enormous naked woman, sudsy-wet from
the shower, coming towards him. In panic, he threw his
sandwich at her then screamed. But a ham sandwich,
even with that much mustard, was no defence against
the soapy behemoth.

ART saw a rotund, limping figure that he
recognized among the reinforcements. It was the Pasta
King, firing on the defenders of the gate. He was the
next nearest, but much further away that his two
previous targets. Art aimed high with both pistols
(all that pasta made him a two-barrel target) and
fired. Milo toppled like a tree, face forward, into a
patch of stinging nettles.

MICKEY saw Dash tending to Revox.
"We're all out! Let's go!" she shouted.
He smiled and waved to her, then turned back to the
reinforcements. A big man fell silently without either
he or Maurice firing a shot. Art was doing a good job.
There were only about five left. He thought he saw a
kid amongst them, dodging out from behind a tree. Or
was that Inspector Gadget? He took aim but missed. He
really wanted to kill the little weasel, but it was
time to go. He signalled to Maurice.

ART's next target was a petite guy in a trench
coat. He was directing the others from behind a tree,
like a little Bonaparte. Art raised both pistols to
give him a better chance of hitting his target as it
bounced around. He fired and both darts hit their
mark. Art smirked, wondering what two doses would do
to such a tiny person.

MICKEY and Maurice covered each other as they
made the sprint across the open ground where Revox got
shot. They both carefully lifted Revox, while Dash put
Jenny back on her shoulders, then they all retreated.

ART was disappointed. The shooting seemed to
have stopped. The defenders had legged it and the few
surviving reinforcements seemed leaderless and were
milling around or getting into their cars. Art
reversed Mickey's Merc further into the undergrowth
until he found another road.

GRODY had no defence against the slippery woman.
His fists slid off her as she enveloped him in her

307

voluminous soapy breasts and bear-hugged him towards
asphyxiation. He tried biting into the corpulent
flesh, but she giggled as if he was flirting with her
and tightened—
But then she let go of him. She was staring down at
the gardens. There was a vehicle, its headlights
catching flashes of people running from the house,
down the hill into the tree line.
      "The maids?" she said.
Grody squinted and saw a cropped blonde head,
      "and the girls. They're all getting away—"
      "We must get down there, stop them!"
She ran and opened the door to her flat, then stopped,
      "Do you smell something?"

      CHURCHILL hugged Olga like an old friend, and
he saw hope in her eyes.
      "Well done boy," she croaked, "I will reward you
handsomely for your loyalty."
      "Really? How much?"
      "A thousand pounds? Now put me down and we'll go
to my room."
But he didn't. He kept carrying her towards the
stinking room with the spiral staircase.
      "A million pounds! I have a suitcase in my room,
you can have it all."
He pushed the door open and smarted at the acrid
fumes. She struggled against him, but he was strong
and easily lifted her over the rim of the tank and let
her feet slowly sink into the molten, evil broth. She
screamed and the liquid splashed on him and burned but
he didn't care; he just kept slowly lowering her into
it, her flesh falling from her limbs, exposing muscle
liquidising on the bone. She screamed, then pleaded,
then thrashed, then sobbed, and sobbed, and screamed
until her lungs were consumed by the acid.
      "Shall we have one last cigarette?" he said. With
one hand still holding her squirming neck, he put a
cigarette between his lips, then produced a lighter
and lit it. The fag burned brighter than usual as he
had predicted. Inhaling, he saw a lick of light come
through the door, almost like a ghost. It found his
still-lit lighter and smiled, then also inhaled. The
oxygen exploded throughout the entire lower floor,
blowing upwards, collapsing the vaulted ceilings,
igniting the wooden fixtures and panelling from above
into a furnace that no fireman would be able to put
out.

      HANNAH saw the first girls emerge from the fence
and cheered. Her new friend and his family couldn't

308

believe the sight of so many kids flowing down the hill, but they welcomed them by the bonfire with mugs of cocoa and hotdogs courtesy of Hannah and Klaus house. It was all very schmaltzy: Lots of hugging and tears and thank yous between the kids and Dasha and Eva and Mickey and Aji and Amber and Art? No. Where was Art?

She heard a rumbling and turned towards the house just in time to see the cellar windows blow out with explosions of flame. Then fire licking the tall windows of the next floor. Then more explosions as the gas cannisters and the drums of chemicals went up.

DASHA and Amber saw Hannah and CC drinking cocoa and cuddling their younger charges by the bonfire, so they went over.

"Thank you," said CC, before Dash got a chance to speak.

"I would say 'It's a pleasure', like an English person, but it wasn't; so I'll go American instead and say 'You're welcome'."

"What are we going to do now?" asked CC, "go to the police?"

"Do you want to do that?"
Everyone shook their heads.

"Not really - I just want to go home."

"Agreed. Let's save that for another day."

"So, shall we call our parents?"
Hannah saw headlights on the other side of the valley driving towards Klaus house. She jumped up, saying,

"I think I might have a better idea. Come over when you're ready."
She waved to everyone then ran off down the hill and over the footbridge...

MICKEY helped Revox into the back of the 101 and dressed his wound. He seemed fine once he had a shot of morphine inside him. Then Mickey got behind the wheel and trundled across the river with everyone either inside, on the roof or the running boards, watching the house burn and the various gasses and chemicals explode in a myriad of colours.

When they reached the top on the other side, HANNAH was waiting in the car park.

"I've hired this handsome coach driver and his charabanc to take us all home," she said, pointing to it, as the residents disembarked after their A.A. Meeting, strangely bemused by the scene before them.

309

Mickey's Merc drove into the car park and pulled alongside Hannah.

"Take *us all* home?" said Eva to Hannah.

"Yeah, I checked myself out earlier," she said, "I'll go to a meeting tomorrow morning I promise."

"A meeting you say?" said Art, sticking his bandaged head out the Merc's window, "you know, I think I'll join you." He got out and another schmaltzy reunion ensued.

"So who's driving the 101 home?" asked Mickey.

"I will!" screamed Aji.

"Anyone?"

"I will!" screamed Aji.

"Anyone with a licence?"

Aji looked deflated.

"Sorry, you've done a great job. Maybe it's time to relax now."

"As much as I want to go with you in the lap of luxury," said Eva, "as I drove it here, I guess I'd better drive it home."

"Then I'll come with you Evie. Hannah? Want to drive the Merc?"

"Well, I was planning on sitting with Viktor the coach driver, but if you insist. Dash? Want to come with me?"

"I'm gonna go in the coach thanks sweetheart, get the girls' details and take them home to their families."

"We'll come with you Hannah," said Aji, pulling Marcus and Amber behind her.

"Okay great, we'll follow the coach back to the A303."

Once she'd made sure everyone was on board the coach, DASHA climbed the steps and saw all the smiling faces which warmed her heart. She saw Elsie and Jenny and her dad in the back row, so she sat in the next row and shut her eyes and relaxed. The rumble of the engine and the tyres on the road helped her decompress.

EVA followed the coach to the M3 then watched it speed away into the darkness. 40mph just seemed so slow again. She glanced at Mickey and tried to speak, but nothing came out. It was a few miles later before she finally said,

"Mickey, I don't want you to go with Natalie to free Karen. You might fall in love with her all over again and I don't want you to, I want you to stay here with me."

"Okay," he said.

"Okay? Just like that?"

"Of course, I love you and will do anything for you, but I also have an admission to make..."

"What?"

"It's a secret."

She nodded and crossed her heart.

"I've never told anyone this. Not even Joseph, who probably loved her more than I did..."

"Yes?"

"Karen *is* alive, but she's *not* imprisoned. She has a ranch in the mid-west, where no one has ever heard of Vogue or Elle, let alone Karen Ford. We email every so often; earlier this year when Art's book came out and she was a bit freaked out, but she was unaffected, compared to us."

Eva looked into the darkness with her mouth open.

"And the last time we emailed was yesterday, and Karen did vaguely recall a drunken night in a bar recently, where she might have blown her cover and told many a tale to an attractive stranger, *and* had a sudden revelation about the bearer bonds."

Eva was shocked.

"Oh fuck Mickey, I wish you'd told me years ago. I've been fretting about you and her all this time..."

"Sorry Evie, I didn't realize you felt insecure about her. You can be a bit of a closed book sometimes—"

"Me?"

"Yes."

"I can?"

"Yeah, we're like two peas in a pod aren't we? But you have nothing to worry about. I love you, and only you."

She smiled.

"I have a secret for you."

Mickey nodded and crossed his heart.

"Artie sent a copy of his 'Head' book to your parents; so they'd know the truth and contact you."

Mickey nodded slowly,

"The sneaky fucker."

DASHA dozed with her head gently bouncing off the cold coach window. She felt someone sit next to her and opened her eyes. It was Art, looking terrible but smiling shyly at her. She smiled back. Their hands touched then their fingers slowly entwined.

Epilogue

A couple of days later.

DASHA sat in Lisboa drinking her coffee, while watching the world pass by. Eva sat next to her, reading various newspapers she'd found. Dash was still traumatized, mainly by her *own* behaviour, but marvelled at what her spirit had made her capable of. But was she any better than any other torturer? Maybe other torturers didn't even think of such things? Other *torturers*; what a horrible sub-section to be part of. Did they meet up at conventions and all get drunk and...

Eva held up the Sun and read aloud:
"SEX-SLAVE-SICKO'S HORROR MANSION RAZED IN HELLFIRE!"
She opened the paper:

> *"Young girls who had been imprisoned in glass cages for the delectation of billionaire pedos, made a daring escape from their twisted captors on Sunday night, resulting in the mansion being destroyed in explosions caused by the gasses used to subdue the children.*

> *The venue, claiming to be a repatriation centre for immigrants, was breached by distraught parents, who took over the centre and freed their children. Their escape was thwarted by pedo guards who besieged the perimeter and a fire-fight broke out. Bodies of pedos were found at the scene, along with a tiny policeman (their ringleader) and celebrity chef 'Pasta King' Milo Pucini (investor).*

> *In the cellar, girls told us, was a vat of acid where unwanted 'merchandise' was disposed of. DNA, semi-dissolved bones and jewellery (including a pendant engraved with the word 'Olga') have been recovered.*

> *The billionaire pedos would visit from all over the world and bid on the young girls in a sick auction of flesh, then the winner would drag his prize to his helicopter and fly away, according to the girls.*

> *They have reported the crime to the Sun and various police stations to make sure that:*
> *"There was no chance of suppression of the story, and that the politicians and policemen who are involved are brought to justice. As evidence mounts, speculation about who visited*

> *these twisted auctions is rife, with*
> *descriptions coming in from the victims blah*
> *blah blah..."*

Eva dropped the paper and asked.
    "How was the journey home in the coach?"
    "It was surreal, and endless, but also very
satisfying:
Some of the girls were ecstatic and some sat quietly
and watched the lights go past, like I did. I couldn't
get my head around what I'd done. I still can't."
    "And the girls? Were they okay?"
    "They did seem okay. Some couldn't remember much—
"
    "Which is a blessing."
    "and we spoke to them and found out where they
wanted to go, and how they felt about it. All of us
had been taken from Greater London, so Elsie in
Windsor was the first to be dropped off. Her parents
were weeping with joy, and so was she. And the other
drop-offs went a similar way, except for Amber, who
went home with Aji; and the twins who decided to stay
at their dad's hotel in Mayfair, as they'd get a
warmer welcome there, and already had a suite waiting
for them."
    "Did you speak to Art?"
    "He came and sat with me, but he seemed
traumatized as well? I got the impression that
something horrible had also happened to him?"
    "He didn't tell you?"
    "No."
Eva leant forward and whispered,
    "So, you know he answered my S.O.S. to help save
you on Thursday..."

HANNAH and Art were leaving the Chelsea Theatre
at World's End. It was quite like old times them going
to N.A. meetings together, though neither of them had
yet spoken or picked up their white keyring. She got
out a packet of fags and offered one to Art who
declined. She popped one in her mouth, then thought
better of it, and gave the packet to the cluster of
smokers outside the door.
She looked wistfully over her shoulder as they walked
towards the King's Road.
    "So I think I need to start coming to S.A. too."
Art nodded,
    "It is our *go to,* once we're abstaining from the
drink and drugs."
    "Let's go later, yeah?"

313

They stopped next to his bike and she waited for a
black cab to pass. She looked into his eyes, then
said,

"Want to go to Mona Lisa's and tell me what
happened to you?"

"Not today," he said, so she hailed a cab, kissed
him and said goodbye.

ART stood by his bike in a daze, his brain a
jumble of disconnected wires, shorting and sparking
and making him twitch. Trying to fathom everything
that had happened was impossible for him in that
moment. All he had to do was stay clean.

He started his bike and let it warm while
watching the people, then he carefully pulled his
helmet over his bandaged ear. A curvy older woman was
approaching that he recognized. Was that Lori's cook?
He called,

"Cookie!" but she didn't respond. He stepped
nearer as she passed and said,

"Catherine? Cookie?"
The woman smiled, but veered around him,

"No darling, you're mistaken,"

"Are you not a housekeeper for a family around
here?"

"God no! I can't boil an egg. I'm an actress. On
my way to a casting for Oxo. Fingers crossed!" Then
she hurried on.

JOSEPH sat at his desk in Ebury House and read
the paper. The news about the *House of Horrors* was
incredible, and timely considering the business with
Natalie. Had Mr Gustav been involved? Maybe he'd just
let her in the window then let her out the door, as
she had hoped? But then why did he say nothing when
questioned by the police?

He saw someone approaching and went to open the
door. It was Kirsten, the model who had helped him
find Natalie. She smiled as she walked in and held out
a magazine to him. He didn't recognize the name
(Wallpaper*) but he certainly recognized the full-page
photograph of Karen Ford's apartment.

"They didn't use me on the cover unfortunately,
but there's plenty of me inside—"

"That was quick!"

"Oh, I'd already sold them, before we made our
agreement; in fact, before we'd even come and shot
them."
She saw the look on his face and said,

"Sorry. But it'll be great publicity for your
place, look at this centre-spread!"

Mr Gustav entered and loomed over her shoulder.
    "That's Ford's apartment isn't it?" he said,
lifting the magazine from her hands.
She cringed, then mouthed the word 'sorry' and ran.
    "It says here that the apartment is open for
viewings like some common attraction? That is
forbidden. Their lease could be revoked, and your
contract certainly will be."
    "I understand Sir."
    "Is that all you have to say?"
    "No Sir. A woman came by last week. She said
she'd met Karen Ford quite recently, who told her
about that famous day. Karen said she'd climbed out of
her window and crawled along the ledge to your window,
and that you'd let her in."
    "Really?" said Mr Gustav, twirling his moustache.
    "Yes, but the next thing she knew, she was
imprisoned and then sold to an Arab."
    "Really?" said Mr Gustav again.
Joseph picked up the newspaper with the front-page
headline
    SEX-SLAVE-SICKO'S HORROR MANSION RAZED IN
HELLFIRE!
    "Is that all you have to say?"
Mr Gustav slowly shook his head, then walked to the
lift. Joseph sat back at his desk and picked up his
Blackberry. He'd been practicing typing with his
thumbs and was ready to start his novel...

    AJI was standing outside her dead grandfather's
house with her dad.
    "Do you want to go in?"
Art shook his head.
    "Just into the garage."
He unlocked the door and stood looking at the
motorbikes and then at the ceiling. She saw a little
black motorbike with a chrome tank. It looked the
right size for her diminutive stature,
    "I like that little black one. Can I please have
that one?" she said pointing.
    "The Vincent Black Shadow? Worth twenty-four-
thousand pounds? Of course Sweetheart, a perfect first
bike."
She shrugged. Worth a try. He was staring at the
ceiling again.
    "What are we doing?"
    "Oh, sorry, just getting a spade."
Aji watched him search for a while then unhooked the
spade from its bracket on the wall.
    "So what are we doing with it?"

"Going to Holland Park. I buried something there, many years ago."
They set off up the hill and into the park.
"So I'm following in your footsteps," said Aji, "I'm writing a kind of journal, except now it's called a *blog*."
"Oh yeah, I've heard of those."
"It's online and I'm already getting a lot of hits."
"That's great sweetheart. What's it called?"
"Watching TV and Movies with Boys."
"Nice."
Aji was slightly disappointed by his reaction but decided to give him a break, what with everything that had happened.
"What about you Dad? What are you going to do?"
"About what?"
"Dash?"
"That's not really up to me is it?"
"I guess not."
"But to improve my chances, I'm gonna go to lots of meetings and stay clean; and I'm gonna stop working for a certain magazine—"
"Sex-Doll-Horror monthly?"
"You know?"
"Of course I know. You think putting a bit of red felt over your drawing board will do anything *other* than make me want to know what you're hiding?"
He nodded and shrugged,
"Sorry."
She nodded,
"And, of course, I'm gonna write another book, detailing these last ten days, if everyone agrees to be interviewed—"
"Awesome."
They got to the statue by the duck pond then climbed over the railing and walked into the undergrowth. He seemed to know where they were going so she followed along. He was muttering:
"The frog pond squares are where we start..."
What was this? A treasure hunt?
"Walk downhill but do not fart..."
Huh?
They meandered through the undergrowth until they came to a patch where the ground had been disturbed. There were a lot of holes. Someone else had been digging. Her dad shook his head and muttered 'no' a number of times, as he thrust the spade into the ground and the various holes. A metallic ding caught his attention and he dug until he revealed a biscuit tin.

"What is it?"

Art rubbed the earth off the lid to reveal childlike writing:

"Time Capsule - do not open until after the apocolips"

He turned the tin and ran his thumb along the tape, still sealing the lid in place.

"Can I open this?" asked Aji.

"Is it after the apocalypse?"

"No, but I'm going to open it anyway."

He nodded, then started searching again.

Another metallic ding. More digging. Another tin. Aji watched him as he gave it a little jiggle, then started to shake his head. He dropped it and walked away. Aji opened it. Inside was his Anthology, open to a particular page. In the header was a chapter title: *Bartholomew Mistletoe's Schooldays.*

Aji took the book and read it aloud:

> *"Being on the Junior Shooting Eight meant it counted as my daily dose of compulsory sport. While Hew and the rest of them changed into their sports kit, I would collect my ear-plugs. While they muddied themselves, chasing a ball for hours in the wind and rain; I would amble down to the range, knock off twenty rounds, then spend the rest of the afternoon in the Art School, where I could smoke and drink undisturbed, and knock out a Spiderman poster for a tenner.*
>
> *In my second year I was promoted to the First Eight, thus had keys to the Armoury, and could sneak in at night. I'd found an old Webley Service Revolver rusting on a bottom shelf, and had moved it into a dark recess to see if anyone commented on its absence, but no one did. Then, as I restored the Revolver, every week I moved one .45 round from its box to the recess. By the end of the year I had enough ammo to pop every boy in my house, but I didn't want it for that. I wrapped the gun and the ammo in an oily rag and calmly packed it in my steamer trunk. When I got back to London I buried the bundle in a biscuit tin in a deep hole in Holland Park. What did I want it for? In case of war or revolution? No, I had a deep-seated feeling that one day I'd need it for something much closer to home."*

Appendix

1. from page 14
"I didn't fake it, I accidentally overdosed—"

An excerpt taken from "I'm Keeping the Head" by Artemis Grime.

"When the anthology came out, the book tour almost killed him. Wherever he went everyone wanted to buy him a drink, stuff coke up his nose, drop acid under his tongue and pump smack into his arm. In fact, the tour did kill him.
In Detroit, he hit up a snowball in the green room then went onstage and greeted his fans. His plan to read the story of him in Beirut overdosing and projectile vomiting onto a bunch of strangers was thwarted by him actually re-enacting the scene instead. He was pronounced dead by a doctor from the audience; a big fan apparently - but not big enough to resist demanding money from the PR girl for his dry-cleaning bill. A local reporter caught the whole thing and syndicated it immediately. It wasn't until 20 minutes later, when everyone had gone, and he had almost crossed the Styx, that the paramedics paddled him back to safety. But by then the news of his death had traversed the globe.
His publishers dropped the tour (as book sales had gone through the roof, and they didn't need him alive and screwing things up)."

2. from page 16
"He travelled the world looking for trouble, and invariably caused it" was the long-winded title of his anthology of 'But I digress...' articles written for various huge-selling magazines in the 80's and 90's. Available from many a bookshops' Bargain Bin - 99p.

3. from page 26 & 164

"'Arthur', as she called him mistakenly."

From the series of articles entitled: 'But
I digress...' by Artemis Grime.
An excerpt from:

*Bartholomew Mistletoe-Grimstone's
Schooldays.*
*"Yes, that is my given name. The hyphenated
name comes from the merging of two great (as in
sprawling) families: The Mistletoes of West
Sussex famous for nothing; and the Grimstones
from Streatham, also famous for nothing. But my
mother, even though she took his name, was
adamant that I should keep the Mistletoe, for
which I am eternally grated. Mistletoe? What
schoolboy wants to have a name like that?
Grimstone, on the other hand, is a name to be
given to an undertaker or a carver of
headstones, in an Algernon Blackwood novella. So
no winners in this story.*
*How did my beautiful fragrant Mother,
Marylin Mistletoe end up with an oaf like Frank
Grimstone? He hid his true nature while he wooed
her, then reverted to type. The only excuse I
can think of for their bad choices, their lack
of communication, their staying together, was
that they grew up during the Second World War,
and I suspect they were both suffering from
PTSD. They saw terrible things that they would
sometimes whisper if they were drunk enough.*
*But no one had invented PTSD then; there
was its predecessor called 'shell shock' but
that was reserved for the most traumatized of
Trench Warfare victims. Normal-everyday horror,
like the sound of a Doodlebug running out of
fuel overhead; a severed head lying in the
street; a child's bloody hand waving from within
a pile of a thousand bricks; this was just
standard wartime fare. They just got on with it.*

*When I'd arrived at my boys-only boarding
school, a flint pile in the hinterlands, I was
still small (and cute, apparently) and had
attracted the attention of all the perverts,
Seniors and Masters alike.*
*The school was visually very similar to
those featured in the movies "Tom Brown's
Schooldays" and "If", but their fictional new
boys had had to learn the names of the Houses,
the Masters and their Wives, the slang (and the*

*finer points of toast-making etiquette), whereas
the only names I'd been taught were of those who
to avoid:*

> *"Never get left alone with Smythe-
Troutly or Reverend Rumbolt or Mr Rush or..."*

*Unfortunately the list was infinite, and
sometimes I hadn't even been introduced to the
person who'd just cornered me in the Boot Room.*

*No wonder I associated the smell of shoe
polish with sodomy. Not mine, thankfully; I was
scrappy and had managed to fend off the unwanted
erections springing from unbuttoned flies.*

*I'd wondered if the perpetrators actually
did use boot polish as lube? It was kind of
slimy. Then they'd have a black cock for a
while, which'd make them easy to pick out from a
line-up.*

*The Notice Boards were full of various
activities we could join to keep us out of
trouble. As a twelve-year-old, Guns and Boats
were my immediate choices, but whether they'd
keep me out of trouble was debatable. Then
another caught my eye: It involved slashing
stuff with Machetes! I signed up and a week
later set off on my bike in my regulation camo
and steel-toed boots full of hope!*

*'T' was a kindly old gentleman who looked
after a forest near our school. Part of that
forest was a spinney of Hazel trees which he
maintained for a certain type of bird to nest
in. I don't remember what kind of bird, but they
were very picky: They only liked to screw in
three or four year old Hazels. Maybe it turned
them on? The way the June '77 centrefold did me?
Or maybe they found it more comfy to nest in?
Like me and my beanbag? (it was the '70s).*

*'T' had the whole spinney marked out and
every year he would tackle two of the areas (to
give them a choice – who did these birds think
they were?) and needed my help. Actually, there
were other boys there, but I have airbrushed
them from my memory. So my/our remit was to
clear the undergrowth and cut the Hazels almost
to the ground, slashing with the machete. This
was called Coppicing (and most likely, still
is). It was very satisfying. Then we'd bundle up
the branches for the Weaver's Circle and stop
for a break. This entailed building a fire to
boil the kettle, then making very sweet tea and*

drinking it, accompanied by orange Club
Biscuits. This was when they were mainly
chocolate with a skinny biscuit inside, not like
now when they've reversed the recipe. Man, that
was good: Sitting in the forest, a warming fire
burning while intaking Tea and orange Clubs with
'T' (and others apparently).

'T' was a good man, who cared for the
'outdoors' in a way I'd never encountered
before. He chatted away in a manner that my
father never did; treated me like an equal, not
an annoyance. I loved him, in my slightly O.C.D
way.

My mother loved her garden and tended it in
a similar fashion, but not for the benefit of
animals. She started buying Orange Club biscuits
too though, at my request. When I was at home, I
never wanted to leave. I hated going back to
school. I just wanted to stay with her. I cried
in the car on the way back at half-term, maybe
to try to persuade her to turn around.

At Christmas, before my second term I had a
monumental growth spurt and my father started
looking at me differently. I was suddenly taller
than him, and seemingly, he wasn't happy about
it.

A new year, and a new term beckoned and my
Father announced he alone, without my mother,
was taking me back. He threw my trunk and tuck-
box in the back and off we drove. No long
goodbyes, no nonsense. He gave me a lecture
about growing up, being a man, and got quite
heated and talked between gritted teeth. As I
watched him go I thought how much I despised
him. Then I turned and walked inside, a kind of
oedipal rage growing inside me. As I climbed the
stairs a boy greeted me, then said,

"Hey Artie, I'm sorry to tell you this but
'T' is dead." I laughed. My big hearty duck-honk
laugh.

Alone in my new study, I unpacked my things
and wondered why I'd done that. It really was a
turning point for me though. It marked the
moment I stopped being a Mummy's Boy, and became
instead, a monster.

It was when I started drinking, started
getting in trouble and getting suspended a lot
(weirdly, my father didn't like this version of
me either. Never happy, that old cunt), and when
I started my program of revenge upon those who'd

wronged me, bullied me, tried to rape me.
Suddenly I was inches taller than my seniors and
could easily rain pain upon them if I so chose.
But I also liked more nefarious punishments: A
tube of my mother's hair removal cream that I
purloined in the holidays, smeared on the head
of my sleeping victim had hilarious results;
joining the Camera Club and learning to develop
my own photos gave me the means to capture the
perps in action, and either blackmail or expose
them by placing the photo in a Hymn book which
would then be passed around the whole chapel
during Morning Prayers.

My House Master, Lovely Phil, during yet
another disciplinary interview and caning, had
concluded that I was a nonconformist, and I
thought that was about right. The idea of being
like everyone else filled me with dread. I
counted myself lucky we didn't wear uniforms.
The only mandatory kit was the gown, and I'd
hated my brand new 'Starless & Bible Black'
edition. I coveted well-worn ones owned by the
seniors, especially Greystoke's old faded
version with sown rips and patches.
Coincidentally Greystoke was one of the perps
upon which I needed to revengerize myself. One
night I went to the sleeping boy's room, and was
torn between gluing his hand to his face, or
taking the gown. Finally, I took the old thing
from its hanger. Then I went to the changing
rooms, unpicked the name labels from both gowns
and swapped them. The sowing had to be perfect,
which took all night, but it was worth it. Then
I set about making my new acquisition unique to
me: By burning holes in it with Sulphuric Acid
in the Science Labs, which Matron could then
patch with random squares of dark fabric, culled
from ancient corduroy trousers, silk
cummerbunds, and leather bustiérs. Greystoke
seemed unaware of what had befallen him, or what
could have, but our House Master was: He with
the massive brain and penchant for perfect
stitching.

I felt I had found my niche as the one who
would stand up to the bullies and performed my
new vocation with zeal. I was the defender of
the oppressed, the Robin Hood of 'H' house. But
the oppressors didn't see it that way. I was
spoiling their fun and getting a reputation at

the same time. It just wasn't the reputation I
wanted (it wasn't until after I'd been thrown
out that I met a boy {junior to me} in London
who told me he thought I was the bully, that
he'd been told not to make eye contact with me,
and that one occasion he had turned his head to
the wall as I walked towards him down Blood's
Passage. I guess the seniors weren't likely to
say why I'd attacked them were they? And did it
matter if they were older than me if I was the
one doing the intimidating?)

    When Lovely Phil finally accepted that
beating me for my infractions was useless, he
decided to call me into his study and speak to
me. I remember fondly our discussions, in which
Phil had treated me like an equal. It had
immediately tempered my destructive urges.
Pleased with the results, Phil then gave me some
responsibility. I was put in charge of Lost
Property; an awful job of collecting abandoned
clothes and belongings from the changing room
and other common parts. The previous incumbent
posted the weekly list so:
          'Sock, blue. 2p fine.'
          'Rugby shirt, soiled, size small. 8p
      fine.'
    Thus no one ever looked at the notice, nor
collected their clothes.
    I decided it needed more zing, pizzazz,
chutzpah, and maybe the occasional illustration?
Thus:
          '1. A shrivelled blue sock, the size
      of Stu's cock.
          Used for the wiping of bogeys on the
      ankle,
          and maybe the occasional wankle.
          Smells of trombone oil. 5p';
          '2. Small Rugby shirt, with large
      muddy hand prints
          where boy may have been carried aloft
      heroically,
          or held down during the act of
      'lerrrrve'. 10p.'
    It was my first writing commission, and
proved very popular with the boys, who egged me
on to greater depths, but not so popular with
Phil, who took the Rugby shirt for
fingerprinting.

Oh, but I digress – From Bartholomew to
Bart to Art to Artie, plus the Mis of Mistletoe
and the Grime from Grimstone."

4. from page 172
From the series of articles entitled: 'But
I digress...'
An excerpt from:

Bartholomew Mistletoe-Grimstone's
Schooldays. (cont)
"The school had a Shooting team and my try-
out had been a breeze: Lining up the dots in the
gunsights with the target came naturally and I
was immediately signed up, and thus given
training in the use of the armoury's cool
selection of guns: Bren guns, which because of
their recoil, would force me slowly backwards as
I lay behind it; Sten guns, which wanted to fire
upwards into the air for the same reason; AK47s;
Armalites; Lugers, and even a Bazooka. My Lee
Enfield .303 rifle was my favourite though. We
were encouraged to give them names, thus I
christened mine 'Lori'. Going to Bisley and
punching a hole in the centre of a target from
500 yards gave me great pleasure, and a lot of
burst blood vessels in my shoulder. The
Brigadier said I would make a great sniper,
alone in that tower block with Lori.
Being on the Junior Shooting Eight meant it
counted as my daily dose of compulsory sport.
While Hew and the rest of them changed into
their sports kit, I would collect my ear-plugs.
While they muddied themselves, chasing a ball
for hours in the wind and rain; I would amble
down to the range, knock off twenty rounds, then
spend the rest of the afternoon in the Art
School, where I could smoke and drink
undisturbed, and knock out a Spiderman poster
for a tenner."
To be continued...

5. from page 174
Aji's first name on her birth certificate was
Aja, after the 1977 album by Steely Dan. When
the word was sung by Donald Fagen he pronounced
it like the continent, 'Asia', and Art liked
that. But most everybody wasn't aware of Donald
Fagen's nasal vocals and pronounced it like the
beginning of 'Adjective', with a hard 'A' at the
front and a hard 'J' in the middle, 'Adja',

which *was just wrong*. Luckily it quickly morphed
into having an 'I' at the end, and everyone was
happy.

6. from page 174

From Bartholomew to Bart to Art to Artie, plus
the Mis of Mistletoe and the Grime from
Grimstone.

7. from page 208

An excerpt taken from "I'm Keeping the
Head" by Artemis Grime.

"The stealing. Art had forgotten all about
that:
Richard had an idea and said he needed
Artie's help, but implored him to make a special
effort not to allow Lori to follow them on their
mission; so, they waited until she was ensconced
with her mother then bolted back to Artie's
house and out the front door. Richard wanted to
go to a newsagent south of High Street Ken, and
when they got there, he asked Artie to buy him a
Caramac and a quarter of Lemon Drops from the
big jar behind the counter. The purchase
complete, but unable to find Richard in the
shop, Artie went outside, and found him skulking
around the corner. Richard showed him what he
had acquired: One magazine called Mayfair and
another called Men Only, both with naked women
on their covers.
"We're going to rent them out at school and
make a fortune!"
Richard looked quite like the boy on the
'Mad' magazine covers, and in that moment Artie
had thought he was mad. But Richard had been
right. They had made a fortune. The next time it
was Artie's turn to do the stealing. He was very
nervous and had to build up to it, first donning
a disguise and casing the joint. Then Richard
distracted the owner by asking for more Lemon
Drops. That was Artie's cue. He stood on a pile
of newspapers to reach the forbidden fruit, then
plucked a couple and tucked them into his
satchel, before legging it. He had procured a
Fiesta and a Club International.
Yeah, he'd had no qualms about becoming a
thief and a pornographer..."

8. from page 259

From a series of articles entitled: 'But I digress...' by Artemis Grime.
An excerpt from:

'Tokyo Tights' or 'Thirty minutes older, but none the wiser'

"Apparently, it can be hard to buy drugs in Tokyo.

I write 'apparently' because I've never had a problem buying drugs. I have an innate radar for the dealer, as do they for a high-rolling punter. It's the addict in me, which acts as a kind of magnet to other addicts. We are drawn together, like moths to a flame, like flies to a turd.

But as a newcomer to any city I wouldn't just walk up to the first guy that prickled my radar. I'd hang out at the station and watch the action. Within minutes I could tell who's selling what and whether it's any good, but also who's on the grift, who's a common thief, and who has murder on their mind:

There's always the opportunist junkie who will promise you the earth then take the money and never return; the team who will sell you brick dust or cheese, then when you complain, threaten you with violence; the singular quiet one who will beckon you to follow him to a house round the corner, down a dark alley until... These are not recommended. Look for the professional - the friendly dude who gets his hand shaken as the punters palm him the money and 'ask for directions' while he counts it; the subtle gesture with fingers as he points out where they need to go, then watches as they go 'shake hands' with another dude down the street.

Next is working out what they're selling, which can be indicated by the state of their customers: Ramshackle - Heroin; Agitated - Meth; Hyper - Crack, etc. or maybe a combination of these, depending on the city.

As a confirmed Drug-Pig on my first mission, 'One of each' is always my request (it's like a Lucky Dip!) or more likely, 'Two of each'!

Before making the approach, work out the currency and the notes. Don't use a big note as these dudes don't give change...

But I digress, as luckily for me I wasn't there to embed myself, but to speak at a

*Godzilla/Gundam Convention; meaning my readers
knew I was coming, and had already been leaving
presents for me at my hotel. I say that, as if
it was an everyday occurrence, like being U2 on
tour, but I must admit I was surprised by the
amount I got, and for a moment I did feel like a
rock star. I hadn't realized my popularity in
Japan, though I should've had an inkling by
being flown across the world and paid a tidy sum
for just one day's work. I laid the presents
along the wall in order of size and gave each a
number. No Fruit Baskets for this notorious
waster: mainly bottles of alcohol (numbers one
to seven), or smaller presents that could be
secreted inside a 'Hello Kitty' Pez dispenser
(eight to ten), or even smaller that could fit
in a tiny envelope (eleven to sixteen), or
'microdots' that could be hidden under a postage
stamp (seventeen). Plus a lot of tights and
knickers; used knickers, with a photo attached
of the owner wearing said knickers, under those
weirdly Victorian sailor suits that Japanese
schoolgirls wear. Some were not; but others may
actually have been schoolgirls.*

*I laid out the polaroids on the table
(numbered eighteen to thirty), emptied the Pez
dispenser down my throat (thanks number nine),
washed the pills down with a swig of Saki
(number three?), then studied each photograph
with a connoisseur's eye. They brought many a
question to my mind. I rolled myself a joint
(from number twelve) and pondered these
important* conundrums while staring out over the
city skyline:

- *Why 'used' knickers?*

- *Was it Tom Jones who had
knickers thrown at him while onstage,
with hotel room numbers written inside?
Were his 'used'?*

- *Were these girls propositioning
me, or was this some kind of uniquely
Japanese ritual?*

- *What were these girls (and one
boy) doing reading my drivel?*

- *Did they borrow their dad's mag
or buy their own?*

- *What was the magazine even
called? (note to self: I must ask while
I'm here). I got sent it every month and*

328

loved the Kanji typeface they used - so much more interesting than our own boring alphabet. But it also used a lot of English words dotted around in different typefaces like The Face did, but most of the combinations of words made no sense: 'Whacky Lemon Surprise' for an article on the Tour de France (a ref to the Yellow jersey maybe?); 'Plectrum Momentum' for one about nail salons (plucking guitar strings?), and my favourite: Used as the banner atop my article on The Reading Festival, 'Book Ripen Orgy' (no fucking idea, though, upon reflection I did write about the Sex and the Drugs {and the mud and the mud wrestling}, but hardly mentioned the Rock'n'Roll at all).

But I digress...

Thirty minutes older, but none the wiser, I resolved to make 'used knickers' the focus of this article. My sponsors, the kindly folk at 'Grammy Moon's Tokyo Experience' may want to add this to their tour by the time I've finished, you never know.

First call, the room-service dude who'd brought all the presents to my room. I showed him the polaroids plus accompanying undergarments, and he laughed. We opened a couple and he sniffed, saying 'burusera'. I sniffed too. There was a mild odour, but nothing to write home about (even though I am doing exactly that). He didn't speak English, but wrote a couple of sentences and an address on the hotel stationary, then put his favourite packet of particularly pungent panties in his pocket and left.

My first lead.

I showered, dressed, then went down to the Taxi rank and handed the note to the driver, who smiled and winked. I was expecting a short ride to the neon wonderland that is Akihabara, but instead I was taken out of the centre, into the suburbs, where all the telephone wires, power cables, corrugated plastic tubing and their accompanying junction boxes were above my head on spindly poles, instead of underground. I think I have mentioned my many phobias to you before haven't I? Well, here's an update on another three: Jumbles of knotted wires and cables regularly appear in my nightmares, as do spiders webs, and large heavy objects

*threatening to fall on my head. This street was
an ominous combination of these plus a few
more... but I digress.*

*My driver Lenny, parked on a T-junction
(the air clear above) and pointed at a shop on
the corner opposite.*

'Burusera' he said.

*I showed him one of the sealed bags I'd
been sent. He gawked at the photo, read the
accompanying note, then looked at me with open
mouth. He held the packet and raised his
eyebrows. I nodded and he unsealed the plastic,
shoved his nose in the bag and inhaled deeply.
Then he reclined his seat and got out his
cigarettes. Was that it? He wasn't even going to
get them out of the packet?*

*We sat and smoked Larks while we watched
the scene, him chatting away as if I understood,
interspersing his mother-tongue with the
occasional English word: 'buyer', 'seller',
'agent'.*

*Seemingly, the shop sold girl's school-
clothes, judging by what was displayed in the
windows. The weird thing was that all the
customers using the door on the left-hand corner
of the shop were men, who'd leave with a
discreet bundle; while on the right-hand corner,
girls would enter empty-handed and leave
counting wads of yen. I lit another Lark and
then it dawned on me. They were selling their
knickers; plus sometimes other clothing too;
sometimes their complete school uniform. They'd
go in wearing one set of clothes and leave
wearing another.*

*Lenny got out and beckoned me to follow. We
walked over the road and went in. It was a
typical second-hand clothes store in many ways
with racks of girls' uniforms, shelves of skirts
and blouses all wrapped in plastic; but the
browsing customers were all male. Also, I forgot
to mention, the clothes weren't clean and the
prices got higher the dirtier they were (I'll
try to crowbar that into the previous sentence
if I get a lucid moment).*

*The Underwear Section differed in that they
were all packed in vacuum-sealed plastic
envelopes, with a photo of the seller carrying
that day's newspaper in front of their face.
Some of these were pricier than a whole uniform.*

*The counter with the till was in the far
corner. Behind that was a door that must have*

led through to the other part of the shop. It occasionally opened and a woman would bring new stock through.

Lenny introduced me to the owner. His name was Tekin and he spoke good English. I picked up a bag of tights from the 'impulse buy' rack next to the till and shrugged,

"You're doing good trade here, but I don't get it. I don't understand the appeal."

"Yes but you are still young. You are not in need. Yet."

"In need? of what?"

"Mementos of life long ago, the fountain of youth."

"Ah, that's what you're selling here?"

"Yes."

"Not pervy, fetish-wear for dirty old men?"

He laughed and shook his head,

"We have two distinct groups of clients, maybe three," he said gesturing towards his customers, "the largest group are the Salarymen; they work long hours, six days a week, never taking a holiday, for life. They may be single, or widowed, or married, but they come here to remember the last time they were truly happy: When they were at school, when they first fell in love, lost their virginity, or maybe had a fumble under the bleachers with their new girlfriend, or were given a pair of these as a memento. It reminds them of when they were alive."

"So it's not about sex?"

He shook his head,

"The second group are a sub-section of the Toaist religion, who adhere to the tales of Shoki. He wrote about a man who went in search of the Fragrant Fruit of immortality. Eventually he found the Eternal Land where he inhaled the Fragrant Fruit and became forever young. He returned with the secret of the source, which was then available to all." Tekin held up a packet from the 'impulse buy' rack.

"This is the fragrant fruit?"

Tekin nodded.

"So it's not about sex?"

He shook his head,

"No, that's our third group. For them, it's all about sex! Sexual gratification, but not in person. We have our two separate doors for the men and the girls, but maybe we don't even need it; when I look out the window and I see them

331

*cross on the corner, they both look at the
pavement and nod respectfully. The Japanese
population are slowly disengaging from one
another, the birth rate is falling, people are
remaining single and forgetting how to interact
in person, and I believe it will happen in other
countries too, very soon—"*

*That was the moment the police burst into
the shop and arrested us all. It was a shame,
because I was enjoying our illuminating
conversation. Luckily I didn't have anything
incriminating on me, but I was still deported
the next day. Never to attend the convention.
Never to be allowed back into Japan. Never to
find out why they'd sent me their 'used'
knickers. I like to think they admired me so
much they wanted me to stay Forever Young, and
I'm okay with that. But hey girls, if you're
reading this in Japan in a couple of months'
time, drop me a line (usual address).*

9. from page 302
"You stole my girl."

From a series of articles entitled: 'But I
digress...' by Artemis Grime.
An excerpt from:

'Sliding the Cigarette through the Suez
Canal'.

*"Personally, I thought my last article
about the charming but ruthless slave-trader 'M'
was a masterpiece, but the magazine's editor has
proclaimed that it was below par and less an
exposé of much other than my own insatiable
over-consumption of any mood-altering substance.
Oh yeah, and that it encouraged our readers to
do the same.*

*I myself objected vociferously and urge you
to follow suit (usual address).*

*So for this month's article he sent from
his office to my home, the fragrant Betty
Balderdash, an ex-shot-putter and part-time car
jack.*

*Her mission: To extract a coherent,
punctuated story of no less than two thousand
words. Unfortunately, not by using drugs and
drink as bribery, but by taping me to a chair
and forcing me to dictate. The indignity! But*

seemingly it worked. We'd knocked out (how many words have we written so far Betty?) 151 words in less than an hour. That's another seven... That's another three... I could go on...

It was during this ordeal that the phone rang and Betty answered, saying I was all tied up at the moment and could she relay a message? She put her hand over the receiver:

"It's the man himself. He's in London on business and wants to meet at One-Nine-Two at seven."

I put two thumbs up, Macca style, but she couldn't see them as they were gaffered to my thighs, so I nodded instead.

My heart was pounding. Did he just need drugs? Or had he been told who I was and what I'd done, and was here to kill me?

I'd last seen him a month or so ago. I'd called him and told him I'd split up with Nina, had a minor habit and needed somewhere to clean up. He'd suggested I come to meet him in Lamu, as long as I brought a week's supply with me. That sounded fine to me; I didn't even want to clean up, and I'd smuggled drugs through customs so many times that I actually enjoyed it.

I flew to Nairobi, hopped an ageing Cessna to the coast, then sailed to the small island nestled in a river-mouth. It's your classic colonial desert island with white sand and palm trees, and that's where I found Pepperoni's Hotel on the waterfront.

Now I'm sure I've said this before, but if you're an addict like me, you'll know how you can walk into a party and be immediately drawn to a stranger on the other side of the room, who of course, turns out to be the guy/girl with the drugs. We seem to magnetize each other and become fast friends; and this hotel had that same quality and everyone I come to mention had been magnetized to this venue, including its owners, blonde and bronzed brothers Ralf and Otto. It was the epicentre of all 'western' (addict) activity, and I was soon embedded alongside Milo and my new friends: Peter B, a charismatic American photographer (famous for the number of supermodels he had bedded), hiding out from the Kenyan authorities for various reasons; Gerard, heir to some architectural monstrosity and half of Scotland, sent into exile by his aged parents; Vanni, the man with

*the biggest cock I've seen (including porn-
stars) and his long-suffering girlfriend Choki;
and of course the charismatic 'M', who had
brought with him the breath-taking Miriam:
Olive-skinned but blonde, blue-eyed and freckly
(are you detecting a pattern here?), she was the
most beautiful girl I'd ever seen, but she
seemed unaware of it. So down-to-earth, so easy
to talk to, so naïve about men's intentions,
including of course 'M', who, if my six months
in his company had taught me anything, was
lining up a buyer for when he got bored of her.*

*A lifetime of David Attenborough narrated
wild-life documentaries had emphasized to never
intervene in the subject's story, but I being
me, thought David was a tosser.*

*Clearly, when I'm embedding myself in a
world, I have to go along with the subject's
fetish/peccadillo/business model; but there
comes a point when the great man's ideology
becomes bollocks.*

*Sure, he could watch a fox enter the
chicken-coop and kill one chicken, but then
could he continue to stand by while the fox
systematically slaughtered all the others just
for the hell of it? Replace the fox with a rogue
tiger and the chicken-coop with a village of
Indonesians.*

*I am an intervener; if I'm not in the
story, is it really a story?*

*Example: Last year's series - 'Arms & the
Man-made Marmalade'.*

*You're with an arms dealer selling an atom
bomb to a eastern-european dictator for use
against his neighbours.*

Do you either:

> *A.   Report faithfully to your
> magazine the excruciating details of the
> deal that led to a million dead.*
> *B.   Foil the plot using nothing but
> a can of hairspray, a mouthful of Bazooka
> Joe bubble-gum and one's own underpants.*

*It's B obviously. Anyone who thinks
differently can meet me outside the Finches any
Saturday night at closing-time for bare knuckle
fisticuffs.*

*But I digress, where was I? Oh yeah,
sitting on the hotel veranda with Miriam
watching her boyfriend and Peter water-skiing
down the estuary trying to out-do one another*

*with their acrobatics as they launched
themselves off the floating ramp. Should there
be a comma in there? Maybe even two? My lovely
assistant Betty will undoubtedly sort that out
later. She has at least untied my hands so I can
have a fag and a chase while she types and
cajoles me with tea and chocolate (a Toffee
Crisp and a Marathon if you must know). I am in
a bad way, but fettled by the knowledge that
she'll type pretty much anything I say. Isn't
that amazing? It's like I actually have a nine-
to-five job and a secretary!*

*Sorry, back to Miriam who, though she had
no idea of his intentions, was under no
illusions about what a cad he was. Thank god, as
I was already falling in love with her. She was
only a couple of years younger than me, but had
had a much better education. One of the first
things she said to me was:*

"It's Ku. You said Klu Klux Klan. It's Ku."

*"But it's so much more alliterative as
Klu."*

*"But you'll come across as an idiot. An
alliterative idiot, but none-the-less an idiot."*

A pedant; truly a girl after my own heart.

*So, as the days slid by, while 'M', Peter,
Gerard et al tried to out-do one another I
became her friend, with the occasional flirty
moment thrown in to make sure she didn't think I
was gay. Or a junkie. Not that flirting would
stop her thinking I was a junkie. I just tried
to hide the fact, but she kept finding me in the
middle of having a hit, and didn't seem to mind;
in fact I think it actually attracted me to her:
The tragic addict who needed saving.*

*A fortnight had passed, when an aged Arab
'Prince' flew in on a sea-plane to have supper
with 'M' and Miriam. 'M' had commandeered the
kitchen to concoct his 'legendary' Puttanesca
sauce for the pasta, leaving Miriam and the
Prince alone.*

*From my vantage point at the bar, it was
obvious to me that he was only there to check
her out, and he liked what he saw.*

*This could have been my big break in the
story. The proof that would convict 'M'. But of
course, for that to happen I'd need photos of
the handover, of Miriam being carted off in the
Prince's sea-plane and of 'M' frolicking in a
mountain of unmarked bills. All well and good*

except I'd just used up my last roll of film on Miriam trying on her new bikini.

Gerard sat beside me, drinking Gin from a Jug, while trying to persuade me to fly to Marseille and drive his new 50 foot power-boat back to Lamu,

"I'll give you a thousand pounds now and a thousand on delivery, please Artie. It'll be quite an adventure."

"Why can't you go Gerard?"

"Oh I'm not allowed more than fifty yards off this island. Restraining order. But can you imagine me blasting the cigarette past here at seventy knots? What a photo that'll make to send to Ma and Pa."

I liked the idea, but I was more interested in his camera.

"You have a camera do you?"

"Yes."

"Can I borrow it?"

"Of course, but it has no film. Do you have film? If not, you should buy some when you get to Marseille."

I decided to tell her:

"Does your family know where you are?" I asked, when she came to the bar for more Perrier. She shook her head,

"No, 'M' asked me not to say, or even tell them that I was with him. Strange really, but understandable, what with the divorce and all..."

I nodded, but then said,

"He's not married. 'M' asked you not to tell them because he's planning on selling you to that 'Prince' you just met. Tomorrow, one way or another, you'll be on that plane flying back to wherever, never to be seen again."

She took some persuading, but the evidence was stacked in my favour.

Once the Prince was tucked up in bed, and 'M' was drunk and snoring loudly, she wrote a note blaming her parents and left it in his cubby-hole at reception. We took a boat to the mainland then a taxi to the airstrip. At dawn, the old Cessna arrived from Nairobi with tourists aboard and I bought her a ticket back to the capital. In a dusty scene reminiscent of Casablanca, we stood on the airstrip.

"You're not coming with me?"

"I can't right now, I'm writing a series of articles on 'M' to expose him, and—"

*"But what am I supposed to do without you?
My parents are going to kill me if I go back to
Eliat now."*

*"Then fly to London and go to my place.
I'll see you there in a week."*

*I liked that she needed me and seemed happy
to go along with my idea. I gave her money and
my address and watched her board, my heart
racing with the idea that she might love me too.
Once she was in the air I hurried back to
Pepperoni's in time for breakfast.*

*'M' and the Prince searched the place and I
helped, looking behind plants, under tables and
in small laundry baskets, until he found the
note at reception. The Prince eventually left,
having spat at 'M's feet. Not a good sign.*

*'M' came and knocked on my door later. In
hindsight I should've got my micro-cassette-
recorder running before opening the door. He
looked me up and down.*

"Did you do it?"

"What?"

"Warn her, and whisk her away?"

*"No, I was as drunk as you last night; you
think she suspected?"*

*"Who would suspect something as outlandish
as that?" he said, "no one would be introduced
to an Arab and think 'I'm about to be sold into
sexual slavery'."*

*"Good point," I agreed, "she didn't say why
in her note did she?"*

*"Just that she was going back to her
parents in Israel," he said shrugging, "fuck,
that's a million lost; let's go to Gerard's,
he's got a parcel coming in on the morning
boat."*

*Betty decided that we'd done enough for the
day and untied me. I walked through to the
bedroom.*

*"'M's in London," I said calmly. Miriam was
anything but calm,*

*"He knows! He knows I'm here and he knows
you're investigating him and he's gonna kill us
both!"*

*"He doesn't know anything," I said, "and
certainly not where I live," I sat on the bed
beside her and took her hand, "you're perfectly
safe here."*

337

"I'll take Betty with me for back-up, and hopefully I'll get enough evidence for Interpol to move on him this time."

"That would be good," she said.

When Betty and I entered the restaurant, 'M' was sitting with Peter B at the coveted left-hand corner table at the back. They sat either side of Jasmine, a beautiful Irish redhead and were attempting to out-charismarize each other. Is that a word? 'To be more charismatic than one another' is so long-winded isn't it? And don't you find charisma over-rated? It's fine for a bit, but it can be so wearing to be around. I prefer being the opposite - being translucent, being generic-looking - able to slide in somewhere unnoticed, being under-estimated; very useful in my line of work. Have you had this discussion with your friends? Which Rolling Stone would you choose to be? It can be quite illuminating.

I sat next to Peter. I'd forgotten he was going to be in town; he'd sent me one of his beautiful letters - a collage on a newspaper article about his persecution by the Kenyans, notated with Indian-ink drawings and comments, plus a few photographs glued on, and drips of his own blood for good measure. They were more a work of art than a letter, so it was easy to miss any actual news therein. But it was good. I felt safer with him and Betty there.

"Is Miriam with you?" Peter asked, while 'M' flirted with Betty.

"I thought she was with you," I lied.

"Well 'M' is convinced you have her, and he's out for blood, so don't find yourself alone with him tonight."

An order? An order not to do something? Challenge accepted.

For my purposes, 'M' and I had hit the end-game a bit too early (damn that Miriam), but I swore I'd squeeze every column inch out of the situation yet. Everything seemed fine except 'M' sent his pasta back twice then insisted on going down to the kitchen to teach the Michelin-starred chef how to do a proper sauce. That left Peter with an open goal for the beautiful woman but he also seemed to have taken a liking to my shot-putter. I left them to it and went downstairs to watch 'M' pontificating, then

338

popped to the Men's loo for desert. 'M' followed
me in and we racked them out. 'M's, apparently,
was direct from Columbia, having traversed the
ocean up a supermodel's anus; mine was from
Afghanistan via a myriad of unknown anuses. All
hail to the anuses!*

Once we'd partaken and the coke and the
smack were fighting for control of my nervous
system, 'M' said,

"I know."

"Know what?"

"What you're writing about me; where you
live and with who—"

"With whom," I said, just to annoy him,
though he already looked very annoyed, and
proved it by punching me in the head. I bounced
off the door and crumpled, unfortunately
obstructing said door as my superhero shot-
putting sweetheart tried to barge it open.
Luckily, my ectomorphic frame allowed her
endomorphic bulk to bulldoze me towards the
tampon disposal bin, and she set about subduing
my attacker. I crawled out and left them to it.

Ironic, finishing our 'friendship' in a
Gents very much like the one in which we'd met
the previous year in Beirut, as regular readers
will know, but to recap: It had been a balmy
night in the club and I'd got waylaid in the loo
by the blackboard and chalk. Having started with
a doodle of what I wanted to do with the curvy
waitress, I'd progressed into full-blown
Bacchanalian orgy featuring all the girls I'd
seen playing beach volleyball earlier, plus the
Ladies of the Choir from the nearby Nunnery, and
two members of Bananarama.

'M' had entered and was transfixed, asking
me to draw him into the mêlée, and we were soon
inseparable. Fate, yet again, handing me such a
rich seam for mining.

As you may remember, drawing had been my
'in' before, when the evil Doctor Koster had
peered over my shoulder in a café in Vienna.
He'd said, 'You aren't drawing what you're
seeing?' and I'd replied, 'What's the point in
that? You can see what I'm seeing as well as I
can.' Instead, I think I had been drawing a
cutaway of a Chevy V8 engine, or St Pancreas
Station or an orgy of Bacchanalian
Bananaramas...

But I digress. I can't tell you where I'll
be for next month's instalment as we are

339

officially on-the-run from the pasta-obsessed madman. Is that my 2000 words?"

*I know it probably should be rectums, but don't you think the word anuses is funnier? All hail to the anuses!

About the Author

Upon leaving school to research his creations, the author went undercover and endured fifteen years of gruelling drug-piggery.

By day, his 'cover' was as a Storyboard Artist, first in Pop Videos, then in Advertising, where he was very picky about his clientele (Marlboro, Messerschmitt, Monsanto, Mekunto, and Mail on Sunday being his favourites).

By night, he was a Comic-Book Artist and while still a spotty youth, he created Bloodrunners, an A4 page for Bike (UK's biggest selling monthly motorcycling magazine), starring Jack Shit, and sold many thousands of T-shirts featuring his anti-hero, alongside fatalistic and/or obscene slogans. Ostensibly about despatch riders delivering live human organs, the characters spent far more time getting wasted than working, which mirrored Andy's own life, and eventually, after three years he was sacked.

This seemed like a good time* to bring his characters to life on Super8 film, so he wrote and directed Bloodrunners (find it on YouTube). *In hindsight, idiotic, but great fun.

Since getting clean in the Nineties, he's created another comic-book entitled Jet Metal, which, for five years, featured in nine monthly motorcycling magazines worldwide, in five languages.

Most recently, his years of undercover 'research' have been collated and distilled (then infused with exotic spices and food colouring) into his book, "I'm Keeping the Head", published in 2017 and now the follow up "The Reluctant Torturer" the second in the series of Artemis Grime mystery thrillers.

This Andy Sparrow should not be confused with his cave-dwelling namesake, who also sells books on Amazon. This Andy Sparrow has never entered a cave. Not because of claustrophobia, nor nyctophobia, but for a nagging fear of a large heavy object falling on his head. This also makes walking in built up areas quite difficult. He lives near the beach in West Sussex, but still won't take off his crash helmet.

Printed in Great Britain
by Amazon

43880501R00188